THE KINGDOM WE RULE

The Kingdom We Rule

HALLE CLARK

IngramSpark

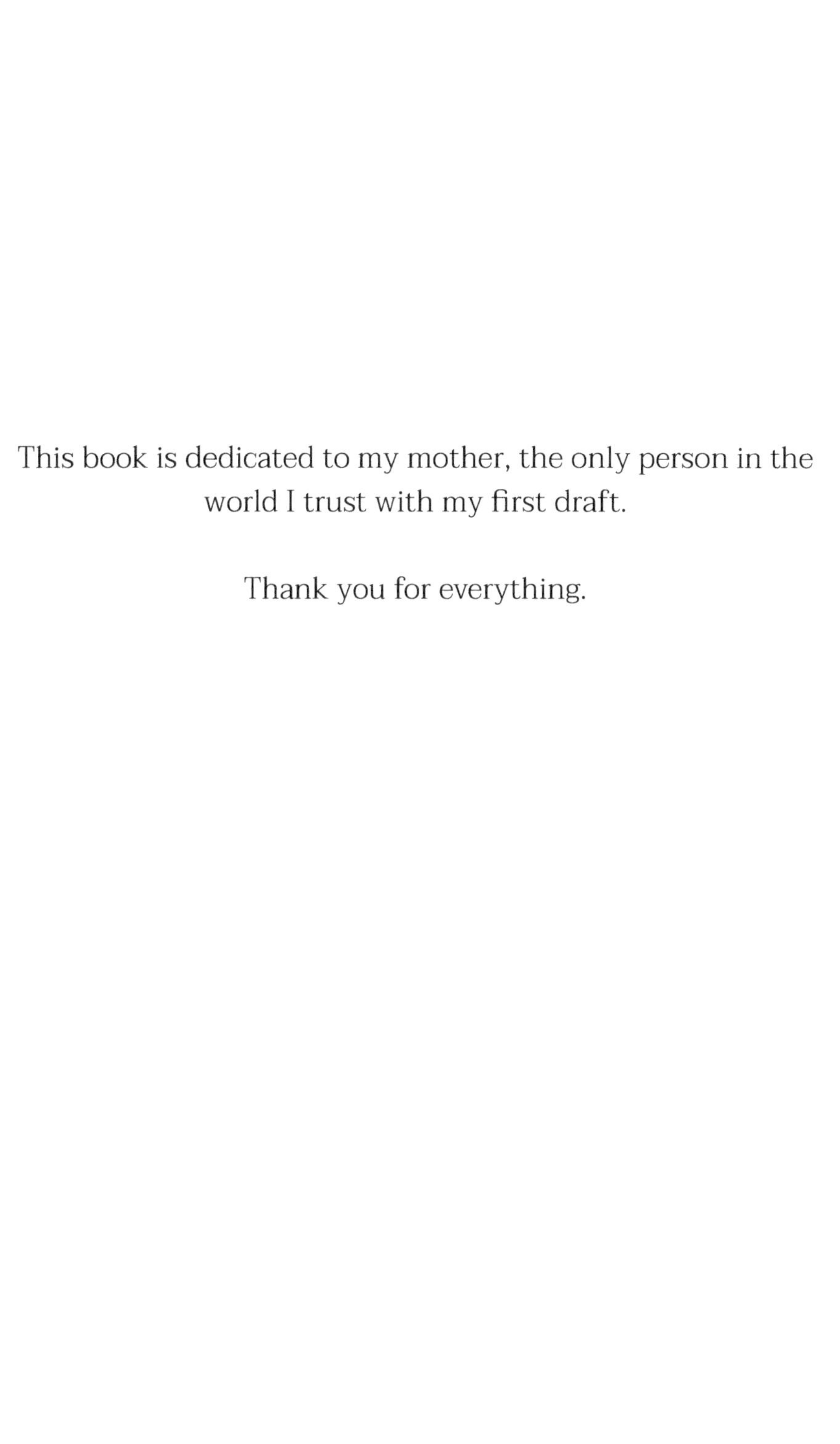

This book is dedicated to my mother, the only person in the
world I trust with my first draft.

Thank you for everything.

Map of the Continent

Contents

PART ONE

Chapter 1

The Changing Times

The passage of time is a strange thing. There have been hours of my life that felt like they could go on for years. There were years of my life that seemed to pass in only a matter of hours. Those who have mastered the spirituality of time could perhaps give you an explanation of this phenomenon, but I had not spent any part of my life mastering this spirituality. And, my knowledge of the inner workings of each spirituality, except perhaps the spirituality of life, was only at its most basic level.

So, I did what many do, chalked this phenomenon up to the mysteries of the universe and moved forward with my more pressing issues. Changing Dolma's outdated, corrupt, and unbeneficial laws was the task that got most of my time and focus. With Thomas by my side, and my party finally settling in, two-and-a-half years passed by in a flash. Gods above, even my first pregnancy seemed like a mere blip in the timeline of my life. During this period, we made all the most necessary changes to provide housing, clean water, and an abundant and sustainable agricultural system to benefit our people. We also granted greater protections and care for the workers of Dolma.

It was not perfect, but it was at least a start. It was a baseline for the future.

I also grew in my relationship with Thomas. We did not have any grand romance, nor did we fall in love. No, ours was not a romantic relationship in any sense of the word, but we managed to build a stable partnership. The arguments and insults that had been thrown around before our marriage all but disappeared. We still passionately debated policies and the order in which we believed work needed to be done, but we were a team. We both knew that no matter what we decided, we would be on the same side. In this manner we grew closer, and became friends and partners, ready to work together to help Dolma grow.

It was only after I had given birth to Marcus Alexander Karl Carleon, first Prince of the Crown Prince of Dolma, did time seem to slow down. As such, when Anora wrote to me, declaring her wish that I become the Crown Princess of Agremerre until my goddaughter, Princess Genevieve, came of age, I was ready for something different in my life. I was ready to focus on things beyond Dolma, and I was ready to start raising my child. There was, however, just one small problem with this: nobody else was ready for me to do so.

"What utter nonsense is this?!" Harry roared, as I explained my plan to go to Agremerre for a year to receive their Crown Princess training. "You're the Crown Princess of Dolma! You can't just leave!", the older man continued, his brown eyes sweeping over me like I had just gone mad. Although, knowing Harry, he likely truly believed I had gone mad. In fact, I was fairly certain that the King of Dolma had decided I was absolutely insane nearly two years ago when I led a campaign that "forced" the courtiers to actually start doing work around the country. Admittedly, only about 42% of the courtiers had accepted this campaign over the past two years, but it was at least better than the 0% that had worked prior to my arrival in Dolma.

"Ava, dear," Priscella cut in, looking at me nervously, her long neck and thin face reminding me briefly of a startled herring. "You just had a baby," she continued as if this changed anything about my plans.

"I had a baby two months ago. I have physically recovered - well, mostly," I said after catching Thomas's pointed gaze. "Nevertheless, I am well enough to travel and begin my training as Agremerre's Crown Princess. Plus, I am sure Genevieve and Marcus will become fine playmates during the year I spend there."

"You're taking the baby?!" Priscella screeched.

"Well, yes, he is my son," I said, calmly. While I was more used to life in Dolma than I had been when I had first arrived, there was still an underlying confusion when someone was so shocked by something I had considered natural.

"But, he is the first Prince of Dolma! Second in line for the throne," Priscella impressed upon me. "He can't just leave!"

"Does this mean I am coming too?" Asked Thomas eagerly, butting into the conversation before I could respond to Priscella.

"Well of course you are welcome to join me," I said with a slight frown, "but I had thought you'd want to stay here and continue your work as Crown Prince."

"Then I will come!" Thomas beamed at me. "I can take care of the tiny one while you work!" Thomas had taken to fatherhood unexpectedly well, after he got over his initial fears of "screwing the kid up." He had diligently begun learning from the nurses and nannies employed by the palace, and even started a lengthy correspondence with my own parents on what skills he'd need to learn. And, I must admit, his patience for crying babies was far superior to my own. Mother had assured me that my feelings were perfectly normal, and promised me that I could still be a good mother even if I was annoyed by the amount of poop and tears my child produced.

With this in mind, I smiled at Thomas and accepted his offer to join me. "Well of course he is coming!" Harry shouted, "He's now Agremerre's Crown Prince, and -"

"That's not the way succession works in Agremerre," I quickly interrupted. "In Agremerre, you can not gain a title through marriage. So, while I may be Agremerre's current Crown Princess, that title does not pass on to Thomas. He technically has no standing within Agremerre's hierarchy."

"Well that's just ridiculous," Harry argued.

"Perhaps to you," I said simply.

"Hold on!" Priscella exclaimed, "If Thomas is not required, then you can't both go. Who will do the duties of the Crown Prince?"

I felt the need to remind her that, prior to my arrival in Dolma, the Crown Prince didn't actually have any duties, but before I could speak up, Thomas jumped in once more. "Ollie will do them," he responded confidently.

"I'll what?" Ollifelle stuttered from her spot across the room. The quiet, but insightful girl looked completely panicked about being forced into the conversation at all.

"Ollie is a Princess of Dolma," Thomas continued, unfazed. "And, she has been learning from Avalynn and Lady Lucy for two years now. She can easily do the work."

"Your sister is to be married!" Harry exclaimed.

"But it's not like you've found her a suitable Prince to marry her off to yet," Thomas argued.

"There are discussions in the works!" Harry blustered.

"Surely those could be put off a year," I pointed out, leaving out the "or more" I desperately wished to add. Seventeen still felt far too young to get married. "Of course, this all depends on whether or not Ollie agrees to the job," I said, turning to the girl. "I think you would do excellently, should you desire the position, plus you will have Lady Lucy, Lord Xander, and Sir Abel to help guide you. And, I am sure Chanti would help you, too." I said, as Ollifelle blushed. Ollifelle and Chanti, Solista's younger sister and one of the two girls I had brought to Dolma's Royal Palace three years ago, had developed a friendship over the past two years that had, in my opinion, greatly benefited the two girls, even if Priscella found the whole thing "unseemly".

"I - I would like to help," Ollifelle said, a determined flash rushing through her brown eyes, looking eerily like the gleam

I'd seen in her father's eyes when he felt particularly powerful. Oddly, I found the look far more reassuring in her eyes than I had ever felt with his.

"Well then that's settled then!" I declared.

"No it absolutely is not!" Harry raged. Except it was, and two weeks later, I set out with my son and my husband into the sweltering early summer heat to be educated as the Crown Princess of Agremerre.

"Avalynn!" came Anora's excited cry three days later when she met us at the Agremerrian border. "I am so glad that you're here!" she continued, boisterously. She reminded me a lot of Father, with her overwhelming presence and excitement. It was a rather comforting sensation. Thomas, however, looked as though he might disagree with me. While I was now more accustomed to the life and rituals that ruled over Dolma, my husband had very little experience with the culture of Nevre-merre, and of the similar culture found in Agremerre.
"I am very happy to be here, Queen Anora," I said, earnestly.

"No, no, child, you are the Crown Princess. Well, at least for the next 19 years or so. You are family, and we can address each other as such!" Anora pushed, beaming at me. Three years had changed very little in the Queen's appearance. She still had smooth brown skin, with only the occasional visible scar from her military and combat training. There were a few wrinkles around her deep brown eyes that were new. "Indicative of a life of smiling," Mama had said about her own wrinkles several years ago. Anora's dark hair showed the most obvious signs of change, with a few graceful strands of silver sparkling against her normal brown tones. Still, she looked healthy and happy and the ease at which we settled into her life and home was exhilarating.

We spent the rest of the day making camp with the Agremerrians, as Anora introduced us to the knights and aides who followed her as she moved around the kingdom to where she thought the need would be greatest. I brought with me all my knights who were originally from Agremerre, and who were now happily bonding and reconnecting with their old friends. And, in Challa's case, family, as his older sister was a knight of Agremerre. It was a day filled with laughter and ease as we discussed the plan for the next year and at the end of the night, Thomas and I were led to a tent that brought back fond memories of my childhood traveling all around Nevremerre.

"They are so nice. Even to me," Thomas pondered as we prepared to retire for the evening. Marcus was asleep in his arms, swaying peacefully as Thomas paced around the tent.

"Of course. Why wouldn't they be?" I whispered softly, moving to join them and stilling Thomas's trek around the space.

"We weren't very kind to you," Thomas said, as I stared lovingly at the face of my little boy. Marcus was the spitting image of his father, asleep like this. His white blonde hair was finally starting to fill out and move away from his head. Asleep, you couldn't see his only physical nod towards his mother, a mix of green in his blue eyes that matched the emerald color that ran through my own.

"That was Dolma," I finally said, remembering the conversation Thomas had started. "This is Agremerre; things are different here," I replied simply.

"I think I can understand now why Dolma was such a diffi-cult place for you," Thomas said, finally looking back at me.

I smiled at him, holding his ice blue gaze with my own. "No you don't. Not yet anyways. You've only been here a day and I promise there will be more to come that will surprise you. You will understand more why I am the way I am."

Thomas laughed softly, his voice carrying around the tent like chimes rustling in the breeze. "I suspect I will be trying to discover what makes you who you are for the rest of our lives, Avalynn. And, I do suspect I will rather enjoy doing it. Come, we will need our rest for tomorrow," Thomas said, without giving me a chance to respond. He shifted Marcus to one arm so he could reach a hand out to me, and pull me gently towards the mats and sheets that made up our campsite bed.

Letting him pull me down on the soft pillow, I turned to face Thomas once more, watching him lay Marcus gently between us. "Dolma is still hard for me," I informed him quietly.

"I know," Thomas sighed, placing a gentle kiss on my fore-head, "but we'll make it easier, with time."

"Yes. Yes we will," I agreed as I drifted off to sleep.

Agremerre was a breath of fresh air compared to my life in Dolma. Traveling around the country as I had in my own child-hood, Genevieve followed us along, diligently trying to repli-cate her mother's actions, while Marcus continued to grow, even laughing for the first time when one of the camp's dogs licked the back of his hand. Thomas was settling in well, even if his face seemed to have permanently settled into a look of confused determination. Even his homesickness seemed to be shorter than mine had been. Something he had politely credited to the presence of me and the baby, although I privately suspected that he found it a little easier to leave his parents than I had leaving mine.

My work with Queen Anora was going well, my family was happy, Oberon, Challa, and Hugo were thrilled to have some time back home, and in just two weeks we would go to the Nevremerre and Agremerre border to celebrate the Unajo festival, and to see my family again. All was well. I was exuberant, and everything felt right with the world. One would be forgiven for thinking that, with the way my life had played out up until this point, I would be used to the unexpected happening. Sadly, that never did become the case.

Chapter 2

The End of
the World

We were working on building houses in a coastal town only a day away from Pantheo, Agremerre's capital. The town, Nagoya, was beautiful - colorful houses lined the cobblestone streets, and the ocean's glimmer could be seen from every part of the sloped town. The ocean itself was a sparkling teal color that glittered like it was full of gems as it reflected the sun. It was easy to see why the ocean's distinct color was the inspiration for Agremerre's blue and green flag. Genevieve and Marcus were at a child care center, and Challa and Leonard were playing catch with a hammer, laughing boisterously behind Oberon, Thomas, Anora and me, as we discussed the merits and problems with a new building style. After Maychula suffered from a massive Earth tremor a few weeks before Marcus had been born, Anora had declared that Agremerre required a different style of housing that would be able to survive any Earth tremors that came to her country.

It was not, of course, realistic or feasible for every house in Agremerre to be knocked down and rebuilt, so Anora just settled for building community centers in each town where people could go in case of an Earth tremor. The buildings had been designed by looking at which buildings had survived the Earth tremor and the three lesser tremors that had hit May-chula. The poor people of Maychula could not get a break it seemed and the King, King Azerel, had sent letters to every country on the continent asking for aid. Something Harry insisted reeked of desperation and weakness, but I found to be a smart plea for the sake of his people.

Needless to say, Thomas and I were very interested in these community centers and had already decided to incorporate them in Dolma as well. We had spent countless hours debating what other uses they should have in the community, much to the initial chagrin of Marcus, who woke up crying more than one night at the sound of our heated debates. I now rather thought that we had mastered the talent of the whispered argument. And, it was an oddly satisfying feeling when we finished our debate without the baby waking up, no matter who was the victor of our particular discussion. Thomas seemed to agree with me on this, as we both could be found smiling triumphantly at the end of each disagreement where Marcus never woke up. It was much more enjoyable to fight when everyone was happy, no matter what the conclusion.

So, we were happily discussing building design when the world ended. Or, at least that's what it seemed like at the time. For how else could you explain a bright sunny day being taken over by clouds darker than night and haloed in an orange light in a matter of mere minutes? I consider myself to be a reasonable person, but when the clouds took over the sky and the cheers and laughter that once echoed behind me fell to a roaring silence, I truly, honestly, and completely believed the world was about to end, and we were all about to die.

Then came the screams. Terrifying, haunting screams from children, men, women, anyone and everyone. And, suddenly, all I could think about was Marcus. My mind went blank, and my soul screamed that I needed to find my boy and then it bounced to Genevieve, I needed to find her too. And Oberon, Hugo, Challa, Anora! And, I needed Mateo, Ana, Galileo, Leonard, Miri, and my family and friends in Nevremerre! My family! Were they safe? Would I see them in the afterlife? What would become of us all and the world we lived in? And, then, I managed to breathe. My shaky gasp filled the air, and a smokey taste fell upon my lips. Fire. There was a fire.

Oddly, for a brief moment, I felt better. A fire was not in fact the end of the world. Of course, I then remembered that a fire was still an emergency, and I jumped into action. "Fire, there must be a fire!" I yelled, turning towards Anora.

She gave me a wild-eyed panicked gaze before she registered my words, and turned herself once more into the confident and assured ruler that I knew her to be. "Yes, knights," she called out, her voice echoing over the area as all heads turned towards her. "Get everybody into their homes and out of the smoke. I do not feel heat, so the fire is most likely not nearby. So, inform the people that this is just smoke from a fire, and we are working to put out the flames as we speak. Crown Princess Avalynn, Crown Prince Thomas of Dolma, and I will start searching for the source of the fire. When you have finished alerting the people, come help us find the fire," Anora commanded.

"Yes, Your Majesty!" came a chorus of voices as everybody moved to start enacting Anora's orders.

"What of Marcus and Genevieve?" Thomas asked, as the three of us moved to our horses.

"The best thing we can do for them is to stop that fire," Anora declared, and Thomas and I nodded in agreement.

"The clouds - er - smoke came from that direction," Thomas said, pointing to the east side of the city, pointing out the location the fire was likely to have begun in. With another nod of agreement, we took our horses and rode East. And, we kept riding, East, West, North, South, all over the surrounding area looking desperately for any signs of a fire. The black clouds made it hard to see much in the surrounding distance, but we failed to find any of the bright orange flames or even a pervasive heat that would suggest a fire capable of causing the clouds that swallowed us now. If anything, the lack of a visible sun was making the whole area cooler.

"We have runners coming from across the nation saying the sky has gone black," Sir Horatio, one of Anora's knights reported, as we made our way back inside for the night.

"And we still have no idea of the source of the fire?" Anora asked, indignantly.

"None," Sir Horatio replied.

"Could the fire be somewhere other than Agremerre?" I speculated.

"It would have to be an incredibly large fire," Thomas said in disbelief.

"Still, it's possible," Anora conceded, looking tiredly around the room. "Send runners to each of our neighbors. See if they have more information. And, print out a message to the people to stay indoors as much as possible until we can deal with the fire and smoke pollution."

"Yes, Your Majesty, shall I send word to the High Judges?" Sir Horatio asked.

"No doubt they are already aware, but I shall draft a letter to them myself. Ava, I'll be sending Genevieve to you this evening, if that's alright? I need to keep working on this, and I trust you to keep her safe and happy in the meantime."

"Oh yes, of course!" I replied, still astounded in her trust in me.

"Good," Anora nodded, "Well, let me love on her a bit before I send her your way."

We agreed and Thomas and I nearly bolted up the stairs to where Marcus was waiting for us, having picked up Marcus from his childcare earlier in the day. When we got up to our rooms, Marcus lay nestled on Challa's chest, completely oblivious to the chaos around him. He was reaching his tiny hands up to follow Challa's large fingers as the giant man made soft little cooing sounds. Beside him, Oberon and Hugo sat, Oberon sleeping soundly on Hugo's shoulder and Hugo looking intensely at a spot on the floor, his mind clearly worlds away from his surroundings.

On a normal day, I would have enjoyed seeing my knights caring for my son and each other in such an unusual manner, but today all I wanted was my son close. I moved quickly and deliberately to Marcus and Challa, holding my hands out impatiently for my son. Once he was in my arms, I pulled the still cooing baby closely to my chest and breathed in his scent and softness, letting the life in his little body calm my unsettled soul. Strong arms came up around me, pulling myself and Marcus into them, as Thomas' head of white blonde hair flopped down against my shoulder.

"He's quite alright, Crown Princess," Challa smiled at Thomas and me. "Doesn't know anything's different."

"Thank you," I said, meaning the words with every fiber of my being, and holding a gratitude for him that the words "thank you" seemed ill equipped to fully represent. My eyes filled with tears I hadn't realized I had been holding back and I worked to blink away the liquid quickly pooling in my eyes. A small mumble came from my shoulder of what I was sure was meant to be gratitude.

Challa gently roused Oberon, and pulled Hugo from his thoughts before patting Thomas gently on the shoulder. "Any time," Challa told us quietly, before guiding Hugo and Oberon out of the room.

Thomas and I just stood there for a while, holding Marcus as he fell asleep. The both of us were simply mesmerized by the movement of his chest and his occasional sleepy gurgles. We could have been there for hours, or perhaps merely a few seconds before we were jolted back into reality with a knock on the door. "Come in," I called out, clearing my throat from the emotions of the day. The heavy oak door creaked open to reveal Anora and an excited Genevieve.

Genevieve bounced into the room with a brightness that seemed to have left the adults I'd spent the day with. "Godma!"

she cried out, her dark brown hair flying behind her as she attached herself to my leg.

"Hello darling," I smiled instinctively at the adorable toddler that had just come my way. "We must be quiet now," I whispered to her, "Marcus is sleeping."

Genevieve looked up at me, her dark brown eyes identical to her mother's as she nodded seriously. In fact, most of Genevieve was nearly identical to her mother. From the brown skin, to the sleek and straightness of their brown hair, Genevieve was practically a miniature version of her mother. The only discernible difference was Genevieve's broader and flatter nose, adorably filling out her round face.

"I will be going now, Geni, so be good for your Godmother and Prince Thomas," Anora whispered, stroking Genevieve's hair gently.

"Yes, Mama," Genevieve beamed. Anora kissed her head before nodding at Thomas and me as she left the room.

"Godma, Prince Godma," I had to force down a laugh at Genevieve's nickname for Thomas. Godmother wasn't quite available in her vocabulary, so I had been dubbed Godma in the early days of our arrival to Agremerre. And, despite being regularly told, Genevieve had yet to grasp the idea of who Thomas was. Thus, Prince Godma was dubbed, and even though we'd been here for nearly two months, the name still made me laugh each time I heard it.

"Yes, Princess Kiddo?" Thomas grinned. He, for some reason, was thrilled by his nickname and was delighted by every small thing Genevieve did. A warmth filled me as, not for the first time, I recognized what a wonderful father Thomas is and would continue to be.

"The sky went black," Genevieve exclaimed, and I immediately felt like I had been doused in ice cold water. Beside me, Thomas had stiffened and was giving me horrified glances over Genevieve's head. Genevieve, however, simply kept talking. "All the ofer kids got scared, but not me!" she said proudly. "I was brave! Like a knife!"

"Knife?" Thomas mouthed at me.

"She means knight," I mumbled back.

"That's great, sweetheart!" Thomas said loudly, picking up Genevieve and flashing her a blinding smile.

"Yes, we're very proud of you, but remember, dear one, bravery is not the absence of fear, but what you do in spite of it," I responded, moving towards the cradle, and laying Marcus gently down in it. Genevieve nodded vigorously at my words, but I belatedly realized that everything I had just said may have been too complicated for a three year old. I once again thanked the Gods for Thomas being such a natural with children because I was not convinced I was really doing the best job. "Come now, let's get you ready for bed," I smiled. If I couldn't understand the best way to communicate with babies and almost three year olds, I could at least make sure they ate, slept, and bathed the appropriate amount.

Thomas looked after Marcus while I took Genevieve for a bath. "Godma, when will the sky go back to bwue?" My mind went blank, my hands, which had been washing Genevieve's hair, stilled, my heart froze in my chest, and I could do nothing but stare at the back of Genevieve's head as I tried to force my brain to function once more.

"Uh -," I said, dumbly. I was not prepared for this. I was not prepared for this at all. How was I supposed to answer honestly in a way that wouldn't completely traumatize this child? How was I supposed to explain to Anora that I scared her precious daughter? Could I lie? If I just said that it would come back eventually, would that work? Was it morally wrong to tell her that it would come back tomorrow, and then, if it didn't, tell her that tomorrow hadn't happened yet? Toddlers couldn't have an accurate perception of the passage of time, so I could probably get away with it.

"Godma?" Genevieve questioned, turning her head to look at me from her place in the tub.

"Yes, well, I'm not sure when the sky will be blue again," I answered finally, trying to sound as nonchalant as possible while I finished washing her hair.

"Oh, well I hope it comes back soon. I like bwue skies the best. Does the bwack sky mean rain like the gray sky?"

"Oh, uh - no, no I don't think so. Usually it means there is a fire."

"A fire!" Genevieve turned towards me, her eyes wide.

"Not that that's always a bad thing!" I scrambled trying to take back what I just said. "In certain areas fires can help promote new growth and improve soil quality." Genevieve continued to stare at me. "So the fire helps the plants!" I pushed forward. "Well, only if it's controlled and contained in a timely manner, and doesn't grow overly large. Although for smoke clouds to be this thick, it probably is a large, uncontrolled fire," I mumbled more to myself. Genevieve still just stared at me. "Er - well, the knights, your mother, Thomas, and I checked and there is no fire in this area, so we are very safe here." I finally, helplessly, concluded.

This seemed to satisfy Genevieve as she nodded and went back to playing with her wooden bath toy. I sighed in relief and felt the panic that had filled me when she asked her question dissipate. I was lulled into a false sense of security, believing all was well and that I had successfully managed this crisis, until Genevieve refused to get out of the bath.

"Genevieve, darling, please, it's time for bed now," I tried to soothe.

"NO!" The toddler screamed again. I resisted the urge to bang my head against the tub in frustration. Each time I went to pick her up, she screamed her little lungs out with an impressive amount of force and stamina for someone so small.

A knock came from the door as Thomas came inside, cradling a fussy Marcus to his chest. "Everything alright here?" He asked cautiously.

"Genevieve doesn't want to leave the bath," I sighed.

"Understandable," Thomas nodded, "Tiny one here will need to be fed soon."

"Ah," I said, grabbing Marcus from his arms.

"I can't leave the baf!" Genevieve wailed, "It's the only place I am safe from the fire!"

Ah, I have traumatized the child in just a few hours. Clearly I am excellent at this whole parenting thing, I thought sarcastically. Thomas, however, just laughed. I stared at him in shock as he beamed down at me. "Well, Princess Kiddo, that would be accurate if there were a fire here, but there is not, so you're perfectly safe."

This, I thought, was not technically accurate. If there was a fire in this building, she would also have to worry about the building collapsing, smoke inhalation, and the fire causing the water in the bath to boil, but I figured now was not the time to inform her of all of that. Instead, I nodded and echoed Thomas, "Yes darling, as I mentioned before, we are all perfectly safe here."

"But what if the fire comes closer?" Genevieve sniffed.

"Then, I'll let you in on a little secret," Thomas said, leaning towards her. "I am the ultimate firefighter! Fire is so scared of me that it runs the opposite direction whenever it sees me! As long as you're with me, sweetheart, you'll be just fine." Thomas gave her a dramatic wink as Genevieve began to giggle. "Now will you let Godma get you out of the bath?" Genevieve looked hesitant for a moment before she finally gave her nod of consent.

Passing Marcus back to Thomas once more, I quickly dried off Genevieve and put her in her night clothes before settling in to feed Marcus. Thomas tucked Genevieve into bed, telling stories that had her giggling happily before she drifted off to sleep. "You're so much better with them than I am," I sighed to Thomas as we watched Genevieve turn in the cot that had been brought in while she was in the bath.

Thomas looked at me in confusion, "Ava, you are currently feeding our son, from your body. Something I could physically never do. You are patient, kind, and, most importantly, you are trying everyday to be here for our son and rule a country! You don't have to do everything perfectly. Everything you are doing right now is exactly what needs to be done. I can take care of all the rest. Neither of us really knows what we are doing, but we are trying our best and that is all we can do."

I smiled at him, already feeling easier. It was remarkable how just having him by my side and having the support and encouragement he seemed to maintain each and everyday made everything in my life so much simpler. He was a rock that helped stabilize all the changes I wanted to make and I was eternally grateful for his presence. Soon Marcus was done feeding, and we all fell into a deep sleep brought on by the exhaustion and fear this day had brought and by the comfort that was found in the four of us being in the room together.

When I woke the next morning, I was convinced it was still night. The sky was so black and there was a stillness in the air that I could never have attributed to daytime. No birds chirped, no insects buzzed, and even the plants seemed to hush their usual rustle of leaves and branches. The madness of yesterday's struggles, the sky's sudden blackness, and the ashy texture of the air filled my memory. And, next to my son, Genevieve, and Thomas, I had this dreadful fear that the dark world would be permanent. Perhaps we were never to see the sun again.

I spiraled from there. With no sun there could be no food, no food meant starving, and so my thoughts circled endlessly. When Thomas woke beside me, he was met with a wild panic in my eyes as my thoughts took morbid and horrible turns. "Breathe, Ava," he whispered to me. "We have only the now, we don't know anything about the future."

The first deep breath I took felt like it might kill me. The inflow of air to my lungs pressed against my chest and pushed at my stomach as though my whole body would erupt. But, I kept breathing. Slow and long, and slowly I began to right myself. Just in time for the woeful shrieks of Marcus to ring out from beside us, in turn waking up Genevieve who began to cry herself.

I can't say I was ever truly prepared for the chaos of parenting, but there is an added benefit that you really cannot focus on anything else. Being forced into the present moment, and away from the dark idea of an unknown future did wonders for the growing pit in my stomach. So, with diapers changed and toddlers soothed, Thomas and I sat quietly together while I fed Marcus.

"You have been spending too much time with Abel," I accused Thomas playfully, readjusting the baby attached to my breast.

Thomas laughed, "If I hadn't spent time with Abel, I would have never grown into the man I am now. But, it was not him I was quoting today. I do believe you were the one to say those words to me a year or so ago when I stood against my father to get our education bill passed."

I stared at him in awe for a moment wondering how on earth he had remembered what I said over a year ago now. "So I did," I smiled at him, "Maybe I am spending too much time with Abel."

Thomas laughed, "He would be very sad to hear you say that. No, I'm afraid we must resign ourselves to having a litany of soothing things we will say to each other at any given point in time. Right Geni dear?" He turned towards the still half asleep child in his arms, who only gave a sleepy nod in return, her brown hair flying out in so many directions it appeared as though it might be learning to defy gravity. I laughed at them both and we began getting ready for what would doubtlessly be a long, busy day.

As soon as we got downstairs, Marcus and Genevieve were whisked away by nannies. Before I could even ask where I needed to be, I was practically dragged by Anora toward another room in the inn that looked to be hastily arranged to accommodate all 28 High Judges. I was vaguely aware of Thomas being pulled off in the direction of some knights before Anora all but kidnapped me, but I never did get around to finding out what they were doing. Upon arriving in the room, Anora and I were hastily directed into chairs, and High Judge Adelaide stood up to speak.

"So far, we have only received reports from Nevremerre, Calvine, and Dolma," High Judge Adelaide began. Her voice was smooth and steady. The sharp confidence and countenance of her tone would give you the impression that the blackness we suddenly found ourselves in was completely normal. This steadiness was something I might have attributed to age, as the dark-skinned woman was only half a decade shy of 80, but sitting to her right, High Judge Zenareth, nearly two years her senior, was possibly the most nervous person at the table.

"Well what did they say?" High Judge Zenareth squeaked, his blue eyes going wide as he flailed his hands wildly around him. His flighty energy and near constant movement gave me the impression that if we weren't all sitting at the table, he would be pacing around the room like a caged animal.

"If you would wait just a moment, Zen, she would tell you," High Judge Ketiana snapped. The youngest judge was glaring at Zenareth's fidgeting hands as though she was contemplating the best way to rip them off.

"Well there is no need to be rude about it," High Judge Miraz said, radiating a similar nervous energy to Zenareth, if slightly toned down.

"We can't get anything done if we just argue with each other about manners," High Judge Kazi said dutifully. Which of course was followed by a litany of bickering High Judges. At this point, I wasn't surprised. When I'd first come to Agremerre, I had expected the judges to work with the same smooth efficiency of Nevremerre's High Council, where disagreements were paused to return as structured debates and personal dramas were handled elsewhere.

This was not the case.

When actually put onto a task, the High Judges of Agremerre worked in ruthless efficiency. Working together seamlessly to create new laws, settle disputes, and manage crises. However, it did seem to take them some time to actually get on task. How long they were off topic largely depended on how long Head Judge Michael took to bring them back to the issue at hand. Michael had said these moments of chaos were vital for keeping everyone focused later, but I rather suspected that he enjoyed seeing the drama of some of the smartest and most well respected people in Agremerre arguing like children. Even now, Michael was grinning mischievously at the judges in front of him.

After a few more minutes, Michael met Anora's glare and he moved to calm the High Judges before him. "Yes, well I am eager to hear the reports from our neighbors," Michael nodded.

It was as if the room had suddenly been replaced by completely different people. Even the most animated of judges stilled, quieted, and focused on Michael. They sat tall and held their heads high as information was passed along to them. "Reports from Dolma and Calvine suggest similar conditions to ours," High Judge Adelaide spoke once more, all eyes in the room flicking onto her. "However, reports from Nevremerre indicate that regions further out from the continent still have blue skies. They also report that clouds past the Hallea region are more gray than black, seemingly becoming lighter in color the closer they get to the western ocean."

"That's consistent with the idea of a fire then," Zenareth nodded. His hands now still, and his voice strong. "In localized fires, the smoke closer to the source is darker, with the smoke becoming lighter further away from the source."

"It must be a strong and large fire to cover this wide of an area," Kazi pointed out.

"And not one in Agremerre. We've had runners check all over our country. The fire must be somewhere else," Anora agreed.

"There are reports that the sky is darker in the Northern part of the country," said Adelaide once more. "Perhaps the fire is in one of the kingdoms to the North East."

"It will take days, if not weeks, to get information from those countries. It's quite a lot of land for a messenger to cover," I pointed out. "What news from the islands?"

"Both of Agremerre's islands are unaffected," Ketiana reported, "Although they can see the clouds that cover the mainland."

"Well that's something," Miraz nodded. "What is the infrastructure like there? Could they support it, if we sent some of our most vulnerable over? The elderly and the very young should not be exposed to the smoke."

"The smoke is not as high as we might believe, very few people report trouble breathing. However, we must also think of those who are ill," High Judge Westin pointed out, from his spot in the corner of the room.

"We will send knights out to the hospitals, have them create priority lists of who may be the most susceptible to smoke inhalation," Michael ordered as the table nodded in agreement.

"We need to have an idea of the timescale we might be working within," High Judge Eloise said, "If we can have an idea when the clouds will dissipate, then we can take more effective actions."

"But how can we possibly predict that? We don't even know where the fire occurred, or when it will be put out," Zenareth pointed out.

"We can work with Nevremerre," I answered almost immediately. "If there are places in Nevremerre with no or limited smoke clouds, we should be able to track the movement of those clouds to see how long it takes for them to dissipate. We can then calculate how long the clouds may last here. It will also let us know if the firefighting efforts, wherever the fire may be, are going well."

"Good idea," Anora nodded. "We will also send knights up to the North East. Then, when we know where we are going, we will set off to help control the fire." There were nods of agreement all around.

"The people will turn to religion in times like these," Westin said seriously, "Have we heard anything from the temples of the spiritualities?"

"No announcement has been made, yet," Michael said uneasily, "But no doubt they will release something soon. In the meantime, we will release news of our three points of action: 1. Getting those in the most danger to the islands, 2. Working with Nevremerre to track how long the smoke will last, and 3. Sending knights to the North East to help fight the fire when we find it." Everyone agreed, and Michael divided up tasks as the High Judges chatted amiably with each other. Despite the pre-meeting bickering, I was always astonished to find the entire group of High Judges got on remarkably well.

Chapter 3

The Rest of The Continent

Three days passed and things finally began to look better. Thomas and I headed up North with the Agremerrian knights, as well as some of the knights from Nevremerre, who had a similar idea of giving firefighting aid to whichever country needed it. Among the knights sent to Agremerre were Alveron, Azar, Carlos, and Elise. Seeing my brothers and my friends was a wonderful experience, and they were all very happy to dote on Marcus and Genevieve as we waited for news of where we were to be sent. Beyond the blinding joy that came from being with the people I loved and trusted, we also received the news that the clouds were starting to dissipate in the Southern regions of Nevremerre and Agremerre rather quickly. This gave us hope that the black clouds would soon leave both countries.

So, it was a surprisingly cheerful crowd that gathered around the Agremerre-Calvine border, waiting to hear where we'd go next. Our campsite was bouncing with noise and excitement. I don't think there were many who became knights without looking for some kind of adventure. And, practically no one with us had ever passed through the border into Calvine, much less towards the countries that bordered Dolma or beyond. Given the serious nature of the current disaster and considering the black skies that still covered all of Calvine, we had been given permission from the King and Queen of Calvine to take our knights through their country toward the site of the fire.

As such, the whole party was itching to go. Even my own brothers had only been to Calvine once (Azar) or twice (Al), as Father would only let us go to Calvine with him on official business if we were of age. And, personally, I was excited too. While I was content in my choice to live in Dolma for the rest of my life, and I would have been happy to live and possibly rule Nevremerre for my lifetime as well, I had always been curious about other countries. I had been disappointed to learn that, despite bordering more countries than either Nevremerre or Agremerre, the nobles of Dolma held a rather firm belief that the King and royal family should stay in the country. So, more often than not, diplomats from other countries came to Dolma vs. the other way around. It was perhaps for this reason that I was so adamant about wanting to go on this mission of aid. Because, when the messenger finally did arrive, reporting the disaster came from Maychula, I did have a choice. In fact, several people argued for me to stay behind.

Nana would say that we all have a choice in any situation, and this, I have always believed to be true. But, for most of the people I was with, the choice was to go on this expedition or to not be a knight. While they would have been supported in entering another occupation, the time, effort, training, and dedication it takes for a person to become a knight of Nevremerre or Agremerre is not something that is easily given up. For my brothers, the choice was to go on this expedition or potentially not be seen as a viable candidate for the throne.

Both still wanted the title enough for their choice to not even be a question, and, of course, the belief they would be helping the people made going on this expedition the only logical thing to do. Anora didn't even consider another option. She had made her choice a long time ago, when she had become Queen. She would always make the best choice for her people. She would always go where she was most needed.

I, however, was different. I was the only person in the group in fact who was different. Contrary to all I thought I would do as a child, I was not a knight of Nevremerre. How could I have been one while living in Dolma full time? I was also only a Crown Princess of Agremerre, not a Queen. It was not expected that I would leave on this trip. Not to mention, it was also very possible that I would never become the Queen of Agremerre. Once Genevieve turned 21, it was highly likely that my position as Crown Princess of Agremerre would end. Also, as Alveron repeatedly pointed out to me, I had just had a child four months previously. A child who was still nursing. A child for whom everyone would understand if I stayed behind to care for. Finally, it was also mentioned to me that fires are incredibly dangerous things, and my presence on this potentially dangerous mission could possibly deprive Agremerre of two potential Queens.

Yet, none of this could deter me. When Thomas gave me a gorgeously gentle smile and said, "I will support you, no matter what you choose. Stay and we will coordinate relief packages and transportation to less smokey areas for people in Agremerre, Nevremerre, and Dolma. Go, and I will do that and care for Marcus and Genevieve. I will take them to your parents and ensure they are safe and happy while you battle the cause of all of this," Thomas said, gesturing to the sky above.

Well, with his support, my choice was made. It is so much easier to make choices when you are supported so strongly. So, I left. I went out on an adventure to places I had been itching to see, and to help people from all the countries I worked for. We said goodbyes to Thomas and the children who set off for Nevremerre, much to Anora's delight, as Nera was currently cloud free, and she worried for Genevieve's health. And thus, I was solidly a part of the party of knights as we set out to Maychula.

I will never regret my decision to go to Maychula. I gained too much to ever regret my presence there, but I do sometimes wonder about my decision. For on some nights, even now, I wake still smelling the burning flesh. I so violently remember the echoing screams, and I can still see all that happened so vibrantly I can practically taste the ash and smoke in the air. I do not regret going to Maychula, but I sometimes wonder if I might have slept better in the following decades had I stayed behind.

We traveled forwards for about three days before anything seemed amiss. We eagerly took in the new scenery of Calvine and enjoyed seeing the still snow covered mountain tops the Northern country enjoyed. In the sunlight, I imagined Calvine must have been breathtaking, but the sky was still covered with the same clouds that blanketed all of Agremerre that very first day, and the sky was only getting darker as we moved across the land. We crossed Calvine with a surprising efficiency for such a large group. Of course we were still slower than the runners. However, we moved fast enough that upon reaching the Calvine-Andaluca border, we were forced to wait for permission to cross into their land.

Elise had been our runner, this time around, sent ahead by the rest of us after we first learned that the fire was in Maychula, and that we'd need to pass through Andaluca to get there. We were all pleased to see her ride up to our party only a few hours after arriving at the border. No one had a desire to wait particularly long when there was work to be done and help to be given. Still, our excitement was tempered when we noticed that she was not riding to our camp alone.

"Greetings Your Majesty, Your Highnesses," Elise bowed to us upon arrival. "I have brought with me Sir Princeton Langinly, who would like to speak with us before we enter Andaluca."

"Certainly," Anora replied, "We would be happy to hear what you have to say." Her voice was regal and confident, and somehow completely lacking the annoyance I'm sure she must have felt at managing to be delayed on such a crucial mission.

"Yes, well is there a place we might speak privately?" Sir Princeton asked. He looked like a rather fragile man to carry a title most commonly found in knights. His round face was puffing out with each breath, and he was dabbing a sweaty forehead with an intricately embroidered handkerchief as if he had been the one galloping instead of his horse.

"As you wish," Anora replied, nodding to me and my brothers as we followed her into a tent we'd set up in case we needed to spend another night in Calvine.

"Good, good," Sir Princeton agreed.

Once inside the tent, we moved to look at Sir Princeton who looked suddenly rather nervous in the face of all four of us. "Well, what did you want to say, Sir Princeton Langinly?"

Azar asked. His face modeled Anora's polite indifference, but I could hear the impatience in his voice.

"Andaluca does not require people to say last names when addressing an individual, as long as they retain the person's title," I corrected automatically, thinking of my time with Priscella as she spoke of her home. Azar shot me an impatient glare in response.

Sir Princeton missed this, however, and merely nodded. "Crown Princess Avalynn of Agremerre and Dolma is correct. However, manners are not what I have come to discuss with you today. You have been granted passage through Andaluca if you wish, but there are some things you should know about the disaster in Maychula," he paused for a moment, breathing heavily before he continued once more.

"First, we do not believe that the incident in Maychula is a fire. Or, at least, it's not like any fire we have ever seen. Our knights have been helping those survivors who made it to Andaluca, and the stories they report are... confusing to say the least. There are tales of people turning to stone, of lakes of fire, and of people being swallowed by the ground itself."

I looked at Azar to see his reaction to all of this, for the words out of Sir Princeton's mouth sounded far too much like the fantasy tales Azar had loved as a child. Before me I saw not a giddy child, but rather a grown man, seriously nodding at the Andalucian representative. He'd grown up, I'd realized with a jolt. Even just a few years ago, Azar would have found some humor or excitement at this mystical sounding news, but now he mirrored Father in his focused attention and concerned analysis of Sir Princeton's words.

"We have not allowed for any of our knights to go into May-chula for fear of a similar fate," Sir Princeton continued, causing me to turn my attention back to him. "You are welcome to cross through our country, and even help us provide aid to the survivors, but we wanted to warn you of the dangers you may face in Maychula before you go."

"Thank you for the warning, Sir Princeton," Anora replied after a moment. "We will continue on into Maychula, but I will make sure that all of our knights heed your warning."

"If you must," Sir Princeton sighed, clearly skeptical of our choice, but I was far more wary of their choice not to even try to go into Maychula and help the people there. "The second, and final request is that you and your party stay at the Castle Andaluca when you return from Maychula. You will be treated as personal guests of the King, who is eager to meet with you all."

"That is an easy enough request," Anora conceded. "We will send a runner as soon as we learn when we are expected back to Andaluca."

"Brilliant!" Sir Princeton brightened. "I will leave you with your... camping... for the night then." Sir Princeton scrunched his nose in disgust before he bowed and left the tent.

"People turning to stone and eaten by the ground?" Al questioned after Sir Princeton had left. "Sounds a bit like their knights have been drinking as opposed to helping the survivors."

"They wouldn't have told us if they didn't believe the information to be at least somewhat credible," I pointed out.

"It does sound rather fantastical, however," Anora argued.

"Perhaps they have another reason for not wanting us to enter Maychula," Azar hypothesized. "They could be responsible for all this in an attempt to gain more land."

"They would have made more of an effort to stop us if that had been the case. Sir Princeton seemed merely to be a messenger. He accepted our decision to go into Maychula the first time we said we would enter," I argued.

"Plus, if they were trying to stop us, no doubt they would have sent someone with more power," Anora agreed.

"They could still try to stop us on the way to Maychula," Al mentioned.

"It is always wise to be on guard, when traveling through unfamiliar territory," Anora nodded. "Ava, you seem to know of Andaluca, what can you tell us of their governing system and military style? What should we be looking out for as we travel?"

"I only know what Queen Priscella has told me, given this was her home country -"

Azar made a disapproving tsking sound at my words and mumbled something about "another children-selling country" under his breath before I could continue.

"Beyond that," I continued, sending Azar a disapproving look, "I only know what was in Dolma's files on neighboring countries and given the state of their Agremerre file, I'm not convinced their files are wholly accurate." Fixing Dolma's files on other nations had been one of the many tasks I was planning on working on after finishing my year of training as Crown Princess of Agremerre.

"Hmm, then perhaps just give us any information you received from Queen Priscella," Anora decided. I complied with her request and told them whatever limited, but guaranteed to be accurate, information I had gained from my time with Priscella. It honestly wasn't much, and I could tell from the frowns on everyone's faces that I had not said anything that could be used to guide us through Andaluca.

Eventually we agreed to use the same protective measures we'd used while traveling through Calvine and we then informed the knights of Sir Princeton's warning about Maychula. The knights reacted, for the most part, how I had imagined Azar would have reacted. They cracked jokes at the fairy tale nature of it all and blustered about how they would soon be "real" heroes. There were made up stories where we fought dragons or creatures of magic and darkness in Maychula.

"If it were really magic we were fighting," Anora testily argued as we were riding, about two days after we entered Andaluca, "then the temples would have sent masters of the magic spirituality. Instead, they confirmed that this, whatever it is, falls under the spirituality of nature. In their announcement, they confirmed that our response is best focused on helping other living beings while the land and the world readjusts itself to an appropriate balance."

"Yes, Your Majesty," the knights called out, becoming quiet for a few minutes before chatter broke out once more.

That evening, we began the usual preparations of food and shelter at our newest campsite. There was a casual and easy atmosphere around us. Not long after we'd eaten, we were all scattered about the campsite relaxing and chatting happily about what we would soon encounter. I was just moving to sit by Carlos and Azar near the fire when I heard Carlos ask Azar why he wasn't joining in with the other knights as they jokingly told dramatic stories of what we might be facing, and I found myself moving closer to eavesdrop on their conversation, fascinated by the character change my normally silly brother was displaying.

"Oh I have plenty of tales to add," Azar laughed, "but I'll save them for when we are all back to safety."

"He's really changed a lot, hasn't he?" Al's voice rumbled behind me. I nearly yelled out in surprise, my face going red at being caught snooping. "He reminds me of Father. It used to be that they only looked alike, but now he really acts like Father too." Al continued, ignoring my surprise.

"You can be a lot like Father as well," I said, finally returning my heart rate to its normal pattern.

Al tilted his head at me, "Do you think so? I suppose it would be impossible not to pick up on some of his habits after being raised by him, but I don't think my personality is really like his. I've always thought I was far more like Aunt Olivia."

"What?" I said loudly, causing some heads to turn to us. I quickly apologized and more quietly repeated, "What?". I couldn't seem to wrap my head around the boisterous and loud Aunt Olivia compared to the careful and calculating Al standing before me.

Al just smirked at me before responding. "It's about values," he explained. "Aunt Olivia may be more carefree than I am, but our values are more aligned. We both value ingenuity and our family above all else. Azar and Father value the country as a collective and hard-work. Ari's values I find to be closer to Mother's, in that they both value intellect and economic stability. And you -" Al paused looking at me once more.

I stared back into his dark eyes, hooked on his words. I was not expecting an in-depth analysis on the morals of our siblings and myself from Al, but he was often considered to be the most observant of the four of us, so it was undoubtedly a valuable insight. "You remind me of Nana, you value the individual and compassion. To you, the plight of one person is just as valuable as the plight of thousands," Al said seriously.

"And do you suppose that since Azar's values more closely align with Father's that he is the best fit to be King?" I asked, not addressing his assumption of my values, as I found him to be correct.

"No," Al replied simply. "I don't think there is any one set of values required to be a ruler. There are some things that a ruler shouldn't value - or should, at least, not believe to be a priority, but as long as you are working towards the highest and best good of the people you are trying to serve, the specifics of your values are inconsequential. That being said, Azar would make a great King."

"Oh," I said, turning to look at Azar once more. "I'm quite sure you did not always think that, so what made you change your mind?"

"He grew up. He worked to change what he felt he was lacking and he grew up. He is 24 now, a phenomenal knight, a kind man, and a well-trained leader. He would be a great king."

"And what will you do to best him then?" I asked, thinking of their famous rivalry.

"You know, Ava," Al replied, "I think I will do nothing." I looked at him startled, but Al was still staring at Azar. "I used to believe I had to save you from the burden and struggle of being King or Queen, but I failed at that. I failed at that before I had even expected the real battle to begin."

"Oh Al, you never...," I began, but Al interrupted me.

"I was convinced you would be unhappy," he continued, "but you aren't. I don't know if you are as happy as you can be, but you are happy." With a jolt, I realized that he was right. Despite my rough start in Dolma, despite the many, many concerns I had and still have about the country, I had made a life there. The work I did, the people I'd found—they did make me happy. Fixing a broken country was incredibly enjoyable in its own slightly (largely) chaotic way.

Nodding my agreement at Al, he continued, "So, you see, I had to reevaluate my belief, and I found it to be wrong. So, I find the throne doesn't matter to me nearly as much. Oh, I'll stay in the running for the position. I could do some great things as a King, you know, but I'm rather neutral about the final result. Great Uncle Asher is getting on in age, and he doesn't have any major candidates for his dukedom. So, I've put myself forward. I expect in the next year or so I will take over his position. I can still become King, if I am chosen, but I believe I will enjoy the work of a Duke either way."

"Really?" I asked, unsure if my question was related to the shock that Al was considering taking over Great Uncle Asher's dukedom or if I was asking about his assertion he would enjoy being a Duke.

"In smaller roles, it is easier to prioritize things like family. Of course, I will still have to leave in emergencies, but it will be a smaller region that will make it easier to return home. I can do work that interests me, and invest more in experimentation, something that is more difficult to do when you must ensure the safety and security of the whole nation. Yes, I've spoken often now with Great Uncle Asher, and I do believe the role will suit me well."

"That's wonderful then," I congratulated, even though I was still a little shocked at all that had transpired.

"Yes. I think so too," said Al comfortably. He looked very relaxed in his position, perhaps he was lighter after releasing made-up burdens he'd given to and taken from his siblings. "Now," he said, turning back to me, "Are you not at all worried about your husband?"

"Thomas?" I asked, very confused about where this conversation was supposed to be taking me. "Not really, why?"

"He's going, alone, to Nevremerre for the first time. Considering your experience in Dolma, I would have thought you'd be more concerned."

I laughed at this. "Oh, no. Thomas will be fine. He is a smart man and has listened to me tell so many stories about Nevremerre he is far more prepared on what to expect than I ever was. He's gotten close to Father through letters and he has always been interested in how Nevremerre and Agremerre rule. He may be nervous at first, but he will be far more accepted in Nevremerre than I was, and sometimes still am, accepted in Dolma. I trust that he will learn a lot and enjoy his time there."

"And you trust him?" Al questioned.

"Yes, I trust Thomas completely."

"Why? How can you trust him when your arrival was so -" Al paused as he struggled to describe my first year or, honestly, first two years in Dolma.

"Torturous, painful, calamitous, odd?" I supplied.

"You know what I mean," Al said angrily.

"I trust him because we have the same goal: make Dolma a safer and more secure place for its people, and also to raise Marcus with love and care. We've discussed it, agreed on our goals and what each term means. And, he is on my side. He's been on my side since our wedding night, and he has worked on showing it every night since. In just about four months, we will have been married for three years. How can I not trust him after all of that?"

"And if he does betray you?"

"Then I have the power and the support to survive it. But, I do not regret trusting him as he is now, and I won't regret trusting him in the future. He shows me who he is working to become every day, and I am thrilled to have someone like him working beside me."

"Very well, Ava," Al said, giving me a quick hug, "Just know I am always here if you need me."

"I know, Al, and I do love you for it."

"I love you, too.

"Did I miss out on a sibling moment?" Azar's voice called out distraught from beside us.

"Yes," Al declared, pulling me closer, "Ava just declared me her favorite brother."

"Oh stop it," I said, pushing myself away from him.

"How could you say such a thing?" Azar swooned dramatically. "Did he force you to? Will I have to fight him? For we both know his words aren't true."

"You stop it, too!" I cried out. "And here I was thinking how much you two had grown up."

Azar laughed. "Only around others, Ava girl," he called out, "Only around them." Al nodded in agreement and gave me a quick wink before I mock stormed off and left the two of them laughing behind me.

Chapter 4

The Survivors

The final day before heading into Maychula was much the same as all the others. The knights were loud, but cautious as we moved through unfamiliar territory. There were several shrieks of unbridled laughter and tales of adventures past. There was an infinite duality about the women and men we traveled with. They could be joyful and carefree in one minute and become serious and focused in the next. So, when we reached the camp the Andalucian knights had set up at the border of Maychula around midday, the tone switched once more. The usually jubilant knights moved through the camp in a somber silence. Next to us sat rugged and worn down survivors who'd made their way into Andaluca.

At that moment I was transported to another time in my life. I had been traveling with my parents and the knights of Nevremerre, nomadically ruling Nevremerre, when we heard news of a fire breaking out in Merino, a town to the east of Nevremerre. When we got there we found nothing but destruction. We spent several months working to rebuild the town. During that time, Nana, a spiritual master, recommended that I use my aptitude for the spirituality of life to do work as a transitioner, someone to help counsel the people of Merino through their grief.

Nana had taught me that trauma manifests itself differently for different people. "You can never truly know how a person will process tragedy until it occurs, Ava dear," Nana had told me, her voice more serious and strict than usual, "And death, be it death of a loved one, death of a part of someone's life, or death of the person themselves, is the most unpredictable trauma experience of them all."

We'd been surrounded by death as she taught me. The black husk of buildings, the flowing petals of ash swirling around us, and the soft crush of black soot that coated the once green and brown Earth. The fire in Merino had looked like something from a nightmare and the haunting aftermath mixed with the winter chill that had clung to the air had sent shivers down my spine. Nana's initial words did little then to ease my fear, but, as was so often her way, she was not done explaining the world around her.

"Life is the most serious of all the spiritualities. Not because life itself is serious. No, no, life is one of the most joyful, play-ful, and silly things there is, if you chose for it to be. No, life is a serious spirituality because it cannot exist without death. But death, my songbird, can be a joyful thing as well."

"When a part of your life dies," Nana continued, pulling me to her and lowering us onto the ashy ground. "It gives room for something new to begin. Even here, this fine ash is rich with nutrients. It may take some time, but the plants and animals who chose to reside in this area will know an abundance they hadn't known before. When people die, their souls go back to the universe, where they are welcomed by souls who love them unconditionally and who first celebrate with them that they have lived, that they have endured, and survived through another lifetime in a physical body. Then they can decide if they will live again and gain a whole new adventure."

"However," Nana's voice grew solemn as she turned towards me, her blue eyes holding onto my own. "When you work with people who have just experienced death, they do not know yet of the joy that is still to come. Some may even go the rest of their life without realizing it. As a transitioner, it is not your job to be their joy or to even tell them of the joy that they will eventually receive. You have to meet people and souls where they are. They will be lost, sad, angry, relieved, frustrated, haunted, scared, and so much more. Maybe they will feel everything all at once, or maybe they will feel a hollow echo of nothingness ringing through them."

"To transition someone to the next part of their journey, you must mirror their emotions. Grasp them, empathize with them, and understand, to the best of your ability, what they may be feeling. Then, you need to let go of those feelings."

"Let go of them?" I'd asked her, confused.

"Yes. They are not yours to hold; you just need to acknowledge and work with them in the other person to facilitate their healing. To work with a person as a transitioner, you must meet them at their level and their level is where they are emotionally."

I was terrified. This was all very vague instruction really. I mean I had been told how to tune in to people's emotional state prior to our arrival, but to then have to go out and do it, to provide advice, or whatever it was that transitioners do, felt insane. Nana, however, just laughed at me. "You'll know what to do when the time comes, songbird." And, amazingly, I did. Sometimes I just listened, sometimes I talked through the person's experience, and once, I sat with someone in total silence for three hours as he contemplated the sky above.

To be a transitioner, to master the spirituality of life was to understand death.

I don't know if I really understood death after the fire in Merino, but I certainly came to understand people, to understand traumatized people who had just lost their homes or loved ones. So, when we rode up to the survivors camp in Andaluca, I stopped. I sent my horse off with a very confused Azar, who was still following Anora to the camp center where we'd discuss final preparations with the leader of the Andalucian knights. Then, I did what Nana had taught me all those years ago, I worked as a transitioner.

The first thing one should really know about the spiritualities is that it is exhausting work. You know what to do because you are being guided by the universe and the Gods. So, as you do the work it may seem easy, and, in some ways, it is. However, it is entirely and completely physically draining. After my first transitioning session, I slept for nearly ten hours, and my body felt as though I'd run for miles.

As with any activity, the more you do it, the greater endurance you have, but even the most experienced spiritualists can only do so much. I knew all this, and still, I was lucky when Al pulled me away several hours later insisting that I rest. Before I could even inform him of some of the troubling things I'd learned, I had fallen into a deep sleep.

I held the whole party up that day. We were meant to have left and entered into Maychula that afternoon, had I not transitioned several people and used up all my energy. With me asleep, and rather dead to the world, it was decided around me that it was best not to split the party at this stage. The rest of the knights would help at the campsite and we would regroup and head into Maychula the next day.

Under normal circumstances, I would have felt embarrassed by this delay I had caused; however, these were not normal circumstances. Early the next morning, hours before anyone in our party would have awoken, the Earth began to shake, and there was a loud booming noise that broke over the campsite. Followed by ear shattering screams. Everyone was now awake, but there was nothing, nothing at all to be done. After all, you can't exactly fight the ground.

The shaking lasted only minutes, but panic still raced through the camp. "That was the sound! That was the sound!" a young boy squeaked, his eyes wide with terror as he looked helplessly around the camp.

"It's happening! It's happening again!" A middle aged woman said, frantically running around the campsite. Her uncontrolled limbs nearly hit a lantern hanging beside her, and I was jolted into action before any other tragedy could occur.

"Quiet! Quiet! Everyone, please be silent and listen here," I tried to command, my voice still a little dry from not having used it since the day before. Panicked people, I soon realized, were not very easily commanded. Some turned to face me, mostly those who were shocked and confused, but those struck by a greater fear could not be touched by my words.

"The mountain is not exploding!" I yelled again, throwing my voice as far and as loudly as I could.

The people beside me flinched, but this time I did have more success in getting the attention of the people around me. Unfortunately, this also meant that they now directed their fear at me instead. Azar, who had apparently been sleeping in the tent next to mine, had just enough time to ask a confused, "What?" before we were swarmed by the masses.

"How do you know?" The flailing woman I'd seen before demanded.

"But it was the same sound!" Another called.

"And the Earth was shaking!" A third person called out.

"Please, quiet down," I said, a little bit desperately. "I will explain everything." This time my words were obeyed, and I was able to more calmly address the crowd. "When the mountain exploded before, you saw a stream of orange fire, do you see that now?"

There was a collective shaking of heads. "And you also felt a huge wave of heat, some even said it felt like burning. Do you feel that now?" Again heads were shook, some even shouted out relieved answers of "No."

"There you have it then," I continued, "Perhaps, Mount Evermay is exploding again, but," I added quickly, pulling up the information I had heard during the transitioning sessions I did the day before. "You are in Andaluca now. The explosion never reached here. You are safe here."

There was silence for a moment, and the crowd calmed slightly before someone spoke. "Well what about the Earth shake then?"

Azar came in for this one. "I spoke with the captain of Andaluca's knights yesterday, he reported that before the black smoke took over the skies there was a similar Earth tremor."

"Earth shake," someone in the crowd corrected. Azar looked utterly bewildered by what to do with this interruption.

"In Nevremerre we've called them Earth tremors," he said, effectively derailing the conversation.

"Yeah, well here we call 'em Earth shakes," the man continued, "And, I think we'd know 'em best." There were nods of approval from all around him.

"Regardless," I jumped in before Azar could respond, "what we are trying to say is that the Earth… shakes, happened before, and this land was not as affected by the mountain exploding. So, we are all safe here. Please continue to rest, the knights of Nevremerre and Agremerre will be heading into Maychula in the morning and we will send a report back as soon as possible." The finally satisfied group began to return back to their respective tents. The only real comment was the many people who gave us solemn nods to be careful before they went back to sleep.

"Damn stupid idea to go back there," the Earth shake arguer declared, "but hopefully, you'll do something good." He nodded before heading back to his tent.

"We'll try," Azar called after him before turning to me, "Mountain exploding?" he questioned, as we were joined by Al and some other knights who had been calming panic in other areas of the camp.

"That's what the people who I worked with yesterday called it. One even declared that the top of the mountain came right off," I told him.

"Hmph. Well, I'm not entirely convinced we can trust them based on what they call things," Azar said, shaking his head before he mumbled "Earth shakes", under his breath. I could only stare at him in response. "Well I guess we'll know for sure later today," he decided before yawning.

"Back to bed then," Al agreed, winking at me as he grabbed Azar's shoulder guiding him back to his tent.

A few hours later, we woke up and went into Maychula, and about half a day into our ride I realized that, had I not fallen asleep the day before, we all would have surely died.

The first thing I experienced and truly noted was the smell. It wasn't the scent of wood burning or an overwhelming cover of smoke. In fact, the smoke was far less intense than I would have associated with any normal fire. No, the burning scent that filled the air in this part of Maychula was like that of rotten eggs mixed with an earthy scent. Not in the way of fresh soil, but rather the same mountain scent that filled the air at mines. It had that chalky mix of breaking rock, but somehow the smell that those rocks were burning. For the whole place was covered by the scent of perhaps the inner core of the Earth itself being burned.

The next thing I noticed were dark black rocks, black lumpy rocks that were strangely smooth. They surrounded the area we were currently in, making what almost could be considered paths around us. They almost looked like a river, like a stream made of stone. The combined assault on my senses sent fear rushing into my very core. Intellectually, I knew that if I'd just traveled back towards where I came I could see sunshine and normal activity, but somehow there was this pressing weight on my chest that screamed that I would die here, that the world was ending and I should run far, far away.

"What are these?" asked Dame Clara, staring down at the stones.

"Ouch," came the startled cry of Dame Lillielle. "They're burning!" she cried out in confusion, showing us a slightly red hand. Indeed, her hand looked exactly like one that had been placed on a heated stove just a fraction too long.

"I think they are slightly cooler back here," Carlos' voice called out behind me.

"Why would you touch them if she just said they were burning?!" I shouted at him. Carlos just shrugged in response.

"Let's just try to avoid any rocks like this for now," Anora sighed.

"Knight Fern, please take lead, keeping an eye out for these rocks. Everyone follow their lead," Al called out, putting one of our more noble riders up front.

It took me a while to notice the increasing heat. I realized that the heat had in fact been increasing as we moved closer to where I assumed the disaster was. It must have been, for I never felt a wave of heat hit me. No, I only had the sudden and shocking realization that I was in fact hot. I was most certainly warmer than I had been a few minutes before. Yes, I was quite certain that heat had been steadily increasing.

Finally, we began to see people. At the time I was shocked that it took so long to find anyone. I had assumed that there would be masses of people running away from the devastation, but now we were only met with one or two souls looking desperately lost. When we eventually amassed groups of five or ten of these people, we would send a couple of knights to escort them to Andaluca.

There were also bodies. Not many, but several looked to be days old. These people, despite soot and ash on their clothes, didn't seem to have died in a fire. They had no burns or even the singeing of clothing that were common on the bodies I had seen in Merino. These people had likely died lost and dehydrated while trying to find some help. It was a terrible thought. When we saw the first body, we stopped to debate what to do with the bodies we would find. Some, perhaps, could still be identified by loved ones. Others had been consumed beyond recognition by the nature around them. However, in the end, our priority had to be the living. Only later could we give proper send offs to the dead. So, we passed the corpses and helped the people we could find until at last we saw what had caused this all.

I had never seen anything like it. I had never even dreamed of anything like it. Neither had anyone else. We stood with some of the best knights in the world–people paid, trained, and encouraged to act in times of crisis and we just stood there in complete and utter shock. Being completely unprepared, we had no idea what to do. Before us, Mount Evermay stood, pouring black smoke into an even blacker sky. From its tip, bright orange, and oddly solid looking liquid descended down the mountain and into the already decimated town below. However, the solid liquid that burned before us had masses seemingly floating on top.

From our viewpoint, standing slightly above the once populous valley below, these black shapes looked almost like burnt trees, floating along the orange river that was slowly consuming all it touched. However, I was disabused by this notion when the orange matter hit a tall tree, toppling it, and causing the once living creature to burn away. I noticed what I had assumed to be black logs were slowly disappearing as well. They were just not burning as quickly as the tree. Besides nature, I watched houses be consumed by the orange liquid. Bricks, stone, wood, and even metal the orange river slowly devoured them all. It was something, I realized instantly that we would never be able to stop it. We had traveled for days, walking or riding for hours on end to witness a phenomenon that we had no power over. We were powerless here.

I can never decide if I should feel bad about how long it took me to notice the people. I mean, I was after all witnessing a phenomenon I had not even known was possible prior to five minutes ago. Yet, the occasional shrieks from the former town could be heard from even where we stood, and, once one got over the shock of the orange river, the constant motion of little black dots in the valley below was difficult to miss. The knights appeared to be torn with this conundrum as well. Some, like Azar, Elise and Queen Anora were already running down the hill, ready to save the fleeing people. Others like myself, Al, and Carlos lingered behind, still trying to wrap our heads around the insane reality we were currently seeing.

After what seemed like ages, Al's voice rung out around me. "We need to help the people make it up to higher ground," he said. His voice felt distant, like he himself couldn't believe he was actually speaking, but he recovered himself with a little cough and then he motioned us forward.

"Wait," I called out, my mind finally catching up with the world around me. "We should leave the horses here, it will be easier to maneuver around whatever is down there, and the orange matter doesn't appear to be moving so fast that we couldn't avoid it." Al agreed, and we left the horses under the care of Oberon as we followed Azar and the others who were already rushing into the valley.

There was a lot more smoke down here, I quickly realized, as the burning smell of rotten eggs infiltrated my body and I had to cough smoke from my lungs. Al noticed it too and called out to the group, "No one should stay down here too long. Get a few people up to safety and then stay up for a bit to recover from the smoke down here."

"Yes, Your Highness," came the chorus of voices around us. We continued our descent into the valley. At the bottom we immediately began to help those who had made it to the base of the hill. Many were carrying large bundles of things they must have rescued from now demolished houses. Some were leading pets or carrying infants. We immediately took steps to lighten their load. Carrying bundles or even the people themselves up and down the hill.

Over and over we climbed that hill. Trekking our way over rocks and crevices that were quickly becoming familiar. Until, finally, a few of us were able to move further into the remains of the city. Here, an oppressive heat buried its way into my skin. I briefly pondered if this is what it felt like to be cooked like a dish in the oven.

"We have to keep pushing forward," Anora's voice called out from beside me. "The people here can be aided by other knights, but there are undoubtedly slower people closer to the source of this disaster who require our more immediate help."

"Right you are, Your Majesty," Sir Argeon agreed, followed by Azar, Elise, and another knight, Dame Mastoria.

"Then let's go onwards," Anora pledged as we pushed forward into the city.

Anora's prediction was right as we soon discovered lost children, elderly, and injured people who were struggling to breathe and move in the smoke. Anora and Azar both gave up their horses to some of those in greater need, and sent word to the knights behind us that more people would be needed to assist those here. Still, our small party pushed forward, paving the way for those behind us. Until, eventually, we hit a fork in our path. Anora quickly divided us and sent Elise and Mastoria to the left, Azar and I down the center, and herself and Sir Argeon to the right.

Azar and I pushed along our path in a determined race of endurance; we paused only occasionally to aid stragglers who had fallen or to check for signs of life in a few poor souls. We pressed forward, having decided, by Azar's suggestion, to only stop when we hit the orange river. For only then would we be able to save those who were closest to the damage, and then work our way back up to the front. The first time we saw the orange matter up close, we still had a ways to go before our path would be completely covered by the glowing substance, but a small stream of it flowed slowly along a small gutter. Azar kept moving forward, but I paused to examine the strange substance. Up close, the glowing orange matter looked thicker and heavier, rolling and seemingly crashing over itself as it pressed onward in its path. I had a strange desire to touch the hot substance, which almost looked like jelly as it moved passed me.

"Ava!" Azar's panicked voice called out from somewhere ahead of me.

"Azar!" I cried out, running towards where his voice had called out for me.

When I finally found him, Azar was surrounded by the orange substance. He stood dutifully in a small pocket of un-touched space in the center of an expanding pocket of the flowing orange matter. In his arms he carried a small child. Behind him lay the body of a woman whose limbs were already eaten by the substance surrounding us.

"I need you to catch him," Azar yelled at me. He looked at me fiercely as his words resounded around us. "I can not jump with him."

"Okay," I agreed. My voice sounded foreign to my ears, and there was a horrible knot deep in my stomach. My heart pounded recklessly in my chest, and my palms were sweaty beside me. We were in danger, I realized with a start. I don't know why I hadn't realized it before, but I certainly knew it now, watching the solid liquid encroach on Azar and the boy.

I watched Azar with fear exploding out of every part of me as he threw the now silent child. The weight of him hit me solidly in my chest, knocking the wind out of my lungs and almost throwing both me and the child into the orange matter before us. I overcompensated slightly in my attempt to keep us out of the burning matter before us, and I fell on my back with the child whimpering on my chest.

"Ava!" Azar cried.

"I'm okay! I'm okay!" I cried back, trying to breathe again, and pulling myself back onto my feet. "Now come back Azar!" I desperately pleaded with him, determined to get him back to the side of the orange matter which had an escape route.

Azar nodded, and prepared to leap, pushing his legs out in front of him like a long jump as he flew through the air. I stepped back, still clutching the child at my breast, but Azar didn't land on the untouched rock before me. Instead he landed in the molten cascade of orange matter just before me. His scream was like nothing I'd ever heard as he scrambled out of the orange matter. His skin was peeling off of him as he finally made it to safer land.

"Azar!" I screamed, using a free hand to pull him towards me. His skin was like fire on my own, and I found I could not touch him for long as he toppled over towards me, a hand still spotted with orange brushed passed me, causing me to scream as well as it melted my clothes and dug deep into my own skin. I jumped back instinctively as Azar fell to the ground.

I was back toward him in an instant rolling him over as I watched his labored breaths start to stutter and increase in frequency. Shock, I realized from somewhere far removed from myself. He's going into shock. "Breathe, Azar!" I found myself saying, "You have to breathe for me!"

Something hot and wet was flowing down my face, but I hadn't the time to figure out what as I desperately tried to figure out how to make Azar's chest move once more. A burnt hand moved beside me, reaching towards me before it fell with a slight thump. In front of me, Azar's eyes went glassy, and I realized with a jolt that he was gone. A numbness washed over me as his chest moved a few more hollow breaths, still programmed to function even if the soul had vacated. Then, it too stopped.

I stood up, suddenly, desperate to put some distance between me and the corpse. I hardly even remembered the child until he whimpered quietly in my arms. "Oh," I said, numbly, "Oh, are you alright?" I asked, more emotion leaking through this time.

"They're dead," the boy said softly, "and it's hot." Perhaps he was feeling as numb as I was, as his voice, too, felt distant and far away.

"Yes," I agreed, "Yes they are dead, and we should leave." But, I did not move, my eyes instead watched Azar's disfigured corpse get taken by the orange matter once more. It was at this point when I finally realized this matter was not a liquid, for instead of being swallowed by the substance, Azar's body rolled neatly on top, and I suddenly knew what the black masses that floated on top of the substance were. They were the burning bodies of its victims.

With this knowledge, I finally turned my back on the scene, and carried the child and myself away from the disaster we found ourselves in.

Chapter 5

The Aftershocks

I could not tell you what happened in the three days following Azar's death. For I was in a state of hollow-being that fell indiscriminately over our group of knights. During the days we tried to help people get to Andaluca, maintaining a base camp at the top of the hill, in the hope that any remaining survivors would find us. At night, I crawled close between Al and the child I had rescued, all of us unable to cry, but desperately in need of comfort. We had knights out day and night searching for survivors from the town and searching for our own missing people, including Queen Anora who had never returned from where she had split off from Azar and I on that very first day. Running around to any place we felt we could get to safely. And, sometimes, going to places that were not safe at all in hopes of finding the people we'd lost. At the end of the third day, we knew we had to go home. The orange matter had cooled slightly, most of it turning to black, and Mount Evermay had stopped smoking.

The locals that still waited with us informed us that this was the first time the mountain had stopped smoking since this ordeal had began. We then knew we had no choice, but to call off the search for those who had never returned. We lost eight, in total. Azar, Sir Laurence, Dame Lillielle, Sir Rodriguez, Dame Rachelle, Dame Cassi, Sir Argeon, and Queen Anora. Of the eight, only two deaths had been witnessed, Azar's and Dame Lillielle. For all three days, hope rang out for the other six.

The decision to leave was made jointly by Al, the senior knights of Nevremerre, Agremerre, and myself. As we told the knights of the decision, we were greeted by sad nods of agreement, until one lone voice broke over the solemn crowd. "I give my regards and loyalty to Avalynn, Queen of Agremerre," Oberon's voice called out before he kneeled before me.

It was like a bolt of lightning struck us all as I realized what had just occurred. Before me, all knights and people from Nevremerre, Agremerre, and Maychula echoed Oberon's words before they kneeled as well. Even Al dropped to his knee and muttered his respect for Queen Avalynn. The hot, wet, liquid returned to my face as I let out a small, little, "Oh."

Al stood up once more, pulling me to him. "We'll talk about it all later, Ava dear, but we must go now," he whispered in my ear.

"Yes, yes," I said more loudly, moving away from Al. "Thank you, for all of the work you have done here in Maychula, now we must prepare to go home. We will first stop in Andaluca where we can get proper treatment for all those who were injured here," I instructed as the crowd began to move.

"Including yourself, Your Majesty," Challa stated, in a tone that suggested he would not be argued with. Again, the crowd fell silent.

"Including myself," I agreed, looking down at the bandage along my stomach, where Azar's hand had brushed against me as he fell. The crowd nodded, and we made our way back to Andaluca.

Grief is terribly, terribly odd. For the three days we were still searching for survivors I couldn't feel anything at all, or rather, I wouldn't let myself feel anything at all. We had work to do, so I could distract myself. And, yet, I was so terribly clumsy and I kept forgetting things and I was hardly able to recognize that life still moved on around me. I felt so disconnected from the world, but grief cannot go on in the same manner forever.

I, as it turns out, could only make it through three days before my emotions toppled me down. When we arrived at the camp in Andaluca, we gave the Andalucian captain there a report and the burn on my stomach was treated. I was then brought to my tent. Even if it was a tent, it was a Queen's tent. As a Princess, I never lacked for luxury, even as we camped around Nevremerre, but there was no denying the materials that frequented my parents' tents even surpassed my own.

Thus, I felt oddly sure that I was being granted the height of luxury in this room. An actual wooden framed bed was placed neatly in the corner of the spacious area. On it were piles of outstandingly soft furs that weren't really any use to me in the heat of summer, but that would keep me comfortable all the same. Rugs coated the tent's floor, leaving my bare feet steeped in constant comfort anywhere I stood. I was also given a writing desk, chair, full wardrobe, and a full length mirror.

I felt wildly out of place. The few changes of clothes I brought on this journey seemed far too small to deserve an actual wardrobe, and my person far too dirty to touch anything in the clean space. I knew my whole body to still be covered in soot, dirt, and sweat from the past three days. So, when a group of people came in a moment later, I felt sure they were here to lead me somewhere else. Somewhere smaller and dirtier where I was sure to fit better.

Instead, the people just bowed, silently placed a tub in the center of the tent and filled it with water. One took my bag, and graciously explained she would wash my clothes. One brought in bandages and ointment for me to rewrap my wound once it was cleaned. They seemed to do all of this in next to no time at all, and suddenly they were gone without me even having said a word. Although, admittedly, I'd had really very few words to say at all as of late.

So, I bathed and dried myself with a clean towel that had been left on the bed. Then I moved to dress my injury. My body moved automatically, I don't think any thoughts ever entered my head. I went to the mirror to take care of my burn and... and suddenly I was drowning.

I was drowning.

All my emotions came bursting out at once and my sobs took over every inch of me. My shoulders shook and my knees trembled and my legs could no longer keep me standing, buckling as I hit the floor. Somewhere in the back of my exhausted mind I became grateful for the luxury tent with its plush rug that softened the blow of my knees. It was also, I realized, far nicer to break down amongst nice things.

Even in my tears I tried to avoid the crux of the problem, but I couldn't. I really, truly couldn't because there, burned into my side, scaring my skin forever more was the thumb, forefinger, middle finger, and a partial palm print of my dead brother. Burned into my side was Azar's half palm print, placed there as he died. As he died right before my eyes. Burning, flailing and screaming after saving the life of a young boy. A boy who got to live, when he hadn't.

I do wish to clarify that even in this moment, I never regretted saving the boy. Not once, not even for a moment. My grievance was with the universe, for surely there was a way that both of them could have survived. Where Azar had made his leap successfully, and we had brought the child to safety together. But, that was not the reality we lived in.

The physical pain that tore into my body at the knowledge that Azar was dead was unbearable. My chest heaved, my stomach was rioting in my skin, and my lungs seemed incapable of ever breathing properly again. It was only then that I also remembered Anora was gone, as well as several others, and I cried even harder, a feat I had not thought to be possible until that moment. I had this vague sensation that I would never be able to survive all that was happening in this moment. Surely these feelings would kill me too.

But, they did not, and some time later, I found I had nothing left in me to cry. And, I did not feel numb. I, in fact, felt more human and real and grounded than I had since Azar had died. I wasn't back to normal, or whatever my new normal would be, but I was more. I'm not sure what I was more of, more of myself? More complete? More alive? I didn't quite know. All I knew was I was more than what I had been these past few days, and I could work with the more I had.

Slowly, and very unsteadily, I rose off the floor and I kept going forward. I put ointment on and bandaged my wound,

I dressed myself in clean, but far too big clothes that had been set out for me. And, in that moment, clean, dressed, and more exhausted than I had ever been in my entire life, I knew I would be okay. Not now, likely not tomorrow, or the next day, but someday this pain would pass. Oh, I would never forget my brother or how much I loved him. And, undoubtedly there would be moments where I missed him desperately, but I would get better. It wouldn't always hurt as intensely as it did now. I would laugh and be happy again, even if it seemed impossible now. I would someday be okay again.

I also realized I was starving. Well, not literally starving, but I was very hungry. I was also very tired. Grief and sadness are arguably the most exhausting emotions. I had absolutely no energy to go out and search for food around the campsite, but I also didn't really want to go to bed hungry. Finally I decided that food was in fact vital to survival and moved my lead like feet through the tent so I could put on my boots and find food.

As it happened, I did not have to go very far. When I opened the tent I came face to face with a young girl who immediately curtsied, "Good evening, Your Majesty, are you done with your bath?" My immediate reaction was that I am not "Your Majesty", until it hit me in the next moment that I was Queen now. I was in fact to be addressed as Your Majesty.

"Yes, thank you," I managed, still feeling a little dumbstruck by my new title. "I would like some dinner now if you can find it."

"Oh yes, Your Majesty!" The girl replied, looking oddly happy about the request. "And, I'll bring people to take care of the bathwater too."

"Thank you - er - Miss?" I questioned more than a little awkwardly.

"Cora, Your Majesty."

"Yes, well, thank you, Cora," I said, attempting to give her a smile before retreating back into my tent, removing my boots and collapsing on top of my bed.

Soon people came to remove the tub. They were not as efficient as I remembered from when they entered my tent, and I was forced to wonder if grief also influenced your perception of time. Still, I was not waiting terribly long before I was alone once more. This however, also didn't last long as I was soon faced by the boy who had been almost constantly by my side since I'd caught him after Azar's toss.

"I do not know your name," was my first response to his sudden presence.

The boy looked just as startled as I felt at my words, but he did manage to rebound quickly. "Alder, my name is Alder Evermay. I'm six," Alder declared.

"Oh, nice to meet you. I'm Avalynn, Avalynn Carleon. Evermay is the same name as the mountain that just exploded," I commented. This was probably not the thing to say to someone who had just lost his home and family to said mountain, but Alder didn't seem to mind.

"In Maychula your last name is the region you were born in," Alder explained dutifully. "The mountain was named after the town... or at least I think it was."

"Alright," I nodded, "How'd you get in here?" I finally had the presence to ask.

"I snuck in," Alder replied.

"Oh, nicely done."

"Thank you."

"Did you get a bath?"

"Yes," and he did look cleaner. He was dressed in a single clean shirt that must have belonged to an adult man as it covered his tiny body completely and the sleeves were rolled up around his arms. His skin was slightly lighter now that he wasn't covered in soot, but not by much. His black hair was short and curly atop his head, the same texture as Al's. He had a slight frame and a broad nose, and his dark eyes held both determination and fear as he continued to talk to me. "Some of the old ladies made me wash."

"Well, it must feel better to be clean."

"Yeah, but mom's dead," and then Alder began to cry. I suddenly didn't feel so tired as I moved to pick him up and pulled him onto the bed with me. "They're dead," Alder cried onto my shoulder, "and that man, your brother is too," he sobbed.

"I know," I said softly, my own tears resurfacing to fall on his head.

"I don't want them to be dead," Alder cried.

"Me neither," I agreed. We sat like this for a while before both our tears slowed.

"You're a Queen," Alder stated, when he could finally manage a sentence without hiccuping.

"So it would seem," I replied, still unused to my own title.

"That means you'll go away. I don't want you to go away like mom did." This, I had to remind myself, was a child's way of processing death and that Alder did not actually believe I would die if I went to a different place than he. Or, maybe he did, but only because he was a child still processing grief.

"You could come with me," I responded.

Honestly, I wasn't thinking about the very valid reasons I should pause and do some research before taking in a random child. In my defense, I was grieving, and, after being thoroughly scolded by Oberon about making promises without having done proper research, we did the due diligence required to ensure that Alder did not have any other family members looking for him. Nothing ever turned up, and Alder declared he had never met any other family members besides his mother. So it all worked out in the end. Which was good because I'd loved him as my son since I asked my ill-thought question, and he had responded, "Yes, please let me come with you."

A few minutes after Alder had accepted my offer to come with me, Alder's breath slowed beside me, and the quiet rumbles of his chest saw him soundly asleep. I felt exhausted, the intense rumbling of my stomach quieting, so that I too could have fallen asleep. And, I did. Although, I didn't even notice it. All I knew is one moment I was sitting with a sleeping Alder, and the next I was jerked out of a dream-like state by the sound of crying somewhere around me.

It was a jarring experience, my body felt lifted off the bed, but also somehow magnetized to the ground beneath me. It was as if I inhabited two worlds at the same time, and it took me a moment to return my split soul back to the reality I was currently experiencing. When I did so, I realized it was Al crying beside me. His big shoulders hunched and shaking as he kneeled in the center of the room. Beside him was a tray of food, a simple meal, just some stew and some bread. Something for me, I understood with a jolt. Al had been fulfilling the request I had made to Cora earlier.

Trying not to disturb Alder, I gently made my way from the bed to where Al was. I picked up the tray he had carried from its spot on the floor, and moved it to my desk. The smell of which wafted around me reminded me painfully of my empty stomach. There were more important things though and it didn't take much effort to turn back towards Al. I wondered if he even knew I had moved. He remained in the same spot I had originally seen him in. He looked almost like a painting, alone in the center of the tent. I could not let him stay alone though.

The only thing I knew how to do was to follow my instincts as I quietly threw my arms around him. He pulled me close instantly. His large body nearly crushing me with his desire to be near me. We knelt there for who knows how long before Al pulled back, looking at me with a tear stained face and puffy eyes.

"I didn't mean to wake you," he began, his voice a trembling whisper as he looked at me with an odd sort of terror in his eyes. "But, when I saw you and you were safe and you were healthy and you were breathing, I just couldn't help it. I'm just so grateful. So Gods-be-damned grateful that you are alive. That you didn't die as Azar did, and it was so overwhelming because -" Al breathed in deeply, looking away for a moment before looking determinedly back at me.

"Because I feel like I must be some horrible person for feeling so happy that you're alive even though Azar is dead. I hate that he died. It feels like I am falling apart without him here. It feels like I won't ever be whole again, but - but we could have lost the both of you. And, I can't help but think about what it would be like to have come back without either of you. I've been thinking about that for so long that when I saw you, safe and breathing and alive, I couldn't help but feel overjoyed. Of course, then I felt guilty for being so happy when Azar was dead. Do you think I'm a monster for thinking like this?"

"Oh Al," I said, throwing my arms around him. "If you're a monster, then I must be too because I am so happy to have you and Ari and Father and Mother and Mama still with me. I couldn't stop those feelings even if I tried, but I wouldn't try. I have enough love in me to be grateful and joyous that I have you, and to deeply miss and grieve for Azar. I will admit though, it feels so much easier to bear when you are here with me, Al."

Al cried into my shoulder, and I watched again as my own tears joined his. I had never been aware that the human body could produce so much water. Later, Al wordlessly climbed on my bed, cradling Alder in his arms, and I, ravenous as I was, ate the now cold stew and bread Al had brought. Despite the cold broth feeling sticky and bland down my throat, and the stringy meat that moved tough and chewy beneath my teeth, I soon found the whole bowl gone. Only then did I join my brother and newfound son on the fur covered bed before drifting off to a dreamless sleep.

When I woke, I had to lead; I was a Queen now–the highest ranking person on this whole campsite, even if the Andalucian knights and the Maychulan refugees weren't technically under my command. I started by telling Al and my knights about my plan to adopt Alder. I then had to pause for several, admittedly well deserved, lectures on appropriate child adopting etiquette, and some, admittedly accurate, comparisons to my Father's adoption of me. A group of knights went to Alder to start making absolutely sure we weren't taking him away from any loving and living relatives. Then, I met with the captain of the Andalucian knights to discuss what was to become of the Andalucian refugees. Next I worked with Al and some of the senior knights from Nevremerre and Agremerre to discuss plans to go home. Here I was also thankfully reminded of our promise to the Andalucian King, as I had completely forgotten we had promised to visit him after our aid mission had been completed. Finally, I decided that four of our riders would be sent back as messengers to Agremerre and Nevremerre to relay the news of the disaster, our impending visit with the royal family of Andaluca, and to let the people, the Agremerrian high judges, and my family know about the eight people we had lost. And, of course, someone would be sent to inform the Andalucian royal family of our impending arrival.

My next task should have arguably been the easiest. All Al and I had to do was decide who we would select to break the news of Queen Anora's death to the High Judges and Azar's death to our family. It seemed easy enough, I had a good idea of who I thought would be the best candidate, Al agreed, so it was definitely a surprise when both of our first choices for this task refused. Oberon's refusal, in hindsight, made sense. I may trust him implicitly, but he was, as he promised three years ago, my knight, not Agremerre's. Although, now being the Queen of Agremerre, this felt like a rather minor distinction.

It was more surprising when Knight Zelle, my second choice in relaying Queen Anora's death to Agremerre, and Agremerre's most senior knight on this mission, also refused. They insisted that I was the new Queen and their place was by my side. I did have the brief thought that, as the new Queen, surely I was also meant to have my orders followed. However, considering this was more of a request versus an order, I was able to quickly brush the thought away. Knight Zelle then helped me find two knights whom we both felt were suited to the role, and they both easily agreed to the task, preparing to set out for Agremerre right away.

Carlos, in my mind, was the obvious choice to send to Nevremerre. He was Azar's best friend. He was close with everyone in our family. His father was on the council. As far as Al and I were concerned there was no one better to send. Frankly, it was the easiest choice I'd made in awhile.

"No."

"What?" Al responded, blinking at Carlos. He had not even paused to think about it before his response was given. I was shocked, and I was practically convinced that I had not heard him correctly.

"No, I'm not going," Carlos declared again, his voice sounding astoundingly confident even if he folded his arms across his chest like a petulant child.

"What?" Al repeated, still blinking at Carlos like he couldn't understand what was going on.

"Er - why?" I asked, sharing in Al's confusion.

"I just won't. I won't do it," Carlos declared again. Al and I just stared at him. We sat like that for a while, stuck in some sort of weird staring contest. Finally, Carlos spoke again, letting out a large sigh, "I can't. I can't do it," he almost whispered to us. His arms falling down by his side as he spoke, "I don't know how. How am I supposed to tell your parents that their son is dead? How am I supposed to tell Ari? Or the Dowager Queen? I don't know how."

Al finally moved at his words, sighing to himself, "How are they supposed to hear it from anyone else?"

"Perhaps with greater ease than they would hear it from me," Carlos insisted. "I can barely keep myself together. The world feels sideways, and I'm so tired all of the time. They will want a report from someone who can give them the information they need without falling apart. And how do you expect me to ride all the way back to Nevremerre like this? I don't want to leave alone. I want to stay with the two of you. With people who loved Azar, just like me. Then maybe the world won't feel as empty."

"Does it feel less empty when you're with us right now?" I asked.

"Of course!" Carlos responded, instantly, "Doesn't it for you?"

"Yes," I responded instantly. I had not thought about it before, but I knew his words rang true the moment he asked the question.

"I can't ride away to be alone with all this," he demanded, gesturing chaotically to himself.

"No. No, you're right," Al agreed, doing a complete 180 from his views just a few minutes earlier. I could hardly complain however, as I found myself switching my view as well.

"I'm sorry," I said. A guilty feeling wormed its way through my body. "We were so busy thinking about our family that we forgot about what this may have been like for you. You will not have to go. We can choose someone else."

"And perhaps you are right. Maybe it will be easier for our parents to hear it from someone less attached to the news," Al pondered.

"Perhaps, although, realistically, there isn't anyone here who could truly be called detached from this. We all lost someone. With eight people dead, it will be difficult to not be attached," Carlos pointed out.

"Yes," Al sighed, "Yes I know. I really, really know."

We sent Dames Ihram and Elise back to Nevremerre in the end. We spent only one more day at the refugee camp before the remaining members of our party were guided towards the Castle Andaluca, where we would stay with King Bradeon and Queen Christine of Andaluca.

Chapter 6

The Transition of Queen Anora

Andaluca was a pretty country, or rather, I imagined that it would have been had the sky not still been covered in smoke. Still, Andaluca was a pretty country, and I had no choice but to acknowledge this fact as we rode towards Castle Andaluca. There was, as it turned out, nothing to do but admire the view as the whole ride was eerily silent. A harsh contrast to the noise we demanded from each other on the way over. But, we were grieving, everyone here had lost someone, most of us had lost many people we were close with.

Over the course of my life, I have done quite a lot of work as a transitioner. Even during my short period of time living in Dolma, and, three years really is a short period of time in the grand scheme of things, I did some minor transition work. Even after this tragedy, or rather, especially after this tragedy I would do the work of a transitioner. However, despite all of this, despite all the people I know I have helped, despite all the study and research I have put into transitioning, I have never been able to say that I truly understand grief. Death I understand. A transitioner's job is to understand death in all its many varieties, but grief has constantly eluded me. Grief, I've now come to believe, was never meant to be understood. Its purpose is to simply exist, to be as it will be, to do as it will do, and to do so in new and inventive ways in each person it lands in.

It is a hope rather than a belief that this is why it took me so long to acknowledge Anora's death. The grief of losing Azar, the trauma of watching him take his last breath, his hand burnt into my skin, I hope that the grief of my brother is what made it take so long to realize I had lost Anora too. For I am not sure that I could bear the idea that her death meant less to me somehow. With all that Anora had given me, my grief for her had to be just as important as the grief for my brother. So, it must have been the grief that made me take five days to truly realize that Anora was dead too.

My realization was so innocuous, so wildly different from the dramatic tearful breakdown I had experienced in Azar's death. I was simply riding in silence when I suddenly remembered that Anora would likely require some information on King Brandeon and Queen Christine. As he was Priscella's brother, I knew more of him than I perhaps knew of other neighboring monarchs. So, I opened my mouth to tell her of this. I turned to where she had ridden by my side for this journey, for the past few months really as she taught me of Agremerre. She had been at my side through all of it, teaching me about the country she so deeply cherished, a country she had known she would rule at just five years old. Even though she had an older sister at the time, Anora said she was so sure she would be the next Queen that no other candidate even mattered to her. She knew she would be Queen in the same way she knew her name, or that the sun would rise the next morning. She'd known it in a way I certainly had never experienced. Yet, she taught me the passion and love she had for Agremerre, quietly lecturing me as we rode around Agremerre, even as we rode to Maychula. And, now, when I looked beside me to speak with her, she was gone.

In whatever jumbled and seemingly dysfunctional mess my head was in, my next move was to look for her. I swung my head around, scanning the knights around me for a glimpse of her. Then, and only then did I realize that she was gone. The sky seemed to crash down around me, and at the same time the ground collapsed beneath me. Right, I thought, Anora is gone. That is why I am Queen because Anora is gone. I couldn't say dead. There was no body recovered. Of course the same could be said of Azar, but I'd watched Azar die. Perhaps Anora was still out there. In my fog over Azar's death, I wondered if I had looked for Anora hard enough? What if I'd missed something?

I felt a desperate sort of panic course through me as I fought the urge to ride back to Maychula. To look around just one more time, for I must be able to spot what everyone else missed. Surely, I could find some clue that the finest knights of two different nations missed. A logical voice somewhere in the depths of my brain informed me that these thoughts were false, but my heart screamed that they had to be true. The only other alternative was that Anora was dead and truly gone and would never be coming back. The thought of it was too terrible to give much thought too.

Yet, I couldn't go rushing back. Well, I suppose, physically, I could, but I was also now Queen of Agremerre, on my way to meet with foreign royalty, with whom maintaining diplomatic relations would be important. Nor could I make the knights turn around to go on a wild goose chase. To insinuate that in the three days we spent searching for survivors they somehow weren't doing their absolute best to find our missing knights and the woman who had ruled Agremerre for the past 20 years. No, no I could do nothing but carry on.

An, in a weirdly foreign and yet totally predictable turn of events, despite my mental breakdown, the world kept turning. My horse kept walking forward, the plants by my side kept fighting for life in the smoke covered sky, and Andaluca remained a pretty place. A pretty place in which I felt utterly broken. It was cruel, I realized suddenly, it was the most insane form of cruelty that one would inherit a throne after the death of the previous monarch. How terribly cruel that I must now take the place of a Queen while still muddled by the grief of my own loss. Of the loss of Anora. I couldn't even begin to think of what this must have been like for Father when he lost my Grandfather. He'd always said it had been difficult, but words meant little when I had no connection to the man. Now though, I felt I could finally understand what he may have gone through. You cannot control death, and if you could, I know Anora would still be here today, but, if I were given the opportunity for a long and healthy life, I would abdicate before making one of my children go through something like this.

With that thought living like a fire in my belly, giving me something firm and solid to hold onto, we passed the rest of our silent journey until we at last reached the Castle Andaluca. The cool night's air wrapped around us in a startling contrast from the oppressive heat that the explosion in Maychula had imprinted on my skin. Odd as it may be, this brief chill was an almost comforting reminder of the change that would come. That I would not always be unstable. That Maychula would someday become more of a far away nightmare than the all consuming terror it was at the moment.

"Welcome Queen Avalynn of Agremerre, Crown Princess of Dolma, and Princess of Nevremerre," a voice called out, forcing me into the present moment. I looked up to find King Brandeon smiling at me. He was truly Priscella's twin, with the same brown hair and blue eyes. Except there was something much softer about the man. He smiled easily and his shoulders lacked the tension that permeated Priscella's every move.

"King Brandeon," I replied, almost bowing before I remembered we were of equal standing now. "Thank you and Queen Christine for welcoming us into your home." I nodded to the woman on his right. Queen Christine was a serious sort of person. She did not smile at us, as her husband did, but she quickly and easily directed workers to start taking our horses and bags to the appropriate places. "Let me introduce the rest of my party," I continued.

"Oh no need, no need," King Brandeon waved me off. "I've been told of everyone you travel with, and of course I welcome you, Crown Prince Alveron of Nevremerre."

"Thank you, King Brandeon," Al bowed, "But I am not the Crown Prince of Nevremerre."

"But you're the eldest son?" King Brandeon questioned.

"Nevremerre is a merit based monarchy. No Crown Prince or Princess will be decided until my youngest brother reaches 21 years of age," Al explained, his tone was exceedingly polite, but after knowing him my whole life, there was a familiar weariness in his tone that I recognized having also needed to explain the Nevremerre monarchy multiple times.

"Please let me introduce you to the rest of my knights," I insisted, refusing to let any of these people go unnoticed. King Brandeon was impatient as I named the 14 knights that were still with us, but he let me finish all the same. When I was done, he opened his mouth to speak some more when he was interrupted by Queen Christine.

"You must be very tired from your journey," she said rather pointedly, "and we were very sorry to hear of the losses you have suffered in trying to aid Maychula."

"Oh, yes, very sorry," King Brandeon agreed, his face briefly morphing into some kind of mock sadness that didn't fool anybody before he bounced back to speak once more.

He was cut off once again by Queen Christine, "As such, we will show you to your rooms where you can rest for the evening. We have nothing planned for the evening, so feel free to take dinner in your room if you desire. Of course, you are all welcome to dine with us, if you so desire."

"Thank you Queen Christine," I responded quickly, rudely hoping I could prevent King Brandeon from speaking, not quite ready for his exuberant personality at the moment. "I believe everyone here would be glad of the rest."

This time, King Brandeon's face showed genuine disappointment as he reluctantly had maids guide the knights to their rooms. Al, Alder, and I were guided by Queen Christine herself, while Oberon, Challa, and Hugo followed diligently behind us. I felt certain I did not require all three of them, but they seemed to be in some kind of agreement about the matter as they all followed me without my asking for it.

"I apologize for my husband," Queen Christine said as we moved through the gray stone castle.

"He seems very nice," I said, diplomatically, and, really, that was true. It just wasn't the best time for me to appreciate this fact in the midst of grief.

"Nice isn't everything," Queen Christine mumbled, and I got the impression that we were not in fact meant to have heard her words. Beside me, Al raised his eyebrow as he shot me a look confirming I had heard the comment as well. I nodded back quickly before Queen Christine spoke once more. "He is very excited to see you, Queen Avalynn. He is eager to hear more about his sister. We haven't had the pleasure of her company since your wedding, and even then, well I'm sure you know how hectic weddings can be."

"Yes," I agreed. "I would be happy to discuss Queen Priscella's welfare with him."

"Good. His two elder sisters and their spouses will be coming to dinner tomorrow. I am sure we will discuss her then."

"Of course," I responded simply. While I knew Priscella was once close to her siblings, her life had changed quite dramatically compared to theirs, and she purposefully maintained low contact, finding it difficult to communicate with them. Other than reporting that she was physically well, I was not comfortable sharing much else with her family. I sent a silent prayer to the Gods that Priscella would not be a long topic of conversation.

Queen Christine showed Alder and Al to their respective rooms, maintaining nothing more than polite small talk the rest of the way. By the time she showed me to my room I was more exhausted than I had been on the whole ride over. While important in polite society, small talk had never been on my list of skills, and it was tireless work to think of neutral topics of conversation. This got even worse when the weather, still hidden by the smoke clouds, was crossed off the usual list of safe topics. I truly felt I must have been terribly uninteresting with my series of neutral and basic responses, but I had simply no idea how to contribute more.

I was overwhelmed with relief when we finally reached the room I was staying in. I dismissed the plethora of servants who'd been assigned to me with instructions to bring me dinner and let me rest. Then I collapsed onto a large couch, drinking in the stillness of the room around me. Of course, I really only got about a minute of solitude before the door opened once more and Alder appeared.

"Your room is much bigger than mine," he commented, by way of greeting.

"I think that happens when you're a Queen," I replied, not moving from my place on the couch. I hadn't really bothered to look around the room, but I was sure Alder's words were true. "They can't risk offending me and causing a war."

"Would you go to war over a room?" Alder asked. His tone was curious, but I heard a hint of worry in it as well.

Despite his concern, I couldn't help but laugh at the question, "If I went to war every time I was insulted, Dolma would not exist anymore. No, no, war is not something to take on lightly. I have made some of the most important choices in my life in avoidance of war. I have no intention of jeopardizing peace over something so trivial."

"Oh," Alder said, contemplatively.

"How's your room then?" I asked.

"Big," he responded. "I've never seen a room so big, but yours is bigger."

"Just wait until you see Dolma," I laughed again. "I've yet to see anything as big as the royal palace there." Alder nodded as though this was a very serious conversation. "You can't stay here tonight," I told him after a moment. "We all need to learn how to function on our own once more, but why don't you get Al, and we can all eat together?"

"Okay," Alder hesitated for a moment before he agreed and left to grab Al. We all ate together and it felt more comfortable than I had been in awhile, even if we didn't speak much.

When I told Al of my thoughts on sleeping alone once more, he just ruffled my hair and said, "Oh Ava, we're never on our own," but he did leave me to my own company as he carried an exhausted Alder away. So, yes, I was never on my own, and my solitude was a welcomed respite from everything else, and it was also when I learned what it truly meant to be a transitioner.

Nana had always told us that dreams were the universe's way of communicating. Spiritualists in all five spiritualities were taught early on in their studies how to interpret and read their dreams. As a child, Azar found this aspect of the spiritualities especially absurd. He'd come to Nana with increasingly bizarre "dreams" that he'd had, demanding she interpret them. Nana however, always knew exactly when he was lying. As a child, it was a frightening ability. As an adult, Azar was in fact, a terrible liar.

Personally, I had never given much thought to my dreams. I had real, physical things to worry about. Of course Nana would say that the spiritualities were real, but I had, at this point in my life, found it difficult to give much importance to things beyond the physical. So, when I closed my eyes that night and felt my body be transported to another place, I assumed it was just another dream, something to be forgotten when I woke up the next day. Never mind that it didn't feel like any other dream I experienced. Never mind the fact that I could simultaneously feel the soft sinking of the luxurious bed and a solidness under my feet as I walked around the place my soul had taken me. No, this was simply just another dream. At least, that's what I thought when it first happened.

I've not put too much thought into what the space in between life and death looks like to others with my ability. But, to me, the place I exist in, or was brought to, changes depending on what my purpose there is. For this first experience, I was brought to a place I have only ever been to twice in the years that followed this moment. The space around me seemed vast, a circular light yellow floor pulsed with energy as I moved around it. The energy was almost bouncing against my touch, yet somehow still stable beneath me. The walls, if they could even be called walls, moved from a purple to a dark and empty black that seemed to extend endlessly around me, but somehow still pulled me into this exact spot. The above, for ceiling was a wholly inaccurate word for what lay above me, was a pulsing and endless sea of blue. And, directly in front of me was Anora.

"I was not done teaching you," came her smiling voice. She looked healthy, and beautiful, in flowing robes that looked so soft compared to the normal armor she usually wore. Despite her words, which normally would have been laced with annoyance or pain, Anora looked relaxed, and at ease. There was something about her, beyond her appearance that made me sure that this was Anora, but perhaps not exactly the Anora that I knew. Nana would later inform me that someone's true soul often had a slightly different personality than the one they would adopt in their lifetimes.

"I wish you were here to teach me more," I finally responded, sadness filling my being.

Anora gave me a sad smile, but her voice was still light as she spoke once more, "It is no matter, you will learn, with or without me. It's only that I am still attached to my country." At this point, Anora held out her hand and on it I saw a long red string, tied gently to her wrist and leading down to somewhere beyond the floor.

"Oh," I remarked, unthinkingly, reaching out to grab the string. In touching it, the floor rippled and opened, showing the string connecting all the way down to a floating orb, Anora's string landing on a large green mass. Around us, the walls turned into pictures. Anora's life as a Princess then Queen flew around us. Her feelings washing over the space as I caught glimpses of her life. I saw the work she put into becoming a great Queen. Hours in libraries and on training grounds. Nights spent studying diplomacy and memorizing the main imports and exports of each town, city, and village. I saw her punish criminals, save children from potentially deadly accidents, help adults learn new skills and find their passions and jobs. The whole time the honey-covered feelings of excitement and joy rang through the room. Ruling was never a duty for Anora; it was a pleasure and a passion that she was thrilled to take on.

"Agremerre," Anora said, basking in all that was going on in the space. "You will take care of it, won't you?" She asked me. Her voice was soft, yet when she spoke, the whole space stilled, deadly silent in want of my response.

"Of course," I said, only focusing on Anora, "I will give Agremerre everything I have to give to keep it and its people safe and thriving."

Anora beamed at me, "Good, good. I had hoped you would," she nodded. "You may cut the string now." Beside me a plain pair of silver scissors appeared, I moved to grab them and did as she said. I cut the string and watched as the soft material disappeared from around Anora's wrist, and the end connecting to the land simply fluttered down back to the world.

Anora and I watched it fall, me with a sort of dazed confusion, and Anora with a relaxed sigh. The space reverted to its original form. Quiet and calm around us. "I have one more," Anora called out, in a sad whisper that filled the space. She held out her other arm, revealing another red string. I did not have to touch it, as Anora herself revealed its meaning to me.

"It's Genevieve," Anora said, pulling her bound wrist to her chest, cradling it with her body. "She will have a long life, if everything goes to plan. Not like me," Anora scrunched her face, "Well it was not supposed to be this short. I had, in fact, planned to be around a while longer." Anora's face relaxed once more, "Although, I never had any intention of living very long. I have other things to do, so I never wanted a long life this time around. A solidly middle-aged death, that was quick and easy for all involved, was what I had planned," she said, tapping a spot on the back right of her head for some reason.

"You can't control everything," was my response, although I had no idea where the words came from.

"No," Anora agreed, "Although you plan for more of your life than most people believe. Next time I will just have to ask more questions about possible volcanos before I go down."

"Volca -" I began to question before I was cut off.

"But this is about Genevieve," Anora said, her voice suddenly more serious than it had been this entire time. "Her soul has plans for her, and you must let her live them, no matter what they may be."

"Of course," I responded. This felt obvious to me, and I wasn't sure why she was telling me something I already knew. Plus, I imagined it would be incredibly difficult to prevent someone from accomplishing their soul plans.

"And," Anora began, before softening once more, "And be sure she knows that I love her. That I will be watching her from the beyond and that I will be so proud of her no matter what she does. Make sure that she is loved, and that she eats well. Please make sure she lives with knowledge of me and my love for her."

"Of course," I said again, there was a pleading tone in my voice as I continued to speak. "I will tell her everyday how loved she is, that I love her and I will continue to love her with all the love I have within me. She will know of you and she will be loved by many, especially me. We will take care of her, I promise."

Anora beamed at me once more. "Okay, okay, then you may cut the string." Again the scissors appeared, and I had the odd realization that I had never noticed them disappear. Again, I held Anora's string filled with love for Genevieve, and once again, I cut the string. This time, instead of watching the string fall, there was a rush of movement in the room as a thin strip of shining paper ran through Anora, on each connecting page a scene from her life played out before rolling itself into a tight ball sealed in a case of metal which deposited itself into my hands.

"I think this is for you," I said, after everything had come to halt.

"Yes," Anora smiled at me softly. "Yes it is, and I am ready to take it."

I handed her the metal case when the above suddenly opened before us. "Until our next life then," Anora said to me as a shiny golden brown staircase opened up in front of us.

"Yes," I agreed, in awe of what was happening in front of me.

I watched Anora climb the stairs, walking freely and easily to the opened area. When she finally entered I was overwhelmed with emotion. Beyond the entrance there were cheers and shouts of joy and the space was filled with so much love I felt as though I would burst. There was a happiness and abundance so pure I felt tears streaming down my face and then the above closed. The room was empty again and I was cut off from the world and emotions the above was holding. Those cheers and that moment was not for me. Not yet.

I then found myself back in the room in Andaluca. The sky was still dark around me. My face was still wet from tears and there was an exhaustion that filled me as if I had not been asleep at all. After a few deep calming breaths, I turned on my side and fell really and truly asleep. I woke late into the next morning, refreshed, but still sad for all I had lost. And, I remembered every moment of my strange "dream" from the night before. It would haunt me, not in an unpleasant way, but certainly in an unforgettable manner for weeks until I could finally speak to Nana about it. Of course, in those weeks in between, I still had duties to attend to, so I could not think of this "dream" for very long.

Chapter 7

The Family of Queen Priscella

My first task, for our first morning in Castle Andaluca, was yelling at my brother, Oberon, Hugo, Challa, and Carlos (just to make sure I had everyone) for letting me sleep so late in the day when we were supposed to be maintaining diplomatic relations with Andaluca. The responses, however, were really not in my favor. Al sheepishly admitted he'd woken only thirty minutes or so before I. Oberon, Hugo, and Challa all seemed to be under some pact to ensure I got the "rest and energy you need to be healthy, Your Majesty." And, they all had the gaul to look happy about it. Carlos simply said it was not his responsibility as he was not one of my personal knights. He somehow managed to also imply that I should hire him for that role.

"For a Queen, not a lot of people listen to you," Alder commented from the side of the room, having presumably snuck in sometime during my rant.

"No, no they do not," I huffed in frustration. I grabbed Alder's hand and stalked out of the room, "Come along. We're going to get dressed and go meet with the King and Queen."

Admittedly, I was not really thinking when I dragged Alder down the halls of the castle. I was far too concerned with trying to prepare a suitable explanation for why I was late and still in traveling clothes. But, the heavy velvet monstrosity that the maids had first put me into this morning was far too heavy to wear in the summer heat. A summer heat that was only amplified by the still lingering heat from the eruption of Mount Evermay, I might add.

Alder, to his credit, followed my rapid pace with a quiet determination, but he stopped short before we could enter the room with the Andalucian royals. "Am I really supposed to go with you to meet the King and Queen?" he asked, as though I was guiding him to this room just for the sake of company on my walk. Company besides Oberon, Hugo, and Challa that is.

"You are a Prince," I declared. A cough from Oberon caused me to reevaluate my words. "Or at least, you will be, as soon as we are finished doing the proper due diligence regarding your adoption," I quickly amended. "The point is, one day, if you wish it, you will be a Prince, maybe even a King if we change the rules in Dolma. Until then, you will still be considered a representative of the countries in which you hold a title. You will need to learn the ways of a court and diplomacy. I won't force you to say or speak in a way that is untrue to what you wish to be, but I will ask that you learn how to be around people with power, and to learn that they are nothing more and nothing less than what you are: human."

Alder nodded as he digested my words. Then he spoke once more, "Assuming I get adopted by you, what country am I representing?"

This was an excellent question and behind me Challa snorted with laughter before answering the question for me. "When you're adopted by the Queen, you will be a Prince of Agremerre as the son of the Queen. However, given her parentage, Crown Princess apparent Genevieve, and your new younger sister will technically outrank you. So, you will represent Agremerre. However, as the son of the Princess of Nevremerre, you, Crown Princess apparent Genevieve, and Prince Marcus (your new younger brother) all share the same rank of Duke/Duchess of Nevremerre. If the Queen becomes Queen of Nevremerre as well -"

"Not likely," I interrupted.

Challa just grinned at me before continuing. "If the Queen becomes the Queen of Nevremerre as well, you will all rise to the rank of Prince/Princess of Nevremerre. Thus, you represent Nevremerre. And, finally, as the son of Queen Avalynn and her husband Crown Prince Thomas of Dolma, you will gain the title of Second Prince, ranking below First Prince Marcus, but above Crown Princess apparent Genevieve. So you also represent Dolma," Challa finished.

"And Maychula," I added, "You may not have had a title there, so you don't represent their policies, but you are from there, so you can represent their people, if you so choose."

"Got all that, kid?" Oberon laughed.

"No," Alder said, looking very confused at all the information that was just thrown at him.

"Well you don't have to think too hard about it. We can go over it again later. Just follow my lead and everything you do will be fine. Now, let's go greet the King and Queen of Andaluca!"

Unbeknownst to me, it was not in fact just the Kind and Queen of Andaluca in the room we had just entered, but the whole extended royal family. The sheer number of people in the supposedly private chamber was briefly off putting, but before I even had a chance to think about it, I was enthusiastically greeted by King Brandeon.

"Queen Avalynn!" He exclaimed, rushing towards me and grabbing my hand, patting it roughly as he moved to greet Alder. "And..." there was a long pause as King Brandeon clearly went through a mental panic at how to address Alder. "This young man!" He eventually mustered.

"Prince Alder is acceptable," Alder said with a sudden confidence that I, at this point, had not realized he had possessed.

King Brandeon was also startled by this as he jumped a little before looking at me for confirmation. After I gave him a small nod, he relaxed more, "Welcome in, Prince Alder. Now let me introduce everyone!" With a rejuvenated sense of excitement, King Brandeon went around the room of nearly 30 people introducing every single person. He listed their full names, titles, relationship to himself, and he seemed to have a personal anecdote to share about every single one of them. It was a wonder the heavy set man wasn't completely out of breath at the end of it all.

Now, logically, I can and should acknowledge that King Brandeon really was a very nice man. It was nice that he was comfortable enough to have his whole extended family with him. It was nice that he took the time to make sure we knew a little something about everyone in the room. And, it was nice that he was so easily accepting of Alder's new change in status and title, something that in another place, with another ruler, would not be accepted so easily. King Brandeon was very nice, but there was not much else that could be said of the man.

"Now tell us, tell us of your trip! Of what adventures you saw in Maychula!" King Brandeon demanded, and several excited faces turned towards me. Behind me, I could practically feel the bodies of my knights stiffen. I looked down at Alder whose open face held a dumbfounded expression that didn't quite fit the intelligent eyes he possessed.

I held back a smile at the expression and fixed my attention back onto the King. "I am glad I had the opportunity to see more of the world. I had never been to Calvine, Andaluca, or Maychula before this tragedy," I said, politely, sitting down in the singular free chair, seemingly placed so that I might see all of the crowd in front of me. It felt more like I was expected to put on a show than have a discussion with the people in front of me. However, no matter the intentions of this family, I am not a singing monkey.

"While we were unable to do as much as we hoped, I do believe that we were able to help many of the survivors get to a safer place and help heal the injured," I continued.

"I know we did, my Queen," Oberon said from behind me. Taking a quick step forward to speak to me. "A rough estimate put together by Sir Kentin found we helped at least 103 people make it to the refugee camp in Andaluca." Oberon gave me a quick bow before stepping back behind me.

"Thank you Sir Oberon," I smiled at him. I had not thought much of the people we had helped, in all honesty. I was far too consumed by grief and the chaos of all that had come after Azar and Anora's death, but it felt good to hear that we had done something to help the survivors . That our whole mission was not as pointless as I had thought. 103 people was quite a lot too. Although, I suspected that both Azar and Anora would have scolded me for this line of thought. They would argue that even just one person was enough to justify our presence. I wondered briefly if I was a cruel person for thinking we'd need to save at least eight to nullify our presence, and at least nine to justify it. Though I supposed around 103 people saved meant I did not have to wrestle too much with this question.

"I do believe that Mount Evermay has stopped its explosion for the time being, so the sky should hopefully become clearer soon," I finished turning back to King Brandeon.

"Yes, well I suppose that's good. It was very interesting, of course, at first. No one had ever seen the sky so dark! It was quite the exciting thing, let me tell you, but now that it's been here for several weeks, it's beginning to lose its appeal," King Brandeon said, nodding seriously.

I was not a six year old boy, I could control my facial expressions. At least, that's what I told myself as I processed King Brandeon's words. "Will you be needing any relief?" I asked, trying to move on. "Both Agremerre and Nevremerre saw a significant decrease in smoke cover before we left. I'm not sure how the most recent explosion has affected everything, but I do believe our food supplies should hold. I would have to get a full report upon returning, but we may be able to provide aid."

"Why would we need that?" King Brandeon asked, his face wrinkling in confusion.

For the first time since entering the room, I faltered. You see, in my head, we had been invited to Castle Andaluca to help provide aid. The past few weeks without sunlight can't have been good for the agricultural industry here. Even Dolma had begun to prepare for lighter food supplies than in past years, although I had yet to receive reports from them about the specifics. No doubt Thomas would have those by now and would be working to put a new plan in action. Thomas and I had discussed nullifying some of the conditions used to bring me to Dolma in exchange for food from Agremerre and Nevremerre before I had left. It was highly likely that upon my return to Agremerre those negotiations would already be completed.

I had absolutely no idea what other reason we would be called here for. There was no expectation that royalty passing through another country would meet, other than letting a ruler know you were passing through. The interconnectedness of the countries surrounding Dolma meant a large number of nobles from each country regularly traveled between the countries. Never anywhere in my training to be Dolma's Crown Princess had there ever been any mention of visits between royals not for the purposes of trade, treaties, or some sort of negotiations. Why was I sitting here in this foreign castle when my parents were grieving back home and I had a son, daughter, and a husband who needed me as much as I needed them?

My prolonged silence was interrupted by Al before I could collect myself enough to respond. "Apologies for my delay,

King Brandeon, I was checking in with our knights to debrief recent events," Al said, enviously smooth with his words, and easily slipping into a believable lie that only I could recognize.

"Prince Alveron!" King Brandeon bounced with excitement, completely disregarding all I had just said. He eagerly repeated the entire series of introductions that he'd given to Alder, my knights, and me previously, which, admittedly, was helpful, as I had forgotten the names of at least half of them already. "Well, well, do come in! Queen Avalynn was just telling us about what your adventure was like! So, how was it? How was your foray into Maychula?"

For a brief moment I saw a flash of surprise fill Al's face and I felt a sort of perverse amusement fill me as I watched to see how he would answer this tactless question. "It was bad," Alder's voice caught me off guard as I turned to look at the little boy stood by the side of my chair. "A lot of people died. My mother died. Their brother died. The former Queen died. When people die, they don't come back. The village I grew up in is gone. The houses, the buildings, the people, the animals, they are gone. It was bad. The "adventure"- it was bad." His little voice wobbled as he glared at the king in front of him, his eyes filled with tears.

Instinctively, I scooped up the child in front of me and held him close against me. "It is as Prince Alder said," Al spoke next, a dangerous sort of politeness in his tone. "While we were able to do some good, a disaster of unknown proportions has hit what was once a peaceful and happy place. Such a thing brings with it a plethora of tragedies we have only just begun to see the ripples of."

"Oh... well, yes, of course," King Brandeon coughed uncomfortably. "But did you see anything cool?"

"My brother's body burning and floating on top of liquid fire was fascinating," I blurted out.

There was a loud silence in the room, as its inhabitants tried to recover from my words. Al was glaring at me as he tried to hide the twisted laughter I could see him struggling to restrain. Perfectly comfortable in the environment I created, I waited patiently for someone to try and start the conversation once more.

Queen Christine tried to recover first. "Forgive us, we were not thinking. We were all simply curious about the unique event that happened so nearby."

As far as lies go, Queen Christine's was acceptable. Not necessarily untrue, but clearly said only to break the tension in the room. There didn't seem to be any real feeling behind the words she'd spoken, but I wasn't actually looking to cause an international incident. "Of course," I accepted, "Your curiosity is understandable." I didn't bother to point out that, had they been actually curious, they could have sent aid beyond their border, but I certainly remembered their lack of action on the matter.

"I'm sure most of us are eager to hear about Priscella. We hear from her rather infrequently," Queen Christine continued.

"Oh yes. We so rarely hear from her. It's such a shame. She used to love us so much, but such things happen when you move abroad. When Anita moves abroad to marry a foreign

Prince, she, too, will forget us," King Brandeon continued, placing his hand on his only daughter's shoulder.

"Ava - Queen Avalynn has remained close with us despite moving abroad," Al jumped in quickly, so quickly he made a rather uncharacteristic blunder. "She didn't write as frequently in the beginning, but we get a letter at least once a week now. In fact, this trip will be the longest my parents will go without hearing from her in nearly two years. You do not lose connection with your family just because you move."

"Then how do you explain Priscella then?" Antoinetta, one of Priscella's older sisters asked. "Did she just not like us or something?" she glared.

"Queen Priscella," I found myself defending, "was not given the same options I was. For me, I moved to Dolma knowing my marriage was a choice I made. Queen Priscella left for a land she did not know, to marry a man she had only briefly spoken to, all because of a tradition she had not thought she would have to take the burden of.

The practice of marriages arranged amongst royalty is not accepted in Nevremerre, Agremerre, or Calvine. And, work is being done to end it in Dolma as well. Neither Crown Prince Thomas nor I wish to inflict an arranged marriage on our children, and I would recommend reviewing your policy as well. It is hard to be forced to leave your home. It is hard to marry a stranger, even if they turn out to be kind. Even when both parties willingly agree to a marriage, there is effort that must be given to both sides of the relationship.

And, in a strange place with strange rules and strange people, you cannot place blame on a person who finds it difficult to be reminded of the life they could have had. Nor could you blame someone who would write constantly in hopes of holding on to what they had. We must all process and live our lives how we choose. I know Queen Priscella loves you all. She has told me that she does, but, even now, it can be difficult to look back at Andaluca and see something she cannot return to."

There was a long silence in the room, as everyone processed my rather impassioned defense of Priscella. I had to brush off my own embarrassment at having spoken. I had not planned to speak as I had, but it felt as if these people were looking down on Priscella, even blaming her for what I knew to be an incredibly difficult situation for her. No one did get a chance to respond though as Al guided us to a swift retreat, "Forgive us, but there is still much work to be done before we can return to Nevremerre and Agremerre. We will leave you to your own company. Queen Avalynn," Al finished, holding his hand out to me.

I took it, still holding Alder as I moved to stand, "Yes, thank you for the conversation, we shall look forward to seeing you at dinner." With that we swiftly left the room, returning to the sanctuary of Al's room instead.

"Are all royals that stupid?" Alder asked once we got there.

"Yes," came a voice from Al's bed. I looked over to see Carlos casually lounging on top of what appeared to be all of the pillows he could find as he flipped through a book.

"What the fu -" Al caught himself before starting again, "What on the God's living planet are you doing here?"

"I got bored," Carlos shrugged from his self-made nest.

"You didn't meet the Andalucian royals," Challa said to Carlos in response to Alder's initial question. He ignored Al's confusion in favor of joining Carlos on the bed. "And your response to the boy's question was an insult to the Queen," he informed Carlos.

"Technically, she's not Queen yet," Carlos said, pointing at me.

"I was thinking of Queen Elenore," Challa responded.

"Not Queen Diana?" Hugo popped in.

"Her, too, and King Edgar and of course the Dowager Queen Elizabeth, but everyone knows Queen Elenore is a genius," Challa continued.

"King Harry is smart too, although he is rather self serving in how he uses that intelligence," I added.

Beside me, Al just sighed, "Alder, do you think we are smart?"

"Yes," the boy responded.

"Then, it would suggest that not all royals suffer from a lack of basic intelligence," Al argued.

"Although, I was not impressed by many that showed up to Queen Avalynn's wedding," Oberon mused.

"Yes, I am not convinced that age and gender-based succession are worth all the fuss," Hugo agreed.

"So what was so bad about the Andalucian royal family?" Carlos asked, as Al sighed once more, collapsing onto the couch as Oberon, Hugo, and Challa filled Carlos in from their positions on Al's bed.

And so it continued, for five mind-numbing, purposeless days I met with the Andalucian royal family. I spent mornings listening to inane and, oftentimes, tactless chatter about the events in Maychula. About how exciting it was to be the first to host the new Queen of Agremerre. How they were so happy this summer brought something to do. I was no longer a Princess who had only seen Nevremerre and Agremerre. Their thoughtless words and frivolous attitude no longer seemed foreign to me, even if I found the thought of such an ill-equipped ruler a little hard to swallow. But, whether or not I was familiar with their attitude, I couldn't help but find them exhausting.

I hid my way through afternoons, finding places to escape and excuses to give so that I might recover from the lengthy and extravagant dinners that reminded me of Dolma. Perhaps, if one were thinking rationally, one could argue that five days isn't really that extensive of a time frame, but, Gods above, it felt long. It felt so terribly, awfully, dreadfully long, and there was seemingly no end in sight. I could find no purpose for this visit other than to entertain the royals and nobles surrounding us. On top of it all, each second we stayed delayed my much desired return to Nevremerre and Agremerre, to my home and family.

With an autonomy I wasn't used to as a Queen, I announced our departure on the fifth night.

"But why?" King Brandeon called out, practically shouting over the large dinner table, "We've had so much fun here!"

"I have had a wonderful stay in Andaluca," I lied, "thanks to your generous hospitality, but we must return to help our countries during this time and to attend the appropriate death wishes, our ceremonies to respect the lives of our fallen soldiers."

"Oh, I see," King Brandeon pouted, his expression would have led one to believe I had just killed a beloved pet. I almost felt bad for telling the poor man that we were to leave. However, this was not enough to change my mind.

"We will leave tomorrow after lunch," I declared to the table.

"So soon?" King Brandeon exclaimed, "How terribly disappointing when we were all getting along so well." The King looked positively despondent as he mournfully hummed, drawing out this moment of his own sadness for several minutes before adding, "Well... if you must."

With the odd sensation that I had done something grievously wrong, I confirmed our departure once more and the meal continued, pausing every so often so King Brandeon could lament our departure some more. I, however, could not be swayed, and, eventually, the evening ended.

I had hoped that would be the end of it. I, frankly, had had enough of the passive aggressive whinings of King Brandeon and I was more than ready to go home. I had assumed that, bar a few more comments tomorrow morning, I would be done with any sort of pestering to stay in Andaluca. Still, if King Brandeon had interrupted me on my way back to my room, I would not have been surprised. However, I definitely did not expect Queen Christine to stop me as I walked back to my room.

"Queen Avalynn," Queen Christine intercepted me as I walked down the deserted stone corridor that led to the room in which I had been staying. "Might I have a word," she continued seriously. "Alone," she pushed on, looking pointedly at my knights.

"If you wish," I sighed. I had not really spoken with Queen Christine since our first night at the Castle Andaluca and while I found her to be a more engaging conversationalist than many of the other Andalucian royals, I felt utterly drained of life by this point.

"My Queen," Oberon jumped in quickly, derailing my train of thought, "I must insist that if you are to meet with Queen Christine, you meet in your rooms." Oberon looked at me with pleading eyes as he made his rather confusing request.

"As my knight requests," I conceded despite my lingering confusion, "May we hold this private meeting in my rooms?"

Queen Christine thought briefly before nodding and walking towards my room. With a brief questioning look directed towards Oberon, I moved to follow Queen Christine. Upon arriving at my room, Oberon, Hugo, and Challa took up positions in front of the door while Queen Christine and I walked into the room. There was a loud click as the metal latch signaled the closing door. As soon as the door was shut Queen Christine turned to me, "Don't leave Andaluca."

"No," I responded, "It is time for us to leave. Unless you have an important reason for our presence here, I am needed back in the countries I rule and represent."

"You have to stay here," Queen Christine demanded.

"Why?"

"Because I need you here. I know what you did in Dolma. I know it was you who prevented Princess Ollifelle from marrying a foreign Prince. I cannot send Anita away. She's just seventeen! It's too young, far too young, and she shouldn't have to leave. Her brothers don't have to. I need you to do what you did in Dolma. I need you to help me keep her here," Queen Christine begged, well as much as someone in her position could beg. If I were really honest, it sounded more like a demand, or perhaps a rant.

It was also just a little bit insulting and also highly inaccurate. First of all, of all the things I had worked on in Dolma, keeping Ollifelle from an arranged marriage was not even on the top ten things I was most proud of. It was not exactly flattering that none of the other things I'd done seemed to be noticed by Queen Christine. Also, technically all Thomas and I really did was delay Ollifelle's marriage for a year. This was a very uncommon occurrence in Dolma as most Princesses were married shortly after their 16th birthday. I could understand why she might believe Ollifelle was safe from an arranged marriage. Of course, Thomas and I were trying to permanently free her from such a fate, but we'd only gotten so far in that task.

"I cannot help you with that," I finally said, unwilling to explain to her why her claim was wrong.

"Well why not? You must be against arranged marriages. Your own marriage can't be good, and I doubt Priscella's marriage is either!"

"The success of a marriage is determined by the effort both partners put into it, not necessarily by how the marriage came about," I bristled, suddenly offended by her words. "My dislike of arranged marriages is mostly an objection to when they are forced upon children who have not made the choice to enter them. I have never nor will I ever understand the notion that children are political tools to be used and traded away. Moreover, I am quite happy in my marriage, and the marriage of Queen Priscella of Dolma is none of your business."

"So you agree! Anita shouldn't be a political pawn!" Queen Christine exclaimed, becoming selectively deaf to any other point I had just made.

"Even if I did," I sighed, "What exactly would you have me, a foreign Queen do?"

"Help us!"

"No."

"Why?"

"Because I have three countries for which I am in some way responsible. Andaluca and your daughter, lovely as she may be, is not a priority for me at the moment. If you require aid for the food shortage you will undoubtedly have at the moment, I will happily work out an arrangement, but I haven't the time or ability to help Princess Anita right now."

Before me, Queen Christine looked defeated, the once strong and proud woman seemed to deflate in front of my eyes. I sighed before speaking again, "I am not unsympathetic to your plight, but even if I were to agree, I could not do what I did in Dolma here. In Dolma, I am the Crown Princess. I had the support, even if it was behind the scenes, of the King. I am nothing more than a foreigner here, a royal foreigner, to be sure, but a foreigner nonetheless.

If it is your wish, you have more power than I. I know that the status of women in Andaluca is not dissimilar to the status of women in Dolma, that is to say we are not given an equal say, but that does not mean we are without power. You are clearly smarter than your husband. If you truly wish to prevent your daughter from an arranged marriage, then I feel confident you can prevent it."

"Very well Queen Avalynn," Queen Christine frowned. "I will leave you to prepare for your journey tomorrow."

"Thank you, Queen Christine."

"Until we meet again."

We left the next day with little fanfare, swift polite good-byes and the painfully obvious desire of my party to leave this castle. With only a few more comments on our quick departure from King Brandeon, we were allowed to leave. Our departure from the Castle Andaluca was easily the fastest we moved on the entire journey home. We rode as if the castle could some-how pull us back if we didn't get far enough away. Perhaps our eagerness to leave was why none of my party was too fazed when not even five months later we got the news the castle was burned until only crumbled stone remained.

When we were young, Mother once asked my brothers and me, "What do starving people eat?" Just children, we did our best to answer.

"They forage," Azar suggested.

"They hunt," Al declared.

"Do they eat the surplus the Ladies or Lords of the areas have saved?" I asked.

"No," Mother laughed. "No, they've already tried all that. If those worked they wouldn't be starving. No, starving people, my children, eat the people who refused to feed them."

Andaluca stayed in the dark for three weeks after we left, and the following winter was the coldest the country had ever seen. And King Brandeon was nice. He was accepting of people rising through classes. He was welcoming to foreign guests in his home, But, nice was not enough to save him from the people he failed to care for. The people he failed to feed. They used him as kindling instead. Something to keep them warm in the harsh winter.

And, of course, there were rumors. How could there not be when from the ashes of her husband Queen Christine became Andaluca's sole Queen and her sons kicked out of succession in favor of her daughter, Crown Princess Anita. It was, many foreigners believed, odd that so soon after her reign a new source of food was found to feed the people, people who now regarded her as something close to the Gods. However, with a lack of solid proof, and similar issues with cold and food scarcity popping up throughout the continent, the rumors didn't even last until spring.

I did not provide aid to the Queen of Andaluca, nor did I speak to her on any topic ever again, save a few official letters. However, I cannot help but reflect back on our last conversation before I left Andaluca. It most likely is awfully grandiose of me to say that I, in any way, affected the decisions, proven or rumored, of Queen Christine, but it is certainly a strong reminder that even in our smallest moments, our words have power and choices can sometimes affect many more lives than our own. Andaluca survived, and even thrived after its revolution, according to all reports, but that was somewhere far away. And, I had family to see, a daughter to take in, a country to rule, and a journey that would take at least a week to get back to them all.

Chapter 8

The Next Step Forward

The journey back took longer than we had anticipated. We stopped earlier in the day than we expected, our bodies unable to push on. The hours spent on horseback felt suffocating, and the conversation was middling at best. Later, Nana would tell me that "there is nothing so tiring as grief," which would explain everything for me. For now, however, it was incredibly frustrating. There was this thought in the back of my mind that we should be able to do this. We have the ability to travel faster, to push on longer distances, but my body pushed back against me at every turn. There was a small comfort in knowing I was not the only one with this problem, but it still wasn't a pleasant experience.

There was, however, one bright spot on the trip. Quite literally as it happens - we woke up five days into our travels to see sunlight peering through the browning tree leaves above us. When the sun vanished nearly a month ago, I had never really had a moment to miss it. There were things to do, kingdoms to visit, and people to work for. Now, on the warm almost fall morning, I realized how much I had missed its light, and the different kind of heat it gently coated us with. Words will never be enough to describe the floating sensation in my chest at the sight of it. It was an overwhelming feeling of what surely consisted of every emotion I could possibly imagine. Silent tears found their way down my cheeks as I took a moment to bask in the light above me.

"Part of me thought I'd never see the sun again," Carlos's hollow voice circled around me. From the corner of my eye I could see him whipping at his own tears. "I'm glad I didn't die," he said eventually, as we both were hypnotized by the rays of sunlight around us. "I don't think I could bear it if I never saw the sun again."

I finally broke away from the sky's hold on me to turn to Carlos. His brown hair looked even darker with the dirt and soot we had been riding through and his tears left streaks of darkness along his cheeks as they mingled with sweat and grime. "I'm so grateful you are alive - I don't even have the words to describe it." I kissed his cheek where his tears had fallen, before I whispered softly against his ear, "I am sorry that he will never get to see the sun again."

Carlos and I maintained a solemn silence for a while before we had to continue our journey though Calvine. Four days later we rode through the Agremerrian border, and one day later we parted ways with the Nevremerrians in our group. It was a quick goodbye, but, even if we would be seeing them all soon, I hated watching Al and Carlos leave. I couldn't have them with me as I made my way to Pantheo, Agremerre's capital. I had to present myself as Agremerre's new Queen. However, they would be there for my coronation, whenever that was to be.

I'd never felt awkward with the Agremerrian knights until that moment. Before I had always been with Anora or the knights from Nevremerre, and it felt like a given that my presence was to be accepted because Anora and the Nevremerrians accepted me. Now, however, with just the knights from Agremerre, I felt out of place as their leader. A voice inside my head screamed that I would never be a true Agremerrian. This voice said that I could never truly be their Queen. I had never even finished the training Queen Anora had set up for me. A year of training had only lasted three months. A wild panic overtook me. It started in my lower limbs before flying into my stomach, crashing and thrashing around me. I can't do this. I can't do this. I cannot do this!

"Yes, you can," the voice was so clear it was as if it had been physically spoken, yet I knew there had been no other sound beside the clamoring of the Agremerrian knights moving towards the capital. "Yes you can," the voice repeated. This time I took care to bundle up the fear that stormed inside of me, and collected it into a little ball that grew more and more compact in the newly emerging hands of the disembodied voice. Even though I was doing something entirely different, it felt similar to the transitioning sessions I had done previously.

"Yes, you can," said the voice, which was steadily gaining a form in my mind's eye. "Yes you can, or else we would have never agreed to take on this task," the voice said to me, finally taking full form in the shape of myself standing in my mind before me.

"Oh," I responded mentally to the figure. The calmer, more gracious version of myself smiled patiently at me.

"We were ready to do this when we entered this world, this body. This was always the plan. This was the path we have chosen from creation and continued to choose throughout this lifetime. We always have the option to switch paths, but we will always come back to this path because this is our favorite way to help people and to heal ourselves."

"I am scared," I admitted to myself.

"Why?"

"I don't want to let anyone down. I don't want to let myself down."

"You could never let me down, and I am you at your most genuine. I am always on your side. Everything else is just a label formal title for the work you started preparing for at just eleven years old and the work you have been doing on your own for the past three years. It is easy to let fear tell us that we are not ready for change, even when logic tells us the real change has already occurred. However, it is easier to continue to walk down the path you have designed for yourself. The path that will carry you to your highest and best good. You are walking the path you, at your highest self, designed. Thus, ruling will be easier than you believe. You are ready; we are ready. Just keep moving forward."

With this last statement, this wiser version of me left, carrying away my ball of fear and trepidations with her like they were nothing. There were only a few fragments of nervous energy that she'd left behind. Small pieces of fear that I could pick up and expand, or that I could collect and throw away just as my other self had done. I took the pieces out the best I could, well aware that there were smaller sections that seemed as though they could only be removed after my coronation. Still, I felt lighter as this surreal moment came to a close and I was back in reality once more.

It did not help, however, the slight unease I felt riding around with this portion of the Agremerrian knights. Unlike in Nevremerre, these were not people I grew up with. They were not knights who I'd known practically since their introductory tournaments. They were not people who knew me and who'd always known me to be an option to rule the country they'd sworn allegiance to. They were also not, Oberon, Challa, and Hugo, the Agremerrian knights I'd brought with me to Dolma. The ones who had sworn allegiance to me, not to any particular country, but to me as a person. People who had then come to learn who I was as a ruler and who stood beside me in the face of criticism, ostracization, and prejudice, not to mention protected me from a few very poorly planned assassination attempts.

No, the insecurities that nagged at me were that the Agremerrian knights were different. While Anora had assured me several times that her people would accept and love me as Queen, should that ever be the case, there had still not been, in my mind, enough time for me to actually get to know these people and this country that I would now rule. The more confident part of my personality said that if they truly did not wish for me to be Queen, they could simply leave my service while lodging a complaint with the High Court. Nothing, after all, in Agremerre's laws forced them to remain in the position of a knight. However, the more insecure part of me argued that the knights before me may still want to be knights, but may not hold any loyalty or even favor towards me. They made me feel, as I occasionally did, that I was nothing more than a placeholder until Genevieve came of age.

The solution to all this, though, was easy. All I needed to do was talk with the knights before me. To bond with them as I had my knights or the knights of Nevremerre. I could easily strike up a conversation, ask them questions about their lives, let them learn about me and my life. I did not, however, do this. At least not at that moment. Oh, I'd use it later; I'd get to know all of the knights who I now served and who in turn served me. But, not on this journey. There was just something that felt very uncouth about trying to up my standings as their new Queen when the old Queen had just died. So, in the day and a half it took to get to Pantheo, I learned very little about these knights and we instead rode in a semi-uncomfortable, semi-silence for the rest of the journey.

My arrival in Pantheo, Agremerre's capital was rather spectacular, all things considered. Although, had I had the mental capacity to remember much, I likely would not have been so surprised. In Dolma and Nevremerre, death was a solemn affair. More so in Dolma, which maintained strict mourning practices that guided its people through practically every minute of the first month after a loved one's death. Something Whimely once told me was very comforting, that you did not have to think about what to do, you just followed the mourning instructions. In the head space I now found myself in, I could see how that sort of easy structure could be helpful. Nevremerre was more free form in managing grief, but end of life dedications were often held in silent reflections, designed to give peace to the grievers. Agremerre, on the other hand, threw a party.

Death in Agremerre was treated as a chance to celebrate a person's life. The more loved the person, the louder the celebrations must be. As many stories of the deceased as you could think of must be shared. The overarching theme to the festivities was "You have brought joy to my life, thus I shall repay you by giving you joy and love in your death."

A beloved Queen like Anora was celebrated on a truly incredible scale. There were colorful flags flying all around the city. Parties and chatter flew all across the streets, with an odd contradiction of boisterous laughter and hysterical sobbing everywhere you looked. For me, it was a distinctly odd experience, but everyone else in my group seemed perfectly comfortable. They nodded approvingly at the bright decor and the freshly painted murals and prints of Queen Anora. They commented on the "good turn out" for Anora's death celebration and I'd never felt more the foreigner in Agremerre than I had in that moment.

People in the streets paid us little attention, something that never happened previously. I was thankful to Oberon who quietly whispered that tradition in Agremerre stated that I could not be greeted by the public until my official coordination. I appreciated Oberon giving me this information before I let my insecurities run away with themselves. Finally, we arrived at Agremerre's Royal Palace. With a strange jolt, I suddenly remembered that the last time I was here, I was dropping off a baby Genevieve after Anora had given birth. Logically, this event only occurred about three years prior, but somehow it still felt like ages ago.

"Godma!" a little voice screamed out, and I soon found myself holding a bouncing ball of a child, beautifully dressed in Agremerrian blue and green.

"Hello Genevieve," I kissed the top of her head.

"Where's Mama?" Genevieve's big brown eyes peered up at me hopefully. "Kazi says she's dead, so she must have come back with you, right?"

"No, my darling, your mother, the wonderful and brilliant Queen Anora has died. This means that she is not living her life anymore. She has passed through to the realm of souls and Gods, but her spirit shall always watch over us."

Genevieve began to cry, "No, NO!" she wailed. "It's not fair! Why didn't she take me with her? I want to die, too, with Mama!"

With some difficulty, I picked up the screaming child. "Now, now, darling. Death is not quite ready for you yet, so don't go rushing it along. And, I believe your mother would rather see you here than with her. She would not wish for you to join her until you've lived a full and happy life."

Genevieve quieted in my arms. "I am full and happy," she whined. "I wish she would just take me with her when she leaves. She's always taken me before." This was not exactly true, but Genevieve was too young to remember the many occasions when Anora had to work without her. So, I said nothing as I continued to hold her in my arms.

Instead, I finally looked up at the people behind where Genevieve had emerged. There stood the High Court, forming themselves into an orderly line as they silently watched the scene before them. It was more than a little disconcerting to see them so quiet and still before me. It was, perhaps, the most uniform I'd ever seen them. "Welcome back," Michael spoke, his whole body falling into a kneel, one leg bent out in front of him as if I was going to knight the man, "I give my regards and loyalty to Avalynn, Queen of Agremerre." Beside him, the rest of the council and knights around the palace followed suit, repeating his words and positions to the best of their ability. High Judge Zanareth merely bowed, and tapped at his wooden leg still visible underneath his shin length skirt. I understood this to mean the kneel would be too difficult for him.

After I accepted their words, I was ushered into the palace to debrief with the High Court. Genevieve wiggled in my arms and was deposited to the loving care of her nanny with a promise I'd be back to see her soon. She was so cooperative about the whole matter, I suspected that, despite my words, she still did not fully understand what was going on. I did not have much time to ponder it though, as I was soon locked into a meeting room with the entirety of the High Court.

"Crown Prince Thomas and Prince Marcus are both still in Nevremerre," Head Judge Michael began. "We weren't sure when you'd get here and Crown Prince Thomas thought it best that he remain with your grieving parents. Genevieve was brought to Kazi, however, as it felt inappropriate to have the new Crown Princess in another country."

"That makes sense," I agreed.

"We sent for Crown Prince Thomas when you came through the palace gates. He should be here in an hour or two. The Nevremerre royal family is still based in Nera for the time being," High Judge Kazi said kindly.

"Thank you," I gave a half smile back at her.

"Now, as it stands, Genevieve is fully under your care, with Kazi still being her other Godmother. In Agremerre, a Crown

Princess being raised by a member of the High Court would be highly frowned upon as it would be perceived as the High Court grooming what should be a part of our system's checks and balances in our favor. For this reason, we ask that the Crown Princess also goes with you when you go back to Dolma," Michael pushed forward.

"As you wish."

"We also ask that you stay in Agremerre for at least a full year after your coronation. This shouldn't be too much of an imposition, as it really only adds another three months to the time you planned to be here training. We also ask that you spend at least half of the year here in Agremerre, and that you come back to Agremerre whenever there is a crisis."

"I will make that happen."

"We understand that you have adopted a child, that child as well as Prince Marcus will both be recognized as Princes of Agremerre, and any other children you bear will also be Princes and Princesses of Agremerre. However, they will all be ranked lower than Crown Princess Genevieve. If, and only if, the Crown Princess, upon reaching the age of maturity declines or is unsuited for the throne, we will choose between the rest of your children for the next candidate."

"Marcus is in line for the throne of Dolma, surely you won't put him in the running," I pointed out.

"It has been discussed, and we will take his position in Dolma into account, but we will not exclude him from consideration for the throne should the need arise," Michael said sagely.

"That information never leaves this room. For the safety of all three of my children, the public will believe that no one other than Genevieve will ever be considered as an heir," I ordered. The gravity of the situation hit me with full force as I thought what the nobles in Dolma might do if they thought Marcus could rule Agremerre too.

"Yes, Your Majesty," Michael nodded with a small smile.

"Finally, we need to discuss your coronation..." Half an hour later plans were confirmed and I was made aware that I would become the official Queen of Agremerre in a day and a half. The High Court went to work on preparing the final details, and I was firmly, but politely told to go rest. Michael threateningly joked that he didn't want to see me until my coronation, while most everyone else gave me some kind of version of the same message: rest, relax, and recover before we put you back to work.

I did so by introducing Alder to Genevieve, explaining to them that they were now siblings. The two seemed to get along, or at least seemed to understand each other in some way, as an hour later Thomas found us all together, quietly playing with Genevieve's dolls.

"Avalynn!" Thomas's voice cried out, pulling me close to him before I even had a chance to look at him. Between us, I could feel Marcus in Thomas's arms, and I quickly ended our hug in fear of suffocating our baby. Once I had resituated Marcus in my own arms, I clung onto Thomas once more. I felt Thomas' heart beat beneath my ear, and in a move that surprised even myself, I began to cry.

"Oh, my dear," Thomas cried back, his own tears falling quietly amidst my own. "I'm so sorry, my darling. I'm so sorry, but I am also so glad you are safe."

A watery laugh burst up within me. "I missed you," I said, surprised by the sincerity I felt with the words. "I missed you both, so much."

For some reason my words caused Thomas to give his own laugh, as he pulled me as tight as my body and the baby would allow. "I missed you too."

We stood there a while longer, controlling our tears and taking comfort in one another before I whispered to him, "Oh, Thomas, it was so awful."

"I know, my dear, that's why it is so good to have you back," he kissed my head before I finally stepped away from him.

Looking at Thomas now, his eyes puffy and red, his cheeks stained with tears, I wondered how I could have ever compared him to art when he could be so real and warm next to me. Unaware of my thoughts and over arching awe of him, Thomas simply beamed at me with his dazzling smile and said, "I hear I have gained another son."

Introductions were made and talk slowly subsided in favor of reenacting the story Genevieve had demanded of us. There were questions that still needed to be asked, stories that still needed to be told, but nothing in that moment felt more important or comfortable than my own little family playing together in the light glow of the afternoon sun.

My parents and brothers came the next day and Alder looked like he might faint at the sight of them all. Honestly, the poor kid was probably still overwhelmed by the whole series of events, not to mention the large and foreign people whom he could choose to call family, should he wish it. Thomas, gratefully, came to his rescue, politely excusing him and the other children from the room, giving Alder some peace and a quiet place to adjust.

My family was quiet. It was both strange and completely expected. They greeted me with long hugs and all the appropriate words, and then we just sat together. We sat together and simply existed in the same space. We wiped away Mother's silent tears, rubbed Mama's trembling shoulders, and let Father squeeze our hands and bodies so tightly we might break. Ari refused to leave my side the whole time. The silence was comfortable, but not in the usual way. It was not healing or releasing, rather it felt right. It was as if this was exactly what we were supposed to be doing. That this silence was what we all needed.

"Azar's life dedication will be the day after your coronation," Mama's voice broke through the silence an hour later. "We wanted to host it before the coronation, so that we could celebrate you having already put Azar to rest, but Agremerre needs its new Queen crowned quickly." Mama gave me a worried look.

"It's okay," I responded, trying to ease any guilt she might be feeling about my coronation.

"Ava, darling, we are so proud of you and this journey you will be embarking on," Mama rushed on.

"Mama, it's fine, really." Logically I meant it. I knew they had an image to maintain, that they still needed to be mourning Azar, emotionally... well emotionally I had no idea where I was at. I was too tired and too scared to even try to address the feelings I was still holding onto.

"But we will be in full mourning at one of your coronations," Mama pressed.

"It's okay, honestly, someone should be mourning. It feels so odd to have everyone celebrating me, when Anora, Azar, and the others are dead." I said it to make her feel better, but once the words were spoken, I was struck with the knowledge that I truly meant it.

"You will be mourning," Father broke in, "It was the same when your grandfather died. Everyone was celebrating my rise to the throne, but my father had died just two weeks prior. It felt wrong to see them celebrate so, but I could mourn privately. And, I expect many others mourned privately as well."

"That will be true, but it will be nice to see some people mourn all the same," I replied.

"We won't be able to say much to you."

"I am well aware of the mourning practices of Nevremerre, Mother. I know you can not make long declarations or speak for extended periods until the life dedication," I said with a hint of annoyance.

"Don't take that tone with me, young lady," Mother snapped.

"Sorry, Mother."

"And don't apologize to me like that!" Mother scolded, "You are the Queen of Agremerre, you can't just show deference to a foreign Queen like that! We are equals in standing you can not treat me like someone who could order you around."

"Yes, Moth - oh - I mean," I fumbled, not entirely sure how to respond.

Mother sighed, "All this to say, Ava dear, we won't be able to give you our praise, love, and congratulations in full. We can only give our formal speeches of union between Agremerre and Nevremerre. To do anything more at an event so public to Nevremerrians would be considered a slight to Azar. So, we must speak only the bare minimum at your coronation."

"But, now, in private, and among ourselves, know that we know you will be a wonderful Queen, a loving mother to Genevieve as well as your other children, and know that we will always support you," Mama continued, as Mother nodded in agreement.

"As King of Nevremerre, I cannot give you everything you may need as Queen of Agremerre, but as a father, know you have my love, and that I will be cheering you on in every move you make. I wish you the best of luck, my gift. May you shine as bright as a thousand suns in your life ahead."

My coronation passed in a stunning state of perpetual numbness, in which I spent most of my time desperately trying to remember the next thing I had to do. It all accumulated in the feeling that I just ran full speed into a brick wall as Agremerre's crown, golden branches with a brilliant blue sapphire pulling them to a point above my brow, was placed calmly on my head.

A repeating mantra of, "What the fuck. What the fuck. What the fu-," bounced through my head as I worked to keep my face neutral. Around me, in the glorious outdoor pavilion Agremerre kept for large events, thousands of people shouted their recognition of my new status, kneeling down and saying my name and title.

My father then came and we solidified Agremerre's and Nevremerre's partnership and combined history. I shook his hand, and with him cloaked in the mourning tan colors of Nevremerre, we cheered for the bright future of our two nations. This was followed by the only event that took me out of my numbness, a parade down Agremerre's streets, where even more people screamed my name. "Queen Avalynn!", "Queen Avalynn!", the cheers from the crowd seemed so vibrant and joyful that I could almost completely rid myself of the fears that I was unwanted as an Agremerrian Queen.

The numbness returned, however, as I pushed my way through a dinner with all of the nobles and judges of Agremerre, forcing myself to remember prepared speeches and addresses to the people in attendance. At the end of it all, I found myself without a single clear memory of the day's events, save the final words of Head Judge Michael at the very end of the evening which relieved me of my burdens.

"You did perfectly, My Queen," he whispered to me before leaving me in favor of his rooms in the palace. My senses came back to me in an instant, overwhelming me with their power as I collapsed against the wall behind me, but, apparently, that was not where my day could end.

Nana found me in that hallway not too long afterwards, and began pulling me down a hallway. "Come now, Ava dear, it's time."

"Time for what?" I panicked, feeling fairly certain I had already done what was needed for my coronation.

"Time to release Azar," she said.

"That was definitely scheduled for tomorrow," I managed, as she pushed me into the room she'd requested for my coronation. "Oh Gods, is it already tomorrow?"

Nana laughed, "No Songbird, now sit. I will explain everything." Some part of me impertinently reminded me that I wasn't supposed to listen to the orders of my family anymore, but I ignored it and sat down on Nana's bed.

"Azar's soul has not left this plane yet. His body is destroyed, so he can not continue to stay here. I have tried to transition him, but he is requesting that you do it. You transitioned Anora's soul. This is the same process."

"Transitioned - wait, you mean that strange dream?!"

"Is that how you perceived it? Well perhaps that is to be expected. I never taught you about individual soul releases. Why don't you just tell me about it, and I will explain?"

Again, I did as I was told, and I spoke to her about everything. I learned my "dream: was in fact not a dream, but a part of death. Transitioners were tasked with helping souls release any remaining ties to the planet before they could rejoin spirit and the Gods. Each red string, as they appeared to me, was a tie holding them back from death, a true death. That this process was vital as not properly leaving this life could corrupt a spirit, turning it into a vengeful wraith or ghost that would eventually come to remember, oftentimes, only the most tragic parts of their lives, driving them mad. And, now, Azar's soul was requesting that I release him.

This was a lot to take in.

However, I didn't get a chance to process much of anything before Nana was leading me into the conscious process of entering the space between the realm of our lives and the realm of our deaths. Slipping into this realm was easy. So easy it surprised me when, after just a few deep breaths, I found myself back in the yellow and blue space I was in with Anora. And, standing whole and unharmed before me was Azar.

Even knowing I was supposed to be seeing him here, I was still surprised. I had watched him die after all, and yet here he was. His chest moved up and down as if breath still moved beneath him. "It's an automatic response," Azar's voice came out, perfectly and clearly into the space. He spoke with an ease and a smoothness. He spoke as if he didn't realize I thought I'd never hear his voice again. "I still think I have to breathe, see, so I just keep doing it. I don't have to though." With this, his chest stopped moving, and a panic rose through me, as if he wasn't already dead.

A moment later, Azar's soul still stood before me, chest still unmoving, but body still fine. "You died," I finally said, my voice sounding distant in my ears.

"I know."

"I need to release your soul," I spoke again, falling back into myself as I knew what I needed to do.

"Yes, I would be grateful if you did." I moved to him, looking for red threads to cut. "There's just one," Azar said, holding up his left arm. I moved to grab the string and watched as pictures of Alder flashed around me. I looked at Azar in confusion. "I need to know that he is okay. That he will be looked after. He has an important destiny, and I was supposed to be there to help him fulfill it. I need to make sure he's looked after."

"You idiot," this was probably not what you were supposed to say to a dead soul, but it felt like the only thing I could say. "You absolute idiot. Of course he is being taken care of. I am taking care of him. He's my son! I've adopted him! What did you think? That I was just going to leave a child with nowhere to go? What kind of person do you think I am? And, while we're on the subject, why aren't you also tied to your family, huh? What about us?"

Before me Azar burst out in laughter. "Of course you are. Well no worries then, you will raise him well, and, Ava, my family isn't here because I'm not worried about you. I will be watching you all from the beyond, but I know you will all keep going on because to not enjoy your life would be an insult to mine and you'd never treat me that way."

Azar beamed at me, "I do love you so. Cut the string. I am more than ready now. It's time for my next adventure."

It was terribly sad, but also comforting to watch his string fall to the planet below, to watch his memories turn into that metal capsule, and to see his bright smile as the above opened up with its surreal joy and love filling the room. "Until our next life, Ava girl," Azar smiled at me before walking through the above whose doors were closed to me.

I cried when my consciousness returned back to Nana's room. I bawled my heart into her arms as she cried her own heart into me. But, in the morning, when I woke up, I found my grief significantly lessened by the knowledge his soul was safe and loved, ready for the next adventure. In a sea of tan, we mourned Azar, and dedicated our words to his memory along with the rest of Nevremerre, and I finally felt ready to take the next steps of living my life.

It was a good thing that I was ready for life, as not even two hours after returning to Agremerre, Mateo, Galileo, and Leonard showed up with the news that Princess Ollifelle had started a coup and named herself Queen of Dolma.

"I think we should just give it to her," Thomas declared after we'd gathered with Hugo, Oberon, Challa. We listened to Mateo, Galileo, and Leonard give the full report once more.

"What?" I demanded, wondering if he had in fact gone insane.

"I think we should give it to her, well, at least for a little bit. Honestly, I don't think she'd actually want the throne for very long. And, she's not hurt anyone. Mostly she's just kidnapped most of the nobles. As long as she's not harming any of the citizens, I say just let her be Queen for a bit."

"She's 17 and she's kidnapped people!"

"Yeah, but Galileo says they are treated very well. Plus, she's been heavily influenced and in favor of many of your policies, so she will probably continue to help the people."

"She's 17 and some of the people she's kidnapped are your friends! What about Whimely?!"

"Actually, my Queen," Galileo piped in, "Lord Whimely assisted the Princess with the coup and is not actually kidnapped at the moment."

"Of course he did," I rolled my eyes, "He probably thinks this is all some big game! And what of Miri, shouldn't she have had some knowledge about this beforehand? Then there is Lucy, Abel, and Ana to think of; why did you not return with them?"

"Lady Lucy and Sir Abel have been given positions of honor in Princess Ollifelle's court. Lady Lucy says she is securing your position for when you are ready to return," Galileo informed me.

"She what?!" I turned to Galileo aghast.

"Ana, Miri, and Abel also elected to stay, Miri saying she will accomplish all that you need her to from inside the castle. Sir Abel said that Dolma needs an ambassador to Nevremerre no matter who's in charge. Ana said she trusts you will be back soon anyways, so it is not important for her to leave now."

"Of course," I huffed. "You do realize how insane this all is," I turned back to Thomas.

"Well, realistically, where's the harm? I mean, it's not like she's as bad as my father or grandfather for that matter."

"It's not just about that! What of Ollie? Surely this is also dangerous for her?"

"In my opinion, as a knight and as a former strategist for the Nevremerrian army, I believe the Princess is incredibly well protected," Galileo responded. "The knights of the palace respond only to her as she was approved by you, My Queen."

"Oh, then what about the people?" I argued.

"The way I see it," Thomas chimed in again, "We have to stay in Agremerre for a year anyway, what if we let her rule for a year then come back and discuss things with her? She deliberately sent your knights back with word that she'd be happy to speak with us. You have Miri and her network still there to give us information, and Lady Lucy is there to help her rule as you would. So, we let her rule for a year, we keep an eye on everything to make sure the people are okay, and we will interfere immediately if they aren't."

"What are we just supposed to send a note saying, "We'll discuss this in a year,"?" I said sarcastically. Except, that's exactly what we did and one year later, we rode back to a version of Dolma that had, frankly, not changed all that much from when we'd left.

PART TWO

Chapter 9

The Trouble with Coups

A year later, and, despite my better judgment, we'd done absolutely nothing about Ollifelle's coup. In the early days, there were tales of nobles trying to escape their involuntary confinement at Dolma's royal palace, but none proved successful. Thomas told me I should be proud. The knights I had trained for three years proved more than competent during this time. The people who I had been most concerned with were rather blasé about the whole affair. It turns out that the three years of what could potentially be described as propaganda in my favor, set into motion by Mother after my wedding, had been very effective.

Ollifelle had profited off this media campaign by announcing to all that she had been appointed by me to take care of the land during my absence (true). However, she also claimed that her father, the former King Harold, had tried to take this job away from her (unverified), and thus, she was forced, for the good of the realm, to imprison King Harold and all those who followed him (false). This was met with a surprising lack of resistance from the general public. And, despite my lingering belief, or rather lingering feeling that what was happening was bound to end in some sort of tragedy, Thomas assured me that everything was fine, so there was no reason to return before my training as Queen of Agremerre was complete. He also obsessively pointed out that Ollifelle's story proved that she'd gladly welcome our presence back at the Dolma royal palace when we were ready to return. I had thought him insane, but I listened to him.

"You know, we could just not go back," Thomas said to me a few nights before our scheduled departure. We were lying together under soft blankets as the sound of crickets chirped outside our tent. "I quite like Agremerre," he continued, as I began to wonder if I would be getting any sleep tonight. "It's such a great place to raise the children, and it will be much easier for you if you didn't have to keep moving between countries. Ollifelle has done just fine so far, and she did go so far as to stage a coup, so maybe we could just let her have it. I don't have to be King of Dolma."

"You do know that if you give up your position in Dolma you won't have any title in Agremerre," I wearily pointed out.

"You wouldn't grant me one, oh great Queen of mine?" Thomas asked, pulling me closer.

"For what should I be granting you a title?" I laughed into his shoulder.

"Lord Thomas, the best father ever, has a nice ring to it," Thomas declared.

"Lords have to manage an area of land to get that title. Sirs and Dames are titles given on the basis of merit or distinction."

"Sir Thomas, the best father ever then."

"I believe there are those that would disagree with your title, namely most other fathers in Agremerre."

"But, you don't disagree with me?"

"Well, I am rather fond of my own father," I laughed, "but it is really the kids you should be asking." There was a pause and I began to drift off to sleep, "I'm still not giving you a title though."

Thomas laughed besides me, "Well, technically I will still be a Prince of Nevremerre, but I think it's all the better not to have a title. I like the idea of just being plain old Thomas."

I sat up and turned to look at him. This was not very effective, enclosed in darkness as we were, but the attempt felt important, "Do you really not want to go back to Dolma?"

Thomas sighed, "I don't know, Ava," he said, playing with strands of my hair.

"That's not a good enough answer, Thomas," I said.

"I know it's not," he kissed my forehead, "I just know that when we return, I will have to be King. The throne won't go back to my father, not now. Honestly, I'm not entirely sure he would really want it back anyway. It's fine for you, you have been a Queen for a year now, but I'm honestly not sure I am ready for the position."

"I'll be there to help you if it comes to that, but honestly I don't know why you're worried about that when we are not even certain that Ollifelle would give up the throne. Plus, I don't see why your father couldn't take back the throne."

"After all the press about him trying to take away Ollifelle's position? The people are far less likely to accept him now than they ever would have been in the past."

"Maybe so, but we still have your sister to deal with. I am not at all convinced that you will even be the King of Dolma at the end of all this," I huffed.

"I know darling," Thomas sighed at me, "It's just, if I do get the throne, I am not sure that I will have the same passion for ruling that you do." I tried to think of something to say to this, to say something to reassure him that he didn't have to rule like me or to tell him that if he didn't want the throne we could do something else, but he never gave me a chance. "It's no matter anyways," Thomas continued, "We can't leave Ollie there all alone forever. We'll see what she wants and go from there."

"Thomas," I responded, feeling woefully inadequate in what I wanted to express, "I trust you, and we will follow your lead, okay? Whatever you want to do, I'll be here. I want you to be happy too."

"I am happier in this moment than I believed possible just four years ago, you hear me? So, don't mind my ramblings and get some sleep."

With the lingering sensation that I was missing a key element in my response to him, but unable to figure out what, I let Thomas pull my body back towards the pillows. He wrapped his arms around me, placing a hand over my scar, a ritual he'd done every night since I had returned from the newly named "volcano" in Maychula, and I felt his warm breath on my neck as sleep overtook the two of us. Two days later, the sounds of birds chirping and the bouncing warmth of the sun guided us and a large party of knights over the border into Dolma, and Thomas was smiling by my side as if he'd never had a care in the world. But, I felt the indomitable weight of knowing his ease and confidence was all just a carefully crafted facade.

Dolma was, in all honesty, fine. The people waved happily as we passed through, a quiet hush of winter wrapped gracefully over busy town squares as the gentle glow of orange fires sprung cheerfully through cottage windows. Inside our own carriage there was a warm haze of laughter as we played games with the three children to distract them from the long journey still to come. And, in these moments with just our family, Thomas continuously frowned as we watched Dolma pass by.

"Are you okay?" I whispered to him as Alder entertained Genevieve with stories of the winters he'd spent in Maychula.

"We can discuss it later," he whispered back, smiling down at Marcus in my lap, and doing absolutely nothing to assuage the fear that was looming inside of me that something might be horribly wrong. Still, I simply nodded back and we continued to the royal palace.

Between the constantly changing moods of Thomas and the coup still ongoing with Ollifelle, I was beyond on edge as we rolled into Ohmehiu, Dolma's capital. Despite the constant insistence that Ollifelle would be happy to see us, I still felt like perhaps we were all about to be murdered. Not necessarily because I believed that Ollifelle had any desire to kill us, after all, she had yet to kill anyone during her time on Dolma's throne, but rather because every history book I'd read had told me this is what I must expect. So, I can honestly say that I was both incredibly shocked and immensely relieved that, upon arriving at Dolma's royal palace, Ollifelle threw herself into Thomas' arms demanding to know where we'd been.

"How could you?!" she yelled at us, pushing away from her brother and pacing around the gate before us. "How could you just leave me like that? For a whole year no less!"

"Yes, but you did an excellent job," Thomas smiled.

"When one declares a coup, usually one expects a more immediate response from the Crown Prince and Crown Princess who are still alive and well, and who have several well trained armies at their disposal," Ollie argued, very reasonably in my opinion.

"Yes, well there is a first time for everything," Thomas smiled with a carefree attitude that did not match what I had been feeling for the past year. "We can discuss it later. First, we should show the children and new knights around."

"Kids, this is your Aunt Ollifelle," I said, trying to keep my composure in front of the children.

Ollie smiled, and as she bent down to greet the children, her whole demeanor switched from anger to a gentle kindness with frightening speed. It was a skill shared with her brother that never failed to leave me in awe. "It's a pleasure to meet you, I have been most looking forward to it. And, please, feel free to call me Aunt Ollie. I'd be ever so happy to show you around the palace if you'd like."

"Yes please," Genevieve clapped excitedly.

"We would be very grateful for a tour," Alder answered primly, nodding behind his sister. With that we all set off around the Dolma Royal Palace, laughing as the children raced to explore the many, many rooms. Thomas and I also remarked on the emptiness of the front palace, with all the nobles imprisoned in the back half of the palace. I doubted the kids noticed, but I, for one, found it to be a very weird day. Especially when it ended with my family in Thomas' and my old rooms, without even discussing the order of succession, or what had been done in our absence. A very weird day indeed.

"Are you planning on saying something or do you want to just stare at the window all night?" Thomas' voice broke through my thoughts as I turned to look at his reflection in the glass in front of me. We'd just put the children to bed and we were now alone in our room, the same room we'd had when we first married four years and two weeks ago today.

Perhaps it was due to my youth spent in Nevremerre, a place I considered to be fairly stable, but it felt positively surreal to be back in Dolma, to see how much had changed in just four years. Then, to now be at the center of what will likely go down as the most peaceful coup in the history of the entire continent, was mind boggling. I sincerely couldn't wrap my head around all that had occurred. How could we be greeted so kindly by someone who had overthrown the government? A government that we were a part of! And, how, how had we gone the whole day without discussing it at all? I knew nothing of Ollie's motives, of her thoughts or demands, I knew not even of what Thomas' and my positions were in the palace. Say nothing of the positions of the children. I did know they were currently being guarded by some of the finest knights in my employ. It was still all so very strange.

"Ava?" Thomas repeated, pulling my attention back towards his reflection in the window. I could see that he had only slightly begun the process of getting ready for bed. His jacket was open wide in front of him, and the top ties of his tunic were undone. He'd taken off his boots, and held one in his hands, spinning it around as he looked over at me.

I meant to apologize, I think. At the very least, there was somewhere in me happy enough to smile, to apologize for being so distant, and to go to bed. I'd sleep away the weirdness and face tomorrow with fresh eyes. But there was another part of me, a hidden part - at least, hidden from me - that was never going to go along with this plan. Perhaps it was arrogance, well I can probably admit now, it was most definitely arrogance; but it was not a bad sort of arrogance, I don't think. My arrogance demanded that I should have the answers and explanations to why this day had been so weird. I was once Dolma's Crown Princess after all, and maybe I still was, no one had bothered to tell me yet what my status here was. Either way, I found myself staring at the window and saying, "I don't understand. I don't understand what's happening here."

Thomas sighed, and he put down his boot. I watched his hazy reflection sink onto the bench at the end of the bed as he ran his hand over his face. I suddenly had the sinking feeling that my marriage, at least the cooperative and understanding union we'd had so far, was coming to an end. I felt like we were running head first into a crumbling avalanche and I did not know how to stop it. "What do you want me to say, Ava?" Thomas spat at me, his voice laced with so much venom I briefly wondered if he'd ever liked me at all.

What did I want him to say? I numbly thought, unable to think clearly as I tried to process the person behind me through the large window, quickly growing blurry as it shielded us from the frigid outdoors. I was suddenly struck by the feeling that I was falling. I was unsure of Thomas' emotions and very unsure of my own. I couldn't comprehend how we'd gotten to this point. I didn't know what was going on with the country I may or may not be in command of, and I couldn't understand why Thomas was so angry at me for not knowing what was going on. It felt like the world I had built was crashing around me because of just one question. Yet, despite all of that, I, stupidly, pig-headedly, pushed on. "Something to help me understand," I responded, my voice felt distant, like I was speaking through the glass in front of me instead of to the person in the same room.

"How can I explain?" Thomas suddenly yelled. "How can I possibly explain this to you? You didn't grow up here! You know nothing of Dolma, of what it is like to live here! You have only ever seen this country as something to fix. You've never even looked for the things we do well. You've never truly understood our culture or our history."

I wanted to object. I'd studied Dolmanian history *ad nauseam* for three years. I knew their laws better than Thomas did at one point in time and I'd been living in Dolma for three years before we'd temporarily moved to Agremerre. I had spoken with the people of Dolma more than Thomas had. I could hardly be said to know nothing of this place.

Thomas never gave me a chance to respond though, as he angrily continued his tirade, "And, I know that your improvements were for the best. Our people have housing and food that were never available to them before. Crime rates are the lowest they've ever been, and the monarchy has reached unprecedented levels of popularity, but we can no longer move forward your way. You don't know enough about Dolma and you've never truly understood why we reached the point that we did in the first place. Dolma has got to be more than it was before and we can not proceed your way–it would put us all in danger. So when Ollifelle and I planned this coup -"

"What?!" I felt my whole body reel in shock as I turned around to face him. "You planned this coup?"

"With Ollifelle," Thomas said, giving me a confused look, "Isn't this why you were mad at me?"

"I wasn't mad at you! I was confused! I didn't understand what was going on!"

"But you've been distant all day. I thought for sure you had figured it out," Thomas said quietly.

"No!" I roared, "I was in shock! What coup in history has ever been so friendly with the opposing side? It makes sense now though, as apparently, we were in on the coup! Why didn't you tell me?"

"What would you have me say?" Thomas demanded once more, standing up so that he towered above me.

"I don't know, something along the lines of "Hey Avalynn, my sister and I are planning a coup," would have worked. And, then, I could have told you that your coup is totally unnecessary as you are the Crown Prince. You would have inherited the throne anyways!"

"That wasn't going to be fast enough."

"Wasn't fast enough? So the work I was doing was simultaneously not good enough because I am not knowledgeable about Dolma, and too slow? How, exactly -"

"Ollifelle is gay and in love with a servant who has color."

"What?" I said, wondering if I ever, at any point, truly knew where this conversation was going.

"Ollifelle is gay. She's attracted to women and she's dating Chanti. She's the sister of that servant girl you brought in, Solista."

"I know who they are," I replied, still unsure where this conversation was heading.

"Look, you've spent three years changing the physical things about this country which is great, but also easy," I opened my mouth to object, but Thomas held up a hand to stop me. "I mean it is easier than what we are working on next, changing our culture - the parts which negatively affect the community as a whole. There aren't many who will complain about cleaner streets, nicer houses, and a healthier workforce, especially when backed by the King. Yet, the way you've done it, nobles have tried to assassinate you on seven separate occasions."

This, unfortunately for me, was a very fair and accurate point. There had been a series of assassination attempts made on me since my arrival in Dolma and they had only increased in frequency. They had, of course, been unsuccessful, but it did not help my case in this matter. "Now we need to change the culture - something most people, for better or for worse, are extremely attached to. And, we need to work semi-quickly. We may be able to avoid an arranged marriage to a foreign royal for Ollie, but it would still be expected that she marry, and to a man at that. Not to mention that it would still be considered incredibly problematic if she married a man who had color. I refuse to let that happen. Especially when she is in love with a good woman who is here in this country."

I was, of course, in agreement with all that Thomas had said, but I was not given an opportunity to say as much before Thomas continued on. "And, if you had handled it, no doubt you'd be getting more death threats and assassination attempts. Which you will say you can handle, but now we have three children to think of as well, and I refuse to do anything that puts them in danger. Or, at least, any more danger than what usually comes with being royalty. This coup transfers powers to us with little interference and perhaps even with more support given that the coup and the work you did prevented the nobles here from suffering the same fate as the nobles in Andaluca. With this, and my greater understanding of Dolma's culture, I can keep Ollie safe while we change the infrastructure and systems that would prevent her from marrying someone she loves. As well as addressing other cultural matters."

The room was silent for awhile as I processed all Thomas had said. In a devastating blow to my ego, I found all of his words to be true. It was a decidedly unpleasant feeling to realize my actions were actually not the best ones I could have taken. Beyond that, there was this strange sinking feeling in my gut that I was no longer providing any actual value in my marriage, that I would soon be an unneeded redundancy in Thomas' life. Still, morally, I felt I had no other choice but to accept this new background role. After all, I had already admitted to myself that Thomas was right. "Okay," I responded.

"Okay?"

"Okay. Tell me how I can help. I will follow your lead," the words felt uncomfortable in my mouth, and I felt a strange sense of unease fill me as I said them. However, at the same time, I knew they must be said. That these were the right words for my life to move ahead.

"Oh, alright then," Thomas said, a dazed look in his eyes, "There is nothing I need from you right now. Er, shall we go to sleep?"

"Yes," I nodded. We moved towards the bed, and Thomas pulled me in and curled up around me. He placed his hand over Azar's partial hand print that had burned through my skin, as he had done since my return from Maychula. It had never been uncomfortable, although, I was very confused the first few nights he did this, but tonight, it felt as out of place as the rest of the day had been. It filled me with sensations I couldn't name, but it held a strange sense of comfort too. A comfort I had no idea what to do with. I pushed all these thoughts away however, and let Thomas' even breath lull me into sleep.

Chapter 10

The Endless Days

The next day was perhaps the most uncomfortable experience of my life thus far. That's not to say it was bad. In totality, it was a lovely day. The thin layer of snow that coated the ground meant the children and I spent a lovely morning bundled up in warm furs and padded quilts as we rolled around the snow covered ground. I spent the afternoon by the warm fire, reconnecting with the friends I'd made in Dolma, as well as spending time with Lucy and Ana as they told me of the oddly peaceful time they had experienced during the year of the coup. And, I introduced the noble children, who were still keeping up with the tradition of spending the afternoons in my old apartments, to my children.

Both Alder and Genevieve made fast friends with the other children. Although, Genevieve's friends seemed to have been made more by force as she latched onto a few individuals and dragged them (with impressive strength for a four year old) over to play with her. All three children she'd collected seemed perfectly happy though as they laughed and cheered with the porcelain dolls they'd found. Alder, on the other hand, was content to stand off to the side watching the crowd before making his selection and seamlessly integrating himself with a group of boys who looked to be all around his age.

Marcus was too young to fully participate in the crowd in front of him, but that didn't stop him from wiggling frantically in my arms in an attempt to join the fray. He babbled quietly to me about wanting to join in using his broken youthful speech, but I denied his wishes and settled him in my old office with a children's book instead. We were eventually joined by several other curious children each with a lengthy demand of stories they wished to hear. Soon the children were all sent away for dinner, and I settled in my own children for their meal. Thomas joined us then and listened to each kid talk about their day, eagerly asking them questions and laughing and smiling at their stories. He then took care of getting them all to bed, and I stood in the dining room watching Richard, Zenia, and Wilbur, our footmen, clear away the table with no idea what to do with myself.

I had just passed a lovely day with my beloved children and it was uncomfortable for me. I felt purposeless. I had no job to do, no crisis to take care of, nothing. Of course, in Agremerre, days like today had been idyllic, a welcome break from running a country to spend time with my family, but it was always undercut with the knowledge that soon I would be working again. Something, I realized I had enjoyed. I liked being busy, helping people in my lands. Idleness was something I don't think I had experienced since I was eleven years old, since I had decided that I wished to be Queen. It had been twelve years since then, and I had absolutely no idea what to do with myself as I faced the knowledge that, if Thomas truly didn't need me here in Dolma, I'd be spending six months of my life for, at least, the next 19 years doing basically nothing.

Agremerre's system of government meant that I was largely needed as a check to ensure the High Court didn't overstep their role, to be an ambassador for foreign relations, and to be the commander of the military forces. Which meant, in a time of peace, with me holding positions of power in ⅔ of the neighboring countries, that my job while in Dolma essentially boiled down to me receiving letters every so often telling me about a new law or plan that I was then expected to either confirm or reject. It was hardly a time consuming process. Especially as each decision would come with a neatly presented argument both for and against the new proposal.

If my experience in Dolma wasn't needed, what exactly was I supposed to do? My children were, of course, lovely, but even my parents, who I regarded as one of the best examples of parenthood, had raised me while holding their own jobs. They each worked in some area of our government. They all spent their days with some purpose, some goal outside of our family that brought them joy. And now, without that, I felt lost, and wildly uncomfortable in the space before me.

"Your Majesty," I turned behind me to see Kentin, the butler we employed in Dolma. "Do you require anything? We finished clearing away dinner half an hour ago, and you still have not left the dining room." I wasn't sure if this was his rather stiff way of wondering if he could be of any comfort or if this was his polite way of telling me to leave the dining room.

"Oh, forgive me, Kentin. I'm fine, just lost in my thoughts," I smiled, unwilling to part with my feelings of uselessness. They somehow felt shameful and selfish in a way I couldn't fully understand. After all, there were, no doubt, many people in Dolma who had dreamt of an idle life. Especially since we'd only just instituted a mandatory two rest days per week for every hired laborer two years prior. A compromise from my proposed three day rest that I still wasn't quite satisfied with, but it was at least an improvement from the zero days off that had happened before.

"As you say, Your Majesty," Kentin bowed, prompting me to actually leave the room, after thanking him once more. I meandered my way towards my shared bedroom with Thomas, which was where Thomas found me sometime later, utterly failing to read a book whose title I had not bothered to look at.

"The kids are ready to say goodnight to you," Thomas beamed at me as he entered the room. I wondered briefly if I had ever seen him so happy, which made my own feelings all the more uncomfortable as my guilt began to bubble within me. "They are all bathed and in their night clothes. Genevieve has had three stories and suffered through my terrible voice for a whole song, and I read another two chapters of Alder's mystery book. I'm beginning to suspect the count was the murderer, but Alder's sticking with his initial thought that it was one of the maids. Marcus is sound asleep, but the other two are demanding kisses goodnight."

I smiled at them, "Well then, I shouldn't keep them waiting." I closed my book and moved to follow him to the children's rooms.

"Oh," Thomas added as we walked through the carpeted halls of our wing of the palace. "Ollifelle and I spoke with father today, and we decided it's best if we get crowned as the next King and Queen. The coronation will take place in the spring, just a bit after your birthday!'

"What?" I stopped suddenly in the hall and turned towards Thomas, unaware of how to process what he had just told me.

"Isn't it great?" Thomas beamed, "This will make it much easier to change things and it seems like we have the full support of the citizens and the nobles who aided in the coup. They are looking forward to seeing us rule the country. This is exactly the result Ollie and I were hoping for. It is nice to see it working out the way we planned."

"Yes. Yes, I am sure it is," I smiled back at him, not sure of how to process it all. "I don't know anything about what to do at a coronation in Dolma," I said, quickly starting back down the hall.

"That's no problem," Thomas said, easily matching my rushed pace. "I will guide you through it. You'll be the Queen of both Dolma and Agremerre soon, isn't that exciting?"

"Yes," I tried to smile, but, truthfully, I was feeling anything but excited about what my life was to become. A brief and terrifying thought rushed through me as I wondered if I would now take Priscella's role in this country, an ornamental queen with the sole goal of creating the next heir. Something I'd already accomplished. What was left to do in a life like that?

After seeing the children, Thomas and I got ourselves ready for bed, and, in the quiet hours of the night, wrapped in Thomas' arms, I thought, for the first time in my life here in Dolma, about running away. It seemed to me that if I were to have no purpose in this country, wouldn't it be better to just go back to Agremerre? Then I could at least be ruling a country as a Queen. I could take Genevieve and Alder and raise them in Agremerrian culture. I'd take Marcus too, but, given his position in Dolma, no doubt I would struggle to have full custody. Deep inside me, however, I knew Thomas would do everything in his power to keep Genevieve and Alder with him too, and I could never actually leave my children. At least not for any significant period of time.

Not to mention Dolma itself. I'd spent countless hours fighting to make this country sustainable, to turn it into a place where its citizens were all well looked after and could thrive. Would I truly be able to leave it now? Could I even leave Thomas now? After all he'd done to support me in Agremerre and Dolma, could I actually leave him now? No, was the immediate answer. The only answer really, as the thought of it all brought a pain to my heart that I wasn't prepared for. No, no, I would stay. I'd find something to do. I'd gain some sort of value during this time of nothingness. With a slightly lighter heart, I finally fell asleep, and put a graceless end to this uncomfortable day.

To be in this world is to feel, or so Nana had told me ages ago. To live unattached from your emotions was a life akin to death. It all seemed very dramatic when she told me this at age six. By fifteen I was sure I knew exactly what she meant. At eighteen, I felt more confused about the topic than I had been at age six. Now, at 23, I had all but forgotten Nana's words. I was far too busy living my life, at least, that was what I told myself. Now, I wondered if I was perhaps living that life akin to death Nana had told me about all those years ago.

I had tried, at first, to do something with my days. I volunteered at the hospital in the city, but with an ongoing coup, that I was somehow the figurehead of, and being Queen of Agremerre, I was surrounded by so many knights I quickly became more of a hindrance than a help. Next, I thought I'd try to work more with the knights and soldiers of Dolma. Surely, my knowledge and expertise would be of some value. But, it was almost instantaneously obvious that I had nothing to add. The men and slow trickle of women who were being trained in Dolma's military were fully under the experienced and capable hands of Sirs Galileo and Mateo and they were being assisted by Dame Margret and Sir Constantine from Agremerre. They were incredible, teaching technique and theory to eager and excited students. And, I... I was suddenly cognizant that, no matter my teachings, I had never actually been a knight. There was nothing I could do there.

I perhaps might have gone to work at a farm or something, had it not been winter. Instead, I used my money and wealth to send rows upon rows of food and blankets out into the cities and towns across Dolma, in hopes they would help combat the frigid storms of snow and ice that, while not as bad as last year, still attacked the country. And then... then I spent my days hiding from the lack of responsibilities I'd now found myself missing. And, it was easy. It was so terribly easy to lock all my feelings of inadequacy away. To slip on the mask of the woman I had thought I was. To smile at all the right times. To laugh when I was supposed to. To carry on as if I hadn't a care in the world. As if I was this confident, happy person.

All the while feeling my shame and guilt rise inside of me. Shame I was not more helpful, guilty I was not doing more. Shame that I couldn't be an effective Queen here, guilty that I was not as supportive of Thomas as he was to me. Shame that I was not helping more in Agremerre, guilty that I couldn't find more joy in simply being a mother to my beautiful, intelligent, wonderful children. I'd find myself wallowing in these feelings I hated, but I couldn't find a way out of, and it seemed my only option was to bottle them up and hide them away. And, it was so damned easy to do.

I also had this vague hope that someone would notice. They would save me from the monotony. Someone had always come before, Nana, Abel, my parents, or my brothers, someone always seemed to find me when I felt down. But, this time, no one did. Perhaps that was my own fault though. I'd sent Abel and Lucy to Thomas, with all the work he was doing, he'd need them more than I. With my new position as Queen of Agremerre, and the better trained Dolmanian knights, the knights who guarded me were rotated with such great frequency, I was lucky if I saw the same person once a month.

Even my children were busy. Alder would spend most of his days studying, improving his reading, math, history, and all the other subjects deemed appropriate for a boy of seven. He also spent one day a week shadowing Thomas, and I decidedly did not think about how my son had more knowledge of the current workings of the Dolmanian government than I did. Genevieve, far more extroverted and social than I had ever been, desired nothing more than to spend all day with the ever increasing number of new friends she'd made. Marcus, at not yet two years old, stayed with me, and this was perhaps even worse. I was terrified that my emptiness would envelop him as well. Unable to show anyone how useless I felt, I'd take Marcus and hide in my old office. I'd spend the many hours of the daytime reading to him and any other children who wished to join. I watched Marucs play with his toys, and desperately tried not to let my locked emotions loose in the room that no adult could enter without my permission.

In the evenings, I'd sit with my precious mask of fake feelings as my kids shared stories about their days, as Thomas and

I tucked them into bed, and as Thomas eagerly told me only the bare essentials of the work he'd done that day. Work I felt that I had no longer had any right to comment on. Then he'd wrap me in his arms as we slept, and he'd place his hand on my scar, and... and I'd think that perhaps I was doing enough because, for some reason, in this farce of a platonic marriage we had created, I wanted to keep his arms around me. So it continued. It continued like this for months. It continued like this for so long that winter began to thaw into spring, and, without warning, in the chill of early spring, my birthday came upon us. My birthday, not my found day, for as far as anyone here could know, I was born, not found.

Chapter 11

The "Birthday"

My children ran into our bedroom first thing in the morning, jumping on my bed and screaming, "Happy Birthday!". Behind Genevieve and Alder, Ana stood with Marcus in her arms, smiling happily as she watched my rambunctious family. She winked at me as she placed a wiggling Marcus on the bed with my other children, "Happy Birthday, Your Majesty," she said before moving out of the room, continuing on her busy day of being the sole housekeeper for our rooms. And, I don't know what came over me, but I suddenly felt sick. My stomach roared, heaving and revolting inside of me in a way that had me sprinting towards the bathroom.

An acidic bile engulfed my mouth, overtaking my senses, and leaving a lingering taste at the back of my throat. "Are you okay, Godma?" Genevieve asked innocently from the outside of the room.

With tears in my eyes and my body still shaking with exertion I tried to respond to her. "Of course, darling. Something must just not have sat well with me from dinner last night."

"It's a shame that you're ill on your birthday," Thomas frowned as I swallowed down another wave of nausea.

"You didn't eat much last night," Alder said simultaneously, looking quizzically at me with his dark eyes.

"Perhaps it's all the excitement then," I pushed on. "When we were young, Azar used to-" my voice caught for a moment as a wave of sadness pushed through me. "Your Uncle Azar," I began again, forcing my words out over the lump in my throat, "used to get so excited for his birthday, he would run a fever every single year. His birthday would have been only a few weeks from now. He was always so angry at me for being fou - er - being born so close to his birthday."

There was a silence in the room for a moment, and I chided myself for making the mood so melancholy. "Why don't you children let me freshen up, and we will all eat breakfast together?"

"Okay!" Genevieve beamed before bouncing out of the bathroom. Behind her, Thomas called for Peter, one of the footmen, to get Marcus and bring everything down for breakfast.

"I'm sorry your family can't be here," Thomas said to me once the room was empty.

"My family is here," I said with more certainty than I'd felt for anything these past few months. "Well, at least some of them."

"Your parents will be here for the crowning ceremony," Thomas continued, "And your brothers."

"I know, and I am looking forward to seeing them," I said with less certainty. "Do we have to celebrate with a big feast tonight?" I asked, changing the conversation to one I was more comfortable with.

"It's too late to cancel now," Thomas joked dryly. "Besides, we haven't celebrated your birthday -" the nausea hit me once more, "really at all in the past four years."

"I have never needed anything big," I pleaded for what felt like the thousandth time.

"That was fine when you were just a Crown Princess -"

"I am still just a Crown Princess."

Thomas gave me an exasperated look. "But now, we are only six weeks away from our coronation, and you are the Queen of Agremerre. Frankly, I'm still surprised we didn't do something last year."

"It was planting time, we had to help the farmers plant," I insisted. I didn't add that farming sounded way more fun as a celebration than the day Thomas had planned for me this year. Nor did I mention how, last year, the council had wished to celebrate my found day, but I had told them no, out of fear that someone might leak the news of my adoption back to Dolma. I also didn't tell him that I felt I would never celebrate my found day in a happy manner ever again, or that with each passing "birthday" party I felt less and less like an actual child of my parents. That it slowly felt like my unique existence was crumbling, and that my adoption was a source of shame rather than love. I couldn't even tell my children for Gods' sake!

"So you said last year," Thomas continued, "But you will very soon be the beloved Queen of Dolma, and people want something to celebrate. Today, the streets of Dolma are full of love for you! We should absolutely be celebrating today. Now, I'll leave you to change," Thomas smiled as he left the bathroom, leaving me feeling worse than before I entered.

What was there to love? My treacherous mind demanded. I was a useless Princess who had to lie about her parentage just to be crowned. Today the whole kingdom celebrated an event that simply did not occur, for my health on the day I was found clearly indicated I was at least two weeks, maybe even a month, old. So, what could Dolma really be celebrating on a day like this? That even their soon-to-be-Queen couldn't survive here without lying? That even with all this power I was supposed to have, I couldn't do anything to change the celebration of my own "birth"?

Helplessness had become comfortable for me by this point, but my train of thought had led me down a road too melancholy, even for me. So, I got up and got ready, dressing and bathing myself, and giving my body and mind something to do. I languished in the humid silence of the bathroom for a moment, watching my own empty eyes stare back at me in the mirror, and I found a laugh escape me as I remembered Nicholas' words from what felt like eons ago. "Easy to read" he'd called me, and truly, how far I'd come since then. Now, there was simply no one who could read me at all. With that thought, I made my way down to breakfast, wearing a smile no one could seem to see through.

Birthdays, I'd decided, were very odd indeed. At least, they were when I was the one celebrating them. All morning long, I was greeted by people I loved, many of whom I'd scarcely seen since we'd gotten back to Dolma, all of whom wished me a "Happy Birthday", and gave me some sort of thoughtful present before rushing to their next duty. They all had a busy list of things to do, it seemed. Some of the many people who greeted me knew that it was my found day, but said nothing that might indicate the circumstances of my birth. The lies slipped as easily off their tongues as my mask of fake happiness slid onto me.

I suppose, had it been my actual birthday, I would have enjoyed it all. Instead, I felt a curious mix of joy at seeing my friends, and utter revulsion at hearing the words, "Happy Birthday". It got me thinking, as it often did, about who my biological relations may be. As a child, I would fantasize about being a descendent of a powerful spiritual seer, and I'd have a new and fascinating magic no one had ever seen before. But, of course, I was Nana's granddaughter, so technically, that was already true. Then, I thought that perhaps I could be a foreign Princess, hidden away from people who wished me harm. But, of course, I was Father's daughter, so I was already a Princess of my own country, and truthfully, I didn't really think that life on the run from people trying to kill me would really suit my tastes.

No, by the time I turned eight, I was forced to conclude that my biological relatives were, likely, fairly normal people. Around the continent, whispers of postpartum depression and suicide were thrown around, drowning and sailing accidents were also mentioned. Every so often, someone would pop up, claiming to be my relative, but each time, they would be proven false. It got to the point that by my tenth found day, Father declared that he would stop listening to any claims about my true parentage. It was a decision I had always agreed with, I had my real family by my side anyways.

I'd practically forgotten about it all, but with each "birthday" I celebrated, I found thoughts about my birth parents becoming more and more prominent in my mind. This year's was easily the worst, as my thoughts wandered, for the first time really, down a darker path. What if my biological parents didn't even want me? What if they abandoned me because they, too, thought I was useless. A vague voice in the back of my mind screamed at the illogical nature of these thoughts. How was a baby supposed to be useful anyways? But, this voice could not be heard over the wails of my broken mind.

And suddenly, I was standing in my dress as my maids put the final touches on my outfit for the giant spectacle Thomas had invented, and it felt like I'd hit a brick wall. I felt suddenly as if my body was somehow far away, as if I wasn't really there. I could hear the litany of negative thoughts that had been plaguing me, but now they were distant. It was like watching a carriage crash, where you know how it's going to end, but you just can't stop it. Except this was my body, my life, and I had to stop it. I had to. Now, hindsight is a wonderful thing, but you can never get it until you have already acted. And, I, even in the throws of my greatest depression, was a person of action. Unfortunately.

If you are waiting for me to tell you what was going on in my head during this moment, you will be sorely disappointed. I have no idea what I was thinking. All I know is my body still felt distant, and the only thing I could think of was the phrase "I have to stop it", followed by increasingly graphic mental images of a carriage crash, flailing legs, splintered wood, and flying dirt all becoming increasingly vivid around me. I can tell you, however, what I did. I told my maids, minus Erika, a new hire and a rather timid girl at the moment, to leave. Then I told

Erika, when she had a free moment, to get Thomas to bring me Nana. I gave her absolutely no explanation as to who, or what Nana might be before sending her out of the room as well. Then, I climbed out the window.

The two story descent was surprisingly easy. Dolma's Royal Palace was frighteningly ornate after all, and the extensive off-shoots and cut-ins where flowers, swords, and Gods know what else were carved into the stone made excellent hand holds as I scrambled my way down. From there, I gained a mild, but needed, confidence boost at how easy I found it to avoid any and all of the stationed knights and guards casing the palace. I may not have been a knight, but I was pleased to see that all the work I had done allowed me to get the better of them as I moved towards the stables.

The first horse I saw was a chestnut mare, who was incredibly calm as I led her around the back end of the Palace. Soon enough, I was on the darkened streets of the city, guided by a blissfully full moon as I rode off to the Dolmanian countryside. An odd joy filled me as the mare cantered through fields, a delightful chill hitting my whole body, causing my teeth to chatter. But, I couldn't stop smiling. My body came back to me, and my heart begged me not to ever stop moving forward.

Finally, when my hands got numb, and my toes felt as though they might freeze, I began to slow down. The horse beneath me halted gratefully to a stop as I took in my surroundings. It was only then when I fully realized the extent of what I had done. I was alone, with no supplies, not even a saddle, I had no idea where I was, and I, Queen of Agremerre, Crown Princess of Dolma had run away. This was bad.

I did, however, have to acknowledge that I felt much better. In fact, I felt better than I had in months, and stopping the barrage of negative thoughts became much easier. I also had to acknowledge that this was an insane act that I had undertaken and that, frankly, I was lucky to be uninjured after riding without a saddle for such a time. I was also forced to recognize that this evening was about to get even stranger as I turned the mare towards the only building I could see and rode on.

It took perhaps another half hour to arrive at the building, but by then I was positively freezing. The cold I had somehow been numb to during my ride suddenly came back with a vengeance and the thin red dress I was supposed to be wearing to my birthday party was not helping. Still, the freezing I felt made it easier to push past any embarrassment and knock on the wooden door of the house, two glass windows revealing the orange glow of a fire within.

In front of me a door flew open letting a rush of warm air hit me briefly as a large man with a long white beard and a completely bald head looked down at me. "H - Hi," I said, using the remaining energy I had to try and speak without chattering. "Can I stay here tonight?"

Behind the man a much smaller woman popped out, she had long black hair mixed with silver plaited in a braid behind her head, and dark eyes that had the same narrow shape as Charlotte, my old maid. Although, this woman's eyes appeared darker in color. "Well you'd better come in then," she drawled. "Go take care of her horse now," she poked the tall man, who tilted his head at me before walking outside. The woman took my hand and led me in, shutting the door closed behind her, exposing me to the warmth of her home. It was both a relieving heat and not nearly warm enough for me, as I quickly hurried myself closer to the fire.

"It ain't the smartest thing to go roamin' around at night before the summer starts," the woman chided, disappearing into another area of the house.

"N - No," I completely agreed, although my shivering made the word come out more like a question.

"But it's especially silly in early spring," the woman continued, coming back into the room and placing a heavy quilt over my shoulders. "I reckon you might have needed it though," she declared, looking at me up and down. I didn't know how to respond to that, so I just stayed silent as she continued her perusal of me.

"The name's Grace," Grace nodded, as if reaching some kind of conclusion. "That there was my husband, Suzan, and you need rest. I'm gonna get you a pillow, and you can keep right here by the fire, and I don't wanna hear a word from ya 'til mornin'."

"Okay," I said, very confused about what was happening.

"Oi!" Grace barked, giving me a light tap on the head, "that was a word. I'll be having none of that 'til the morning." This time, I nodded my head in response, and Grace gave me an approving smirk. Behind her the door opened to reveal Suzan, who nodded again at me as he came through the door.

"That horse alright?" Grace called as she disappeared yet again into another room. Suzan nodded once more. "Good," Grace's voice echoed from somewhere in the house, and I felt sure that she couldn't have actually seen Suzan's response. She came back a few minutes later with an embroidered flower pillow with frayed edges on most sides and tossed it at me. "Sleep," she ordered, before grabbing Suzan's hand and taking him to the back room, the door closing behind her with a loud click.

Oddly, I did sleep, really only mere minutes after Grace and Suzan left. I found myself drifting into oblivion as the warm fire heated up my freezing body. Even more strangely, I slept so well and so long that by the time I woke up, the fire was out and Grace was humming in the kitchen making Suzan's lunch. "You slept quite a while, you did," Grace told me as she heard me move to get up.

"It appears so," I said, blinking, a little disoriented in the afternoon light. "I apologize," I said again, still not sure what to do in this situation.

"Ah, no matter," Grace brushed me off. "That happens when you're healing."

"Healing?"

"Yes, that's why people end up here, to be healed." I stared at her blankly, and she did nothing to ease my confusion except put a sandwich on the table and tell me, "Come eat."

We ate lunch in total silence, for which Suzan joined us from whatever it was that he was doing outside. I tried to ask about it, but I was hushed once again by Grace. Soon I was washing up the plates from lunch, and Grace was making some tea. She plopped two mugs down on the dining table and not having any idea of what else I could do, I sat down.

"I got color," Grace began as soon as I sat down. I frowned at her statement as the woman in question looked only slightly darker in skin tone than myself. "It's my eyes," Grace explained, "They don't like the shape here, but they tolerated my family. Hard to avoid people with color, really. Then I married a colorless man - this was before Suzan. His name was Eliek and he was a good man. His father was a drunk, and Eliek swore he would never be like his pa. He managed, with the help of some wise folk, to come to the conclusion that in order to be strong, he had to be soft.

It took him ages, but he did it. And, he dragged me along, too, although we were still just friends back then. But, we helped each other be brave in a cruel world. You know what the bravest thing you can do in a world like ours is?"

She paused, waiting for my answer, "I don't know," I responded after a moment.

Grace smiled at me, "That's the last time you say that here." She sipped at her tea, before continuing on, "Bravest thing you can do is be soft. To feel your emotions and let people see the broken parts of you. It can be quite the difficult thing, to speak and be open with those around you, but it's always important."

Grace went quiet, she was quiet so long I went to prompt her myself, "So what happened to Eliek?"

Grace gave me a sad little smile, "They killed him, honey." I felt my blood run cold. "About a week after he married me, a group of colorless men came to our door. He told me to run, and put himself between me and them. I did run, but I heard later that he didn't even fight back. This made things worse, I think, at least for him. However, I was safer, a woman told me later that they'd given up on me. She said they felt bad about Eliek, given he didn't fight at all." Grace scoffed at this, "Like that made it any better."

"I'm sorry," I said, horrified by her story.

"Yeah, well I had to learn how to live again after that. I had to learn how to be soft again after that. That's damn tricky, that is, but I did it. And, after I did so, I looked towards the Gods and said this "Gods, send me those who've lost their way, who've become numb or hard and need help to change. Let me guide those who are ready or need to hear my words. Please bring these people to me." The Gods listen real well to things like that, or so I've found.

In the nearly twenty years since then, only one person has come who didn't need my help. That was Suzan. Nah, Suzan didn't need my help; he was a gift. He still is a gift for me. And, I was a gift for him, too, I do think. Been awful happy with him, you know, awful happy indeed."

"Are you worried about him facing the same fate as Eliek?" I questioned, fear creeping into my voice.

Grace laughed, "Fear's got no place in love, honey. And we live further away now, so it'd be quite the undertaking to get out here. Plus, things been changin' since you came. Got some nobles with color now, don't we?"

"People have tried to assassinate them more times than they've come after me," I lamented bitterly.

"And they've all failed. Plus, they all knew what was going to happen."

"It shouldn't have had to happen! And, I should have been better able to protect them!" I exploded feeling more anger than I'd felt in a long time. Feeling more than I had felt in a very long time. My numbness seemed to be melting in the face of Grace and Suzan's warm home.

Grace laughed at my anger, a full hearty sound that pushed all through the room. "Any person with color knows what it means to live here, as does every woman, every person with an alternate gender, or anyone in a nontraditional kind of love. They all know what they have experienced in a system like ours. There's no such thing as soft change. It don't have to be brutal, but too many will feel a hard shift no matter how slow you move.

Now me, personally, I say just rip the bandage off and let the people settle as they may, but I ain't the Queen. The biggest thing I'd tell you is to have compassion for the people changing. Now hear me on this one: we're doing compassion, not sympathy because things do need to change. But, see most people go hard in the face of a hard world. They see the most disadvantaged person and hold on so damned tightly to anything they think will stop them from ending up like that. Now, that don't excuse any cruelty they inflicted while driven by that fear, but it makes it much easier to understand why they cling so damned hard to something that really hurts all of us in the end."

"So, what do you do to fix it?"

"Now really, that's something I ought to be askin' you!"

"Well," I started after a moment in which I realized she actually expected me to answer the question. "We can increase exposure to people of different backgrounds, colors, and ideas. That decreases fear."

"Not bad, could be tricky to implement in smaller towns."

"Closing the gap in wealth between the different groups of people, having more public examples of women, people of varying genders, and different sexualities," I suggested.

"That will upset many, but it would help. Truth be told, there are a million different ways to change something, and you'll have to use at least 100,000 of them to make sure the change truly holds. And, no matter what you do, people are going to be upset."

"But perhaps I don't know enough about Dolma to make the right choice!"

"Hogwash, you've been living here for years. You have seen a successful version of what you're trying to accomplish and you're not alone; you've got people to help you. Although, really, even them nobles you've got with you up in the Palace would be grossly out of touch with what goes on with the actual people they rule. They spend far too much time locked up in that giant monstrosity of theirs to see what we do. If you want to help, first ask yourself why you stopped trying to do so and why it took coming all the way out here to change your mind. Then, do something about it."

I opened my mouth to answer the questions Grace had posed, but she raised her hand to stop me, "Nah, I don't need to hear 'em answers. I imagine there are some other folks who you need to talk to instead."

"You're probably right," I conceded.

"Suzan drew you a map back to the capital. I imagine they'll be lookin' for ya there, but in the meantime, you're welcome to stay as long as you need."

When I woke up that morning in Grace and Suzan's house, I felt so comfortable and warm, I felt as if I never wanted to leave. Now, I felt that same warmth and comfort, but I also felt an anticipation and flightiness to return back. To start working on myself first, and then work to improve Dolma and Agre-merre once more. So, with plenty of afternoon left, I grabbed my mare and bid goodby to Grace and Suzan, thanking them for all of their help.

"Come back any time," Grace called.

"Safe travels," came a low rumble from Suzan as he nodded towards me once more. I waved at the two of them one last time before I trotted off to Ohmehiu, and Dolma's Royal Palace.

I never did see Grace and Suzan again, but I did come to learn that I wasn't their first or even their last royal visitor and they'd seen their fair share of nobles as well. The story of Eliek and of countless others like him fueled many of the changes we would come to make, but to do all that, I first needed to return to Thomas and life as Dolma's Crown Princess, and future Queen.

Chapter 12

The Confrontation

Coming back into Ohmehiu as a future Queen who had, quite literally, run away was easily the most embarrassing thing I've ever had to do. Fortunately, it seemed as though Thomas had kept my disappearance under wraps, at least from the citizens, who waved me back in the capital with loud shouts and crowding of the streets. However, within fifteen minutes after the first excited exclamations by the people, I was practically surrounded by knights.

"Crown Princess," Galileo said, giving me a tight lip smile as a hoard of knights raced to our location. His use of this particular title brought on the memory of Galileo telling off Leonard and me for racing through the city. Consumed with my good memories, I smiled but my genuine mirth was met with a harsh glare from Galileo. A positively terrifying response, but not nearly as threatening as the visceral storm that radiated from Sir Lemmly, my head knight from Agremerre who was supposed to be in charge of my safety in Dolma.

"My Queen," he yelled with barely contained fury as he stomped - or as much as one could stomp while riding a horse who was unaware of the nuance of the situation - towards me. Suddenly, I was confronted with the sharp realization that perhaps Sir Lemmly's biggest task at the moment was keeping me safe from himself.

"We are to see you safely back to the palace, Crown Princess," Galileo said, his cold anger was no less frightening than the loud rage of Sir Lemmly, who was currently all but shoving other horses away so he could ride by my side. Squeezed between these two knights and surrounded by at least 15 more, I was beginning to feel more like a prisoner than a Princess, to say nothing of a Queen. Feeling oddly emboldened, I said as much to the men beside me.

Sir Lemmly actually growled in response, causing more than one head to turn his way. Galileo, however, simply gave me a deadly smile before calmly saying, "We just want to make sure you get home safely, Crown Princess."

"You haven't called me Crown Princess since I became Queen of Agremerre," I commented idly, still possessed by a blasé attitude I couldn't remember acquiring.

Galileo glared at me once more as we continued riding, but Lemmly turned towards us and hissed, "Queen's don't run away!"

"Well, that can't possibly be true," I said, making no effort to conceal my voice as Lemmly had, "as I have done just that."

Lemmly looked as though he was contemplating the pros and cons of strangling me right this very moment, but Galileo stopped him before he could speak again. "I'm sure we will discuss the matter in more detail when we get back to the Royal Palace," Galileo casually threatened.

"If you insist," I responded, shockingly unfazed by it all. "But, really, if you two were going to be so upset by it all, then you should have made sure I wasn't able to escape in the first place. I mean, really, it's a safety issue. If I, someone who isn't even a knight, was able to sneak out unnoticed, that also means someone could just as easily sneak in," I continued, alerting not only them, but also myself to the security implications of my adventures.

Lemmly had to be physically restrained by Oberon beside him as he lunged in my direction. "Your Majesty," Galileo just groaned. His voice was filled with so much exasperation that I rather thought I should have won some reward, but at least he seemed to have begun the process of forgiving me.

"When we get back, I'm making you take the knights examination," Lemmly grumbled, having now regained some composure. Behind him, I heard Oberon give a stifled laugh. I turned to smile at him, and Oberon gave me a quick wink in return.

In what was likely a great relief to Sir Lemmly's nerves, we passed the rest of the journey back to the Royal Palace in silence. When we finally did make it back, however, we were greeted by the stern, angry, and annoyed faces of Thomas, Abel, Priscella, and Harry. My embarrassment hit again, along with my strange unbothered attitude, which I now determined to be a response to my embarrassment.

With no better response lined up, I simply addressed my comment to Priscella and Harry and said, "Fancy seeing you here." This was probably not the greatest opening statement, but it was also, in my opinion, a rather valid sentiment considering I hadn't seen either Priscella or Harry since our return from Agremerre.

Harry's face turned a curious shade of red as he blustered, "What sort of ill-advised-"

"Not now, Father," Thomas cut him off. "We've sent for the Dowager Queen Elizabeth," Thomas said curtly towards me.

"Thank you," I said back, scarcely remembering why I'd asked for her in the first place.

"Would you come with me please?" Thomas demanded, turning to head into the palace before I'd even responded. Not willing to anger him further, I quickly dismounted and followed him through the ornate halls of the palace, making the accurate assumption that someone would stay behind to care for the horse I had been using. Not too long after, Thomas turned into one of the endless rooms. Once I had followed behind him, he quickly closed and locked the door, effectively blocking the trail of knights and royals following us from entering the room.

"Hold on!" Harry banged on the door, "I want to speak with her too!"

"I will have a moment alone with my wife," Thomas bellowed through the wood.

"But -"

"Your Majesty," Abel's soft voice resounded through the door. "Why don't we wait for His Highness and Queen Avalynn in your chambers?" There was a series of muted grumbles, but shuffled footsteps did suggest that the crowd was moving away.

Thomas waited until the last echoes of their footsteps had completely disappeared before he spoke, his body still turned towards the door. "What in the Gods' names were you thinking?" he questioned, his voice just barely above a whisper.

"I wasn't," I answered honestly.

"You weren't thinking?" Thomas turned to me, his voice gaining strength as his blue eyes bored into me, demanding answers that I wasn't sure I possessed. "Then why did you do it?"

"I don't - I mean I felt I had to. I had to get away, just for a little bit," I responded, pleading with him to understand.

"What could you possibly have to get away from? You are the Queen of Agremerre and very nearly the Queen of Dolma. You are loved by your people and by your children; you are surrounded by luxury; anything you desire people will throw at your feet. Good Gods Ava, what more could you want?" Thomas begged of me.

"I -," any earlier confidence I had at speaking my problems seemed to all but crumble before me. After all, Thomas' list of things I did have was awfully thorough and awfully complete. "I don't know how to not work," I said, my whole body shaking with something I knew was not the cold room.

"What?" Thomas blinked at me.

"Ever since I was eleven years old, my whole life has been working to be Queen. I don't know how not to work. I feel so useless and despondent. I don't feel like I can have a crown if I am nothing more than an ornamental Queen. I don't deserve that title. Not to mention, my whole image in Dolma is crafted on the lie that I am my Father's biological daughter. If I am going to be such a useless liar, I might as well go back to Agremerre to be Queen full time."

Thomas stood in silence for a moment before speaking once more, "Did you think I was useless in Agremerre?" His tone was quiet, and there was a sort of helpless fear in his eyes that also infected me. I had no way of knowing if my response would exacerbate that fear, but I could only answer with the truth.

"No! No, of course not Thomas. You were everything in Agremerre. You helped me stay sane, comforted me as I grieved for my brother, let me bounce ideas off of you when I was stuck on a problem. You were anything but useless!"

"Well there you have it then!" Thomas said, breathing out a sigh of relief.

"But I'm not doing any of that here!"

"You're watching the kids."

"Well yes, but we have nannies and caregivers, I am not alone in that task. I also have a title, Thomas. You don't hold a title in Agremerre; you are not expected to work for that country. But, I am supposed to be the Queen of Dolma, and, no matter what was done before, I was always taught that a title means something. I must be involved in the politics and governance of a country that I will be Queen of!"

"You've completely overhauled several of our country's systems? Isn't that enough?"

"Queen is a job you hold until you are dead or give it up. There is always work to be done. And, besides, even if I wasn't Queen, I am not supporting you in the same way you've supported me. I hardly know anything about your plans or problems!"

"So you don't trust me to handle things on my own?"

"That's not what I said."

"It certainly sounded like it."

"Well if it did, I'm sorry and I do trust you to handle it, but I'm saying that it is my job to handle it too."

"Your method is dangerous!"

"All methods will be dangerous. We are trying to change a culture so accustomed to prejudice and hardship that there will always be those who are angry, no matter how slow we go!" I argued, rephrasing some of Grace's words.

"Yes, but then the danger falls on me instead of you."

"That's not any better!"

"I can't lose you, Avalynn," Thomas roared. "I can not do it. You weren't there, the day we learned your brother died. I wasn't with your parents when they first heard the news; all I knew was that one of their children died. Your father sat me and Marcus down to tell us something, and his eyes were red and puffy, his voice was shaking something fierce, and good Gods Ava, I thought it was you. I thought you had died, and the thought of it nearly killed me. I was so damned relieved when King Edgar said it was Azar who died I nearly laughed out loud.

I need you safe, you see, and so I couldn't have you in a position where people would continue to try to kill you. I just couldn't do that. And then! Then, you go and pull this stunt, and everyone's telling me that you're smart and strong and capable and I know that, but do you know how terrified I was? I just kept thinking what if something horrible has happened? It was awful, Avalynn."

"I'm sorry," I responded, and I felt that regret and apology so earnestly I wished for nothing more than to project my sincerity and feelings onto him.

There was a long silence, in which we both just stared at each other before Thomas gave a large sigh. "I was wrong to try and keep you from ruling Dolma," Thomas accepted, running his hand through his short white hair.

"Running away, even briefly, was not the best response from me either. Although, it did help my emotional state," I partially conceded.

Thomas gave me a weak laugh. "Okay, okay, you will rule besides me, as you were always meant to. Just promise me you will talk to me before you run away again.'

"I promise," I smiled at him, feeling confident that I could keep this promise.

"Then we'd better go and meet with the others. I imagine they too have much to say," Thomas offered me his hand.

I felt my cheeks flush at the thought of facing more of the people who I had left behind in my disoriented state as I took Thomas' offered hand. "Yes, I am sure they do," I sighed.

Thomas laughed again from beside me as we walked through the halls. "I think I will enjoy the sight of it all."

"Traitor," I grumbled.

"Oh no, I think it is my well-deserved reward after spending all night worried about you. And, for covering up your absence with the nobles. If anyone asks, you were ill," Thomas informed me.

"Thank you, and I am sorry that I made you worry. It wasn't my intention to cause you or anyone else pain."

"I know Avalynn," Thomas squeezed my hand, "I know."

We walked down the empty hall in a companionable silence. I did feel like we were heading in the right direction, as both rulers and partners, but there was a sort of odd trepidation to it. It was as if our current relationship was fragile, but, if it were to break, there was confidence that we could put it back together again. We, as friends and partners, would be able to make it through anything. However, this new attempt at ruling together was still unstable and unknown. It was a way of working together that we had never tried before. We would be working together as equals in both knowledge and experience and it was a type of relationship that Thomas had never seen a proper model for, having only spent a few months with my parents at most. I found myself wondering if we could really pull off this new working relationship, or if all we'd be able to do would be falling back into the old pattern we'd grown accustomed to these past three months. I pushed these thoughts out of my mind however, secure in the knowledge that if we fell back into old habits, one conversation with Thomas would put us back on a more favorable track.

I also had to wonder at my lack of hobbies or, frighteningly, lack of personality outside of being a ruler. With my now, thankfully, clear head, I could examine my despondence over the past months, and I found myself lacking the self esteem and confidence I had felt while either competing for or working towards a crown. It would seem that I would have to do something and put some effort in finding who I could be outside of a crown. Beyond my roles as a Queen and a mother, who would I be when it became time for me to release all my titles, for I had no plans to die with them and leave my children in the same position I was in when Anora had died.

My determined thoughts were put on hold as Thomas and I reached the rooms that once, or perhaps still did, belong to Queen Priscella. My lack of knowledge about the current political state of Dolma caused me another brief flare of sadness and confusion as I pondered the ownership of the room.

Instead of leading us in, Thomas stopped me in front of the large doors, and proceeded to read my mind as he spoke. "These rooms will stay in the possession of my mother," Thomas informed me, squeezing my hand once more as he spoke. "My father will also be remaining in his rooms, although the first floor will become the main office of the King and Queen. Traditionally, once we had been crowned, you would have taken over mother's rooms and lived with Genevieve, while she was still young, and I would have taken father's rooms and lived with Marcus. Alder at eight would be given his own set of rooms, but -"

"No! You're absolutely right!" I said, anticipating his next words, "We will not split up the children, and Alder certainly won't be living alone," I said vehemently, practically vibrating with anger at the thought of such an arrangement.

Thomas gave me a sigh of relief as he finally looked up at me. "It -," he faltered slightly, but after a hard swallow that caused the hard spot in his neck to bob, he continued, "It would mean we will keep having to live together."

"Of course," I said, feeling a little baffled by his words, "We're married, and I would never expect you to be away from the children."

Thomas practically glowed in response, beaming at me with such a brightness I thought for a moment he could replace the sun in the sky, "I -," he began.

"Is she here yet?' A loud voice screamed as the doors in front of us pulled open. Before us an enraged Harry trampled out, stopping short at the sight of us. "Oh, Ava, right, well come in," Harry continued, his voice losing all of its former heat.

"I am here, too, Dad," Thomas grumbled.

"You are not in trouble," Harry barked back.

"I am 23 years old. I hardly think I can get in trouble," I said indignantly.

"You're 24 now, darling," Thomas chimed in.

"I am 24 years old. And, you have no power to scold me," I corrected.

"I do!" Lemmly cried out, crashing into the open door in his rush to object. He didn't seem fazed by this though as he just glared at me while rubbing at his forehead.

"As do I," Galileo agreed, calmly walking towards us.

"I am the King of Dolma!" Harry started, before I cut him off.

"I thought Ollifelle was named Queen after the coup?" I interjected.

"That's not important, the point is -," Harry tried to continue.

"It's probably important to Ollifelle," I interjected again. The girl in question was sitting in the room and just gave me a shrug in response.

"Also, in two months, Thomas will officially be King," Priscella chimed in.

"That's not the point! The point is you can't just go running away!" Harry finally finished.

"Why not?" Priscella questioned.

"It does sound rather nice," Ollifelle agreed.

"It does not! It could be dangerous!" Leonard's voice echoed from somewhere in the room.

"She came back," Lucy's voice called out, "and it's not like you haven't had the same thought."

"I certainly haven't," Hugo chimed in, and I was forced to wonder just how many people were in the room I'd yet to walk into.

"Me neither," Mateo's voice agreed.

"I pondered the idea occasionally," Challa's calm voice mused, "but I thought of it as more like a vacation as opposed to leaving for good. Just like Her Majesty!'

"Same here," Oberon nodded, his body just visible from the doorway. "I could never leave forever."

"You and I are different people," Ollifelle told him.

"I'd gathered that much already, Princess," Oberon responded.

"Perhaps this would be better discussed once we are all sitting down in the room," Abel suggested, stopping any further commentary as he pushed past Harry, Galileo, and Lemmly to escort me into the room, and towards a large seating area. Abel gave me a quick smile as he moved to sit across from me, as everyone else took their seats.

Chapter 13

The Fallout

The room, as it turned out, was filled with the Dolmanian royal family, all of my original party who came with me to Dolma, three of my Agremerrian knights - Lemmly, Knight Zelle, and Sir Brighton, and Kentin, my butler. My embarrassment had greatly subsided after my discussion with Thomas, and the odd shouts of agreement that had come from inside the room. There was also the fact that, even in this situation, I felt better than I had in the past three months. I had been drowning, I realized now. I was drowning in emotions of grief and self pity, and I had not realized how deep I had sunk until I'd pulled myself out. Leaving and grabbing Grace's outstretched hand had helped bring me back to life and show me the air and sun once more.

My new-found breath also made me more acutely aware of the possibility of sinking again. I knew that it was, perhaps always, going to be an option for me. It felt like I was just sitting poised at the surface of a lake and I could feel the watery depression I had been in still cloak my body. At the same time, there was air and warmth to be found at the surface of the lake and if I just put in a little more work, I could find the shore. I knew there was hope for better and brighter things to come.

Feeling all of this, I couldn't regret the actions I had taken. However ill advised or worried it had made the people I love, I couldn't find it in me to want to take back my actions, or even apologize for them. I felt guilty for making everyone worry, that I would apologize for, but I would not apologize for running away. I needed to run away. I needed that escape and I needed to feel something else before I lost myself completely. Now, I was faced with the task of explaining this need to the people around me and I had to hope they would understand.

"Now," Abel said, turning the attention in the room back towards him. "Who would like to go first?"

This was the wrong question, as it turned out, as the room promptly exploded into chaos. Practically every person in the room attempted to speak over each other. Thomas and I sat silently together, watching it all, and Kentin soon brought us some tea. Abel too, was silent, almost gleefully so, as his dark eyes twinkled in enjoyment as the room descended into further and further madness.

"Isn't it his job to prevent all this?" Thomas asked, looking inquisitively at Abel over the top of his tea cup.

"You would think so," I agreed, holding a similar confusion. I, however, was also filled with gratitude that the eyes in the room had moved away from me as everyone chose instead to argue with each other.

"I imagine this confusion is necessary, Your Majesties," Kentin declared, standing primly behind us.

"How so?" Thomas pressed as we both turned to face my serious butler.

"Her Majesty's leaving stirred up many emotions for the people here, not all of which were about Her Majesty herself. While Her Majesty was gone, many here felt they could not express those emotions, but, now that you've returned safely, Sir Abel is giving them leave to do so. Without all of their emotions being directed solely at Her Majesty, of course."

"Then what of you, Kentin," Thomas asked, "Did Her Majesty's departure cause you any emotional disturbance?"

"Well, she will need to apologize to Erika. Erika was rather distressed at Her Majesty's departure, especially after being the last person to have seen her before she...departed. Erika seems to believe that it was her fault Her Majesty had disappeared since Erika couldn't figure out what a "Nana" was. She was quite inconsolable about it, not to mention she was convinced she would be held responsible for the whole affair."

"Well Ana and you would never let that happen!" I countered, despite the shame that had begun to rise in me.

"Of course not, but she only started working here two months ago, Your Majesty. It is my, and, I believe, your desire not to drive away good staff members. Next time, please do entrust a more seasoned member of staff with the task."

I blushed at his words. "I will apologize as soon as I can," I assured him.

"As you wish, Your Majesty," Kentin bowed. "Then, Your Highness, to answer your question," Kentin said, turning back to Thomas, "I support Her Majesty in all of her choices."

"Even running away?" Thomas asked incredulously.

"Yes," Kentin responded, without explaining himself further. "There is fresh orange poppy seed cake prepared, if you'd like some, Your Majesty," Kentin then informed me.

"Oh, yes, of course I would like some. Orange poppy seed is my favorite," I said, surprised by the sudden change in topic.

"I know," Kentin bowed, walking away towards the kitchens.

"Why do I get the feeling he's rewarding you for this?" Thomas demanded, still staring at Kentin's retreating form.

"Because I think he is," I replied back in equal shock.

Around us, the shouting continued. Despite all the commotion and noise around us, regardless of who was speaking, or who was being spoken to, there was no real malice behind anyone's words. However, the emotions they spoke with were very real, and I suddenly found myself wondering if I was not the only one who'd become overwhelmed, despondent, and closed off during this time. For, looking at these people, I got the sense they were all breaking down, in one way or another, save Thomas and myself. And, really, I was only able to remain calm by having had my break down yesterday.

"I don't like celebrating my birthday," I suddenly said to Thomas, moving away from the chaos in front of me.

"What?" Thomas blinked at me, tearing his eyes away from the yelling mass.

To him, my words were probably quite random, and I couldn't blame him for that thought. But, as I watched those around us lay out all of their buried feelings, I felt the inescapable urge to speak about all of my problems too. "I don't like celebrating my birthday. Specifically, I don't like that we are celebrating my birthday and not my found day. It makes me feel like an imposter, it makes me feel like I am lying to the world, and it makes me feel scared," I told him. "I want to tell people I am adopted. We've adopted Alder, we've adopted Genevieve. I don't want people in Dolma to think that Alder and Genevieve are somehow less than Marcus."

Thomas stared at me quietly for a moment as he contemplated my words, "Okay," he said, simply, "We've spent too long hiding it anyways. Actually, your father gave me something for your birthday that may help."

I felt instant relief. My breathing eased, my neck and shoulders relaxed, and I realized I'd been carrying the weight of my "birthday" and the lie this celebration forced me to tell for so long I'd forgotten the extent to which this story had truly burdened me. Like so many things these days, I was struck with the ease at which I had forgotten my pain. For almost five years now, I'd ignored how much this issue had really bothered me and I'd grown accustomed to its weight. Right then and there, I vowed to forever more be more conscious of these weights and burdens I placed on myself and I refused to let them lay on me for any longer. I could do better for myself on this matter and I had no desire to go back to what I had done before.

"What did Father send?" I asked, after I dissected my relief.

"It was actually something he'd given me when we saw your family before leaving Agremerre this winter. He wrote down his story of finding you."

"What?" I asked in shock, I hadn't heard that story since my 19th found day. A wave of nostalgia, and grief hit me as I thought of the once integral life tradition that I had thought had become all but forgotten.

Unaware of my feelings, Thomas simply answered my question rather nonchalantly, "Yes. I thought the whole thing was rather sweet. I'd never heard the story before, but your Father said I could read the letter. I was thinking we could publish the story, tell the whole country, in your Father's words, about where you're from and show how much he loves you, all in the same breath."

"That's a brilliant plan," I smiled. Thomas beamed at me in response. "Have I really never told you of how I was found?"

Thomas just shrugged. "You never say much about your birth - I mean found day. In hindsight, I suppose I should have guessed you didn't like celebrating it as a birthday," he frowned.

"How were you possibly to know my feelings on the subject if I never told you?"

Thomas stared at me for a long moment, his face filling with some emotion I couldn't name, and I could have sworn he was searching for a way into my very soul. "Yes, I suppose I wouldn't know," he finally said, his voice so quiet and distant, I wondered if his words were meant for me at all. We continued to stare at each other for a moment after that, for what reason, I couldn't say. All I know is that it took a great deal of effort and energy to pull myself away from his gaze.

It was only later, when Kentin was pouring me another cup of orange and cinnamon tea did the fighting people in the room seem to remember their ire was supposed to be directed at me. This shift, in my opinion, was caused entirely by Harry, as somewhere in the midst of shouting with Ollifelle over something, he rather abruptly turned towards me. "Well, what do you have to say about this?" he demanded, in a voice that somehow managed to cut through everyone else's conversations.

After his words, a, now foreign silence hit the room, as everyone else ended their discussions to turn towards me. I quickly tried to busy myself by taking a sip of my slightly too hot tea. Harry's question, in my mind, was hardly fair. There was no answer I could give that would not end in another round of the loud chaos that had filled this room just moments ago.

Also, if I were really honest, while I cared for everyone in this room and their presence surely indicated that they cared for me too, I wasn't prepared or even comfortable, giving them full access to the fragile mental state I was in when I'd run away. After all, I was really only just starting to make sense of my mental state myself. Perhaps when Nana arrived she could help me understand it all. She could and would - if she thought it necessary, help me craft a concise and easily digestible statement that my allies could use to understand my actions. But, she was not here yet and I felt as though I would need novels to describe how I felt.

Instead, I simply said, "It was never my intention to make you worry." It was, in some ways, a hollow reassurance, considering that what my intentions were hardly mattered when my actions had caused the opposite response. Still, I felt the words had to be said and I was honest. Whatever feeling or answer I had been searching for when I had left had made my actions feel like an act of self preservation. There was no malicious intent, just a desire not to suffocate any remaining parts of myself. "I am sorry for causing you to worry," I concluded.

"How can -" Harry's anger was cut off as the gentle voice of Galileo spoke over him.

"You're only apologizing for causing us to worry?" It was hardly a question, the way Galileo had said it. In fact, it was almost as if he was simply confirming my intentions as opposed to searching for further apologies.

"Yes." It was the only response I had to give. My choice to run aways was an entirely selfish maneuver. I had not, at the time, thought of anyone but myself, I am not even sure I had the capacity in that moment to think of any one else. But, running away had helped me. The physical act of leaving, the guidance from Grace, the choice to return had all but brought me back to life, and it did so in a way I'm not sure I would have been able to achieve if I had simply stayed in the palace.

There was a terrifying thought that, if I had stayed, I would have continued to find it easy to hide away. It would have gotten easier to smile and pretend that all was well, even on days like my "birthday". It was a horrifying notion because I now remembered that each day like that felt like a slow and painful death. And, I swear, I think it would have killed me. I think it was killing me. At least it was in all the ways that matter. Running away was an entirely selfish move and I would have reconcile that with the pain I'd caused to the people I love. But, sometimes, just sometimes, when all other options seem hopeless, selfish moves are a necessity that the soul can not afford to do without.

Galileo looked particularly heartbroken at my response. It was an emotion I failed to really understand, especially when he simply bowed and said, "I understand, My Queen. I hope to serve you better in the future."

I couldn't understand what his words meant or, more accurately, why they were the words he'd selected in this context. I couldn't fathom how me running away could possibly translate to him not serving me well. And, when his sentiment was echoed by every other knight in the room, it only served to further my confusion. It would take another few months, and several long talks with Nana to fully understand his words. It was a message that I, frustratingly, had heard countless times before, but couldn't manage to make stick inside my head. Somewhere in my downward spiral, or perhaps even as far back as my crowning in Agremerre, I'd forgotten that I wasn't alone in this journey. I'd forgotten that these knights, at least, didn't serve Dolma, some didn't even serve Agremerre, they served me, as an individual.

For these knights, my vanishing act was a failure, as my actions suggested that I had not been able to trust them enough to tell them or take them with me when I left. It was also, once I learned the meaning of Galileo's words, not something I could immediately correct. For, in all honesty, when I left the palace that night, I hadn't trusted these knights. I hadn't trusted anyone. I was so sunken in shame that I felt that I could trust no one to see how truly broken I was feeling. I didn't trust them, even though I loved them. This knowledge, once I acquired it, was a bitter tea to swallow.

Harry, on the other hand, was not satisfied with this inter-action, and was rather vocal in his criticisms. "Why should we care if you hurt us or didn't? It's not about what we feel, it's about the fact that you ran away! You left, Avalynn! How was that even possible?"

"Yes, next time you chose to run away, please let us know, the knights of Agremerre will be sure to come with you!" Lemmly nodded, his voice far more even in tone than Harry's.

It was at this point that I realized that there were a large number of people who seemed to believe that I would run away again at some point. I, to this day, have no idea how they got this notion. In my mind, the matter was solved. I'd gotten the freedom I needed to clear my head. I would go on to have some transitioning sessions with Abel and Nana. I'd do the work needed to heal myself and no one would ever have to be worried about the runaway Queen again. However, it seemed that no one else seemed to understand that this escape act was a one time thing.

"Wait, that's not the point! You're not supposed to go with her!" Harry yelled.

"We definitely are though," Knight Zelle said, "She is the Queen of Agremerre. We are Agremerrian knights, we are sup-posed to follow her everywhere. Although, you do bring up a good point, we will need to know exactly how you managed to leave the palace unseen. We will need to update the security."

"Does that mean we can now all try to escape the palace?" Ollifelle asked, looking rather excited, "You know, as a security drill or something... to test the palace for weaknesses!"

"Oh, that could be fun." Lucy agreed eagerly.

"We are losing focus!" Harry yelled once more. The indulgent silence that followed his words suggested his volume and aggressive tone could no longer inflict the fear it once had. "The point," Harry continued angrily, "is that you need to tell us why you left."

"And will that help you, King Harold," Abel jumped in, speaking up for the first time since we'd all entered the room, and allowing me time to think of a possible answer to Harry's question.

"What do you mean?" Harry sputtered, "This is the most important question!"

"That didn't answer my question," Abel responded calmly. "What we are looking to do right now is to soothe the hurt that Queen Avalynn caused by leaving so suddenly, as well as soothe the hurt she must have felt to have left the way that she did. Some hurt has already been discussed, and we'll now have to go through its healing process." Beside Abel, Galileo nodded, and I struggled to determine what pain he suffered that we had already discussed. "Now," Abel continued, "We are trying to isolate why this incident has caused you pain, King Harold."

You would be forgiven for thinking Abel had spoken in a foreign language with the way Harry was looking at him right now. His mouth hung open and he could do nothing more than blink at Abel for several minutes, during which no one else in the room dared to speak. Finally, the silence was broken by none other than Priscella, when she turned to me and asked, "Why did you come back?"

"I'd like to know the answer to that too," Ollifelle chimed in.

This, I felt I could answer. "I never intended to leave forever," I responded confidently. I may have not known this when I first escaped the previous evening, but when I had calmed down, I had always known that I would return home. "I could never leave you all, my family, or this country forever. I guess I mostly just needed a little bit of space, then I met this wonderful woman called Grace, and everything just sort of fell back into place. Then I was ready to come back home."

"Grace, as in Grace and Suzan? The couple who run that farm a few hours north of here?" Mateo asked, and I turned to gape at him.

"Yes! How do you know them?" I asked, shocked that he knew who I was speaking of.

"I accidentally came upon their place after stopping that noble uprising a few years ago," Mateo answered casually, "They're lovely people and Grace really helped me out with her advice."

"Yes! She gives great advice!" I agreed enthusiastically, excited to be talking about the new people I'd met.

"Avalynn will be, once again, taking a more active role in the changes we are making to Dolma," Thomas said, effectively putting an end to what would have likely been an animated discussion about Grace and Suzan between Mateo and me.

"What do you mean once again?"Challa asked, looking confused. Shame and embarrassment filled my body once more, and I had the strong desire to simply disappear as the heat and discomfort of the emotions twisted inside of me.

Beside me, Thomas stiffened slightly as he took in the confused faces of those around us, only Ollifelle looked comfortable, smiling at us both and responding, "Oh, that will be good. I kept telling you that we should work with her more."

This time, Thomas blushed, before quickly working to calm himself. "Why wasn't Avalynn working with you?" Harry asked, his voice almost quiet compared to his earlier tone, but still maintaining his original intensity.

"Well -," Thomas began.

"This can't be that much of a surprise," I suddenly cut in, unable to stay silent in my shame, "I haven't done any work since we came here this winter, surely you all have noticed." My embarrassment subsided slightly as it was replaced by astonishment. In my head, I had been so sure that everyone had known that I hadn't been working. They had to have all known that I was practically useless in this country, since we had arrived. It was incredible for me to think that this was a shock to the vast majority of people in this room. "How could you not have known that?" I demanded, incredulously.

The embarrassment that I had felt seemed to transfer to the others in the room. Even Hugo's usually unflappable face gained a pinkish hue. Lucy, however, was unbothered, "I was working with the nobles in the outer regions," she explained, brightly absolving herself of further inquiry.

"Yes, thank you for the work you do," I quickly agreed. "I suppose it doesn't really matter," I concluded, "I will be working again in the future, and I came back to do that work."

"But why weren't you working previously?" Harry questioned again.

"That's not a question that needs to be answered at the moment," Abel jumped in once more.

"Are there any questions I can ask?!" Harry grumbled, but Abel just smiled at him in response. "Fine then! I guess I'm done here," Harry huffed. "Don't run away again," Harry ordered me before getting up and marching himself up the stairs.

"Why is he going up into my rooms?" Priscella questioned, a hint of irritation lacing her voice as she watched Harry disappear.

No one answered her, and instead, Galileo turned to me saying, "There will be some reorganization of the knights, Your Majesty."

"If you think it is necessary," I said, not entirely sure why he would think this was needed. "I trust your judgment."

Galileo frowned at me, but continued, "I would also like to request a meeting with you in which you show Sir Lemmly and myself the route you took to exit the palace grounds so we may increase security in the weak spots you have found."

I accepted his request, and he left the room, taking many of the knights with him. With their departure, more and more people began to trickle out of the room. I stayed behind with Kentin, Thomas, and Abel as we finished the cake and tea that had been brought earlier. "You knew I wasn't working," I said to Abel when the room was quiet once more.

"Yes," he smiled calmly at me.

I was quiet for a moment, as I weighed my words, "Did you - did you also know that I was struggling?" I asked. The words felt harder to say than I was initially anticipating.

Abel's smile fell as he stared at me for a long moment, "Contrary to popular belief, Your Majesty, I am not in fact a mind reader, and while I can, on occasion, correctly infer mental states of individuals I know or work closely with, I was not, I am ashamed to say, focused on you these past few months."

Relief, more than anything else, filled me with his words. It would have been far worse if he had known of my distress this entire time and still done nothing. "You didn't have to look after me, that's not your job," I instantly went to reassure him.

"My official job title might be ambassador of Nevremerre," Abel said, giving me a sad smile, "but that does not mean it is my only responsibility. Still," Abel brightened, "You came back, and Betty is on her way, so I know your soul and mine will feel healed once more." Abel stood then and bowed before me, "I am infinitely grateful to have you back safely once more, Your Majesty. Please do remember I will always do whatever is in my power to assist you should you require my help."

"Thank you, Sir Abel." We exchanged smiles, and he too left the Queen's apartments.

I sat with Thomas for a little while longer before we too left to go back towards our rooms, Kentin and some of Thomas' knights (who had been waiting outside the door of Priscella's apartments) followed closely behind us. When I returned to our corner of the palace, I was quickly greeted by the children who were under the impression that I was still sick and in bed. I only spoke with them briefly before Thomas grabbed my hand and excused us both to his office. He brought me in alone and locked us both inside as I took a look around the room. Neat stacks of papers and books sat on an overcrowded desk. Red chairs and curtains gave the space a serious feel, but Thomas seemed to relax in the warm room. He walked gracefully over to his desk before turning towards me, "Well then, let me catch you up with what I have been doing." It was a simple phrase, but with it spoken, I felt like my world was set right once more.

Chapter 14

The Recovery

Slowly, I began to reestablish myself as the person I had once assumed myself to be. I worked with Thomas and Ollifelle; we brought in others like Lucy and Whimely and drafted new laws to push forward the new world we all dreamed of. I trained with the knights most mornings, and I spent the evenings with my family. It was a familiar order and by no means an unpleasant one. The knights' schedule had been changed, so now I constantly had two Agremerrian knights, two knights of Dolma, and two knights from my original party by my side. It was almost surprising, the excitement I felt upon seeing my old friends so often. When Mateo and Galileo showed up to guard me again after only two days off, I very nearly cried.

I had thought, at one point, that this would be all I needed. I was working in a job that I cared about; I had a family I loved; and I saw my friends much more often. Three months ago I was sure that this was all I needed. But, perhaps I wasn't the same person I was three months ago, or, perhaps, the hole I dug for myself during these past three months was harder to come back out of than I thought.

I comforted myself in the knowledge that I was doing better, each day no longer felt like a slow, torturous walk towards death, but I still did not feel normal. I still retained a sort of hollow feeling and I'd catch myself, every now and then, falling back on the same masks of joy and politeness that I didn't actually feel. There was another emotion added to the mix though: determination, fueled by a greater understanding of my predicament. Determination molded to my consciousness and was guided by the firm hand of hope. Nana was coming, and I knew with every minuscule part of my body that she could help me feel right again.

Seven days later, a white figure on a white horse came running to my rescue. She rode up to the palace with a bright smile and a knowing look in her eye that could only be gained through years of experience and dedication. When she held me in her arms, I thought that there was no greater and more wonderful feeling than the love that is born from asking for help and having someone answer that call. "Hello, my Songbird," her throaty voice echoed melodically in my ear. "You've been awfully busy, haven't you?"

"Oh no, Nana," I cried, feeling tears roll down my cheeks, although I was unsure of what emotion triggered the response. "I've not been working at all! That's why there was a problem!"

Nana laughed, the sound of it blowing across me like a warm breeze, carrying her love up into the heavens around us. "Oh, my dear, not all work is physical and not all work is positive, although all of it will help us grow. Believe me, dear, when I say you've been working very hard indeed." She released me and raised a wrinkled and slightly calloused hand to my cheek. "But, we will discuss all of that in time. First, you must let these old bones rest and pay me for my trouble with the smiling face of my great grandchildren and some warm tea!"

My own laughter merged with hers as I led her into the palace, "Of course, Nana."

Nana did not address any of the problems I had for a full five days. Instead, she spent her time playing with Alder, Genevieve, and Marcus, all of whom were delighted by her presence. She ate meals prepared generously by the positively besotted chef, who had been a fan of Nana's since Nana had healed the chef's niece from a depressive episode two years prior. Nana also brought Chef Augustine fresh thyme each visit, an unnecessary, but clearly a still appreciated bribe for the old chef who had been exclusively cooking Nana's favorite dishes for the past five days.

Then Nana was held up with a whole series of tasks. She had long talks with Abel that always seemed to end in uncontrollable laughter, transitioning sessions with at least 20 knights and Ollifelle, and she practically flirted every day with a very stiff Kentin. Frankly, Nana seemed to be talking with the entire palace except me! I was more than a little jealous, although I worked very hard to dismiss these feelings, knowing very well of Nana's love for me and how each of her talks with others was a healing process for them. Still, I was the one who called her here, for me, so I did think I deserved just a little bit of her time.

Finally, on the morning of her sixth day in Dolma, I got a bit fed up, and pulled her to my study after breakfast. "Can we please discuss my problems now?" I demanded, my temper flaring up in a way I hadn't remembered since my childhood.

Nana raised an eyebrow at me, as she suppressed a smile on her lips, "Are you ready to be helped then?"

The question threw me off guard as I stared back at her. Was I ready? I felt ready, there was an impatience in me that demanded I release all that weighed down on me. There was also a more logical side of me that wondered if this was some kind of trick, did Nana know something about me that I didn't? A part of myself that apparently had never left Mother's school room thought this might be a question with a right and wrong answer and I desperately did not want to get the answer wrong. "Yes?" I finally answered, hoping this was the correct response.

"Oh Ava," Nana sighed, kindly, "Sit down my dear." She led me to the red velvet couches that filled my office, placing me in one couch and positioning herself opposite me. "My dear, Ava," she began again, once we were both situated. "It seems to me as though you have become rather passive in your own life."

Passive was not a word I had ever thought to use while describing myself, nor had I ever heard it used in reference to me. If anything, I thought I'd be more accurately described as assertive or even aggressive in my actions and behaviors. "Passive?" I echoed back, unable to say anything else in my confusion.

"Darling," Nana explained, a softness and caring tone washing over the room as she spoke. "More often than not, the things that have brought you to this point have been things that have just happened to you. You were asked for in a treaty with Dolma; you were told you were to become Queen of Agremerre. While you have agreed to take these things, and more, they were not roles you actively went to seek out. These great, life changing moments were simply the byproduct of life's never ending chaos. While you have made the most of these events, when you first decided to come to Dolma you gave up the only active goal you've ever had and since then, you've struggled to know how to replace it.

"That's not true," I argued, "I had the goal of improving Dolma. I worked on that for three years!"

"And then you accomplished that."

"Not really, there is still a lot of work to be done."

"Yet, you let yourself be talked out of that work."

"I got back in," I said, rather defensively.

"Yes, after breaking down, sinking into depression and running away. Physically leaving everything and every person from your current life behind," Nana pointed out strictly.

"I was not depressed," I argued, "and I did come back. I wasn't even gone a full day!"

"Avalynn, you isolated yourself from others, stopped doing activities you previously enjoyed, you slept more, ate less, and you felt the need to hide your true emotions from everyone around you. These are all symptoms of depression. There are more and different symptoms of course, but illness of the mind manifest differently in each individual person."

"But I wasn't sad," I defended.

"Weren't you?"

"I -," I began, "I was numb. I'm not sure I could have been sad, I just felt empty."

"Avalynn, suppressing our emotions does not mean that those feelings have disappeared, and locking them away means locking away all of our emotions and our true feelings," Nana responded gently.

"Well, I know that now," I huffed.

Nana smiled at me. "You know it intellectually, not emotionally, but that's alright, we will get there. So much has happened to you in the past five years, Avalynn, I wonder if you ever stopped to truly process it all." The answer was no, as it turns out, and Nana stayed for six weeks helping me do exactly that, before moving my care over to Abel who'd added my transitioning as a job to do along with his ambassador work.

When Nana did leave, much to the disappointment of the entire place, there was hardly time to wallow in our sorrow as the whole country was set to prepare for Thomas' and my coronations. So, her departure was followed by the pressing arrival of delegates and royalty from six different countries - including Maychula, our relationship becoming much closer after the events of their volcano. Not to mention the first introduction of the new nobles we had appointed, as well as the careful release of the nobles who'd been basically imprisoned in the back of the Palace for the past year and a half.

I was reminded heavily of my wedding, running around with too little time to talk to anyone for very long, Thomas constantly by my side. Although, being the Queen of two different countries - nearly - did put me in higher demand. Not to mention that after Queen Christine's takeover and matriarchal restructuring of Andaluca, Queens and women in general were treated with more respect and a little more fear, from the more patriarchal societies like Dolma and Experion.

Despite this now being my second coronation, I did, I confess, feel rather minimal excitement from the whole ordeal. I was far more focused on the guests, the schedule, and the organization of the whole elaborate show, and it really was a show, Dolma put on to crown its next rulers. At least when I received my Agremerrian crown the High Court was in charge of the ceremony, although that coronation had been less than joyful for different reasons.

All this is to say that by the day of the actual coronation, I had almost no conscious recollection of the proceedings. I know Thomas and I were bejeweled in the most ridiculous amount of heavy jewelry I'd ever seen in my life. We also wore huge blue and red cloaks of dyed fur that smelled like dust and nearly made me sneeze on at least six occasions, and that caused us both to practically melt in the overly ornate throne room. The throne room seemed to stretch on for miles as we were forced to slowly march to the opposite side where we vowed to serve Dolma with all we had. We were then given the crowns of Harry and Priscella, who now became the first living King and Queen dowagers in Dolma's history.

"Presenting King Thomas Harold Rayforth Ecardio Davenforth Carleon and Queen Avalynn Priscella Carleon," a herald announced to the crowded room as we received our new names to show our new change in status. As per tradition we were to have the names of the previous King and Queen placed as our new middle names. I felt a little bit weird about having a shared name with Priscella, but I wasn't about to change this centuries old tradition, not when I was already changing so many others.

That was all I could remember of the ceremony. I know I spoke to people and words were spoken to me, but it all flew by so quickly and there were still so many things to do that I basically missed the entire part that made me Queen of Dolma. This meant that when Thomas and I changed clothes and were riding far more comfortably out into the city to greet the people, I found myself initially turning and looking for Harry and Priscella when the masses of people shouted praise for their King and Queen. We spent hours dancing and eating with the nobles and royals we had invited and, like my wedding I was never without a partner, although fortunately my stamina for the whole event seemed to have improved. Then, finally, Thomas and I were able to retire for the evening. So, as we collapsed onto our bed, still dressed in our nicest clothes, I had the odd realization that we'd just completed the first non violent coup I'd ever heard of. The strange thought carried me to sleep after what felt like a very strange day, in which I'd yet to completely comprehend I was now Queen of Dolma.

Chapter 15

The Divorce
of Dolma

As it turned out, being Queen of Dolma changed my life in absolutely no significant way whatsoever. Not only was all the work that I'd done in the past five years practically the work of a Queen to begin with, but Thomas had been basically running Dolma as King for about a year and a half anyway. So, our final month in Dolma before moving to Agremerre was very joyful and easy, all things considered. It seemed everything was going smoothly as we excitedly packed for our stay in Agremerre. So, it was a bit of a surprise when a week before our departure we, or more specifically Thomas and Ollifelle, encountered a large roadblock in our normally peaceful life. This time it came in the form of Priscella and Harry - announcing their divorce.

"What?" Thomas yelled, so loudly that the small room that Priscella and Harry had chosen to make this announcement was unable to properly contain the volume of his word, and I felt my ears ring uncomfortably beside him.

"You can't!" Ollifelle countered at the same time as her brother, her eyes filling with tears.

Harry and Priscella looked taken aback by this reaction and I found myself agreeing with their surprise. I was never under any sort of illusion that Harry and Priscella were a love match. Frankly, I wondered if they even liked each other, or if they simply got along just enough to keep the country together. Given Dolma's attitude towards divorce - unfavorable - I was a bit surprised that two of the most traditional people I'd ever met had chosen this outcome. However, they were no longer King and Queen, and I had no doubt that this decision would lead to the greater happiness of both parties involved. As such, Thomas' and Ollifelle's reactions were a mystery to me. This was, in my mind, a very plausible and practical move for the two dowager monarchs.

"We are divorcing," Harry repeated, looking cautiously at his children. "We married to forge an alliance between our two countries, an alliance which is no longer needed considering I am no longer King and Andaluca's monarchy has been almost entirely restructured."

"But you can't divorce!" Thomas exclaimed.

"It's better for everyone this way," Priscella said, bluntly.

"But, where will you go?" Ollifelle cried.

"For goodness sake! It's not like I'm kicking her out of the country!" Harry snapped. "She's the Dowager Queen of Dolma, she'll still have rooms in the palace, she will just now have more freedom and the ability to marry someone she loves."

"But, you love her, right?" In moments like this, I do believe the sensible approach is to be compassionate and understanding of the emotional nature of the people in the room. All of us, however, failed spectacularly at this task as we stared in confusion and horror at the sheer stupidity of Thomas' words. "Er - no - hold on, I didn't mean it like that," Thomas desperately tried to back pedal.

"Well, what did you mean?" Harry demanded. "You didn't actually believe us to be in love?" Harry looked disgusted at the thought.

"You don't need to make it sound so impossible," Priscella huffed.

"But, it's true! I don't love you," Harry pointed out.

"Well obviously, but it's not impossible!" Priscella persisted. Harry looked at her in exasperation.

"Right," Harry continued, opting not to continue the current argument with Priscella, "Well the moral of the story is we are getting a divorce."

"But why?" Thomas whined.

"Because your Father is a bad husband, and I want to have my own life," Priscella said, primly.

"Well you didn't have to say that so harshly!" Harry turned on Priscella, looking supremely offended.

Priscella just shrugged in response. In front of me, Thomas got up and started pacing around the room. "This can't be happening," he muttered, seemingly to himself as he walked.

"Thomas," I started, a bit hesitantly as I went to grab his arm, "This is your parents decision and it isn't exactly a huge shock considering the way they got married in the first place."

The way Thomas looked at me, I might as well have suggested that I horrifically murder all three of our children. "How could you say that?" Thomas demanded.

"Maybe we should take a minute and talk about this more tomorrow?" I suggested gently, "It seems like perhaps everyone needs some time to digest everything."

"Well… fine then," Thomas huffed before storming out of the room himself.

"How are you doing, Ollie?" I asked, trying to ignore the baffling behavior of Thomas.

"I'm okay," the teenager said, wiping her tears off her face. "It's strange, I know this is the right decision and I never believed you two were a loving couple, but I still feel upset."

"Oh, Ollie," Priscella said, patting her daughter's hand. "It was a hard decision for us too, or for me rather, as it was my idea, but I think both of us deserve relationships that will make us happy. Your brother has made it so that you will not be sent away as I was, and now I wish to take the steps required to live a life of my choosing, even if that life is not one I can clearly see at the moment."

Priscella's words struck something within me, and I, for the first time, felt something akin to admiration for the woman. While I'd been compassionate about her experiences and the choices she'd made in ruling Dolma, I also knew that my model of being Queen looked entirely different than anything she was doing. Looking at the woman before me now, however, I thought she seemed awfully brave. She was changing her life drastically by making a decision that, even as little as a year ago, would have ostracized her from all of Dolma. And, she was working towards a future that she couldn't yet imagine, but had faith that it would be better than her life now.

I found that I honestly believed in her faith as well. Even without a true idea of what Priscella's future looked like, I too shared her confidence that it would be bright. I also felt hope and joy that she now felt she could make this decision. I knew that the only reason she felt she could do this was because of the changes Thomas and I had made. It was also likely that her choice would inspire other people in unhappy marriages to go their own separate ways. This, undoubtedly, could lead to greater freedom in who married whom and increase the over-all happiness of those who felt trapped in marriages that no longer served them, or in which they were being abused.

However, my admiration and hope was somewhat dimin-ished by the notable exclusion of myself from Priscella's speech about finding happiness. It seemed as though whatever Priscella believed about the divorce of a Dowager Queen, the current Queen of Dolma was not allowed to divorce her hus-band. Not that I had any desire to divorce Thomas, but I did wonder at my own happiness in this arrangement. Nana had spent six weeks with me working on how I could more actively work towards my own future, and chase my own happiness.

But, I still struggled to label exactly what that happiness might be.

"Thank you Mother," Ollifelle said, breaking me out of my own thoughts as she went to hug Priscella. "I think I will be alright. I'll go and spend the day with Chanti, and I'm sure I'll feel better in no time." Ollie beamed at us both before leaving the room as well.

I had just started to leave myself when Priscella spoke once more, "I was not expecting the children to take the news so dramatically."

There was a lingering silence in the space before I realized I was expected to respond to Priscella's statement. "Yes, well change can be difficult no matter how prepared you are," I rushed out something that sounded vaguely right before attempting to leave once more.

"Thomas took the news especially hard," Priscella spoke again.

"Yes, he did seem to," I replied awkwardly. I had no explanation for Thomas' behavior myself, so I could hardly give an explanation to Priscella.

"You will help him to understand, won't you Ava?" Priscella said to me, a pleading look in her eyes that looked uncomfortably onto my core.

"He will have to process his feelings about the subject on his own terms, but if he comes to me I will argue in support of the divorce," I conceded.

"But, you can talk to him now," Priscella pressed, grabbing my hands and staring intently at me. "You can explain this to him. He listens to you, Ava. He will understand if you speak to him."

"I can't make people process their emotions," I hurriedly explained, pulling my hands out of Priscella's grasp. "I support your decision and I will tell Thomas that, if he wishes to discuss the divorce with me. Now, if you'll excuse me." With that I fled the room, moving in a manner similar to Thomas' exit just a few minutes ago.

"Are the dowager King and Queen really getting divorced?" Lucy asked, taking me by surprise not even five minutes after having left the small sitting room in which I'd learned the news.

"How can you possibly know that?" I asked in shock.

"Miri told me, but it was so surprising I thought I'd better confirm with you," Lucy shrugged.

"Why's this so surprising to everyone? I never got the sense that the two of them particularly liked each other," Knight Zelle said from behind me.

"It's shocking because in Dolma people don't get divorced... ever," Sir Duketan, one of my Dolmanian knights answered.

"Miri is supposed to be in Agremerre, preparing any information I need for my return," I started, walking purposefully down the halls towards my rooms. "And how do you know about this? None of you were in the room with us," I asked my knights.

"Miri came back early, she left a report on Agremerre on your desk," Lucy supplied, only really leaving me with more questions.

"And, Princess Ollifelle told us," Challa informed me, "She told us about it almost immediately upon leaving the dowager Queen's sitting room."

"That can't be how the Dowager King and Queen want this information to spread," I muttered, "I'm sure I can count on you all to keep this information to yourselves. And, how long has Miri been here that she already knew this information?"

"It's too late for that, Your Majesty," Sir Ingron, my other Dolmanian knight, said, "Princess Ollifelle also told her knights and Sir Jason is a terrible gossip. The news is probably halfway around the palace by now."

"And, Miri only just arrived back today," Oberon added, "She reported back to Galileo this morning right before you and King Thomas went to meet with the Dowager King and Queen."

"And, she already knows about the divorce?"

"Apparently most of the servants already knew," Dame Natalie, from Agremerre, supplied.

"Then how did we not know this before?" I asked.

"Miri is just better at knowing things than us," Lucy supplied.

"You're trained in getting information! And," I added, pulling Lucy close and whispering towards her. "We have other spies."

"Yes," Lucy agreed, nonchalantly, "but their main priority is ensuring your safety as opposed to trivial gossip."

"Then what about you? You love trivial gossip! You think it's helpful for exciting people and understanding the truth in various situations!"

"The Dowager Queen was very good at hiding this," Lucy shrugged.

"You just said most of the servants knew!"

"That's probably just an exaggerated number based on the people claiming they knew now that the information is out," Oberon theorized.

"It's all getting very complicated," I sighed.

"Yes, but that's what makes it interesting," Lucy agreed. "So, with the dowager King and Queen divorcing, will you now divorce King Thomas?"

"What?" I stopped walking suddenly, causing Knight Zelle, who was walking behind me, to slam right into me. After taking a moment to right myself, I turned back to Lucy, "Why would I divorce King Thomas?"

"Well," Lucy explained, "the Dowager King and Queen are divorcing because arranged marriages don't lead to the happiness of the people involved; it's not inconceivable that you and King Thomas might do the same. Surely with you involved, you could make appropriate arrangements for the kingdom. You could easily rule together, even if you weren't married."

A strange sort of panic hit me as she spoke, "Arranged marriages are not doomed for unhappiness," I instantly defended. "Thomas is a fine partner and husband, and it would be easier for both of us to do our jobs if we are married. One divorce is enough at the moment, I should think."

Having finished my defense, I continued our journey to my rooms. My speech itself sounded confident enough, but I couldn't help but wonder if Thomas would have agreed with my sentiments. We had not married for love, it's true, but I was content, happy even, in the relationship we had built for ourselves. Thomas was supportive, intelligent, nurturing, kind, and happy to adapt to my "new" ideas and my demanding schedule as the Queen of two different countries. Not to mention he was a loving and attentive father to our children. I cared about him, in truth, and the idea he would not remain at my side was not a pleasant one. Still, I refused to dwell on our marriage when Thomas was not here to speak for himself.

I then went on with my day, and I tried, and then failed, to put Priscella and Harry's divorce out of my mind, or rather, what their divorce meant for my own marriage. I wasn't so out of touch with my own desires to know that I would like a love match. I did want a marriage with someone who I loved, and, equally importantly, who loved me. I also knew that if I ever chose to think about it, if I ever stopped and examined my own feelings on the subject, I would likely find that the relationship I was in was a lot closer to that love match than I wanted to admit, at least on my part. So, I would not examine those feelings. I couldn't. Doing so would ruin the stability we had and I found that, for the moment, I valued that stability more than the potential happiness I could find elsewhere or even in this same relationship just with different parameters.

So, I kept focused on my insane task of trying to push Harry and Priscella's divorce from my mind, an exceedingly difficult task when everyone from Ana to Alder came up to me wondering if the rumors were true. I was awfully curious as to when I became the official source for Palace news, and I mentioned as much to Whimely - the 12th person so far who came looking for my verification on what seemed to be the news of the century.

"Well, it's not like I can ask Thomas, Miss Queen," Whimley pointed out using the new, rather condescending, title he'd given me since my coronation. I had hoped he would have given up on the moniker by now, as I had done my best not to take the bait and react to the name, but no such luck.

"Well, I don't have a different answer for you than I had for the last dozen people who came before you," I huffed, "It is not my place to comment on the Dowager King and Queen's relationship."

"You know that's practically confirming the whole thing," Whimely pointed out, unhelpfully.

"Well what would you have me say?" I demanded, "Honestly, you'd think the world was ending the way people keep badgering me about it. And, really, why can't someone else verify the rumors? Why not ask Ollifelle? I hear she's the source of at least half of what's been spread around."

"She's their child!" Whimely pointed out, "It would be terribly rude to ask her, Thomas, or frankly the Dowager King and Queen themselves this question."

"I'm their daughter in-law!"

"Think of it this way, Miss Queen, you're a more approachable person to the masses such as myself!" I gave an aggravated sigh in response. "And you're a lot easier to read," Whimely continued.

I was not so easy to read three months ago when no one realized I was depressed, I thought bitterly. But, he was correct, apparently the return of my mental health also meant the return of my "easy to read" facial expressions. I wasn't trained, as Thomas and Ollifelle had been, to not react when people try to tell you things. "Still, if people just waited a little bit, no doubt an announcement of some sort would be made," I finally responded to Whimely.

"Queen Avalynn," Whimely said, suddenly serious, "No noble in Dolma has gotten divorced in 146 years, and even that was a case in which the wife had gone insane."

"Given Dolma's history, I do question whether she actually was insane," I interrupted.

"Perhaps she was not, but it was the last successful divorce in Dolma and it's worth noting that no royal in Dolma's history has ever gotten divorced. It's easier to claim your wife cheated on you and have her executed or imprisoned. And, any woman who asked for a divorce, prior to the changes Your Majesties have made, would be thrown out onto the streets, stripped of her title, with no access to money or her children."

"Goodness, Dolma must have seen rather large numbers of their nobles die from "household accidents"," I half sighed.

"Why would you say that?" Whimely asked, confused.

I stared at him in awe for a moment. "I'll explain it another time," I eventually decided. "Continue with your point."

"Well there isn't much left to say other than this is a big deal. I mean have any of the royal family of Nevremerre gotten divorced?" Whimely continued.

"Of course," I responded easily, "and at least three did so while they were reigning King and Queen. Several Princes and Princesses have divorced as well."

"Of course they have," Whimely sighed, letting his head fall into his hands as he pinched the bridge of his nose. "Right, look, I know things are different for you, but here, divorce doesn't happen. Not for us. Not for nobility and definitely not for royalty. And, they say the Dowager Queen is to keep her place at court? To not lose her title, her money, or access her children? If that's true, do you know what that means?"

"Of course she won't just be kicked out on the streets for a divorce," I said, before quickly adding, "which I am not confirming. I mean really Whimely, we have been putting in place new divorce laws for the past two years, what did you think was going to happen?"

Whimely just shook his head. "It's one thing to say a divorce will now be kinder to the people, especially women involved, it's another to watch it happen to a royal family member. To see the divorce of the second most famous couple in all of Dolma and to see the family be accepting of it."

Acceptance had yet to be determined, if Thomas' reaction today was anything to go by, I thought to myself. "So do you think a divorce like this would trigger a chain of divorces?" I asked, although I privately believed this would be exactly what would happen.

"Among other things," Whimely nodded, "Honestly, this is a great way to show the country just how different things will be under your reign, which could be very useful moving forward. Still, it's likely this will dominate all news for a long time to come. Not to mention as King and Queen, you are the only one high enough ranked to oversee the divorce proceedings. Are you really able to go back to Agremerre amidst all of this?"

"I'd forgotten we'd be in charge of the divorce legalities," I sighed. "If one took place," I added, albeit rather pointlessly at this point. "We do need work on Dolma's judiciary system," I lamented, feeling a tad overwhelmed at the thought. "But, I am still the Queen of Agremerre. I have a duty to Agremerre, and to Genevieve, to spend six months there."

"You took a year away from Dolma when you first became Queen of Agremerre, maybe you could do the same thing now."

"Dolma has the Dowager King and Queen and Princess Ol-lifelle to oversee the country in our absence and Thomas is available to return whenever needed. Agremerre, at the time, had no other alternative, plus I was only Crown Princess of Dolma at the time."

"They had their High Court and still do."

"That's an entirely different branch of government and one that is not meant to serve as a complete ruler," I sighed once more, mirroring Whimely's gesture of running my hand over the bridge of my nose from earlier. "Look, I can not make any decision until I have more information. Something I will not gain until at least tomorrow."

"Ah, so there is something going on tomorrow!" Whimely said, exuberantly.

"You were at Ollifelle's rooms before coming to mine, don't act like you didn't know this," I grumbled, feeling a little disappointed I'd let the information slip regardless of whatever he might have known previously.

"True," Whimely confessed, "but it always feels more accurate when I hear it from you, Miss Queen." Oddly, Whimely's words made me feel better, and the man in question gave me a low bow and a kiss on the hand before seeing himself out. I was able to go back to reviewing Miri's reports from Agremerre for about a half hour before Leonard and Mateo came in with the exact same questions. It was proving to be a rather difficult day in the long run.

That evening was not much better. A sullen and withdrawn Thomas paced around our shared room in a brooding manner, that was eerily reminiscent of Alder's when we'd "made" him eat dinner rather than allowing him to read his latest book two nights earlier. I did try, multiple times, to break through Thomas' disturbed grumblings, but I found no success in the matter. Eventually, I resorted to loudly declaring I was going to bed and blowing out all the candles as Thomas continued to pace. I don't know when he came out of his musings, but when

I woke up the next morning, I found him in his usual spot next to me, his hand resting gently against my scar.

Despite the normal position I'd woken up in, the next part of the morning was far from standard. For starters, Thomas somehow managed to stay asleep as I began to prepare for my day. This was not completely unusual but, even after I dressed myself and the usual time for breakfast with the children was fast approaching, Thomas remained asleep. Deciding he needed his rest, I ate with the children on my own, but was surprised to see that several hours later, Thomas was still not out with us.

With just an hour left before we needed to meet up with his family, I left the children in the capable hands of Meredith, our Agremerrian nanny and went to find Thomas. This was not a hard task, as it turned out, for I found him almost exactly where I'd left him earlier this morning. I was pleased to see that he had woken up. However, he appeared to be only half dressed. His green embroidered tunic was only partially laced at the front, and he was missing at least one shoe. None of this seemed to be of much of note to the man in question however, as Thomas appeared practically frozen in place. His hand was held expectantly on the lace of his tunic, but his face was turned towards the large window by our bed.

I watched him silently for a moment, drinking in the perplexed look on his face, and the helplessly lost look in his eyes. He was beautiful like this, the gentle glow of the morning sun bathing him in a warm honey color. Conscious of the time, I moved quietly into the room. I was careful not to startle him too much, well aware that he had likely not even heard me enter. I wondered if I needed bother though, as when I finally went to kneel before him, he didn't even blink at my presence.

"Thomas?" I asked, gently, reaching out my hand and laying it on his cheek, guiding his gaze towards me.

Thomas' own hand reached up to meet mine, holding it tightly against his face, and causing my fingertips to brush through the soft strands of his hair. He sighed lightly into my palm, causing my body to shiver as the hot breath tickled my hand. "I have a plan Ava," he said quietly to me, resting our joined hands together in his lap. "But, I am not sure it will change anything."

"It's not your job to change your parents' relationship," I said, softly, doing my best to remain compassionate in light of the heavy feelings practically radiating off of Thomas. Feelings that I was failing to fully comprehend.

"I'm King," Thomas responded.

"And theirs is a personal relationship."

"I do not wish for them to divorce. It won't be easy for them."

I sincerely doubted this would actually be true, but I tried to avoid saying that to Thomas. "That is their decision to make and have we not been working to make it easier for people in this country to get divorced, should they so wish?" I pointed out instead.

Thomas stood suddenly, dropping my hand and moved across the room, "Yes, but I didn't expect my parents to be the people to use that service!"

I sighed and picked myself up from the floor, shaking my legs out from the hot numbness that came from kneeling too long. "I am sorry that this has hurt you, " I said, unsure of how else I could kindly reply to a situation that, to me, seemed like a very obvious outcome. "I am sure that wasn't your parents' intention."

"I am going to have mother come with us to Agremerre," Thomas said, in what felt like a complete non sequitur. "Maybe with some time away from my father, they may make a different choice."

Now, I would never confess to be an expert on the psychological make up of any being, however, it was my opinion that Thomas' plan of action would likely have the opposite effect of what he was intending. For starters, any doubts Priscella may have about living alone would promptly vanish during her time in Agremerre. Then, there was the fact that Harry and Priscella hardly ever spent time together anyways. I don't believe either of them had ever had a great desire to see each other in their time away from their duties - official and unofficial. Still, Thomas seemed rather dead set on this particular plan.

"Thomas, while I would be happy to have Priscella join us and the children would likely be very happy to have their grandmother with them -"

"I don't see why, she's not very good with the kids," Thomas interjected, and I suddenly found myself fascinated by what this man had managed to observe while being so oblivious to the situation his parents were in.

"My point is," I continued, "Are you really sure your plan will help? It may be, and, honestly, it seems likely, that you are only delaying the inevitable."

"I know," Thomas relented angrily. I almost expected him to stamp his foot in protest, but instead he just crossed his arms and glared at the floor. "But I have to do something! Don't you see Ava," he pleaded at me. "I have to do something."

I did not see. "Yes, of course you must," I said, despite myself.

Thomas gave me a satisfied look before trying to leave the room, and, after reminding him he was still missing a few key details in his state of dress, we both made our way back to Priscella's rooms, where the family would meet up once more.

This time, the mood in the room was far less chaotic. The break seemed to be beneficial for all key players. Ollifelle seemed brighter, and looked to be almost excited by how this particular brand of family drama would play out. Thomas was determined, looking at least vaguely confident in his "plan". Harry too mirrored his son, looking like he was prepared to fight, although I'm not sure about what. Priscella was calm and collected, every bit the dignified Queen she'd felt forced to play and now was desperately trying to throw away.

"Right," Thomas started talking immediately upon entering the room, "I will of course accept the divorce, but mother must come with us to Agremerre first."

Priscella stared at him, "That won't change our minds, Thomas," she said.

"It doesn't have to," Thomas unconvincingly declared, "but, it will allow you to experience what life is like apart from each other, at least for a little bit. This will help you make a more informed decision. Plus, this is not a matter we can fully resolve before we have to leave for Agremerre, so it would have to wait until our return to Dolma anyways."

I decidedly did not mention that Thomas could easily take an extra week or two to deal with this, while I went on ahead to Agremerre. I did feel a little bit of pride at suppressing this thought, and, therefore, supporting my husband in this matter. I thought I'd done very well, so far, in hiding my utter lack of comprehension as to why Thomas felt so adamantly that his parents shouldn't be separating.

Priscella frowned at Thomas' statement, and Harry was looking intently between the two of them. I was beginning to suspect that Harry had little to no say in the matter of this divorce, but it didn't seem that he really cared either way. "Very well then," Priscella nodded, and Thomas gave a satisfied grin.

"Wait, why does she get to go to Agremerre?" Harry asked, finally advocating for himself in this matter. "Why can't I go to Agremerre?" Oddly, Harry seemed far more passionate about going on this trip than he did about his marriage.

"You are always welcome to visit," I told Harry.

"But, you are also needed to help watch over Dolma while we are gone," Thomas finished for me. "You and Ollifelle are to make sure things run smoothly in our absence, and to ensure emergencies are swiftly dealt with in the time it takes us to come back." I nodded my head in agreement.

"Oh very well," Harry huffed. "But, I want to come next year."

"I am sure we can find a way to make that work," I placated while Thomas stared at his father in astonishment. Finally, after a few more days of frantic preparation, we were all packed and ready to head back to Agremerre.

Chapter 16

The Changing Succession

With carriages packed and knights all around us, we set off towards our next adventure. The mood was high and bright. While I was becoming more comfortable living in Dolma, I still found it easiest to live in Agremerre. There was just something freeing about returning to a place that was more intimately familiar to me, and it appeared that I wasn't alone in this thought. Beside me, my knights from my original party looked incredibly happy, laughing and joking with each other. Genevieve also looked thrilled, cheerfully telling Marcus about all the people she was excited to see, as my young son kept attempting to toddle around the carriage.

Both Alder and Priscella seemed rather indifferent to the whole affair. While they didn't bring down the mood of the rest of us in the carriage, their lack of excitement was much more noticeable because of the joy felt by the rest of us. Priscella, I could understand, after all, she had not intended to be on this trip. Plus, I suspected she'd never truly rid herself of the prejudices and biases that Dolma had once held against Agremerre. Alder, on the other hand, was a bit of a surprise.

Now, obviously, Alder had come to Agremerre at a tumultuous time of his life. Really, in the space of just a few weeks he'd lost his mother, his home, and several close friends. Then he proceeded to get adopted by a Queen, became Prince of two kingdoms, and gained two younger siblings. However, from the beginning Alder was sent to work with a transitioner, and Thomas and I did the same thing so that we might raise him and Genevieve better. Still, we had now spent almost two years with Alder, and while there is always something more to know about your children, I did feel as though I knew a lot about Alder. So, I was very surprised to see him looking less than enthusiastic about this move.

"Alder," I called out, determined to discover why my estimation of his character seemed off. "Are you not excited to go to Agremerre?" I asked.

Alder just shrugged. "Well it's not really all that different from Dolma, is it?"

Every adult in the carriage simply stared at him in shock. "What?" Thomas responded, his face utterly devoid of any cognizant thought as he blinked at Alder.

"Well," Alder rushed to explain, always quick to pick up on social cues, "It's not like my schedule will really change. I will just be learning from my Agremerrian tutors. There's not a big place for children like there is in Dolma, so I'll mostly be spending time with everyone here."

"Oh, well yes, I suppose that's true," Thomas agreed, looking like he was coming back to his normal self.

"Yes, well I suppose when you're wealthy nothing much changes no matter where you are," Priscella agreed, simultaneously.

"Don't be ridiculous," I said, absolutely not in agreement with the Dolmanians in the carriage. "You're almost eight years old, you will need to start knight training and begin performing some of your royal duties."

"What?" Thomas was back to looking shocked.

"Well, of course," I responded, a little bit surprised as to why this would even be a question. "Alder is a Prince, and he really should have begun knight training last year, but given that we were all still adjusting to Agremerre, it made sense to wait. Also, while the knights of Dolma have certainly improved, it would be best to start his basic training with the knights in Agremerre. Then of course there are his duties as a Prince of Agremerre. Alder is old enough, and adapted to Agremerre enough, that he is ready to begin taking on some light duties as a Prince. I imagine he can also take on some duties in Dolma when we return."

"Really?" Thomas asked, his surprise now morphing into interest as he thought about the prospect. "I didn't start with the sword until I was nine, did you start sooner?"

"We all started at seven in Nevremerre, and he won't have to pick the sword. Azar and my father both fight with a hammer, but there are also bow and arrow, spears, axes, and so on. Technically he doesn't have to specialize in anything since right now it's about keeping him active. Alder, dear, if you'd like to choose another sport after you've tried combat classes, you most certainly can."

"And, what will he do for his duties as Prince?" Thomas asked eagerly.

"Well -" I began.

"What does it matter if I do any of that?" Alder asked, angrily folding his arms and slouching down in his seat. "It's not like I am a Crown Prince."

For a brief moment, anger filled my entire body. How dare any child of mine even dream of shirking off the duties that allow them to live the life of luxury and abundance that was provided to them. I then had to calm myself as I remembered that it likely was difficult for Alder to be the only one of his siblings to not be addressed as Crown Prince or Princess given that Agremerrian and Dolmanian law placed Genevieve and Marcus respectively above him in rank. There was also the fact that no one other than Thomas and myself knew that Alder was a possible candidate for succession in both Agremerre and Dolma. The latter after we revised an old law that allowed male children born out of wedlock to inherit a title to also include adopted children. Then there was the fact that Thomas and I were working on changing Dolma's succession laws completely, but that too was a secret, although I'd bet money that the people from both Nevremerre and Agremerre would have already guessed that Alder had the potential to gain the throne in both countries given time.

Instantly, I suddenly became immensely sympathetic to my parents as I debated the pros and cons of informing Alder that his position was far more powerful than he realized. Like my mothers, I had no desire to push someone I knew to be an ambitious child towards trying to rule a kingdom. It was a quest that took up, upon greater reflection, too much of my childhood, and I did not want to inflict the same situation on my children. However, I also knew of the political landscape that occurred in every country and I knew that, at least in Agremerre, someone would one day make Alder aware of his potential as a King. If we weren't able to teach him well enough, they could use that knowledge to manipulate him.

My eyes found Thomas' who seemed to be thinking of the same thing. As our eyes met, I realized instantly that we both knew what we wanted to do. "Close the carriage windows," Thomas instructed Priscella and Alder, sitting across from us. Both gave us curious looks before doing what they were told.

"Now, the first thing I want to stress," I began, looking sternly at Alder, "is that you are a Prince. You are a Prince of Dolma and Agremerre, and a Duke of Nevremerre. Each of these titles give you land, money, power, and education, a comfortable living area, and any sort of clothes, food, or possessions you could wish for. However, this wealth also comes with responsibilities. Regardless of what position you may hold in the future, it is our duty to give back and protect the people who enable us to hold this position and the luxuries that come with it in the first place. So you will take on the responsibilities of being a Prince."

"Yes, Mother," Alder conceded, and even if half a year had passed since Alder had decided to give me that moniker, the sound of it still made my heart flutter.

"That being said," Thomas continued, "there is something you should know, but before we tell you, everyone must promise to not tell anyone else, this is for your own safety, do you understand?"

Instantly, Alder and Genevieve sat up straighter, both waiting excitedly for the new information they were about to hear. "Yes father," Alder said, as Genevieve responded, "Yes, Papa."

Thomas gave them both a stern look before looking at his mother, "The same rule applies to you as well."

"Yes, yes," Priscella agreed, "I'll keep quiet."

Thomas suddenly looked unsure, "I mean it, this could be dangerous."

"I would never do anything to harm them, Thomas," Priscella said, looking slightly taken aback.

"Why is it so dangerous?" Alder asked, looking back at me.

There are moments when parenting in which you are suddenly intimately aware that your next action or inaction could potentially harm your child in the future. To tell Alder that his right to the throne could make some people, especially in Dolma, want to hurt him was not an easy conversation. To not tell him though could leave him open to manipulation. With Genevieve, it was important that she knew that becoming Queen was a choice, and despite her current title of Crown Princess, she still had options. However, we also did not wish to foster any feelings of competition between the two.

With all this in mind, I hesitated for just a moment before I began to speak, "Alder, if something were to happen to Marcus," I paused for a moment to look at the sleeping boy beside me. "You are next in line for Dolma's throne. And, should Genevieve ever decide she doesn't want to be Queen, Agremerre's High Court has decided that you and Marcus will both be considered as the next possible candidates."

"Can I do that?' Genevieve asked, "Not be Queen?"

"You don't have to do any job you do not want once you turn 21 and come of age," I told her.

"So, I can be a mermaid?" Genevieve asked.

"Of course," Thomas responded, before I could break Genevieve's heart over the human inability to become a mermaid.

"I don't understand," Priscella said, "Alder is not related to Thomas by blood, how could that work?"

"We can explain the legality of it all later, but it's essentially the same thing that makes Avalynn eligible for the throne of Nevremerre. Adopted children are still considered the children of the parent. Sharing blood is no longer a requirement for succession," Thomas told her, before looking at Alder. "Are you okay, kiddo?"

"Don't people in Dolma not like me because I'm a dark color?" Alder asked us, and I have never felt more unprepared for anything than I was for that question.

Obviously, my first instinct was to say "no". No, of course not, why would anyone dislike you for something as silly as that? But that wasn't true in Dolma. While we were working on changing things in the country, there was still work to be done, but how was I to describe this to a child? How was I to describe it when I couldn't even understand it myself?

Thankfully, Thomas stepped in to answer the question for me. He did it brilliantly, in my opinion, although my opinion was likely the least important in this whole matter. He spoke to Alder and Genevieve (who would all too soon have the same questions and ones about her gender as well) about Dolma's history, about the fear of the colorless men in charge that led to policies of discrimination. He told them, in no uncertain terms, how wrong these policies were, and how we were working to fix them.

"But people are scared," Thomas finished, "and they don't yet understand the idea of how a society can function without the powerful stepping on the backs of the weak. They believe that if things change, they will be the weak, that they will get stepped on. Because of this, there may still be people in Dolma, of any rank, gender, or skin color, but mostly those who look like - well me, I suppose - who say or do things that might cause you emotional pain. If any of them say anything, you can come straight to me and your mother, and you can be sure it will be dealt with so that it doesn't happen ever again. However, please remember that if someone does say something mean about your color or gender, that it will never be true, and it is never a reflection of you as a person. Do you understand?"

Alder and Genevieve both nodded, but I suspected we would likely have to have this conversation again someday. "So," I transitioned, "Alder, please tell me why you will be taking on the duties of a Prince?"

"Because I am a Prince, and it is my responsibility to help the people of the countries I hold a title in," Alder nodded, and I felt a curious mix of pride and sadness at the seriousness of his tone.

"Oh, me too!" Genevieve cried out, "I want to help with royal duties too!"

"Your fifth birthday is only a few months away, you may begin some duties after that, you will start seeing tutors around that time as well, so it will be a big change!" I told her.

"Why didn't I start when I was five?" Alder asked, and Thomas and I both looked like we'd run into a brick wall. Looking at Thomas' face, I felt a bubble of laughter rise inside of me. "Wait, don't answer, I know," Alder said, frantically waving his hands while his face took on a slightly darker hue. Thomas gave a relieved sigh before we opened back up the carriage windows and played some travel games until it was time to stop for the evening.

"I want to have a word with my mother," Thomas whispered to me once we reached the inn. Priscella had been rather silent as we rode towards our destination, so I nodded at him and took the children in by myself. Together, the knights and I had a lovely dinner with the kids. Then, alone, I bathed each child and got them ready for bed. I read stories, and sang them to sleep. Exhausted from travel as they all were, they did not comment on the unusual absence of their father. I, however, thought of little else.

After the children fell asleep, I said good night to Elise and Ben who were guarding them this evening and went in search of my missing husband. I did not have to go far until I heard his and Priscella's voices muffled through the door of our room.

"And, why does that matter?" Thomas yelled from inside the room. The outrage in his voice was palpable.

"Don't treat me as though I am the villain here, Thomas," Priscella snapped at him.

"Aren't you?" Thomas roared angrily back at her.

"Of course not," Priscella insisted, "I am just pointing out the very real and honest reactions that people would have if they ever learned that boy was in line for Dolma's throne."

"Don't you dare call him "that boy"!" Thomas fumed, "He has a name, Alder, and he is your grandchild. They all are! You cannot continue to only want to see Marcus, don't think I haven't noticed how little attention you give to Alder and Genevieve!"

"Yes, well they're not really your children, are they?" Priscella screamed at him. As I continued to listen to their conversation I felt a rush of nausea fill my body. Logically, a part of me rationalized that I was listening in on what was clearly the middle of a very long and heated discussion which undoubtedly frayed the nerves and sanity of its two participants. Emotionally, I was on fire. How could someone say something so cruel about my children? How could Priscella say they weren't really Thomas' children when I knew the love, dedication, and energy he poured into them every single day? How dare she speak this way about my kids!

"You will never say that to me again," Thomas' voice was so low I had to press myself against the rough wooden door to hear him. "In fact, you will never say that ever again, or I will cut off any remaining funds you may have."

"You wouldn't do that!" Priscella exclaimed, but she didn't sound as confident as she had even just a few moments ago.

"I would," Thomas reassured her, his icy tone leaving no doubt to his sincerity. "I will not let anyone hurt my family, verbally or physically."

"I am also your family."

"Which is what makes your claims all that more confounding! I thought you liked the children. I thought you liked Avalynn!" Thomas' voice returned to normal.

"I do! Genevieve and Alder are nice enough, and I agree with the changes you and Avalynn have been making! But, really Thomas, how much more of this will you really put up with, and what is to become of you once all these changes have been made? You are becoming redundant in your own kingdom! What will you do if Avalynn leaves you, if she takes over your kingdom, what will happen to you then?"

"Like you leaving Father?" Thomas shot back, an odd sort of bitterness in his voice.

"I have always been redundant in Dolma, not like Avalynn. And, I will never have the support nor power she wields."

"Enough!" Thomas yelled, sounding both angry and exhausted at the same time. "We can talk about this more later.

In the meantime, you will give Alder and Genevieve the same level of attention and care you give Marcus, as little as that might be." I had only a few moments' warning to position myself slightly back from the door before Thomas threw it open, and I was met with the enraged faces of Thomas and Priscella.

"Ava," Priscella gasped in surprise.

"Priscella," I acknowledged, "I just put the children to bed, I hadn't thought you'd still be here."

"Yes, well, I was apparently just leaving," she said with a small glare at her son. Thomas too glared at the retreating figure of his mother, before I walked inside our rooms.

"Did the kids miss me? Should I go say goodnight now?" Thomas asked, his voice becoming soft as he gazed down the hall towards the children's room.

"No, they fell asleep so quickly they hardly had a chance to notice you weren't there. They'll be fast asleep now and delighted to see you in the morning, of course."

"Yes," Thomas frowned slightly, but moved to close the door. "I wasn't aware it was so late. I'm sorry I missed tucking them in."

"These things happen, it is not reasonable to expect to be able to be there 100% of the time," I said as the door clicked shut.

"Yes," Thomas said, turning once more to face me. His soft tone vanished as his gaze swept over me with a heightened sort of intensity I didn't know what to do with. The room was silent, and I felt hot and tense as he continued to stare at me. My mind frantically searched for something to say. Had he known I was listening? My skin prickled uncomfortably, as Thomas' eyes continued his silent assault of me.

Then, he moved towards me, and my mind went blank as I tried to come up with a suitable excuse for my eavesdropping. "I -," but I was cut off by Thomas' lips crashing down on my own. His smooth hands came up to my face, threading gently over my check before his fingers put a firm and pleasurable pressure on the back of my head. I gasped at his movement, and Thomas only used this to deepen the kiss I wasn't prepared to understand the meaning of.

I couldn't think of anything as Thomas kissed me. Or, rather, I refused to think of anything. I wanted, desperately, to be kissed by this man. I wanted, I tragically realized, to be loved by this man, but that wasn't possible. He'd told me so all those years ago. He was right then; we were better off being friends. It was safer if he was just my friend. No one could be hurt if we were friends and I could keep him in my life if we were just friends. But, Gods above, I loved him.

I loved the way he kissed me. I loved the way he held me at night. I loved his passion and his dedication. I loved the way he loved our children. I loved the way he constantly supported the work we were doing to change the country he was born in. I loved the way he laughed and smiled. I loved how he always tried to move forward with a positive outlook on life. And, I loved the way he chose to learn and grow alongside me.

It was so ruthlessly tempting to just keep kissing him. Kissing him, however, meant acknowledging those feelings of love I had been so desperately shoving down, with the futile hope that if I didn't name them, I wouldn't have to deal with them. It was a bit too late for this, I realized as my hands roamed Thomas' chest. For a brief moment, I toyed with the idea of just hiding my feelings. Even if I couldn't hide them from myself, I could hide them from Thomas. I could let him continue to kiss me like this and no one would need to know. It would be a pleasurable sort of torture, I thought, but it would still kill me at the end of it all. So, I built up my strength, and pushed Thomas away from me.

He still cradled my head when I pushed him away, his blue eyes looking at me so softly I felt I might cry from the gentleness that countered the abruptness of his earlier motions. "Thomas," I said, softly, as I tore my gaze away from him, suddenly losing my ability to look at him. I watched his blue tunic instead, my hands nervously fiddling with the ties at the front. "What are you doing?" my voice sounded far away. It sounded foreign, even to me, as I practically begged for an answer.

"I won't lose you, Avalynn," Thomas said, his grip on my head becoming stronger as his voice intensely berated my ear.

"So you kiss me!" I demanded, anger filling the fear and anxious sadness I'd held before. Anger was the easier emotion to focus on here, so I let that anger fill me. It whispered, irrationally, that Thomas must have known about the love I held for him, the love I'd never admitted, even to myself, until about two minutes ago. He must know, and he was kissing me to use my love as a weapon so I would have to stay by his side. It had to be true because this thought was easier to hold onto than anything else.

"Yes," Thomas said, and I looked up to find his eyes still locked onto me. And, when I brought my face back up to look at his, he kissed me again. His mouth was passionate yet gentle against my own, it was as if I was simultaneously something fragile and delicate he needed to protect and something he wanted to devour. Even pressed up against him as I was, I still did not feel close enough. My concentration on anything that wasn't him seemed to seep away from me, flowing out of my brain like falling sand as he continued his exploration of my mouth. I never wanted him to stop.

But, he did. His mouth left mine, and his hot breath and his warm lips kissed their way across my face. And somehow, I wondered if this was even more blissful. He kissed my cheeks, nose, and forehead before he made his way down to my neck, letting his hands fall down to my arms, running his warm fingers along my exposed skin. His lips were almost tantalizingly light against my neck, causing my whole body to shiver as a heat took over my chest, radiating through my body.

"Thomas," my voice called out, and in that moment, I could not tell you if I was begging for him to stop or to keep going. With that thought I realized that I did in fact need this to stop. "Thomas," I repeated, more firmly this time. Once again, Thomas stopped, but he remained firmly latched onto me. Not letting his hands leave my body, and keeping his head so close to my neck that with each breath I took, I could feel the tickle of his fallen hair and the brush of his nose against my skin.

I stepped away from him, and wondered when such a simple movement had become so difficult. "You can't do that," I whispered to him. "Anyone would fall in love with you if you kissed them like that," I half warned, half confessed to him. My body was trembling, and my heart was thrumming so loudly it was practically the only sound I could hear. Thomas' eyes narrowed as he walked towards me once more. He grabbed my waist, cupped his hand on my face, and pulled me towards him once more.

"Don't," I begged of him, his lips mere inches away from my own, "Please don't be that cruel." Thomas sighed, before backing away slightly and resting his head against my shoulder, his warm breath fluttering on my neck as he hugged me close to him. I felt infinitely fragile in that moment, as if in my next breath I would shatter all over the wooden floor of the inn. I imagined pieces of myself lodged in the floor, sticking out of the polished bed frame, and shattering the window, creating an even larger wreck in the room around us. And, yet, I stayed whole. I was still put together in the moments Thomas held me, and I had no idea how I'd managed it.

"Let's go to bed," I told Thomas gently, after what felt like eons just standing there. Thomas nodded silently against my shoulder. I gently pushed him back and we silently got ready for bed. There was only the slight creaking of floor boards and the occasional hoot from passing birds to accompany our motions.

"You haven't eaten," I suddenly realized as we both re-emerged in our night clothes.

Thomas shook his head in response, "It doesn't matter now," he said. He latched onto my body once more.

"But -", I began to argue before Thomas picked me up and carried me to our bed.

"It doesn't matter, Avalynn," Thomas repeated, laying me gently on the bed. He soon joined me, pulling the covers around us and wrapping his arms around me, keeping a gentle hand resting on my scar. My heart pounded dangerously in my chest, and I thought I would never fall asleep. Yet, hours later I was comfortably woken by the soft golden glow of the morning sun, and the inn's maids, knocking on the door to signal it was time for us to prepare for the next leg of our journey.

Chapter 17

The Key to Marriage

As it turned out, actively acknowledging I loved Thomas did shockingly little to change the day to day structure of my life, or at least our lives when traveling. It did not make it any harder to raise the kids, or to discuss the state of affairs in Dolma. He continued to help me figure out the nuances of problems and the plans I was working on for Agremerre. Sure, my heart rate rose in his presence and I was filled with an obnoxious joy when I saw him do anything I found endearing, which, as it turns out, was quite a lot of things.

It took six days to return to Pantheo, where we would spend a few days catching up with the High Court before roaming around the country to areas in need once more. And, in that time, Thomas never revived the argument he had with Priscella and we never discussed the kiss we shared. The stalemate silence that was created on both these issues was not something that could last forever. I knew I could not continue to love Thomas in silence and I also knew that I could not continue to leave Priscella's words unaddressed.

I procrastinated both these tasks by telling myself that these discussions were not something to have on the road—an excuse that felt like both a blessing and a curse when we rode up to the Agremerrian Royal Palace days later. Still, I steeled myself for the conversations ahead. I was ready to face the two situations that had been pulling on my emotions and daring me to speak my truth. I was ready, but apparently nobody else was, as I was immediately pulled into meetings upon my arrival and I scarcely saw anyone other than the High Court for the next three days.

If my busy schedule was just another method of procrastination for talking about my feelings, it hid itself well, as I was thoroughly exhausted when I came to bed each evening. Still, three days later, I found myself with an unheard of break in my schedule and found Thomas, my children, Priscella, and my mothers all playing together and enjoying some afternoon tea and new cupcakes supplied by Aunt Olivia. Mama and Thomas were playing with the children, running through manicured lawns with such raucous laughter, Priscella declared it gave her a headache and left for the quiet haven of the castle.

"An unpleasant woman," Mother commented brazenly, "A divorce will do her good."

"I have never found her unpleasant," I said, in awe of her words, "well, I suppose until recently."

Mother's eyes narrowed, focusing on the retreating figure of Priscella. "She is afraid of the divorce, she is afraid of what it will mean to be alone, and she is afraid of happiness. She still will want to go through with the divorce, but in the meantime she is attempting to control all that she can, and it makes her more annoying than usual."

"It sounds like you don't really like her anyway," I pointed out.

"She was content to live forever in a horrid system solely because it did not punish her as much as everyone else. I can have some compassion for the circumstances that led to this belief, but I can never like her or her soon to be ex-husband as people. Do be sure Thomas and you issue apologies for the pain Priscella's and Harold's rule, and those who came before them, caused. As a leader, you now shoulder the burden of all those past mistakes."

"I know, Mother, we already have apologized for things done in the past under the name of the King and Queen, and we are prepared to do more if it is required."

Mother gave me a small smile. "Nicely done," she nodded as I took a sip of my tea, "So, when did you fall in love with your husband?"

I spat out my tea, coughing hurriedly into a napkin while Mother sat peacefully beside me. I glared at her while I got my breathing back under control. "How did you know?" I demanded.

"Oh, Ava, darling, I am your Mother, I could see it on your face a mile away. Plus, you've started smiling whenever you see him."

"I do not!" I uselessly objected, feeling embarrassment well up inside of me. "Oh well, maybe I do," I conceded almost immediately after, "I admitted it to myself a little over a week ago, but it's probably been longer than that."

"And, you haven't told him yet?" Mother asked me, setting aside her tea with a frown.

"I've been busy," I obfuscated.

"I can't say I ever thought you would be this shy in love, Ava," Mother hummed.

"Well, I suppose you told Father and Mama right away when you decided you loved them," I said sarcastically.

"Yes, I did," Mother said, throwing my sarcasm off. "I was the first person to confess in both cases."

"Were you not nervous?" I demanded, looking at her with astonishment.

"Ava, I was born to love those two people. Nothing was or would ever stop me from marrying and growing old with them."

Mother was a terrifying person, I decided right then, although it really shouldn't have been a surprise. She was also, however, clearly not the right person to discuss this with. "I'm not sure I have the same certainty that you did."

"Well that's not required," Mother said in a slightly exasperated tone. "Ava, when you love someone, you love them independent of their response to your love. They are not required to love you back or to stay with you just because you love them. When I decided to be a partner to Edgar and Diana, I chose to utilize my skills and passions to put myself in a place in which marriage was an option, but the choice to agree to our union and to commit to our relationship is something that we all agree to every single day. As long as we all continue to be our honest selves, and respect the relationship and individual boundaries we each have set, our relationship is able to thrive. So, be honest about your feelings, and then create the individual and relationship boundaries you need based on whether or not he loves you, too."

"You make it sound so easy."

"It is," Mother replied simply, "The emotions around the conversation may be overwhelming at times, but the task itself is frightfully easy, although it will need to be updated from time to time."

"Okay, then," I surrendered, and Mother nodded once more before we turned back to watch our family playing out in the summer sun.

In what felt like an ominous coincidence, but could have just been my own nerves. Thomas and I had several hours of free time later that evening. The children were being entertained by their grandmothers, I had successfully caught up with most of the work that required my in person attention, and the hot summer sun was beginning to fall. Thomas and I found ourselves walking in the palace gardens, away from anyone else.

Being alone with Thomas, I felt a strange sense of trepidation. There was this clumsiness to the way I spoke and moved that was wildly uncomfortable. I knew it was because I loved him. I knew the only cure was to tell him I loved him, but the discomfort I felt in my uncoordinated nerves was nothing compared to the abundant fear that held me back from stating my love aloud.

"- like the gardens in Agremerre have. The colors of the wildflowers -," As I was lost in my emotions, trying to build up my courage, or to come up with a better method of hiding my feelings, Thomas had been commenting on the garden. His smooth voice was like a melody, softly rushing its way through my subconscious. "And, I remember you telling me about the bees being more abundant when they are surrounded by -".

"I love you," I blurted out, shocking myself in the process. My fear instantly filled me, demanding that I take back my words somehow. It was easier to push aside that fear now that I had already begun though. "I love you," I said again. Just because I wanted to. Just because I needed to show the fear that it could not hold me back. Just because it was true.

"What?" Thomas said, he looked like a strong breeze might topple him as his blue eyes stared almost blankly into mine. His body was frozen, one hand still lost in mid air from where he was pointing at one of the flowers.

"I love you," I repeated, "and you don't have to love me back. You don't have to do anything really. My love for you won't change your life at all. You can still love someone else, if you find that someone. But, I just thought you should know that I love you." I rambled, filling the silence with a monologue of my own thoughts.

"I'd like.. I want to be able to express my love for you in a romantic way. I want to kiss you and hold you, and be by your side. However my love for you will still exist if you'd prefer us to maintain the platonic relationship we have now. My love for you can remain platonic, if that is what you need. I just... I just want you in my life forever. And, ideally that would be romantic, but I also very much enjoy the platonic relationship we currently have. What comes next is up to you really. We can do everything the same, or we can work out something different, if you'd like. I guess I just thought you ought to know."

The truthful nonsense that spewed out of me fell silent as I ran out of words to say. I watched Thomas for what felt like eons as I waited for a response. But, the wonderful man in front of me was seemingly content to mimic a statue for the rest of the evening. As I looked at him a sort of calm elation ran through me, and I could not help but smile at him. I then placed my hand on his warm cheek, and then ran it down towards his still dangling hand. "Come," I said, gently guiding his arm back down to his side. I gave a gentle tug of hand as I took us back from this paused moment in time towards the garden once more. "You were saying that the gardens in Dolma need more native flowers like we have in the Agremerrian garden?"

I pulled us down the rows of flowers, hearing the heavy thumping of Thomas' footsteps. His still loose grasp on my hand informing me that, should I let go, he would likely stand frozen once more. Still, even if Thomas never responded to my declaration, even if he turned me down, even if he accepted, I found myself completely calm. There was this sense of deep understanding within me, a trust and complete and utterly filling certainty that whatever happened next, whenever it would happen, I would be okay. We would be okay. "I agree, having more native plants will increase the number of pollinators and allow our non-native plants to prosper as well. Perhaps we -," I was stopped by the feeling of something wet and warm gliding access the hand entwined with Thomas'.

"Thomas?" I paused our walk to face him once more. His pale skin was stained with silent tears that sparkled in the light of the setting sun as his shoulders shook with the weight of his emotions. "Thomas!" I gasped, releasing his hand in favor of his face as I stroked the tears from his cheeks.

Thomas' hand grabbed mine, pressing my palm further into his cheek as his tears increased. A stuttered breath escaped him as he cried. "Say it again," he whispered to me between stifled sobs.

I briefly questioned if he was really that concerned with native pollinators before my inner self slapped some sense back into me. "I love you," I told him calmly.

"Hugh -," Thomas wailed before pulling me into his chest, holding me hostage against his body.

"I love you," I repeated, and even though the words were muffled by my head on his chest, he must have heard me because he squeezed me as if I would simply disappear if he ever let go.

After a while, his tears slowed down, and he let go of me just enough for him to reach a hand to my chin. His grasp was firm as he carefully guided my mouth towards him. He kissed me as though I was something precious, delicately exploring my lips and pulling me towards him. I let the pleasure of his mouth radiate through me for a few moments before I pushed him away.

"Thomas," I said, taking in his darkening eyes still wet with tears, "I love you, you cannot kiss me without telling me where you stand in all of this."

"Why not?" he questioned, his voice a little raw from crying. If someone else had asked me this, I would have run away.

It's the sort of phrasing that, in another context, could imply that just because I loved him, he could do whatever he wished with me. A thought that was so ridiculous it didn't even merit further discussion. But Thomas, Thomas was so genuine in his question, so innocent even as he probed for an answer. I was suddenly struck by what felt like a lightning bolt of understanding. It was such an obvious realization that it was almost equally as shocking that I hadn't realized it before. Thomas had no model of what loving someone romantically looked like. He had not grown up watching the healthy relationship that I had seen. He was abused by his first partner, and he was now healing and walking blindly into an honest and unconditional love for the first time.

I couldn't help the loving smile that held my face as I explained. "Thomas, if you wish to show me romantic physical gestures, but do not love me in a romantic way, I will get hurt. It will hurt me. We would be in an unequal love and it would cause me unnecessary pain. I will love you no matter what, but boundaries are vital in any healthy relationship. Boundaries allow love to thrive without causing unnecessary pain. You do not need to decide if you love me romantically right now, or if you want to try a romantic relationship with me. But, you cannot kiss me until you have made that decision. I am happy to wait."

"Oh," Thomas replied, looking a bit panicked, "Did I hurt you just now?"

"No," I smiled at him, "but don't do it again until you've made your decision." I turned back around and offered him my hand. "Shall we continue our walk through the garden?"

Thomas nodded, and hesitantly took my hand once more. We strolled silently side by side for a while longer. I was just about to suggest we head inside, as the sun was practically gone, and we'd, no doubt, soon be plunged into total darkness, when Thomas stopped me once more. "What if I am not good at it?"

"What? Love?" I asked, a bit confused. Thomas nodded vigorously in response. "I'm not sure there is such a thing as being good or bad at love," I told him. "I don't think it is possible to love someone badly. The physical act of love making can be bad, but I greatly enjoyed our time together when we made Marcus. So, I don't think you have anything to worry about on that front." Thomas blushed from beside me, but gave me a smug little smirk despite his pink ears. "There is, however, unhealthy love, but that can be fixed by respecting boundaries and having clear communication. If love is ever unhealthy, that is when actions must be taken to step away and sometimes leave the other person behind. However, I believe you will always do your best to respect any boundaries I set, just as I would respect yours. Am I wrong?"

"No! Of course I would respect your boundaries," Thomas declared.

"Then I don't think you would love me badly," I repeated.

"What if I can't love you as well as you deserve?" Thomas said, quietly.

"That's for me to decide. I will tell you what I need and you will tell me what you need, then we will both individually decide if we can work towards these needs together. Love may not be something we can choose, but a relationship is. A relationship, romantic or otherwise, is a choice we make each and every day. We constantly choose which relationships to keep, and which to let fall away. I would like to choose to be in a romantic relationship with you, but that is not a decision I can make alone."

"I want you by my side."

"I'll be there, no matter what you decide."

"I love you," Thomas told me then. I have never been able to fully find the words to describe what it feels like to have your love requited, but it is a joy beyond all others.

"I love you, too," I squeaked out.

"I want to have a romantic relationship with you," Thomas stated, "I love you."

My heart skipped a beat, "You said that already," I smiled breathlessly.

Thomas wrapped his arms around me and rested his chin on my head, "So I did, but it seems like I'll be saying it again. I love you, Avalynn. So, let's go put the children to bed." I laughed in agreement and Thomas held my hand all the way back to the palace and I felt like I was walking on air given how happy I was.

Life was tinted cherry pink as Thomas and I said good-bye to my mothers and took the children up for bed. I was in such a vibrant and beautiful mood I didn't even know Priscella had been glaring at us, or, more specifically, me, until Dame Remziah, who'd been standing guard within the palace told me the next day. She was concerned for my safety around Priscella, something I greatly wished I could have laughed at. Her imparting this information to me was a bit late, you see.

Since Dame Remziah was a bit late in her delivery of Priscella's glare, I spent the evening completely oblivious to her movements. Thus, I nearly jumped out of my skin when she grabbed me suddenly as Thomas and I were leaving the children's room. Thankfully, I had managed to suppress the impulse that led me to bruising Thomas' leg all those years before, so Priscella came away from this incident very much unharmed. "Priscella!" I gasped at her instead, "Goodness whatever are you doing, scaring me like that?"

"Mother," Thomas' voice called out from beside me as he regarded his mother in confusion.

"Oh," Priscella coughed, loosening her grip on my arm slightly, but leaving her hands planted on my exposed skin as she stood up a little straighter. "Forgive me, Thomas, I just needed to borrow your wife for a little bit."

Thomas gave her a quizzical look before saying, "I don't know why you're talking to me, it's Queen Avalynn's forgiveness and permission you need." Thomas gave me a nod before leaving us both in favor of our bedroom.

"Well, what is it you need?" I asked, my eyes still following Thomas' retreating form.

"Come with me," Priscella insisted, tugging me down the corridor towards the guest room she was staying in.

"Priscella!" I urged as she pulled angrily on my arm, "You don't have to drag me, I can follow you of my own accord!"

Priscella paid no attention to my words, however, and continued her hostile rampage through Agremerre's royal palace. At some point, my arm became sore from the awkward way in which she held it. Occasional stabbing pains rang through me, but I just continued to follow her, telling myself it must be an important issue for her to be so insistent about getting me somewhere we could talk alone. The sight of her rooms a few minutes later was a relief, so much so that I actually smiled at the thought of getting there.

She finally let go of my arm as we entered the stone room. Although it was furnished with high quality wooden furniture and decorated with the vibrantly colored silks common in Agremerre, the simple nature of the room looked wildly out of place in comparison to the excessive and large jewelry, hair, and clothing Priscella still favored. I had a brief flash of concern as I thought about whether Priscella would survive Agremerre's far warmer climate for the rest of the summer. Looking back on it now, it was a needless worry.

"What have you done to him? To us?" Priscella demanded, suddenly furious.

"What?" I asked, very perplexed as to the nature of Priscella's words.

"Thomas!" Priscella snapped as though this was obvious, as though the entire inner workings of her mind should have been innately known to me. "He's smiling! He's laughing! Gods above he's practically glowing!" Priscella clarified once it became clear I did not possess the talent of telepathy.

To be honest, I smiled at Priscella's description of Thomas. I felt his ease in expressing his joy was bound to be a sign of the love and comfort he felt around me and our family. "I told him I loved him," I told her honestly, mistaking the anger in her tone as some form of sarcasm. It seemed impossible to me that someone could be angry at joy, especially the joy of their child.

"Gah," Priscella groaned, "Of course you did! You just had to love him, didn't you?"

"I hadn't realized that was such a bad thing," I countered, finally catching on to the fact her emotions on the subject were genuine.

"Of course it is! Avalynn, you'll have the boy wrapped around your finger. This is terrible! Maybe not for you, of course, but for the rest of us, for Dolma, Gods above, for the whole continent, this is a disaster!"

"I can hardly see the flaw in loving my husband," I said, defensively, feeling my own temper rise dangerously inside of me. "And, Thomas is and has been a grown man for years; we are a partnership of equals. We always have been, and we always will be."

"Ugh," Priscella rolled her eyes at me, "That boy would destroy nations for you. All you would have to do is say the word. Now that you "love" him." She practically spat the word "love" out at me. "He'd do nothing short of everything you'd ask. This was never meant to happen!"

"He is a grown man, and do you not believe I genuinely love him?" I demanded of her.

"Avalynn, you're either the best liar the world has ever seen, or you do, in fact, love him. And, having now known you for almost five years I can say with great confidence that you do love him, and therein lies the problem."

"Am I just supposed to live the rest of my life in a love-less marriage?" the unspoken addition of "like you did?" hung ruthlessly in the air.

"It would have been better if you had," Priscella snapped. "You should have been like me -"

"You were miserable!" I shouted, unable to contain myself.

"Yes!" Priscella shockingly agreed, "And I am thrilled to be able to leave after years of stuffing any semblance of a soul into these ridiculous dresses and keeping any thoughts I had hidden behind a mask of ignorance and indifference, but do you know what else I was? I was safe! I was next to power-less, and so no one ever had to notice me! But you, Gods you, Avalynn, are so horrendously loud."

I had not lived such a life that I had never been insulted. In fact, I had always thought I had rather thick skin; two older brothers would do that to you, you see. But Priscella's words cut deeper than I would have thought possible. Loud was not an insult, technically, really it was a descriptor; in some cases, loud was even a compliment. However, when Priscella said it, I felt the weight of the word pierce me so solidly in my chest, my hand came up as though I would actually find some gushing blood. "Loud" was a more haunting word than I could have ever possibly imagined, but Priscella had not finished.

"It was fine to change Dolma. Your changes, in the long run, are actually very beneficial to me, although I did not think they would be at first. No, the problem came when, a year and a half ago, you became the Queen of Agremerre. Then Thomas took control of Dolma, and then, I watched as everything clicked together. I realized what a problem you were."

This was hardly an insult, I was frequently declared to be a problem, ever since childhood, really. True, the word was usually graced with more love and affection than Priscella had given it, but I still perceived it as a compliment. "You cannot run two countries on the continent without catching the eyes of every single country around us," Priscella sighed.

"I had hoped to break your stronghold in Dolma by having Thomas remove you from ruling the country. Had you been the quiet, uninterested ruler I was, no one would have thought twice about you ruling two countries, but, no, you undid all my hard work and convinced Thomas to start working with you again."

"Wait, you told Thomas to stop working with me to rule Dolma?" I cut in, an uncomfortable sense of horror and dread filling me.

"Not directly," Priscella confirmed. "He's a smart boy, Thomas. More often than not, he's on guard for people manipulating him. As such, there's not many who can use or influence him, but it's so much harder to distinguish between manipulation and concern when you are family. Perhaps it was because, at least in this case, my manipulation did come from a place of concern. Either way, several comments about the dangers you or Marcus might face and he changed his tune quickly enough."

"Thomas can make these decisions for himself! Why would you do that to him?" I said, my earlier horror fading, replacing itself with disgust.

"He's loved you for ages, you know," Priscella said casually, as if she wasn't holding information I had been terrified to obtain just earlier this morning. "Love is a terribly powerful motivator, as I said. If he loves you, he'll do anything for you."

"Love is not meant to be so damaging."

"And yet, it is. It always has been, since long before you and I walked this land, and it always will be, for long after you and I are nothing more than dust on the ground. But, it matters not what love ought to be. All that matters now is that it is. Thomas loves you, you rule Dolma at his side, and he will do what you ask because he trusts no one as well as he trusts you. So now, the whole continent will watch as you rule two countries, and the whole continent will start plotting as you add a third to your collection."

"I will not be Queen of Nevremerre," I practically laughed at her, "Unless you're thinking of another country who, for some reason unbeknownst to me, plans to give me their throne. I know you're worried that I'll start some continental war. As the Queen of three kingdoms, no doubt I'd be some sort of threat to the other nations on the continent. They'd band together and fight the woman who controlled a little over a quarter of all the known nations.

But, it won't happen. Nevremerre's a merit-based monarchy and I have two very worthy brothers and at least one cunning and semi-reformed noble who would rule instead of me. No, the other countries of the continent will find me to be nothing more than an anomaly. A holding place until Genevieve comes of age."

"For someone so clever, you can be so frightfully ignorant sometimes, Avalynn," Priscella clicked her tongue at me. "How can you not see that you are the front runner for Nevremerre's throne?"

"Don't be ridiculous! How could I rule Nevremerre when I am already ruling two other countries? Why would they choose me, who will be splitting my time over multiple places, when they could choose one of my brothers who could dedicate all their time and energy solely on Nevremerre?"

"How could they not? If you have already proven yourself an effective leader of two countries, why not add a third? Plus, by the time you actually rule Nevremerre, it is possible that Genevieve will have already taken over as Queen of Agremerre. Plus, for Nevremerre, a Queen who comes not only as a verified quality ruler, but as someone who ensures peaceful relations with a neighboring country, and has the added strength and resources from two additional countries. Why would they ever turn that down?"

"And, have me split my time among three countries? That is a logistical nightmare, for everyone."

"And yet, it's being done with Agremerre and Dolma, and just as you've done with Ollie and Harry in Dolma, your brothers could manage crises in your absence. With you as Queen, three separate countries get easy and free trade of resources and knowledge. Just as Dolma improved with knowledge of Nevremerre's ways, so too could Agremerre and Nevremerre benefit from Dolma. Our dress manufacturing techniques, for example, are truly second to none in production time and quality. You could create quite the boon in all three of our countries, regardless of where you physically reside most of the year."

"Fine," I finally sighed, accepting that her words were not as untrue as I, for the sake of my schedule if nothing else, wished them to be. "Say, for the sake of argument, I agreed with you, what exactly would you have me do? Stop working in Dolma?"

"Yes! If you can show neglect for one of the countries in your care, no one would think of giving you a third. Or, at the very least, that mistake would make your brothers a more promising option for the throne."

"No! No, I could never do that! It wouldn't be fair," I protested, just the idea of neglecting any country I was a ruler of hitting me so viscerally my whole body recoiled.

"Life isn't fair," Priscella insisted. "Do you think it was fair that I was sent off to marry a man who is repulsed by any sort of physical intimacy while my siblings got to marry people they love?"

"Harry is one of the many types of asexual and it does not make him incapable of love. Also, one of your siblings' "loves" may have orchestrated his murder," I derailed the conversation. In hindsight, it was very cruel to bring up the demise of King Brandeon, but in the heat of the conversation I felt more than justified with this addition.

"I know very well how my brother died," Priscella glared, "Very well, since you brought it up, do you think it's fair that I can never return to my home country lest I end up, at best, imprisoned like my sisters or, at worst, killed like my brother? And, what of all the men and women who died in famine or illness, what of those who experience tragedy, is that always fair?"

"I'm not questioning that life can be unfair -"

"Good, so you'll know that, should you take the throne of three countries, your every move, and the moves of every person connected to you will be watched by the entire continent. You will know that you may shift the balance of power in every other country on the whole continent as they strive just to even match the power you hold. That, by making each of your children in line for succession of each country, that they will be the prey of every power hungry person in the world as they might one day hold all of the power you carry. Every fortune hunter will want to be in their inner circle. Should they try to marry for love, they will be met by countless people who only seek their power and wealth. Every single day you live, there will be a wall of people who try to tear you down, for the rest of your life. That is how you and this entire family will live. All of us! Just in the hopes of being somewhere close to you. Fair or not, this is how the world is."

"If I am ever in a world so hopeless and bleak, I will no doubt have deserved that fate. But, the world you describe, while perhaps it will exist, has another side. A side in which I have allies and support and love. I will not face what you describe alone, nor would anyone else who I love."

"So you could live with all of that?"

"Yes, and it would be worth it because I could make the world fairer. I am not so egotistical to believe I could fix every injustice in the world, but as a ruler, I can fix a lot of it. I can work to avoid famine, fund research for curing and preventing illness, provide shelter from harsh weather, and so much more. Countries can fear me, if they must, but success for the countries I rule is global success. The stronger we are, the more resources we will have to help others."

"Hmpf," Priscella crossed her arms in annoyance, but I pressed on.

"Besides, none of this could matter at all. We still have two years before we know for sure if I will be Nevremerre's Crown Princess! And, as you pointed out, my father may very well rule longer than I am in possession of the throne in Agremerre."

"I wouldn't hold your breath for that outcome."

"Are you aware of something that could cause the premature death of my father?" I asked, my voice dripping with sarcasm.

Priscella rolled her eyes at me, "I'm just saying you have two options, stop trying in Dolma, or prepare for the consequences of ruling three nations. Your naive optimism about global strength will not help you if the rest of the world chooses to fight against you.

"I will never abandon my duties in Dolma like that."

"Then start planning for trouble."

"You do know I can always turn down Nevremerre's throne," I said, mild exasperation coating my tone.

"Would you?" Priscella's blue eyes hooked onto mine. Her dissecting stare clawed its way into me, hungry for answers. "I don't usually think of you as power hungry, but I wonder if you could turn it down if it were handed to you."

"I guess we will find out, if I am given that choice two years from now." It was the only answer I could give, as I found myself pondering the question as well. "But, in the meantime, can you drop this quest of yours to lessen my or my children's power in Dolma?"

"Very well," Priscella sighed, "but I have given you my warnings, remember your actions do not affect just you."

I laughed at her, "That has been true for nearly every decision I have made in my entire life. With that said, I left the room.

I believe my younger self would be astonished to find out that putting the Nevremerre succession out of my mind was an easy task. Perhaps it was just more pressing to focus on my family and Thomas. I also had more to focus on when, a year after my conversation with Priscella, my daughter Elizabeth, called Eliza, was born. She was named after her recently passed great grandmother. Three nations celebrated her birth and heralded her as the light that guided us all from the darkness caused by Nana's death. Most likely though, was that I was not worried about the succession because I was busy. I was busy being a mother and a wife, and I was busy being Queen Avalynn of Agremerre and Dolma. I was slowly becoming more confident in my ability to help people and guide both countries towards peace and prosperity.

While hindsight usually tells us change is for the best, I often find it such a shame that periods of calm, peace, and prosperity rarely last for long, and in the winter of my 26th year, change came in the form of Ari's 21st birthday celebration. That winter was, perhaps, one of the most challenging times of my life.

PART THREE

Chapter 18

The Homecoming

In mid-winter of my 26th year of life and after having only spent two weeks in Dolma since returning from our six months in Agremerre, my family was traveling all the way back to Nevremerre in preparation for Ari's 21st birthday. It was shaping up to be the event of a lifetime. According to my mothers: diplomats, ambassadors, nobles, and rulers from all over the continent had written (breaking several etiquette rules, I might add) hoping to invite themselves to Ari's birthday celebration. And, of course, if they happened to stay an extra week and find out who was to be made Crown Prince or Princess, then wouldn't that be nice for them? It was pandemonium and I hadn't even seen it in person yet. Ari's birthday would likely be the most well-represented event in the continent's history. Nine of the eleven rulers of the continent would be attending, counting myself twice as the Queen of both Agremerre and Dolma. Two of the rulers coming were people my family had never even met!

"It was silly to spend two weeks in Dolma when we were just going to be coming back to Nevremerre," I huffed to Thomas, who was sitting across from me. He was looking dedicatedly down at the pile of documents he'd taken to working on while we traveled.

"We needed to focus on Dolma for a bit so we could look into that issue of the collapsing roofs," Thomas said, pleasantly still in spite of my fidgeting movements.

"I have been saying that we needed better infrastructure in the outer villages for years, especially with the harsher winters we've had since Maychula's volcano," I added.

"Even we don't have the resources to completely rebuild eighteen towns in just a few years, we've already made sure we have suitable refuge buildings in each town for those who lost their houses. We also will continue to build with the improved roof design, so we will see fewer collapses in future years. And, so far, this winter hasn't been as bad as the year before, and certainly not as bad as the year before that, so I suspect we are slowly returning to a more manageable season," Thomas proposed, still browsing through the new education decree I'd drafted. His quill rising to make the occasional note as he did so.

"Well, I suppose you can't control the weather," I said, tapping my fingers anxiously along the carriage windowsill.

"A fact you'd know better than most, my love," my heart skipped a beat as he gave me a small smile.

Fighting my urge to blush, I looked back out the window and focused myself once more. "Your parents and Ollifele should have stayed behind."

"There is no way they would have done that."

"We could have ordered them." Thomas just gave me a pointed look. "Between us, our children, your parents, and your mother's latest boyfriend-," Thomas wrinkled his nose in disgust at the notion.

Chartson Mederain Nolaned, former Lord of Dolma, left much to be desired in the way of conversation and company. Not to mention he was only the latest in the seemingly endless line of men Priscella had gone through post-divorce. Mama, very kindly, informed Thomas and myself that this was merely Priscella's way of discovering how to love after having only ever been stuck in a loveless marriage. However, with a new man practically every month, it was getting a little difficult to remember everyone's names.

"- Ollifelle, Chanti, and everyone's luggage, we are taking eight carriages to Nevremerre. Eight! Not to mention we've left Whimely in charge of the country!"

"You like Whimely and you trusted him to handle the rebellion of the old nobles last year entirely on his own. He also only has limited power in case of emergencies and Lucy is with him; he cannot act without her approval and vice versa. This might also give them the alone time they need to finally get together." It was now my turn to wrinkle my nose in disgust.

"You thoroughly misunderstand Lucy as a person."

"I think they'd be quite cute together, and Whimely really respects her," Thomas defended.

"Love and respect are not the same thing," I argued.

"But you cannot truly love someone you do not respect." Thomas nodded seriously.

"Well, aren't you the philosopher?"

"I am a man of many talents," Thomas winked at me. "Plus, when we actually get to Nevremerre, we will only have two carriages. Of all the people coming, only you, the children, and I are allowed to stay in Nevremerre's royal palace. Everyone else and their carriages of luggage, will be staying in Agremerre."

"Well, I suppose that is true."

"You don't have to suppose, Avalynn, my love, as you were the one who made the plan," Thomas had an annoying little smirk as he gave up on his report in favor of staring at me.

"Hmph," I slouched back in my seat and crossed my arms, "Well, it still seems like way too many. It's just a birthday party."

"You're nervous," Thomas smiled, putting all the papers to the side and coming over to sit beside me, pulling me against his chest.

"I am not," I protested, but I did not move away from his grasp.

"Yes, you are," Thomas said, too confidently for anyone's good.

"Oh, I should have just gone in the carriage with all the children," I said, feeling a rise in irritation as I went to half-heartedly push him away.

"So you could put on a mask and ignore your feelings in favor of entertaining the children?" Thomas asked, refusing to let go of me. "They are having a great time with Nanny Jon right now, no need to bother them."

It was a very cruel sort of intimacy that let him peer into my very soul. "I hate it when you do that. There is no need to read my mind."

Thomas laughed at me, "No you don't."

He was, of course, right. His knowledge of me and accurate assumptions of my mood and desires, even if not always correct, made me feel very loved. It was also somewhat frustrating in that I would now have to discuss the feelings I had hoped to avoid, but supposedly talking about your feelings was a healthy and vital part of life. "Fine, I don't hate it, and I do love you."

Thomas kissed my head, and I could feel his smug smile over my head. "So, are you ready to tell me what's wrong?"

"You already know," I said, a bit indignantly, finally moving my head from his chest to sit up and face him. "I'm nervous."

Thomas smiled at me, "So tell me about it, please."

I sighed, leaning back into my seat, "It's turning into a whole big thing."

"In two weeks' time, Nevremerre will appoint its next Crown Prince or Princess. This has always been a big thing," Thomas pointed out.

"Yes, but not this big! I cried out. "In the past, Agremerre's ruler, the High Court, and Calvine's royal family were the only visitors. Now, Mother says they are expecting the total population of Nera to double the week of Ari's birthday and the crowning of the Crown Prince or Princess. It all just seems like it's too much."

"And, you're scared." It wasn't a question as Thomas nodded along with my words.

"Yes. I am not sure what's going to happen next, and I am not sure I know what I want to happen next."

"I'm not sure that's true, Avalynn."

"Okay," I breathed deeply as I prepared to expose the inner feelings I'd hoped had been destroyed ages ago. "I still want it - the throne of Nevremerre. It's hopelessly greedy, and entirely impractical, but I want to be chosen as Queen. I just want to rule over my home country, the country I have been preparing to rule since I was eleven years old. But, I also know that to rule Nevremerre, I would be putting all of us in a more dangerous position. Not to mention adding to our already busy schedule. So, I am scared. I am scared about what comes next.

"Avalynn," Thomas smiled, "that's all perfectly reasonable and all entirely irrelevant. Right now, we are traveling to Nevremerre, and we cannot know what will happen next, so it does not matter right now. And, no matter what happens, I will be by your side, and I will love and support you no matter what. Just as we will love and support the children in whatever they decide to do. We all have each other, my love, and it will be okay regardless of the decision made in two weeks' time." I let Thomas' words rush over me as he spoke, letting the knot in my stomach unfurl as he calmed me with his logical and emotional reassurances.

"You are right," I breathed. I was still feeling a little out of sorts, but I let myself sink back into him anyway. "It will all be alright as long as I still have you and the children." My head fell back on his shoulder, and he gently stroked my hair until the swaying of the carriage brought me towards a peaceful sleep, one that kept my frayed nerves at bay until I was brought back to consciousness several hours later.

I had always been fond of the way Nevremerre chose to govern over its kingdom. Likely in part due to being raised in Nevremerre, I felt very partial towards a merit-based monarchy. I simply believed it was the best way to choose the next ruler, or at least the best way we'd come up with so far. But, now it was time to choose the next ruler, I found I hated the experience. Intellectually, I knew this would pass, that the anxiety and nerves I felt at this moment would leave my body as soon as the new Crown Prince or Princess would be declared. This wait in between that moment and now, however, must be some sort of divine punishment. It physically hurt as each waking and some sleeping moments, were consumed by my own nerves. It felt like I needed to talk myself out of a downward spiral every other minute just to get by.

Distraction became my drug of choice, but even the combined energy of four children could not quell my anxiety for long. Nana would have said and Abel did say - many times before our return to Nevremerre - that I needed to stay in the present moment. I was told worrying about the future was pointless, that no future had been decided on yet. Alder even, horrifyingly, reminded me that the entire country could go up in flames before a decision was made. Abel then had to assure me that Alder continues to transition well in spite of the tragedy he experienced at a young age. Thomas found Alder's remark funny, and, supposedly, Thomas is doing well in his transitioning sessions, too. It didn't stop me from worrying about the both of them though. And, perhaps it was true that they were both doing well, considering that, out of the three of us, I was the only one who was a nervous wreck.

I do think, however, I could have done much better if the topic of Nevremerre's succession wasn't the main topic of discussion absolutely everywhere I went. "Who will rule Nevremerre next?", "Nevremerre's undecided throne", "What Nevremerre's next ruler means for you", and similar headlines dominated newspapers and gossip reels all over both Dolma and Agremerre. Although I had yet to see it myself, I was sure it was true in Nevremerre as well, and other countries too. Before we left, Whimely joked that I'd gotten what I wished for when I first came to Dolma and it was true, suddenly the whole country had turned into experts on merit- based monarchies. The two weeks we spent in Dolma found me fielding questions from citizens, nobles, knights, guards, and staff alike as to my thoughts on who would "win" Nevremerre's throne.

All this news made me realize that there was, perhaps, too much the people of Dolma could know about Nevremerre. There were whole articles written about Al and Ari, discussing their history, their strengths, and their weaknesses. All three of us were in turn compared to each other, all to determine who might be picked. Stories of Father's ascension to the throne and the throne and other past Kings and Queens weren't off limits either, as suddenly dedicated researchers of Nevremerre's ruling history came out of the woodwork to get interviewed in papers all over Dolma. Although I did enjoy the many scholarly articles written by Lady Irisetta, who had turned reading in my library into working as a historian for the Library of Dolma, a position created by Thomas and me for the purpose of research and education four years earlier.

In Dolma, I could at least benefit from a rather biased show of favoritism, as I was often portrayed as the "clear choice" in most publications. Though, I couldn't quite decide whether this obvious sign of support made me feel better or worse. Agremerre, at least, was slightly less obsessed with the results. Thomas attributed this to Agremerrians already being familiar with a merit based monarchy, while Dolma was entranced with the newness of the concept. However, being less obsessed did not mean that Agremerre was free from the chokehold the Nevremerre ascension had over, seemingly, the whole world. The fact remained, that the selection of a new Crown Prince or Princess of Nevremerre was an event that only occurred once or twice in a person's life. It was rare, and had always been an important event to the people of Agremerre, with them being so close, both geographically and politically, to Nevremerre.

Thus, I was asked about succession every place we stopped in both Dolma and Agremerre. It was so frequent and so persistent regardless of country that I felt close to tearing my hair out. And, of course, I had to mask my own anxieties and worries. I had to be polite and kind as I was asked, for the thousandth time, who I thought would inherit the crown. I could recite, "I don't know, but I believe any of us would be an excellent ruler," in my sleep only two days into our journey. I knew that people were excited, but it felt as if I would never be able to escape from their words.

I also kept thinking about Ari, who's coming of age was to be so over shadowed. There was a reason, afterall, that the decision was to be made a week after the youngest child's birthday. It was meant to decrease emotional stress and to prevent having a potentially painful memory be associated with the youngest's birthday, but none of that seemed to work this year. Ari's birthday was to be used, mostly, as an excuse for people and rulers to come to Nevremerre and to stay in Nevremerre until a decision was made. And, Ari, who had never been fond of large social gatherings, was now to be hosting perhaps the largest event most of us had ever been to.

I felt like I wanted to scream at the injustice of it all. But, I knew that, really, there was no injustice. Even if I had not gone to Dolma, even if I was not Queen of Agremerre, this would still be a big event. Maybe not quite as big - definitely not as big - but still just as important. It would still be an international event, with both Calvine and Agremerre involved. And, all things considered, I would likely be just as anxious and nervous.

Still, I desperately wished I could just forget about the whole thing. I wished I could find out later, quietly, alone in my office in Dolma, or in a tent in Agremerre. Perhaps this worry was the cost of wanting to be in a position of power. If it was, it was nothing I wouldn't readily do, but I still wished for a less stressful system.

Thomas must have talked to Priscella and Harry, as they both were uncharacteristically quiet when we traveled together, but I heard them both gossiping about the succession when they thought I wasn't around. It was almost surprising how much closer they had become when they no longer had to be married to one another. My children talked about it, too, also in secret, but I could hear them whispering about it after Thomas and I had tucked them in. The knights were better about sneaking around, but Mateo informed me it was a hot topic amongst them as well. I was forced to accept that, for the next two weeks or so, Al, Ari, and I would be the center of attention for everyone we knew or would meet. It was not the most pleasant thought.

You would think that by this point in my life, I would be used to a certain level of fame and notoriety. And, that certainly wasn't untrue, but the fact remained that more often than not, newspapers and town criers favored other reports. The day-to-day policy choices and government debates rarely held much interest to most people. Not to say it wasn't reported, but "King Edgar puts new irrigation system in place for crops in the Mariposa region" is never as gripping of a headline as "Popular singer, Delia, cheats on her wife with her drummer,". Of course, there were exceptions. We were still royalty after all, and one of us made headlines with a reasonable sort of frequency. But, we rarely stayed in the popular media for long. Notably, my marriage to Thomas dominated the news in both Agremerre and Nevremerre for three whole weeks when I first left for Dolma. However, I never did manage to see many of those headlines as I was much too busy actually moving to Dolma.

In Dolma, I had graced the cover of many newspapers and magazines over the past seven or so years, but there was an isolation that came with living in the Royal Palace that meant that this, too, was rather unimportant in the grand scheme of things. I made international headlines when I became the Crown Princess of Agremerre. Before now, that was easily the most notably famous I have ever been. But, it all felt like a positive sort of fame. I'd already secured my position. I had the support of Anora and the High Court. The people who came to greet me merely wanted to get to know me, since, as only a

Crown Princess, I had yet to have the power to give people all they wished for. In some ways, it was similar to my time as just a Princess of Nevremerre. The fame I had now was so much different.

Clearly, the notoriety I currently had superseded any fame I had previously. The articles, the stares, the crowds that swarmed me now dwarfed anything I'd experienced previously by leagues. The coverage of Nevremerre's succession had been the top story for months. And, even in the ivory tower of the Dolma Royal Palace, I had felt its reach. This time, however, I was not met with light-hearted curiosity, but rather with judgment. The judgment was not exactly harsh, I did have many supporters, but it was still judgment. The world was dissecting my every move for the past 26 years of my life, looking for flaws and pulling out my strengths so I could be evaluated by every literate person in reach.

All this to say, I was overwhelmed and a little bit frightened, and I did not seem to know how to fix it. Despite the fact that I was now considered an adult in every single known country (and had been for at least a year now), and despite the fact that I was a Queen of two different countries and a mother of four children, I was still somehow convinced that my arrival back home to Nevremerre would fix everything. I was sure that being with my parents and brothers would sooth my every nerve, calm my raging thoughts, and bring back the inner peace I had really only just begun to settle into. That's why I felt so grateful as we dropped Harry, Priscella, Ollifelle, Chanti, and most everybody else off at the Agremerrian Royal Palace. With just Thomas, my children, and all my knights from when I first left for Dolma beside me, I felt like I was practically bursting with excitement at being back in Nevremerre.

Chapter 19

The Candidates' Conference

I was happily waving at the crowds of people who roared as I rode past, entering Nera as my family had traditionally done, with Alder and Genevieve riding on their own horses beside me. Thomas stayed in the carriage with Marcus and Eliza, both far too young to ride on their own, much to Marcus' chagrin.

"There is quite a crowd," Genevieve said, her seven year-old voice almost getting lost in the thundering cheers of the people around us. I looked over to see the normally bright and outgoing girl look on to the crowd rather apprehensively as she tried to smile and wave at those around us.

"There is a crowd that comes out to see you as Agremerre's Crown Princess," I pointed out.

"I am not acting as Agremerre's Crown Princess today," she argued back, "and this is a much bigger crowd."

I slowed my own horse down to ride beside her. I squeezed Genevieve's hand that wasn't holding the reins tightly for a moment before looking forward once more. "It is a big crowd. Bigger than we have faced before, but we are all strong, brave, and kind people, we will push past this challenge and become stronger for it. And, you are always Agremerre's Crown Princess no matter where you are. Unless, of course, you decide on another career path."

I'm not sure my words were entirely helpful, as Genevieve still looked rather nervous, and I was unable to do much else as we rode through the crowds. Still, she did sit up straighter in her saddle as she continued to wave.

"We aren't exactly entering Nevremerre as Prince and Princess though are we?" Alder said from my other side. He, unlike his sister, seemed unfazed by the crowd, waving diligently as though he'd done this a thousand times before. "I mean, you are not wearing your crown."

"I am wearing the crown of a Princess of Nevremerre because I am attending this event as a Princess of Nevremerre, primarily. Should your Uncles Alveron or Ari become Crown Prince, then I will don my crown."

"Which one?" Alder sassed.

"Does this mean we are now of equal rank, Godma?" Genevieve giggled at the same time.

"We are always equal," I told Genevieve before sending Alder a stern look, which did not appear to suitably chastise him for his tone. Instead, the young boy stifled a laugh instead. It was hard to be angry when my children were happy.

"I think we're still a lower rank, Gen," Alder called over to Genevieve, "If mother is just a Princess-" I scoffed at his word choice, "- then we are currently a Duke and Duchess."

"That means less work, right?" Genevieve giggled back.

"It most certainly does not," I responded before Alder could speak again. "As Duke and Duchess, you are still holders of titles in Nevremerre, and therefore, you are beholden to the work required to maintain that title. Not to mention that whatever headgear, or lack thereof, that we wear, you both constantly retain your titles from Agremerre and Dolma."

"This is all very confusing, Godma," Genevieve sighed, while Alder nodded in agreement.

"Yes, yes it is," I found myself agreeing, suddenly back to grappling with the conflicting desires about adding another country to the list of places that I ruled and crowns that I wore.

As I had promised Genevieve earlier, we did manage to survive the extra large crowds and make it to the Nevremerre Royal Palace. "Grandmother!" Genevieve practically vaulted off her horse into Mother's waiting arms, as a startled new footman whose name I'd yet to learn scrambled to grab the reins of Genevieve's horse.

"Geni, my girl!" Mother beamed, holding her tightly.

"We would have been scolded relentlessly for that," Al clicked his tongue as he held out his hand to help me off my horse.

"It does seem terribly unfair," I laughed, getting off my horse and hugging my brother tightly.

"She says that grandparents are required to spoil their grand-kids, but I don't think that Nana ever spoiled us that much," Ari commented, before hugging me as well. He'd grown up in all these years, and I did mean that literally, as he stood several inches taller than everyone else in the family, although he was still rather thin compared to Father and Al.

"I must say, I am surprised it is Mother who spoils them so, I thought for sure it would be Mama," I commented, watching Mama lift Alder in the air, and watching, with more than a little amusement at Alder's rather indignant face. "I think he thought he would be too big for her to pick him up now," I commented.

"If he doesn't like it, he should just tell her to stop," Ari said, looking a tad confused. "She is good about that sort of thing,"

"I think, perhaps, you'll find Ari, that he doesn't dislike it as much as he pretends too," Al smiled.

Ari sighed, "That's a strange way to live."

Al and I both grinned at each other, "Yes, yes it is," I agreed, "But he is only nine, so maybe he will work that out for himself later. Come now, while we wait for them to realize that I'm here too, let me speak with that lovely husband of yours," I directed Al, as Mother and Mama continued to coo over Marcus and Elizabeth, Genevieve and Alder still in their arms.

"Cecil," Al called, as his dark haired husband came trotting towards us, a bouquet of flowers tied neatly in his hands.

"Ava!" he cried, giving me a large hug, "You'll love what I brought you this time!" Cecil was the gardener at the Duke's estate that Al now presided over after Great Uncle Asher's death a few years prior. I had never seen Al so smitten and their wedding was truly beautiful. Beyond that, Cecil had a green thumb like no other and he grew and crossbred the most gorgeous flowers I had ever had the pleasure of seeing. I enjoyed his work immensely, and he constantly brought me a new selection of his flowers to enjoy.

I happily chatted with Cecil for about five minutes before Father finally appeared. "I am so sorry I'm late," Father's voice boomed across the courtyard. "Ava, my gift," Father called me as I ran towards his open arms. "I am so glad you are here," he whispered, kissing the top of my head. I released him then, taking a step back to look at him. He looked tired, a sort of hunch held his shoulders, and there were deep bags under his eyes. Still, he smiled at me before beaming at his grandchildren. The years since Azar's death had taken a toll on him, and Nana's death had not helped. I did not have to look at my brothers to know we all had the same concerns about the man.

While my children were being led into the Palace by Father, my mothers came to greet me. "You look so bright, Ava, darling," Mother smiled at me, her strictness that had struck such fear into the nobles and even other royals all but melted away in front of me and my brothers.

"I feel like a wreck," I laughed, although, in this moment, it appeared my prediction held true. So many things could be cured by coming back home.

"It did turn into quite the event," Mama nodded, "I'm not sure any of us could have predicted this."

"I think it might be my fault," I whispered, biting my cheek before I moved to apologize for making this event the ordeal that it was.

"Yes, it is," Ari nodded, and guilt crashed into me, or rather, it unlocked itself from the place inside of me that I'd hidden it away. It felt horrible and I was burning inside as I thought of what this should have been, a celebration of only those closest to us in honor of Ari becoming an adult.

"I am so sorry, Ari," I told him, every minute piece of my body trying to show my sincerity.

"What for?" was Ari's confused response. My mind went blank as I was struck with the knowledge that Ari, like always, meant what he said. In his mind, I was both at fault for the mess this ceremony will become, and in no way responsible for it. In Ari's mind these were not conflicting ideas, and I was filled with a flood of gratitude for my younger brother, who likely would not understand one bit of why I thought I needed to apologize for what had happened.

"I am going to hug you now," I told him, not waiting for a response before I wrapped my arms around him. Al laughed openly as Ari awkwardly patted my head.

"Do you still need a hug?" He asked sincerely after we had been standing there for a minute or so.

"Yes," I told him honestly, but I released him anyway.

"Good, then let's get you all inside. Octavian, his family, and Olivia will all be joining us for dinner tonight," Mama said, "So we will have the whole family here!"

Mama excitedly told us the plan for this evening before Mother soon ushered her and Cecil towards another location. Something about flowers for Ari's birthday, I believe, but, honestly, she likely knew that what we siblings truly required was time alone with each other. Al led the way, as older siblings are want to do. He simply started walking down the halls, and Ari and I could do nothing but follow. It was as if we were kids and Al had come up with a new game, something he was basically solely responsible for at the time. We, or rather I, even left the space that Azar would have occupied as we walked like ducklings behind their mother towards wherever Al was heading.

When we finally stopped, we were in a small sitting room on the first floor, the same one that I remember Mama yelling at Father in, from all those years ago when we first announced I would be leaving for Dolma. In which I had sworn I was ready for all that would come. In which, I had felt very grown up, and in which I now felt very young and very unprepared. I took a seat on the couch, and soon felt the heavy weight of Ari beside me.

"Drink?" Asked Al, moving towards a cabinet and pulling out three glasses before either of us had responded.

"Just some juice," Ari replied, watching Al carefully pour his favorite mango-pineapple mixture with an approving nod.

"Just something light for me," I responded, and minutes later I was handed some surprise cocktail while Al, himself, sipped at a glass of brandy.

"You don't normally drink, Ava," Al noted.

"And I won't again after this one," I informed him, with a sort of definitive seriousness I was sure I hadn't possessed before the children came into my life.

"It wasn't a judgment," Al smiled.

"Given your drink of choice, I should hope it wouldn't be. But, that doesn't change my answer."

Al smirked once more before settling between Ari and me on the couch. I gave Ari an incredulous look as we both maneuvered ourselves into new positions that would give us the space required to breath as our behemoth of a brother took up the majority of the couch. Ari, rather politely, plopped himself up against the arm rest. I, on the other hand, sent my legs sprawling over Al, intruding on his space after he so determinedly took mine. Al gave an indignant huff that only served to make Ari place his overly long legs on Al as well.

We sat there for a bit, shockingly comfortable in our chaotic arrangement of limbs before Al broke the silence. "This is torture, the worst kind of torture." Ari immediately went to remove his legs, only to be stopped by Al's free hand. "I meant waiting for the Crown Prince or Princess announcement."

I hummed in agreement, taking another sip of the lovely sour concoction Al had made me. "It is decidedly unpleasant," Ari agreed, looking down at his own drink.

"You know what the worst part is?" Al carried on.

"What?" I asked superfluously.

"Once the decision is made, none of this will matter. It will all just become some footnote in history. There will be, maybe, one line, "so and so became Crown Prince or Princess after being chosen amongst their two other siblings." I mean that's all it says about all the ceremonies before ours. I know, I've checked. Every now and then, someone like Queen Estelle gets a couple of sentences, but only because she'd already removed herself from candidacy and shouldn't have even been considered," Al ranted, staring angrily at the wall in front of him. "All this anguish and time, and this moment will be wrapped up in a few sentences as just another mundane moment in history. Except, for us, for all of the people like us in all of Nevremerre's royal history, this moment is anything but mundane."

"Historians should write something about all the Kings and Queens who never were," Ari said thoughtfully.

"Nice of you to think up the title for them," I agreed.

"I'm not sure that's the worst part though," Ari almost whispered into the room. Al and I both looked at him, nodding at him to continue. "Well, it's just that, no matter who wins, people will always wonder if we would have still been chosen if Azar were still alive. Just yesterday, there was an article saying we likely wouldn't have had this drama if he was still alive, since he would surely be King. Of course lots of other newspapers say otherwise, but still. Is that a terrible thing for me to say?"

"No, and by Gods, you're right. That bastard took the easy way out and died, so he wouldn't have to compete with us!"

Al yelled, causing me to let out a rather morbid laugh from beside him.

"Everyone is so much kinder to you after you die. He's being reported on like he had no faults, at least he is by the reporters who choose to mention him," I agreed.

"Seriously, fuck him for dying," Al swore, and I thought that I would never agree with anything more.

"It also has never been a given that Azar would win, even when he was alive, he was always considered to be on an equal level to the rest of us. It is upsetting to have our own merits devalued because of his death," Ari continued.

"I miss him, too," I said, and my brothers nodded.

"I can't help thinking I'd be less anxious if he were here," Al said, and Ari and I nodded once more.

"We wouldn't all fit on the couch though," Ari said, causing Al and I to laugh.

"I am sorry this all interfered so much with your coming of age Ari," I said.

"Why?" Ari questioned, once again looking completely un-fazed by the matter. "It was always going to be like this; your choices just made the whole event larger."

"I suppose you could argue that due to the sheer size of this event, my worry about this whole thing only taking a line or two in the history books is negligible," Al pointed out.

"I doubt it. Unless something really dramatic happens with all the countries attending, nothing in the actual proceedings has changed at all. We've been working on crowd management techniques for half the year, so it is unlikely we will have any tragedies caused by the sheer amount of people in attendance. Economically, we might get a bit of a boon, this whole event has the potential to do wonders for Nevremerre's tourism industry. And, areas all over Nevremerre have been reporting an increase of people arriving even now, weeks before the final decision. That'll be your fault as well, Ava," Ari informed me.

"Happy to help," I nodded, taking another sip of my drink.

"It's a great way to show off Nevremerre to the world," Al agreed, "but it could also give us more enemies."

"Yes," I agreed, "What will make this event go down in history is not just the size of the event, but who all is coming, and how their interactions could reshape the continent as we know it. However, that is not a good enough reason for us to stay isolated. If I've learned anything from ruling Dolma, it's that we all benefit from shared connections and open communication."

"Their connections resulted in the bartering of their children," Ari pointed out.

"I didn't say that there wasn't room to grow," I snapped, "and we don't do that anymore. Not since Thomas and I took over anyways." Al snorted from beside me, so I elbowed him in the ribs.

"Careful, Ava," he yelled. "Watch the drink," He added, as if he hadn't already steadied the glass before he could lose a drop.

Silence filled the room again as we were each consumed by our own maudlin thoughts. "So, how is Father?" the tension in the room thickened, as I had known it was likely to do as we discussed our Father.

"Whoever becomes Crown Prince or Princess, should be prepared to take over as King or Queen very soon," Al supplied.

"It can't be as bad as all of that," I found myself pleading, struggling to reconcile the memory of my hearty and commanding Father with the dire picture Al was painting. Still, I cannot say he looked well when I saw him.

"At least, that is what I think, but I have primarily been in the Southern Duchy. Ari has spent the most time with him recently." We both turned to look at Ari then, waiting on any insights he might have.

"I -," Ari began, "I'm not good with this sort of thing. I'm not sure I know what would help."

"We don't need you to come up with a solution," I assured him. "You are very observant, you simply need to tell us what you have noticed about him recently. We will all work together from there."

Ari sat and thought for a moment. "He is slower about things, he stays to work longer, and he doesn't smile as much."

"He should see a transitioner. He's done his best, but to lose Nana and he's probably still blaming himself for Azar's death can't be good for him," I said, immediately thinking back to my own use of a transitioner.

"I'll talk to him about it," Al agreed. "No doubt Mother and Mama have brought it up as well. He may just need an additional push."

"And that will help?" Ari asked, looking back and forth between the two of us.

"It will be a start," Al insisted, "It's up to him to see what he will do from there."

"And what of the throne?" Ari pressed.

"Surely we can't ask him to step down simply because he is a bit depressed. He may be slower in pace, but my understanding is the country is still running smoothly," I interjected before Al could speak.

"Mother and I have taken on some extra work to ensure that is the case," Ari nodded, "It is very manageable at the moment."

"I suppose once there is a Crown Prince or Princess there will also be an extra hand," Al hypothesized.

"Unless it is me, but I suppose that's unlikely," I sighed.

"You don't think that you'll be picked?" Al smirked.

"Do tell me how I am supposed to rule a country I would likely only be in for a maximum of four months a year," I said snarkily.

"It wouldn't be so different from what our grandfather did before Father implemented a nomadic rule," Al argued back, still smirking at me.

"Plus, it might be considered a bonus as you won't require all the same Crown Princess education, seeing as you are already a Queen," Ari pointed out. "You could take over more quickly if need be."

"I'd wager, Ava," Al cut in, "That I am worse off than you."

"You've been successfully managing the Southern Duchy for over two years! How could you possibly be at a disadvantage?" Across from me, Ari nodded his head in vigorous agreement.

"I've also been very clearly highlighting my weaknesses as a nationwide leader. I don't want to move around as much as Father does. While I am good at managing internal disputes, I am reluctant to change or renegotiate with the other duchies. And, frankly, I think I like working on a smaller scale as opposed to a larger one."

"Ruling a Duchy is only one step down from a King," I pointed out, irritation laced in my words.

"It's four times less work though," Ari pointed out. "I mean the King has to work with all four duchies, a Duke only has to bother with his own. However, at least the two of you have leadership experience. I have never held a title in which I bear sole responsibility for a region."

"You've got business experience working with Duke Austin," Al argued.

"And you have been supporting Father with his work for the past few years," I agreed.

"Plus, you'll be taking your knights test before the decision is made. When you pass you'll at least have a leg up on Ava, the only one among us who has never been a Nevremerrian knight," Al goaded.

At 26, I still took the bait. "I've done the work of a knight in two other countries!" I practically shouted at him.

"You're not actually a knight in any of those countries though," Al grinned at me.

"Only because I am Queen! Plus, I can still fight! I've won Agremerre's Open Tournament twice compared to your single victory in Nevremerre's Open Tournament. I'd say I'm very much at an advantage."

"You didn't win last year," Al pointed out.

"I'd just given birth!" I cried out. Laughter erupted from my brothers, and I did my best to glare at them both while fighting against my own smile.

"Eliza is better than a tournament win, I suppose," Al playfully concluded.

"She's better than a billion wins," I agreed, my heart beaming at the thought of my youngest girl.

"But not a billion and one?" Ari smiled. We all laughed once more, and we fell once again into a companionable silence.

"Do we all still actually want the throne?" I finally asked.

"I felt a lot more sure about my answer seven years ago," Al said absently.

"I don't know either," Ari hummed, "It's an awful lot of work."

"I feel as if I won't know until, or rather if, someone actually offers me the role. Surely it will just become clear then if I could actually do it," I confessed.

"I am sure it's some kind of coping mechanism, but I feel the same way," Al sighed.

"If we don't know if we still want it, it won't hurt as badly if we lose," Ari supplied.

"That's it," Al nodded, "Although, I do wonder if it will hurt no matter what happens or what we want."

"It appears we will be forced to find that out," I swirled my cocktail around in its glass before finishing what remained. "Just... just stay by my side, both of you. It will be easier if I have the two of you."

"Of course," Ari agreed.

"With pleasure," Al smiled.

Gracing them with my own smile, I finally moved us along, "Then up we get. It's time we get ready for dinner." It took a bit of detangling, but soon the three of us were moving through the palace towards our own rooms to prepare for the night ahead.

Chapter 20

The Source of Fear

My room was not the room I had known since childhood, but had been, logically, switched to a room further down the same hall. It was a bigger room, a place that could accommodate my new life, and, more importantly, my husband, who shockingly required space, a wardrobe, and his own bath as well! Again, it made logical sense, but it did feel oddly distant from the home I had known. It was really an obvious and, in some ways, painful reminder of how different my life was. There was an odd sort of mourning for the child I had been all those years ago, a child who seemed to me to be a lot more free than I had realized at the time.

There was, of course, another side to these emotions–a pride and a joy that filled me with the person I had become. There was an incredible feeling of love and joy at seeing Genevieve take over my old room while Alder was just down the hall in Al's old room. I got to watch Marcus and Eliza play in the nursery in which my brothers and I did and it was a feeling like no other. There was truly a bittersweet quality to the way life just kept moving forward.

These feelings seemed only to hit me now, walking these halls once more. Perhaps it was the accumulation of all the stress and nerves I felt that brought on this acute nostalgia about the place I was currently in. It certainly did not help my current state of mind, when instead of Ana and Charlotte I was greeted and dressed by two new maids, Leisel and Marie. Again, it made sense, Ana, while in Nevremerre, was currently taking some much deserved time off to visit friends and family, and Charlotte was no longer working for the Nevremerre Royal Palace, having instead opened her own roaming hair salon so she could follow her wife, Dame Elise, around as she and the other knights followed Father around the country. I would, of course, be seeing both of them while I was here; they just wouldn't be dressing me. Once again, I was forced to confront the passage of time in all its amazing new wonders and all of its never to be seen again memories.

I confess I was getting more than a little bogged down by it all. If Nana were alive, I would likely be told I needed to sleep, a surefire way to cure most problems, in her estimation, but I didn't appear to be in the mood to take that advice. So, instead, I put on a green velvet dress sure to keep any winter chill at bay, and went to collect Eliza and Genevieve for dinner. Marcus and Alder would get the pleasure of Thomas' company.

"You look amazing, Genevieve," I smiled as I walked in the room, my mood lightening instantly as I watched Genevieve twirl around in her yellow dress. The bright color matched her bright soul so perfectly and popped against her brown skin.

"Pwetty," Eliza cried from my arms, stubby hands reaching out towards her sister.

"Look Godma," Genevieve beamed as I put Eliza down, "It twirls!" Genevieve spun around in the yellow cloth while Eliza clapped excitedly, clumsily spinning beside her.

"Wonderful, both of you," I gushed. "You look just like your mother, Genevieve, darling. She loved the color yellow as well." Genevieve grinned so wide I could see all three gaps in her smile from her missing teeth.

"Here you all are," Mama's voice echoed from the doorway, as she and Mother filtered inside. "We went to your rooms first, Ava, dear, but you'd already gone." She kissed my head before going towards Genevieve and Eliza, "And look at these two gorgeous girls!" she cried out, easily picking them both up.

"Mind your back, my love," Mother worried as she came in and held me in her arms.

"They weigh nothing," Mama laughed. "Grandkids are no weight at all," she declared, kissing Genevieve and Eliza dramatically on the cheek.

"Gwandma!" Eliza shrieked, while Genevieve moved to give her a bigger kiss in return, giggling the whole way through. Time wasn't such a bad thing after all, I quickly decided.

"You look lovely, Avalynn," Mother said softly, as she turned me around to face her. I basked in the warmth of her attention as she smoothed down my hair, and fixed the wrinkles in my dress with her own well used hands.

"As do you, Mother," I said, admiring her orange dress that paired effortlessly with Mama's blue dress.

Mother laughed, "We nearly match, Ava. Well, except for the color."

I laughed myself as I realized she was right, we'd both chosen the same long sleeved slim fitting silhouette, only mother had opted for a more open back whereas my dress favored a lower cut bodice. "It's almost like you raised her," Mama joked.

"Next time, we should all match!" Genevieve declared.

"What a wonderful idea, little one," Mama shined, "Let's make Grandmother here design something wonderful for us all," Mama gave Mother a flirtatious wink before happily adding, "Aren't girls just the prettiest?"

"Oh yes!" Genevieve happily agreed as we all headed down for dinner.

Dinner was a lovely affair. It was practically a given with my family. Aunt Olivia and Uncle Octavian helped add to the bountiful chaos, swapping stories about their own rambunctious youth and entertaining my children with stories of their Grandfather that seemed to leave them happily baffled. In between it all there was a large catch up chat in which cousin Micheal and his spouse, Ernest, told us about their new millinery store, set to open in the spring. I had not thought of Micheal as a creative sort before, but paired with Ernest's imaginative mind, they could apparently create the most remarkable hats. Cecil and Thomas seemed content in each other's company as they spent practically the entire evening discussing the latest mystery novel by the Agremerrian author, Beniot. I was pleased with this development as Thomas had been nagging me to read it for the last month, and now, at least, he had someone to talk to about it instead of having to wait for me to get around to reading it.

It was pleasant and easy and almost enough to make me forget about my own nerves–almost. Anxiety is a weird beast in that it always appears at the strangest times. Laughing about Olivia pranking Father and Octavian when they were children and then suddenly being hit with the knowledge that soon the Crown Prince or Princess of Nevremerre would be decided was surreal. I caught both Al and Ari in a similar struggle throughout the evening, going from a carefree laughter to a silent brooding sort of look in only a matter of seconds. Each time we caught ourselves in this position we shared supportive nods, pulled in by our shared understanding that only we, and perhaps two others, in this room could really understand. It was, easily, the most violently dichotomous period of my life.

Throughout dinner I got caught up time and time again on the thought that Father might already have an answer to this uncertainty, he might already know who will next inherit the throne. I am not sure if it was cowardice or respect for one another that meant none of us even dared to ask him about the choice he and the High Council may or may not have already made. Then dinner was over, and my whole family fought over who got to tuck my children into bed for the evening, as the kids all smiled and giggled at the crowd of people fighting for their affection. After an exhausting day, both Thomas and I relinquished our parental joys in favor of a blissfully silent night that quickly turned into a hazy maze of scattered dreams and deep sleep as Thomas held onto the scar at my side.

The next day gave way to the feeling of being observed. This should not have been a new feeling, I had, after all, attracted a fair amount of attention almost consistently during my time in Dolma. However, at least there I could retreat to my rooms or office and easily be hidden from inquisitive eyes. I found no such peace during this time in Nevremerre. I did, of course, have an office, generously provided by my father where I could handle the affairs for both Agremerre and Dolma, but I had the utterly irrational thought I was being watched the entire time. Not that I thought there was someone actually in the room watching me, but rather I got the almost paranoid feeling that the routine of my life was being watched. Almost as if someone was standing behind me with a clipboard recording what I was doing at each moment of the day, writing down when I worked, what I did with my free time, possibly even what I ate for each meal. Rationally, this made no sense, but I had trouble shaking the sensation nonetheless.

In my entire life, I had never found being in Nevremerre to be uncomfortable, but it certainly was now. I felt I was being watched in the palace; I knew I was being watched in town, where an attempted lunch with healers Autumn and Murphy saw me swarmed by so many people that the Agremerrian knights, now doomed to follow me everywhere, physically forced me to leave after only five minutes. Murphy and Autumn kindly agreed to come visit me at the palace the next day. And, throughout it all I still had to deal with my own stress that would not go away. It was insanity, and I was constantly filled with the strange urge to bash my head on the nearest surface in the hopes it would take the stress away.

There was hope in the fact I was not alone in my feelings, however, and my brothers and I were soon pushed into a new game of our own devising. Had we ever sat down to name it, it would likely be called "doing absolutely everything in our power to never think". It was a thrilling game, quite literally because fear did wonders at emptying the mind. We sparred more than we ever had in the past, much to the chagrin of the knights now forced to keep up with us. We rode through the woods separating Agremerre and Nevremerre at breakneck speeds, and we relied quite heavily on my young children to use their boundless energy to distract our own spirits. However, it seems that after less than a week, even my own dear children were tired of us. Alder even cheekily suggested we all go read a book instead.

"Still convinced we should have a merit-based monarchy in Dolma?" Thomas joked with me one evening. We were alone together in our room and Thomas was patiently massaging my shoulders as I, once again, complained to him of my nerves.

"Don't ask me that now! I really won't say yes," I told him firmly.

"Oh," Thomas said, looking down on me with more than a bit of surprise, "I didn't think you would go that far!"

I couldn't fault him for his shock. Throughout my entire time in his acquaintance and for all the years as his wife, there was perhaps no greater advocate for a merit-based monarchy than I. Even before coming to Dolma and meeting Thomas, I had always truly believed in the way things were done in Nevremerre. I was now more familiar and certainly fonder of new and different governing styles, but I still had a soft spot for the familiar practices of Nevremerre. Still, I had to confess my love for a merit-based monarchy was crashing at this particular moment.

Even still, "Being able to remain composed in times of stress and pressure is vital for a leader," I conceded, "this is an excellent way to test that skill, and compare my siblings and me.

If the price of maintaining a functional monarchy is for a few people to have a month's worth of stress, it is really not that bad. Also, it's only as bad as it is this time around because I've gotten the whole continent involved."

"Oh, I don't know," Thomas smiled, "I rather think that you and your brothers would be just as nervous."

I huffed, but did eventually have to agree to his point. "I just wish that they could tell us already!" I said, jumping up and pacing around the room. "I mean really, there's no reason to keep us in suspense. An official announcement could come later, and we wouldn't have to be so anxious now. They must already know who will be chosen," I argued. "Ari's birthday is just a few days away, and they only have a week after that to pick the successor. There is nothing in our character that will change so drastically, so either the competition is so tight we are still the subject of heated debates in the council rooms, or, they are keeping us in suspense for no good reason!"

I flopped dramatically on the bed, after my rant, only losing a little bit of drama to the awkward height of the bed itself, which forced me to jump in order to successfully place my body on the mattress. Thomas looked at me with a curious little head tilt before he joined me on the bed, with admittedly more grace than I had managed. "Are you worried that if they don't pick you it means you aren't a good Queen?" he asked, quietly looking at me as he sat down in the chair I had previously occupied.

And, Gods above, if I didn't have that fear before, I certainly had it now. Except, if I really looked at myself, this was my fear. Since I was allowed to stay in this competition seven years ago, this had been my fear. Really, how could I not believe it? All my life I had been told that the High Council and Father would pick the best candidate for the throne. There was a part of me that felt that I had never really been picked for my roles as Queen of Agremerre and Dolma. Sure, technically, I had been hand-picked by Anora, but it was done with the knowledge that I would happily leave once Genevieve turned 21, and took her rightful place, an event that did not feel far away. And, again, I could argue that Harry had gone out of his way to secure my presence in Dolma, but, really, Harry had no knowledge of who I was as a person. He was doing nothing more than placing a large bet on the parenting skills of my mothers and father.

No, now I was forced to conclude consciously something my subconscious had always seen: I never truly felt like I was worthy of being Queen. There was suddenly no doubt in my mind as to why I still wanted the Nevremerrian throne. It had been a question I'd thought of, but never looked into. I had never thought myself to be a greedy person. Nor did I believe myself to have a thirst for power, like Lord Nicholas - who, tragically, was now solidly a member of the High Council as the noble representative and who continued to look all too smug whenever we saw each other around the palace. I also was not really desirous for the additional work that would come with the position. So, I did wonder why I wanted this position, but to look too deeply into the question made me more and more fearful of the truths that I would find. It seemed easier then, to simply not look.

The universe and the Gods, as it turns out, were not so kind as to let my inner troubles hide. They truly must be laughing as I had to hear my greatest fears spelled out in the clearest terms by the beautiful face of my husband, and to now live in the mortifying reality that I would be completely known.

"Avalynn?" Thomas asked again, moving to hover over me in the face of my growing silence.

"Yes, yes, you are right. I do fear that if they don't pick me it will mean I have never been good enough to rule," I told him, staring up at his dazzling eyes. My hand went up to lazily trace the warm contours of his face as I confessed to all the feelings that took up this frightening part of my very soul. After all, what else could I do when I loved him so? "I fear their judgment. I want, sometimes more than anything else, though it pains me to say it, for them to tell me I am enough - more than enough really. I want to hear them say I am good at this job, that I am a good Queen. I seem, in this competition, to care about nothing more than that. I do not wish, at this moment, for Nevremerre's crown, rather I want so desperately for someone to tell me I'm worthy of wearing it."

Oddly, despite the fear I had held about diving into my inner psyche, the moment I said the truth aloud my whole being fell into alignment. My stress crumbled, my nerves vanished, and a sort of completeness came through my body, filling the gaps the other emotions had left behind. With it, I also found a new clarity. My stress was only being amplified by the uncertainty as to why I wanted Nevremerre's crown. I was suddenly certain that as it was with me, the same thought was true of my brothers. We'd all let our undiscovered desire for the throne lead us through a vicious cycle of stress and panic. While interesting to learn, I doubted my ability to lead my brothers through the same period of self reflection Thomas had just led me through, but at least I felt better.

"Avalynn," Thomas began in that tone he used when he was trying to be understanding and compassionate, but definitely thought I was being ridiculous. "You are the beloved Queen of two different countries. Gods, you are easily the best Queen Dolma has ever had." I did not disparage the entire history of Queens in Dolma by pointing out that this was in no way hard to accomplish, although I most certainly did think it. "How can you believe yourself to be unworthy of the throne?" Thomas pleaded.

"Well I didn't say it was a logical thought process!"

"You do realize," Thomas continued, failing to mask the sort of loving exasperation that he held in his words, "that if you are not selected, the biggest, and, in my opinion, only problem the High Council would have is with your time constraints as Queen of two other countries, right?"

"Well not really," I said, "because I think that I might believe that something else might be wrong with me."

"Avalynn, as you always tell me, being King or Queen is a job. There is nothing wrong with you because you are not the best fit for a certain job. It has never been and never will be a reflection of you as a person."

"Oh," I responded, suddenly and almost violently aware that I had never heard such a sentence before, or, if I had, I had never truly absorbed the thought. It hit me now though, being a Queen does not affect who I am as a person. The words clung to my brain, and demanded space and weight as they carved themselves into my very being.

"Though, if it helps at all," Thomas continued, "I can picture no better person than you to rule. However, I can also picture no better person than you to love and raise children with.

Whatever job you wish to hold, I believe you to be the perfect person for it."

"Flatterer," I laughed at him, "but it does help. You always help." I sat up to kiss him. "You know, I've spent the last three years working on discovering who I was if I didn't rule, but even with all of that, I managed to miss how this selection process has affected me."

Thomas opened his mouth, likely to say something kind while reminding me that healing and personal growth take time and we are all subjected to occasional relapses in behavior and thought patterns, but the most important thing is that we continue to recognize it when this happens and work to change it. All the usual stuff he would say as someone who has spent far longer working with a transitioner than I. I did not let him make his speech, however, as I carried on, "But I know that my personal growth has made a difference because as soon as I realized it, I no longer cared. I am a wonderful person, though it still feels strange and boastful for me to say it aloud, and I will still be a wonderful person and a successful Queen with or without ruling Nevremerre. It would be lovely to be able to rule and care for my own country, but I no longer feel I need to rule it to be whole or complete."

Thomas kissed me before reorganizing us both into a better sleeping position and saying, "My love, if you are not a successful Queen, no one is," before blowing out the remaining candles and guiding us both to sleep.

The next day, I was light and delighted. I felt whole and happy, and I was now fully experiencing the joy that came from visiting a much loved home after many years away. I felt confident and alive and blissfully free of all stress and worry.

I was also nearly instantly pulled aside by Al and Ari who told me I was, under no uncertain terms, allowed to withdraw my name from succession.

"I was not planning on doing so to begin with," I said, looking at them both in confusion.

"Then why were you looking so happy?" Ari demanded.

"Am I not allowed to be happy?" I asked, indignantly.

"No," Ari replied.

Al, on the other hand, opted for, "You'd only be so happy if you no longer had to deal with this competition, and since they haven't told anyone who will win yet, you must be planning to drop out. We will not let you drop out because of stress," Ari nodded vigorously beside him.

"Well I'm not dropping out, as I already told you. I simply found the major reason for my stress and now I'm not stressed anymore," I told them, with only a little bit of the annoying condensation one feels amongst brothers.

"How does that make any sense?" Ari demanded.

"Queen Avalynn?" another voice called out around the corner behind us.

We all turned to see Lemmly staring at us like he was unsure what to do next. We must have all realized the hand he kept on his sword at the same moment too because Al and Ari who, just moments before, had been intruding on my personal space simultaneously took several large steps back. A small giggle overtook me as I realized to the outside eye, Al and Ari's sheer size in comparison to my own could make even the friendliest chat look like a threat to my person. It was fortunate that this particular instant wasn't even close to the arguments we'd all had as children. "Yes, Sir Lemmly?" I asked him, still silently laughing at my brothers.

"You are to be meeting with the High Court today, Queen Avalynn," Lemmly nodded. "It is approaching the time we must depart."

"Oh, thank you for reminding me!" I smiled at the still confused looking man. "I shall be right behind you once I finish speaking with Prince Alveron and Prince Ari."

"I shall be here if you need me, my Queen," Lemmly nodded before stepping back around the corner.

"You'd think we were threatening you," Al huffed.

"If I had said I was backing out of the succession, I think you would be," I pointed out. Al only shrugged in response. "Either way, I really do have to get going, so to summarize: I have dealt with the fear I held around whether or not I would be selected. I am no longer stressed, and I highly recommend the two of you do the same."

"You don't have to sound so superior about it," Al said, giving me a stern look.

"Don't scold me because you can't figure out your own problems." Al moved to argue back, but I stopped it. "Sorry, that was mean. I mean I am fortunate to have a loving husband who was able to help me gain some clarity last night, and allow me to give myself the support I was lacking in order to not be disappointed, no matter the result. And, I do genuinely wish the same for both of you, as I know how difficult all this is."

"But I don't have a husband," Ari pointed out.

"The husband was a bonus, but not required for self reflection."

"Then why bring him up?"

"I like talking about him?"

"Oh, okay," Ari conceded.

"Go on then," Al said, apparently now satisfied with my explanation, "don't keep Agremerre waiting." I smiled at them both before running off to find Lemmly and get to Agremerre.

Chapter 21

The Crown Conundrum

After a long walk and conversation to assure Lemmly that my brothers would never be a threat to me, we arrived at Agremerre's royal palace, where we were instantly greeted by Head Judge Michael, who led me immediately into a meeting with all the other judges. "So, will you be Queen of Nevremerre?" Michael asked, boldly and directly as soon as I walked through the council room door.

Taking a quick moment to take in the abruptness of his inquiry, I responded, "I have no way of knowing that yet."

Michael visibly deflated at my words, "So they don't tell you early?"

"No."

"Oh. Well, we should still discuss the possibility of you being Queen." Around him the rest of the room of judges nodded, in a rare moment of complete synchronicity that threw me wildly off balance, Michael took my silence as a sign to keep speaking, "We want to tell you that we are in full support of the merger."

"The what?"

"Well, should you become Queen of Nevremerre, our countries must surely join. We would, of course, spread our judicial legislation throughout Nevremerre, and -"

"Hold on," I interrupted him, looking around the room in utter dismay. "Should I become Queen of Nevremerre, you wish to permanently join our two nations?"

"Yes," Michael continued, as if this were the most natural thing in the world. "We voted on it. Now as I was saying, there are a series of advancements we will need to implement -"

"You didn't ask for this when I became Queen of Dolma," I interrupted once more. I felt entirely discombobulated by the progression of this conversation. It was as if I'd fallen into a different dimension, or been captured by fairies perhaps. I suddenly eyed the tea provided for me with infinitely more suspicion. Although all of my instincts and senses told me this was ridiculous.

"Well, no," Michael said, apparently growing equal parts exasperated and confused by my own confusion. "But, we didn't need to, obviously that was your goal eventually."

"Bring in Sirs Lemmly, Oberon, Challa, and Hugo, please, " I suddenly demanded, and when the High Court didn't move quickly enough, I roughly pulled open the door to the court chamber and asked Amy, the servant on call for the room, myself.

"Why do we need them?" Michael asked, staring at me like I'd grown three heads. I must have been looking at him in the same manner because High Judge Kei soon jumped in the conversation to come to my defense.

"Surely the Queen has a good reason; we simply must wait and be patient," she supplied, in a tone of voice that was undoubtedly meant to reassure and calm those around her. The Agremerrian High Court never had been the sort to function that way, however.

"Why must we spare the time and energy on that though," High Judge Zenareth said in irritation. "We are the High Court of Agremerre. We should act with direction and speed for the good of the country!" This felt a bit rich from a man whom I'd once seen argue with the council over the exact definition of the term worker for an hour and a half while we were deciding on a new labor law. Although at the time, it hadn't felt so trivial as I agreed with him on the importance of having the term clearly defined within the wording of the law.

"It is equally as vital for us to ensure we are thinking clearly and judiciously about each law and political action we put in place," said High Judge Adelaide, High Judge Zenareth's main sparring partner in the worker debate, who believed using a general term would prevent employers from refusing workers their rights by having the labor they provide being just under the legal limits set in place by a specific definition. Also an excellent point, and the debate did, in my opinion, work productively towards a compromise that would positively affect the workers and employers of Agremerre. "We must not make foolish decisions because things were discussed in haste," High Judge Adelaide finished sagely.

"Well, the Queen should at least tell us the reason behind why these knights were requested," High Judge Eloise demanded.

The bickering, oddly enough, seemed to be helping my confused and disturbed mind become more settled and clear. Still, the only answer I could give was, "I require them to ensure I haven't gone completely mad in the span of five minutes. It shouldn't be long, my knights are never too far from me, even here," I reassured, pausing only briefly to wonder at the notion my knights would need to be so close to me, something that had never been required of Anora or Father. I knew the reality much more clearly than I had accepted when I first married Thomas: my rule in Dolma polarized the country to an incredible degree, putting me in more danger than any other ruler I had watched growing up.

As if responding to my thoughts, my Agremerrian knights soon came bursting through the door. "My Queen," Lemmly nodded, seemingly surveying the room for immediate threats to my person. Upon finding none, my knights relaxed, and their expressions changed to those of curiosity and excitement. Challa even gave me a mischievous wink as he observed the High Court.

"Thank you for coming," I began, "Now, please answer this next question honestly: did I ever give you the impression that I was going to combine Dolma and Agremerre to make them one new country, or a larger Agremerre?" As I said the words, I felt a curious sort of apprehension take over me. I knew I was never looking to combine the two nations, but, perhaps, if the High Court had mistook my motives so completely, other people may have as well. Depending on how my knights now responded, I may have to make several very public statements on the subject.

My worries were in vain, however, as Oberon's immediate response was to laugh. Hugo gave a confident, "Of course not," amid Oberon's laughter, forcing the man to sober his mirth.

"You're serious?" Oberon, soon asked.

"I have never believed Her Majesty to even think of such a thing," Challa stated pleasantly, rather obviously hiding his own laughter. Beside him Oberon nodded exuberantly.

"I must concur with the others," Lemmly agreed, "But, Your Majesty, why would you need to ask such a question?"

"What?" came High Judge Westin's shout from behind me, "How could you not be thinking of combining the two nations?"

"How could you think she was?" Oberon asked, and clearly he had been spending too much time with Carlos as of late because I was certain he'd never been so blatantly impertinent before.

"Well, what else should we think?" High Judge Lurece said, his face was frozen in such a manner that you could be forgiven in believing me to have just admitted to some sort of grave crime. Alas, I had done nothing more than simply rule over two countries as distinct and separate entities.

"What of all the improvements you have been making?" Michael asked, his frantic eyes and hunched posture betrayed a similar confusion to what I had experienced when he suggested merging Nevremerre and Agremerre.

"Is it not a Queen's job to improve a place?" I asked. I was starting to regain my equilibrium in this conversation, but I still was mystified by where the High Court had gotten this idea in the first place.

"But the work you've done resembles work we've done in Agremerre so closely," mumbled High Judge Ketiana, it was unclear whether this comment was made to the room or just herself, but I decided to answer it anyways.

"That's because there are several working and successful models in Agremerre that can be used to improve Dolma. You'll notice I've also used practices from Nevremerre and even Calvine in my work."

"Sirs, thank you for answering our questions," Michael suddenly said, standing and ushering Lemmly, Oberon, Challa, and Hugo out of the room in a manner that left no space for argument. Soon, the four knights were out of the room, although Oberon and Challa looked rather reluctant to leave, likely amused by the argumentative and disorganized High Court that was not often seen by the public. After they left, Michael turned back to me, "Do you mean to tell me you have no intention of combining Dolma to make it part of Agremerre?"

"Of course not!" I cried out, "They are two completely different countries! Dolma and Agremerre have two entirely different cultures and government styles. The only thing combining our two countries would do is create large scale and unnecessary conflict," I insisted.

"Now, but in the future, as you continue to change Dolma, things may be different," Michael insisted.

"You must see how converting Dolma over to the Agremerrian system would be better for everyone involved," High Judge Zenareth said with an astounding air of confidence that managed to render his statement as being free from any sort of superiority despite the words themselves having an undeniable condescension in them.

"Thank the Gods none of you are responsible for diplomacy," the words slipped out of me without thought, but the truth they held in them could not be pulled back in. I stared at them all incredulously for a moment before a panicked thought fell through me. "Did you pick me to be Queen because you thought I would allow you to preside over Dolma as well?"

"Gods no, Ava," Michael assured me.

"Besides, we didn't choose you," High Judge Ketiana pointed out, "Complete separation from the judicial and executive branches, a Queen cannot control the courts and the courts cannot control a Queen, unless one part finds the other to be acting in bad faith for the kingdom. Queen Anora was always responsible for picking or creating a successor. The High Court is only to approve the chosen person and to make sure they have the intelligence, personality, and history deemed appropriate for the position. It was our duty to accept Queen Anora's decision. Nothing in your history or skills deemed you inappropriate for the position, so we accepted Queen Anora's decision. Your qualifications were all determined by Queen Anora.

It wasn't exactly a ringing endorsement, but it did ease my worries on the subject, and excitedly, no doubt due to Abel's transitioning sessions, did not cause any of the pain this statement would have caused me just a few years earlier. "Good," was all I could nod in response.

"Just so we are clear, Queen Avalynn," Kei jumped in. "The same holds true for you. Should you believe Crown Princess Genevieve unfit for the position, or should the Crown Princess decide she would rather not be Queen, it is your responsibility to choose the next ruler. Unlike Nevremerre, the next ruler of Agremerre is not a joint decision, the choice is entirely yours. The only thing the High Court does is ensure the person you select is unlikely to abuse or be ignorant of the power they are being given."

"Right, of course," I agreed, feeling very much like I should have known this from the beginning, but, admittedly, there were gaps in knowledge even now, which the premature death of my predecessor had caused. Not that either Anora or I could be blamed for the tragedy of her death, but I seemed unable to escape the pierce of shame that ran through me whenever the High Court or one of my knights kindly explained to me something I felt I already should have known.

"Back to the matter at hand," Michael said, refocusing the group, "You say you won't combine Agremerre and Dolma because the differing cultures and styles of governance would create unnecessary conflict."

"Yes," I agreed.

"Then what of Nevremerre? Our countries have an entwined and rich history, not to mention our values are very closely aligned," Michael explained.

"I doubt the High Council of Nevremerre would be willing to adapt to a judicial monarchy. You forget the history of our nations, our values may be aligned, but there has always been a fundamental difference in how we choose to enact those values. Both of our systems are functioning exactly how we wished them too, and all three of the countries we spoke of today have a level of nationalism that would make merging a difficult affair."

There were several hesitant nods around the room as some of the High Judges acknowledged my words, "Not to mention, should Dolma, Nevremerre, and Agremerre all combine, there would undoubtedly be a war on the horizon."

"What? How would that happen?" Kei asked, looking startled.

"All eyes are on Nevremerre at the moment, surely you've noticed the size of the crowds gathering in Nevremerre and Agremerre to see who will rule next. As the ruler of two countries already, to add a third, and a great military power at that, is exactly what many nations are afraid of. My sources tell me there are already pacts in place by other nations on the continent to join forces in case an attack against us seems necessary. The larger and more powerful our countries, the more others will be threatened by our presence. If I am to be Queen of Nevremerre as well, I will have to prepare a whole series of appropriate statements and send envoys towards several countries all across the continent. To completely combine all three of our nations in more than just the rule of one single person could invite an attack against us."

"I thought the Nevremerre succession must have always been this big," High Judge Ketiana, the youngest High Judge, said thoughtfully.

"You thought that rulers from nine nations always attended the succession ceremony of a country that only borders two countries?" I asked, trying and failing to keep the judgment out of my voice.

"That many rulers are coming?!" High Judge Eloise asked in shock.

"Do none of you pay any attention to global politics?" I asked, rudeness slipping out of my mouth unhindered once more.

"No," Michael responded, entirely unoffended, "That's your job." Given I seemed to be in the middle of all the global politics anyway, I could at least feel confident in my knowledge of the current situation.

"Yes, well, the only country who hasn't, at least, sent a representative is Caperian. Andaluca has sent an ambassador, but the King or Queen of every other nation in the world will be attending. They begin arriving two days from now."

"That's slightly less impressive considering two of those nations are represented by you," High Judge Miraz mused. This was entirely inaccurate, and the feat was no less impressive even with my two titles as Queen. I didn't even know where to begin informing High Judge Miraz of all of this, so I just remained silent.

"Very well, our countries will not merge. So, if you become Queen, we will need to work out how to best divide your time between all three nations," Michael said, with a definitive nod.

"Surely that is a task better done once we know if I actually have the position," I practically begged.

"Always best to be prepared, my Queen," High Judge Westin said, and his statement was punctuated by nods of scarily unified agreement from the people around him. And thus, discussions began.

Two days later, Thomas, my children, and I stood in Thomas' and my room staring at a ridiculous seventeen crowns all sprawled out on the bed, the only surface in the room big enough to hold them all.

"We could switch crowns with each visitor," Alder suggested.

"That's going to get really confusing, really quickly," Thomas pointed out. "Personally, I think my choice is clear. I am the King of Dolma, so I shall be the King of Dolma for this event."

"But, you're also the Prince of Nevremerre," Genevieve sing-songed as she twirled distractedly around the room, followed closely by Marcus.

"Yeah, we should all be Princes!" Marcus shouted, stumbling slightly as he tried to move with the limited grace of a nearly five year old.

"That could be fun," Thomas laughed. "Wear the crown of wherever you are just a Prince or Princess in! That's bound to confuse the guests."

"Eliza and I are just Prince and Princess in two countries though," Alder pointed out.

"Mommy, I'm bored," Marcus whined, apparently, he'd gotten tired of twirling with Genevieve, and was now searching for other entertainment, "Why does it matter? Just wear the pretty one." Much to Priscella's and Harry's dismay, Marcus loved my Agremerrian crown above all else, he would happily sit for hours tracing his tiny fingers over sculpted branches and the sparkling teal stone.

I moved to grab Marcus, lifting him onto my hip, "It matters because when we meet all these new people, we have to show them who we are, and what we represent. We also have an obligation to -"

"Too many big words, my love," Thomas smiled at me as he bounced a sleeping Eliza in his arms. I looked down at Marcus to find him already disinterested in my words, as he was instead gently folding my hair on top of itself in a manner that would surely cause my maids a great deal of grief when it was time to greet the royals and nobility who were coming tonight.

"We'll put the children in their Nevremerre crowns," I decided quickly.

"What?" Genevieve cried, looking almost heartbroken at the thought, "but my Agremerre crown is so much prettier."

She was right, the singular bronze ring of metal that indicated a Duke or Duchess of Nevremerre paled in comparison to the gold and emerald tiara that was traditionally worn by the Agremerrian successor. Even so, I wasn't ready for my children to have to face the world of politics and intrigue. Genevieve and Marcus in particular would be subjected to scrutiny as Crown Prince of Dolma and Crown Princess of Agremerre. No, as simply a Duke and a Duchess, they would be less easily recognizable, and able to spend time, hopefully unnoticed, with the other children.

"Nevremerre crowns it is, darling. You are in Nevremerre after all, and if you're acting as a Princess, you'll have to talk with a lot of adults," I told her. Genevieve scrunched up her face in response.

"Very well then," she huffed, picking up her own crown from the bed. Alder followed suit, and then he and Genevieve helped us place the circlets on Marcus and Eliza's head.

"And for us, my love?" Thomas asked, kissing my head where the crown would be placed. "Shall I be a dashing Prince or a striking King for you this evening?" He winked at me, his voice rumbling deeply as he spoke to me. "I will say," he stepped back, looking seriously at the bed once more. "I would feel derelict if we didn't have a Dolmanian presence here. My parents will be there, but -"

"But, as its current rulers, we will be able to do more as a representative. I have similar feelings about Agremerre. The High Judges will be coming, but they have no knowledge or thought about diplomacy," I agreed.

"Then," Thomas nodded, grabbing his Dolmanian crown, "I shall be the King of Dolma, and you," he continued, placing Agremerre's crown gently on my head, "shall be the Queen of Agremerre." Then he leaned into my ear and added, "And, we can have a scandalous love affair that can span three countries." I laughed at him as he kissed my neck and we moved to get the children ready for the night ahead.

Mother and Mama could only come to collect us briefly, as they'd spent the entire afternoon working as the hosts (along with Father) for what was, in all likelihood, the biggest event Nevremerre has ever held. Frankly, it was a miracle they were even able to stop by at all.

"Most people believe I went to greet another guest," Mother told me, uncharacteristically slouched in one of the chairs in the room.

"I used the back stairs to sneak up," Mama told me, still maintaining an impressive amount of energetic positivity. She looked absolutely delighted by her stealthy escapades.

"And what of Father?" I asked.

"Your Aunt Olivia just arrived," Mama laughed, "She's the perfect bodyguard for these kinds of events."

"We couldn't leave him to anyone else," Mother said, finally sitting up and giving me a stern look, "because none of our children have decided to grace the reception hall with their presence."

Even at 26, being a fully grown adult with a job and a family, I still managed to feel the slight pang of guilt and shame that came along with being scolded by one's Mother. "We're not late," I defended, "We will still be on time for the reception, we just won't be early."

"You speak like you can read your brothers' minds," Thomas laughed.

"I know them well enough to know they won't be late for a big public event," I retorted.

As if to prove my point, a tentative knock at the door brought Ari, Al, and Cecil into our room. "Uncle Cec!" Genevieve squealed, running and flinging herself into Cecil's waiting arms.

"Geni girl!" Cecil roared back, spinning Genevieve brightly around.

"The way she acts, you'd think we weren't her favorite uncles," Al sighed with a click of his tongue.

Ari gave him a bewildered look. "We aren't her favorite uncles," he responded bluntly.

"Well we should be," Al insisted, despite Ari's confusion.

Genevieve laughed. "You are all my favorites," she told him. "But, what are you all doing here?"

"Hiding?" Mother successfully guessed.

Al gave her a sheepish look in response. "No," he said, while Cecil gave a cheerful, "Yes," in response.

"No," Al insisted, sending a stern glance in Cecil's direction which only served to make Cecil laugh.

"We can't be hiding," Ari said, "You can all see us."

"Exactly!" Al confirmed, "We just came to see if we should all go down together?"

"Surely that will just cause more commotion," I said, fear creeping through me at the thought.

"Perhaps, but it will also mean that one of us will avoid the mad rush of being the first of us to enter," Al confidently informed me.

There was a slap of instant dread that hit me at the thought of being the first to enter, and the panic that overwhelmed me ensured that I knew the right choice. "We will all go in together. That's the best option, we should all go in together," I rushed to respond. And, so it was decided. Mother and Mama snuck back into the reception hall, and Al, Cecil, Ari, Thomas, all my children and I were announced to what was easily the largest crowd I had ever seen, at least in the Royal Palace of Nevremerre. When we entered, the eyes of every single person in the room were locked onto us, and I suddenly was incredibly grateful for my early years in Dolma, which allowed me to walk into this drama without any care for the crowd's incessant gazes.

Chapter 22

The Continent's Meeting

Nevremerre had always been a colorful place with a light style of dress that accompanied too hot summers and winters that could only be called cold with the same loving bias of parents complimenting their child. Yes, events in Nevremerre held a colorful and repetitive look. Tonight, however, was a menagerie of styles. At first glance, the room could have been a museum, a violent exhibition of fashion throughout the continent.

Every person stood dressed in their country's version of finery. The delegates and royals who came from Calvine stood comfortably in silk suits, many sporting the short sleeves of people for whom Nevremerre's current winter chill was more aligned with summer weather. The female representatives from Abethy favored the wide and stiff gowns that had been popular in Dolma when I first arrived. Broad shoulder pads adorned the men in their group, so when the delegates stood together they seemed to fit together like puzzle pieces. Those from Experion stood tall in suits and dresses lined with sculpted metal, proudly flaunting the many ores their mines were famous for. Clumped in groups towards the side of the room were two countries whose fashions I couldn't recognize. They would be Lithia and Zolminia, but I did not yet know who was who. One group stood in heavy furs of animals I couldn't recognize, but whose pelts looked luxuriously soft. The other group wore loose fitting fabric draped around their body and wore fabric headpieces that were held together with various pins and jewels.

There were, of course, some familiar styles. Most in Agremerre dressed similarly to those in Nevremerre, although more leather work was incorporated in Agremerre's style. Dolma had long since dropped their overly large dress style, but still kept the overwhelming number of jewels and heavy necklaces that had long found its home in Dolma's noble style. All these styles were only heightened by the fact the room had seemingly segregated itself by country. The only exceptions were the intermixed Nevremerrians and Agremerrians and the infinitely diverse crowd that swarmed my parents.

Just as the presence of each of these countries was novel and remarkable, the absence of others was perhaps even more noteworthy. Caperian, for example, had no presence at all. The country whose military conquests shocked and terrified the Eastern half of the continent, who was rumored to be plotting the downfall of every country it bordered, sent not even one single diplomat. The message was clear, no matter what we did here, even if Nevremerre, Agremerre, and Dolma combined, Caperian was strong enough that it wouldn't matter.

A greater mystery was the absence of Andaluca's Queen. Delegates, ambassadors, even a Prince from the country all attended. Their presence was known. They mingled in all the right places. The Prince, Prince Dane, I believe, was even among those speaking with my parents as we entered, but Queen Christine was noticeably absent. To the others in the room, this was confusing to say the least. No explanation for her absence was given, even to the King and Queen of Maychula, who had stopped over in Andaluca on their way to Nevremerre. Rumors flew of illness, instability, and even secret armies.

Priscella had obsessed over it all with an equally enthusiastic Harry, but no reasonable explanation could be found. The High Council gossiped over it, but never gave it any serious thought, and my parents were just happy to have one less guest to take care of. So, I was the only one who knew the truth. After all, if I were her, I wouldn't want to face the one person who knew I'd arranged for the murder of my husband and the violent takeover of his throne.

It was a secret I would carry even past Christine's death sixteen years later. I simply did not know how to say it. When King Brandeon first died, I had told Priscella I had more information about her brother's death and I'd been resoundingly told to keep it to myself. So I did just that. It wasn't until Queen Anita came to Dolma on a diplomatic mission two years after her mother's death that I spoke of my knowledge again. In a private moment, I asked the young Queen if she knew her mother murdered her father. It was a tactless question, but the child was grown, and the part of me who had been suffocated by my silence on the subject had to know.

"Mother saved me," Queen Anita said quietly.

"An arranged marriage would not have killed you," I pointed out with my advanced experience on the subject.

"That depends on who my partner was," she retorted. "Besides," she continued, gazing intently out the window at the barren trees with their snowy coats, "there is more than one way to die."

"Your father's death was a rather permanent sort," I said, with a blasé ease that I had not then known myself capable of.

Yet, Queen Anita responded with the same tone and I was forced to wonder how we could both be so unfeeling towards this man's death. "Do you believe in the greater good?" was Queen Anita's response "because you must know my country and its people are better off now than they were before."

I could not answer her, for my answer to that question seemed to change every day. It was a question I would never be able to answer. The choice between the greater good and an individual or even a smaller group of people hits differently when you are the one to explain to their family why they had to die. So, the subject was dropped. And the file that Miri and her ever growing spy network put together confirming what I already knew about the days resulting in King Brandeon's death has stayed forever locked in my desk, ensuring no country I ruled, nor any country my descendants rule will ever be harmed by Andaluca, at least as long as Queen Anita reigns.

Of course, back in the reception hall at the welcoming banquet to kick off the three-day celebration of Ari's coming of age, Queen Christine's absence was a pervasive mystery discussed in hushed whispers by all who came. It was never spoken to me of course. No one comes to the Queen of Agremerre and Dolma to gossip, and, as such, when my brother, my family, and myself were announced, the stares turned into a stampede. We were crowded by people in the manner I had thought I would have seen when I first went to Dolma. It was in equal part terrifying and exhilarating to have my conversation so desired, to have my power so recognized. It was also quickly boring. It was very surface level, shallow conversation. People who wanted something and mindless flattery in hope of a connection.

Every now and then I was able to learn something new and interesting. I spoke with King Kumba and Queen Kumben of Lithia, decked in their beautiful headdresses. I learned that once married, the people of Lithia gained a new name to be shared as a couple with slightly different endings to differentiate gender, or, in the case of same sex marriages, who earned more. The Zolmanian's told me of their soft furs and the many beasts that roamed their lands. They valued hunters as we valued our soldiers. King Pier proudly boasted that he and his husband King Meine had personally hunted the pelt they wore tonight, and fascinated us with delightful stories of their daring explorations, and with the reverence and respect their culture demanded of any creature they caught. Nothing was to be wasted on their hunts.

The night, as with any welcoming night, was kept light. No talks of trade or politics were needed, not when everyone here would remain for another ten days until the next Crown Prince or Princess was announced. There was no rush, no demand for time, and dinner was soon followed by dancing, and while I was never in want of a partner, I was not accosted with the political moves that had dominated my wedding. Undoubtedly, they would come, a dance, after all, was the perfect place for a quiet conversation, but this week would be full of dances. So night one was easy, almost joyful for the political minefield it was. And, it was exhausting. I'd only barely changed into my night clothes before I fell into an untouchable sleep.

The next day was perhaps the best of the whole ordeal, for the morning was spent with only my family celebrating Ari's birthday. The morning was its own little slice of bliss. Breakfast was all of Ari's favorite foods and afterwards, we sat in a drawing room giving Ari his presents. Father boldly and fearfully regaled us with stories of Ari's youth that caused even the normally unflappable Ari to blush. However, the problem with being the youngest was that Father wasn't the only person with stories to tell, and perhaps Al and I were becoming nostalgic after all this time. Or, perhaps we were simply completing the age-old requirement of teasing the youngest sibling, for we, too, began reminiscing over stories of Ari as a child. We didn't let up until the room was full of laughter, and Ari's groans. However, despite his face working hard to match the same shade as his hair, Ari's own smile never left his face.

Private life, I easily determined, was by far more pleasant than public life. The intimacy of being with family, even with the expansion of my family, Cecil, and our cousin Micheal's partner, Earnest, and new baby, Gilbert, was of far greater comfort and satisfaction than the rush and flurry of people that made up every ball and dinner that was required from a ruler. While I may have gotten more familiar with the etiquette and mannerisms expected at these events, they managed to drain all energy from me. However, I did sometimes wonder if this had more to do with the people involved than the event itself.

My morning was jovial, warm, content, and those emotions were instantly lost by running into Lord Nicholas. "Princess!" Lord Nicholas said, looking unnecessarily startled, considering he would have known about my presence in the Royal Palace for almost a week now. He would, of course, be involved in picking the next ruler. Something that still didn't sit quite right with me, even if Miri had informed me that he still relied quite heartily on advice from his old mentor Lord Azcarth.

"Queen Avalynn is my new title now, Lord Nicholas," I informed him, attempting to keep the disdain I felt for this man out of my mouth. Alder's curious face looked up at me and his questioning squeeze of our clenched hands told me that I was likely unsuccessful in this endeavor.

"Of course, Queen Avalynn," Nicholas bowed, regaining his charm and composure instantaneously. "And, I should greet your family as well. King Thomas, Crown Princess Genevieve, Crown Prince Marcus, Prince Alder, Princess Elizabeth," Nicholas bowed to each of my family in turn, even to little Eliza, who at barely a year old would be oblivious to him no matter what he did. "I am Lord Nicholas, noble representative of the Nevremerre council, and an old friend of Queen Avalynn's."

"I don't believe we could have ever been considered friends," I told him bluntly. Nicholas just beamed at me.

"Lord Nicholas," Thomas jumped in, "I have heard much about you. I would shake your hand, but," Thomas shrugged his arms where one held Marcus and the other Eliza.

"Of course," Nicholas smiled. "I'm surprised you've heard of me."

"You are the Noble representative of Nevremerre High Court and Queen Avalynn is my wife. I've heard of you for your position and your history with the Queen," Thomas nodded, "I would have expected us to meet sooner, but since you only became the representative this past year, I suppose it makes sense." Thomas' words didn't sound like an insult, but by the Gods they felt like one.

"If you're the noble representative, surely you should know of my Mother, Queen Avalynn's title. She's held it for several years now, it's strange that you should address her by her old title," Alder mused, imitating his father's tone. Nicholas' smile, which had held through Thomas' comments, faltered at Alder's words, doubtlessly thrown off guard by the intense interrogation from a child.

"Yes, please forgive me, I was not expecting to see Queen Avalynn here," Nicholas recovered.

"In our grandparents' home?" Genevieve asked innocently, "Where else would we be?"

I had to hold back laughter as I saw the panic in Nicholas' eyes as he scrambled for an answer. However, even if I still didn't particularly like the man, he was not an enemy, so I rescued him just this once. "It is not a problem, Lord Nicholas, it has been awhile since we last saw each other after all. Now I must go prepare for Ari's birthday tournament."

"Oh yes! I can't wait to see you fight, Godma!" Genevieve squealed beside me, bouncing up and down on the balls of her feet.

"You're competing in the tournament?" Nicholas asked, not bothering to hide his surprise.

"Yes, it's been awhile since I have fought with my brothers, I am excited to see what progress they have made and I will enjoy watching the other knights of Nevremerre," I told him, preparing to walk away. "It was good to see you again, Lord Nicholas, until next time."

Back in Thomas' and my rooms, I turned to my husband and children. "Now what was that?" I demanded, my hands flying to my hips in a picture of a stern disciplinarian I never truly felt.

"I don't like him," Alder replied simply.

"Why?" I pushed.

"Because you don't," Genevieve cut in.

"That's not really a good enough reason," I sighed.

"Yes it is," Thomas insisted, "We trust your judgment, Ava dear. If you don't like someone we can easily decide not to like them either."

"Well, I suppose that makes sense," I agreed, quickly falling out of any semblance of strictness. "Was I really so obvious?"

"Usually you are more reserved when you don't like someone," Alder noted thoughtfully, "but you were more open this time, so we must really not like him."

I almost laughed at my serious boy and his diligent observations of us all. "I don't like him," I said, emphasizing the word I, "but he is not an enemy, so you all don't need to antagonize him."

The children all nodded in agreement, but Thomas snuck behind me and wrapped his arms around me before whispering in my ear, "I most certainly do." He then kissed me before turning to the children, "Come, let's get ready for the tournament!" Leaving me no time to respond to his childish antics with anything more than surprised laughter.

The qualifier event for Ari's birthday tournament, the main event beginning tomorrow, was almost as crowded as the Open Tournament usually was. Thousands of people poured into the stadiums, and the royal box, normally filled with figures from Nevremerre's government, instead was filled with foreign Kings and Queens, glittering in jewels and fashions that mesmerized the crowd. Nevremerre had never been so worldly, with only two countries bordering us, we never needed to be. The influx of visitors with their different ways of speaking, cultural norms, and style of dress were as interesting as the tournament itself. I watched the people of Nevremerre stop in awe as groups of people from other nations walked by, seemingly oblivious to the commotion they caused.

I had never thought Nevremerre to be a very isolated place, but now, as the Middle Arena I would be fighting in filled with people, I watched as the foreigners were treated as oddities, oftentimes given space before a few more curious souls breached the invisible barrier and struck up a conversation. It seemed as though the foreigners were treated with a caution and apprehension I had not previously seen in my countrymen. For all the exhaustion this event was causing, I briefly wondered if it was also doing some good in broadening Nevremerre's horizons.

It was incredibly odd, I also was forced to realize. Nevremerre, to me, had always felt like a warm and welcoming place. This influx of foreigners proved something that I had not thought to believe: Nevremerrians, like perhaps everyone else on the continent, were afraid of things that were new and different. In the conversations I'd heard over the week I'd been here, I wondered if the whole country suffered from the same sense of superiority I'd felt when I first came to Dolma. I watched with some embarrassment as I saw each of my countrymen learn about the rest of the continent and believe they could do better. This embarrassment was heightened with the shame that, until even as little as two years ago, I had thought the same.

As I grew more comfortable in Dolma, and, after ruling both Agremerre and Dolma, I was coming around to the opinion that both countries were better off with the shared knowledge and resources that came from the expanded relationship the two countries now shared. Through this, I now carried a vision in my head of the whole continent like this. An easy and unrestricted flow of information and ideas that would support the health, wealth, and welfare of all the people, while still maintaining the rich and vibrant culture of each individual nation. Given the reaction of the Nevremerrian people to the influx of visitors, however, I wondered if this vision would be harder to achieve than my fantasy would allow for.

If I am really honest, turning that fantasy into a reality, at the time, felt like far too much work. After all, I had four kids and two, perhaps three, countries that I needed to focus on and a vision that involved so many would be challenging to accomplish with just Thomas and myself propelling it forward. Perhaps, for now, bringing Dolma closer to Nevremerre and Agremerre was enough. Surely it had to be enough because I really felt that I could not find the energy to do more. So, despite the fact that there were more leaders of the continent in one place than there had ever been in all of our recorded history, and despite the fact that I had this dream of global peace and cooperation, I did not push for the world I had en-visioned.

Surrounded by the splendor, the stress, and the noise of Ari's birthday and the succession decision, I couldn't even feel upset by my choice - or rather I couldn't let myself feel upset by my choice. I grappled with it later on. It would later nag at me in my lowest moments, demanding of me an answer. If I thought it would help people, my people, why would I not push myself to do more? This was my job, my privilege to help people. Was this not a frightful form of neglect? Surely, I should have pushed myself harder, done more for everyone. When I was a child, Al had informed me that being a Queen was a job that took everything from you. It was tormenting to learn that the "everything" that was taken from me as a Queen was not that joyful moments were stolen, but rather my not having the stamina, resources, or strength to give all that I wanted to give.

Learning to forgive myself for not being able to do all the things I wanted to do was a task I wasn't expecting. It was also more challenging than I would ever have expected. I had grown up with the knowledge that I could do everything. It wasn't thrilling to learn that this was not in fact true. Time would make this lesson easier, but before it would get easier, I had to actively work through the sluggish struggle of healing myself from the long-held beliefs that caused this pain in the first place. The only comfort to be had was the firm knowledge that, eventually, I would succeed, and one day, I would no longer carry with me the guilt I felt at not being able to do more.

Before all of that, before I had even had the time to realize all of those complex and conflicting emotions, I was called to fight in the qualifying tournament for Ari's birthday. I entered the Middle Arena to the roar of a crowd that felt more over-whelming than the ballroom I'd avoided the night before. It shouldn't have felt so unprecedented, after all, I had competed in Agremerre's Open Tournament almost every year since be-coming Queen. I'd only missed last year because of Eliza's birth only a month earlier. I also was not afraid of losing. I was confident in my victory, even if the opponents I was facing in the open battle all stood towering over me.

I was a two-time champion of Agremerre's Open Tourna-ment and opponents of this size were nothing new. No, what unsettled me about this fight wasn't the crowd or the oppo-nents, it was the fact that fighting like this in Nevremerre was exactly what I had once assumed my life would be. In this moment I could almost believe that the past seven years didn't happen. That my life had gone exactly how I'd imagined it would at nineteen, at eleven, or even younger. That perhaps even Azar was still alive, fighting in another arena, as both Al and Ari were. And yet, despite my weird nostalgia, I also knew that the reality I felt so connected to never actually existed, and that, even after everything, I was very grateful for all I did have in this reality.

So, overpowered by my thoughts, I missed the starting call announced by Lord Katz, as Mother was the only one of us not to be competing, and she was opening the Grand Arena. It was only through years of training that I missed the opening blows from Sir Indiga. Mother would have, correctly, admonished me for not giving my opponents proper attention. No matter how much confidence I had in my victory, a sure way to guarantee a defeat would be not to properly focus on my opponents. I made quick work of Sir Indiga, disarming him and knocking him to the ground before surveying the rest of my opponents.

There were 45 total contestants in the arena, including both Mama and Carlos, both engaged in their own battles.

Another knight, Dame Madiline came my way, followed by Sir Xantheon for a two on one take down. All my training with knights of Dolma made me unafraid of the current numbers. I'd trained against more. All I had to do was disarm my opponents and knock them to the ground. Those were the rules for qualifying. Participants were randomly divided into three groups and we'd fight until ten people were left - at least in the Small and Middle Arenas. The Grand Arena, which had the largest number of participants in the qualifiers, would accept twelve victors. Tomorrow, those who qualified would fight in a traditional one versus one tournament style until there was one winner. Until that time, I just had to stay on my feet and remain in possession of my sword. And, although it had been seven years since I sparred against her, I would be best served to avoid Mama.

I was fortunate, for the first half of the battle, that Mama was surrounded by knights who undoubtedly hoped that eliminating her in a group attack would make it easier to win the tournament overall. However, they did not coordinate an attack, as it would be against the rules, and Mama was not a woman to go down easily. Thus the initial crowd was thinned, and Mama, instead of dealing with those who remained, came straight to me.

"Mama?" I asked, startled to see her sword flying towards me, hitting my own with the same impressive strength I remembered from my childhood. An incredibly impressive feat considering the sheer amount of time that had passed.

"Sorry dear," Mama grinned, not even having the grace to sound winded. "But, if I want to win, it's best to defeat you while you are outnumbered." As if to prove her point, I was soon forced to dodge the hammer of another knight. Another one of Mama's opponents, I realized. Those remaining from her initial battles had followed her towards me, and seemed comfortable in taking any opportunistic shots they could at me as well. It was, honestly, a very effective way to fight against me, if highly annoying.

I was tiring far too quickly dodging the multitude of attacks around me, all the while combating the relentless and aggressive onslaught of movement from Mama. If I were younger, I suspect I might have lost hope. I could see myself losing the mental edge as the battle became a more intense version of my younger self, failing again and again and again to land a single blow against the fearsome fighter that was Mama. It was probably even what Mama was hoping for, as if she weren't the person who taught me this trick or the person who taught me the importance of mental strength in any activity. And, if I were younger, it might have worked. But, I had survived the court of Dolma, I'd survived volcanos, childbirth, and the politics of ruling two very different countries. Being outnumbered in a fight whose stakes meant nothing was of no consequence in the grand scheme of things.

All I had to do was wait for a mistake. The idea that I would make one was not even part of the equation. Thus, the patience I had acquired as a result of raising children came to the forefront of a placid mind. I entered a trance-like state that was almost relaxing despite the large amount of energy I was using. I let my body react without the hindrance of consciousness, responding to the threats my body observed before my mind could bring them to my attention and one by one the knights around me fell.

As the number decreased, I could focus more on my attacks. Instead of waiting for my opponents to reveal their mistakes to me, I moved to cause them in my opponents. I pushed them off balance and forced them to move to places that were more beneficial to me. Then there were only three competitors around me and I could not say how long it took to get to this point. Around me, others still fought, but they hardly mattered compared to the three I faced now. Had it been seconds, minutes, hours, since they had come to challenge me? I could not say, but my head was clear and the leather that adorned the handle of my sword felt light and comfortable in my hand, and in the moment, I felt sure my victory against these people was guaranteed. I was so confident, so right in my knowledge of victory that I could have sworn that the universe was forced to bend to the vision. For if that was not the case, I couldn't explain how else my body was able to bound into a only half-understood dream of a plan in which I pushed a dual sworded opponent to the side, limiting Mama's range of movement. Then, before she had a chance to readjust, I advanced, throwing her into the path of the third opponent, whose sweaty grip was causing him to struggle with the hammer in his hand.

Mama's stumble towards him resulted in his own misstep in which he tried to swing his hammer at Mama, but was hindered by his sliding grip, which instead only served to force Mama back towards me where I was able to grab Mama's sword and I watched in near slow motion as she fell to the ground.

A loud whistle shattered the blood rush that had muffled my brain and I looked around to see that with Mama's defeat, only ten of us remained on the arena grounds. There was a loud roar of applause as the commentator struggled to let his voice be heard to announce that we who remained would be competing in the tournament tomorrow.

"Brilliantly done, Ava!" Mama yelled, throwing her arms around me and fully bringing me out of the trance I had been in as we fought. I laughed, in exhaustion and exuberance, as I hugged her to me.

"You were so close to making it!" I told her, a tired amusement colored my tone as I tried to imply that her attacking me may not have been the best move.

"I fought to win the tournament," Mama said, shaking her head at me. "I do not regret an action I took that would bring me a greater victory, if I had succeeded. It is far better to take a risk that would lead to an overall win than to take the safe path that would get me further, but cost me a long term victory. If you don't believe me, then tomorrow evening ask him what he regrets the most," Mama said, nodding to where Carlos was congratulating himself and his opponents on moving on to the final tournament.

I raised an eyebrow in disbelief, but I could not hold it long as I smiled at Mama. She then backed away from me and held out a hand, "Excellently done, Queen Avalynn," she acknowledged loudly.

"The same to you, Queen Diana," I beamed at her, before shaking the hands of Sir Laurence and Sir Andor who I'd been fighting against, as we all moved back to the fighters' tents to rest and wash the sweat and dirt off of our aching bodies. A joyful adrenaline pushed off the worst of the exhaustion I knew was to come.

Chapter 23

The Trials of a Ruler

"Godma!" Genevieve cried, as she flew into the tent, her dark hair blowing wildly around her as she jumped into my arms. "You were so cool! Your sword was thrashing all around and you were spinning everywhere and it was so cool."

I felt my whole body laugh as I held her close, vividly remembering almost the exact same situation between Mama and myself when I was Genevieve's age. "Thank you, darling," I beamed, spinning her around with energy I'm sure I hadn't possessed earlier.

"You were clearly the best," Alder agreed, standing by the tent's entrance holding Mother's hand. "Even Grandmother said so."

I pulled Alder into a hug, still holding Genevieve in one arm. "Oh, did she now? I would have thought that she would be cheering on your Grandmama, or perhaps watching your Grandfather."

"Only when she fights well," Mother smiled, "And I've watched your Father fight many times. I wanted to see you."

"Mama did fight well!!" I insisted, not wanting to cheapen my defeat in any way.

"She did, but you were better," Mother smiled. "I have been waiting to watch you fight for a very long time. I will enjoy watching you win tomorrow."

"You have two other sons who may be fighting tomorrow," I laughed.

"I still think you will win," Mother said.

"Why do I get the feeling you've said that to Al and Ari as well?" Mother laughed at me once more. "Speaking of, have they finished fighting? Do we know if they will both be moving on in the tournament?"

"We were watching you and Grandmama," Genevieve informed me, "so we don't know."

"Your husband and Marcus will be here shortly, and we can all go to the other arenas together," Mother said. "He got caught up with some of the royals from Experion."

"Plus, we need to see Grandmama," Alder noted.

"Yes, we do," Mother smiled.

"Then we have a plan," I agreed, "We will gather the troops then check in to see who else has qualified for the tournament."

Rather predictably, both Al and Ari made it through to the finals. Al had been Nevremerre's Open Tournament champion for the past four years, and he was heavily favored, by at least the Nevremerrian crowd, to win the whole tournament. Most Agremerrians favored either myself or Galileo, who still held me at about a fifty-fifty split. While the crowds had never actually seen him fight, Ari was expected to do well in this tournament. The combination of his being trained by Father and Mama, plus the previous success of both Al and Azar when they first competed, left few in doubt that the youngest would also show the same skill. They were not aware that Ari favored more intellectual pursuits.

Father's success in the qualifiers was a greater surprise. At sixty years old, it was safe to say that Father's physical strength was on the decline. Nevremerre saw no shame in defeat, at least there was no shame in losing a tournament, so there was no expectation that Father would do well in a fight like this. However, Father took his duty to always fight for Nevremerre very seriously. He and Mama had both continued to train whenever possible, even though Father had stopped fighting in tournaments about eight years ago. His qualification for the tournament itself was a sensation.

Even as we exited the changing tents, now accompanied by Mama, Thomas, and Marcus, we heard the loud chatter of Father's qualification. Apparently, he had slayed his competitors down with the force of 1,000 suns, he channeled powers only the Gods could know and guaranteed a victory against all those who fought against him. As we listened to these, constantly more elaborate, stories trickle in from the excited crowd around us, I heard the snorts and chuckles of my mothers beside us.

"This happens whenever Edgar fights," Mother laughed, as she observed the people around us, people too excited to even register that we were walking past them.

"Truly," Mama agreed, "it was ever so disappointing when I first fought him and I learned he was only human."

"Then why do they talk about Grandfather like that?" Genevieve asked, now comfortably settled in Mama's arms.

"Because he is King, dear one," Mother chimed back in. "We may know he is human and fallible, but to the public he is their leader. When they do not know him like we do, it is easy for them to make up stories of his greatness. They do the same with your parents, and, if you chose to inherit, they will do the same to you. Your people will never truly know who you are. If they like you, you will be attributed virtues that no mere mortal could possibly have. Your faults will be thought of with kindness and forgiveness, only serving to endear you to the masses. If they hate you, you will be an irredeemable villain. Your faults will be a death sentence. Every now and then, they will simply forget you. This usually happens when things are going well. It can be, quite successfully, argued that being forgotten is actually the kinder of the three options. They will love you, they will hate you, or they will forget about you, this is the life of the famous."

"What does fallible mean?" Marcus asked, distractedly playing with the embroidery on Thomas' jacket.

Thomas explained the word to Marcus while Alder and Genevieve debated with Mother and each other whether being forgotten was truly the best option. Mother happily chatted with the two of them, probing the holes in their arguments and asking them follow up questions in a manner I so vividly remembered from my own childhood. I watched Genevieve's face scrunch in a familiar frustration as she was forced to think more deeply about her response. We stayed like this until we reached the Grand Arena in which Father and Ari had competed.

We saw Ari first, he was methodically cleaning his sword as he told us about his fights. His descriptions were not good enough for Mama, who asked so many questions that Mother had to forcefully drag her away from an overwhelmed Ari. "Did you enjoy it?" I asked Ari, once Mama and Mother had left, taking the children and Thomas with them.

Ari pondered the question for a moment, "It was interesting to see how different fighters chose to attack me," Ari decided.

"But, you didn't enjoy it," I said more than asked him.

"No," he agreed.

"You know you don't have to compete in these."

"I do, if I am to become King," Ari said seriously. "I will need to compete at least once every three years before I turn 45, then I will need to compete once every five years until I am 60."

"Now, I know for a fact that is not a rule."

"Well no, but I did the math," Ari informed me.

"The math?" I asked. Confusion was not an uncommon feeling when talking with my younger brother. Often, his mind would jump to places that were foreign to me. It felt as though he was starting at the end of a conversation while I was still at the beginning. With some time and a few questions, I could usually catch up to his train of thought, but it was a little upsetting to both of us when I had to ask Ari to slow down the speed at which his brain moved.

"There is a correlation between public approval and a ruler's performance in the realms' tournaments," Ari explained, now attuned enough to me to better infer where in his train of thought he had lost me. "Based on the competitions of previous rulers, I have to get a mean average of approximately sixth place in the tournaments I compete in before I turn 45. After that, my rank in the tournament becomes less important."

"Oh," I responded, unsure what to do with this information. "I'm sure there are other ways to improve public opinion," I tried to reason with him.

"There are," Ari responded, confidently, "I could also have a child, get married, save the country from disaster, or win a war."

"Oh," I found myself repeating.

"Yes," Ari agreed. "Children require a lot of care, having an ever increasing number of spouses seems difficult to maintain. To save the country from disaster, I would have to create the disaster and I don't want to do that, and there is a consistent decrease in popularity for a ruler about two and one-half years after a war is over. They need to fight in a lot of tournaments to recover from that dip. Plus, I wouldn't want to go to war."

"No, war does not sound fun," I agreed, "I can see why you might choose fighting in tournaments over the rest of those options." Ari nodded at me in fervent agreement. "You do know that you don't have to be King," I told him, trying my best to sound both encouraging, should he want the throne and understanding, should he realize he may not want it. My delicate attempt at unbiased support of Ari went totally unnoticed, however, as nothing about Ari's tone, posture, or countenance changed with my words.

"Yes, I am aware of that option, but I won't know if I like it until I try it. This also will not matter unless I am selected."

"How will you try to be King?"

"By being Crown Prince, if I am selected," Ari said, as if this was the most obvious answer in the universe. "Crown Prince is the trial of being King."

I had never thought this to be true. Sure, my work in Dolma as Crown Princess had been what I did as Queen, but that was Dolma, and, as far as I was concerned, Dolma at that time wasn't a good example for any sort of leadership. Crown Princess and Queen were entirely separate roles, in my head. While I could see the logic in Ari's words, I couldn't find it in me to believe them to be true. I would not argue with him though, so I simply nodded and said, "Alright then, shall we go find Father?"

Ari elected instead to go through his usual routine of polishing his own armor and I left him to his own devices while I moved to find Father. I found him alone, which was a bit of a surprise considering that it couldn't have been more than five or ten minutes ago when I sent my mothers and the children to find him. He looked pensive in the dark tent, sitting slumped by a stool, with his head resting in his hands. It was almost difficult to reconcile this man with the Father I had idolized as a child... almost.

I think, had I been younger, still in my teens, perhaps, it would have been unbearable to see Father like this. I would not have been able to comprehend his pain or weariness. It would have gone against everything I had believed him to be. Now, shaped by my own experiences, more aware of my own shame, sadness, and guilt, I felt I could understand this version of my father, even if I felt that he was in danger, as I had once been, of letting these emotions overwhelm him. He, at least, acknowledged that he was struggling, and I had faith he would recover from this soon.

"If I were an assassin, you'd make quite the easy target," I opened, moving closer towards him.

"Oh, Ava," Father smiled weakly, "the guards wouldn't have let you in here if they thought you were here to kill me."

"You never know, I could be trying to kill you to ensure my place on the throne," I joked.

Father laughed then, a rather hollow thing, shaking with the weight of his thoughts. "Another crown to add to the two you have already?"

"It does seem like a bit of overkill doesn't it?" I asked, sitting down on the stool beside him.

"You certainly wouldn't find me begging for another one," Father sighed. "I love the one I have, but will gladly refuse any more."

It was my turn to laugh, "There are benefits," I defended, "but it is a lot of work."

Father nodded, and we sat quietly together for a moment. "Your mothers, Thomas, and the children went to see Al, his qualifier is apparently still ongoing. Or, it was just a bit ago. My guards reported Al was still looking strong."

"I would expect nothing less," I responded sincerely. "It's weird to have been proved so competent with a sword and still have guards following you around," I commented. Nearly seven years since I'd made my way to Dolma, and I'd never gotten used to being followed by knights. I loved my knights, of course, they'd quickly become some of my closest friends and strongest allies, but it was strange to be followed everywhere I went, to have people guard the doors of the rooms I'd entered. There had been knights and guards growing up in Nevremerre, but they only really followed my father, and, even then, he was given more freedom than I was currently allowed. It was generally acknowledged that he could defend himself. I, too, could defend myself, but given my controversial status, I required guards wherever I went. Even today, in Nevremerre, I had four knights, two from Dolma and two from Agremerre, shadowing me.

"You'd think," Father said, leaning back against his seat, "that after thirty odd years on the throne, I'd get used to having them around, but just yesterday. I walked out of my office and nearly ran right into Dame Matilda."

I laughed, "You do have a bit of an excuse, they don't usually guard you in the palace. That's a recent addition, just because of all the foreigners that are here."

Father sighed in response. "Does it ever just kill you, the weight of it all?" Father asked me. His voice was dark and heavy. There was a hardness to his tone that hit me like a fist to the gut, and took my breath out of me all the same.

For a moment, I panicked. I wanted to reassure him. I wanted to pacify him and tell him glorious platitudes like "You're doing a great job," or "It will all be okay,". True, I believed both of those things with all of the energy in my being, but they would also only be said to keep him that indomitable Father that existed in my childhood. So, instead, I told him the truth, "Sometimes I feel like the only thing keeping me from a weekly mental breakdown is the fact that there is constantly more to do."

Father smiled at me, a real smile, the kind that lit up his entire face and brought that roaring fire back into his eyes. "Exactly," he chuckled. "It's like this tournament. I had to fight in this tournament, you know why," he began, and I did know why. His performance was a show of strength. It was a vital presentation to almost every country on the continent that held the central thesis, Nevremerre's current leader is alive, healthy, and powerful. It was a promise that, whoever took the title of Crown Prince or Princess, Nevremerre is and would be a thriving stronghold on our end of the continent. We did not need to threaten the continent with our mighty armies, all we needed to do was show that our sixty year old King was still fit enough to fight competitively and we would send a message: If this is what our King can do alone, imagine how well he can do with armies.

"It was so stressful, Avalynn," Father complained to me. "I had to train for months to get back into a truly competitive form, and good Gods I am truly too old for this. And, today! Today was so nerve wracking. Obviously, I couldn't have anyone hold back in fighting me; it would be a dishonor to all of us, if I even asked. I really had to qualify so that we could send a vital message to every clever delegate and royal in that stadium and to all the many more who will hear about it after. By Gods, I was nervous and I still feel nervous even though it's over! And, now, I have to think about how long I can reasonably hide in this tent until my nerves can subside. Also, there is a significant lack of time available for napping that we really should fix."

I laughed then. I know he was being very honest and vulnerable in his feelings, but my feelings matched his so precisely, I don't think I could do anything else but laugh. "It really is so stressful," I agreed between my giggles. "The whole continent is acting like if I gain one more crown I will come trying to collect them all. Surely they must know the weight of their own."

Father was smiling at me, relaxing his tense shoulders and releasing the tension we had both held onto. "And yet, some of them and some people would. They would take as many crowns as they could get their hands on. What an insane way to live."

"Absolutely mental," I agreed.

Silence fell upon us again, only now it was comfortable and warm, occasionally being broken by a stray giggle. "You're a good Queen, my gift," Father quietly said, giving me a quick kiss on the forehead. "Are you ready to face the world again?"

I was, and we exited the tent to the news of Al's qualification. We met him and the rest of my family in Al's tent as he gleefully told us of his competition. Mama, looking pointedly at Ari, as Al more successfully answered her questions. Throughout it all, Father looked lighter than I'd seen him since my arrival and there was the delightful sensation of being complete and whole as I took in the people around me. Al declared he would win the tournament with ease, and I argued with him with a passion that would make Azar proud as I proclaimed my own victory. Ari said he would aim for third. Father said he would be happy to make it out of the first round.

My kids were all on my side and having three very energetic cheerleaders (and one sleeping baby) worked wonders at overwhelming Al's own voice. He didn't seem to mind though, smiling happily throughout the walk back into the palace. It was an early night for those who fought, a grateful excuse to skip the party that was held for the visiting nobles and royals that evening. Thomas, Mother, and Cecil represented us, while I spent a delightful night reading a romance novel in the solitude of our room. I went to bed early, and, when I woke up, it was time for the real tournament to begin.

Between my talk with Father, my defeat of Mama and my good night's sleep, I was thrilled to start fighting today. My body was thrumming with energy and excitement and I could barely wait to begin. Although I had not fought them in my arena, Galileo, Mateo, and Leonard had also qualified for the tournament. There were several grumbles from my other knights who had been hoping to join the fray, but the rules of birthday tournaments in Nevremerre clearly stated that only those born in Nevremerre could participate. There was a rumor that this almost 300 year old rule was a result of Queen Tillian losing her own birthday tournament to Agremerre's then King, King Barion, but there was no record or writing to actually prove this theory. And, since no one had ever bothered to change this rule, most of my knights were left grumbling in the stands.

I was hoping to get a chance to fight only the friends and family I knew, but sadly tournaments are never so tidy. So, when I received my randomly allocated place assignment, I found my first match was with a knight I'd only met maybe once or twice before, Knight Rixton. It was a bit of a surprise when of the eight people (including myself) I was either related to or was close friends with, none of us would be fighting each other in the first round. It was also highly disappointing to learn that only if I managed to make it to the final four would I be able to fight against someone I knew. And, that was only if Al made it to the final four as well. We were both fairly confident in our ability to get that far, however.

"Looks like we won't be battling it out for the title, but rather to be the bracket leader," Al laughed with me as we both looked rather sullenly at the numbers we'd been assigned.

"That's only if you beat me, Your Highness," Leonard said, appearing from behind me.

"And, if you both beat your first matches," I pointed out, Mother's countless lessons on overconfidence ringing in my ears.

"You better win your first match!" Carlos' exuberant voice boomed from somewhere over Al's shoulder.

Practically all thirty two of us fighting in today's tournament turned to see him pointing his sword at Mateo. "I will try to do the best I can in any competition," Mateo responded, looking especially calm in front of the intense and chaotic energy that Carlos radiated.

"Oh come on," Carlos whined, lowering his sword and practically begging Mateo, "We have a chance to fight each other in an actual tournament! We never get to do this! I thought I'd never be able to actually fight you. You always go off with your family or decide to go live in Dolma of all places!"

I could see Mateo struggle to fight off a laugh. "If you really want to fight me, Sir Carlos," Carlos perked up, reminding me far too much of a puppy Al had gifted to Alder just a few months prior as a ninth birthday present, "Then you should focus on winning your first match."

"Mateo," Carlos groaned. "Alright, but you better win too!" Carlos once again demanded, as Mateo smirked at him.

I practically ran to the arena timetables and was thrilled to see that the match Carlos and Mateo would potentially be fighting would take place at a time that I would be free, even if I won my matches. This was at least one thing to be positive about with my schedule. The tile I'd pulled to give me my position in this tournament was number thirty one. Notoriously, the last two numbers in a tournament were one of the worst, scheduling wise. It basically meant that, even though I was awake and warmed up at dawn this morning, my first match wasn't until the early afternoon. It also meant that assuming I won each match, I would come into the finals directly after the previous two matches. Tournaments were truly nothing, if not a test of endurance.

On the bright side, however, I would now have plenty of time in the morning to watch the other matches. "Who should we go see?" Father asked me, startling me as he all but appeared behind me. I would have thought I would have at least heard his armor clinking behind me, but apparently Father had mastered the art of stealth. "We both have the first match free," Father elaborated, as I claimed my startled nerves, "And Al and Ari are both to fight."

"If I were truly to be competitive, I should watch Al, it is important to discover his weaknesses quickly, but it's Ari's birthday and I've never seen him fight before, so let's watch him," I declared.

Father laughed from behind me, "Very well then, my gift. May I escort you to the Grand Arena for Ari's first match today?"

"Yes please, King Edgar," I replied, taking his offered arm.

"And, I will say that I do not believe you need to watch your brother fight to defeat him," Father called loudly as Al walked by us to head to his first match in the small arena.

"Hey!" Al said with mock outrage, "I'll have you know, Queen Avalynn, King Edgar said the same thing to me just a few minutes ago."

"Oh, but how could that be?" I cried out, as if I weren't absolutely sure Al was telling the truth, "How could Nevremerre's kind and just leader mislead his children in such a way?"

Al cackled as he ran off to the small arena. Father and I wished Ari good luck before Father escorted me to the royal box of the Grand Arena. We were the first to arrive in the box, the visiting royals were either still checking the boards to check which fight they should see, or still sleeping, preferring to watch the later matches. The High Council was potentially in the other arenas as the sheer number of royals visiting, plus the ever increasing size of my family, meant seats in the royal box were rather hard to come by, although I suspected I'd see a few check in for open seats closer to the start of the first match.

"Are you ready for the tournament?" I asked Father as we took two seats in the front row. As we were both competitors in the tournament, Mother would be opening the Grand Arena, and therefore qualified for the main throne in the royal box, at least until Father lost.

"Oh yes," Father laughed, "The pressure's off now. Since I will be 60 this year, it's more than enough to just qualify. Now I am here for fun."

I smiled at him, "Just for fun," I agreed.

Chapter 24

The Tournament of Connections

It did not take long for the Royal Box to begin to fill with people and I was prevented from focusing on the tournament by having to work as a diplomat. It was a frustrating experience –kind of. Truthfully, I rather enjoyed diplomatic work. Learning about the cultures and views of the different countries that were currently in Nevremerre was actually very interesting, after I put aside the feeling that they were all judging my capabilities as a Queen. I could also see how, under different circumstances, a multi-cultural tournament or festival would be a great strengthening event for all.

However, I wasn't just working as a diplomat and Queen, I was also here as a fighter and as a sister. It was frustrating to have to keep switching my brain between these three modes. To have, in one moment, a conversation with the King of Experion about the different fighting styles of Nevremerre's knights in which I had to be cautious about potentially revealing military secrets, to then have to try to maintain a conversation about why Mother opened the tournament while my father was sitting next to her, all while trying to watch Ari's first battle down below was incredibly overwhelming and brought out some rather potent frustration in me.

I was not nineteen anymore, however; so I was rather pleased that I managed not to snap at anyone by the time Ari's match had finished. Unfortunately, this came at the cost of having been unable to devote my full attention to watching Ari fight. It was a shame, really, considering that Ari's ability had improved tremendously since I'd last seen him fight. He'd grown incredibly from the fourteen year old I'd left in Nevremerre to the knight he was now who'd just had his first tournament victory. From the way he fought, I doubt anyone would even think that he did not like fighting. Except, perhaps, Mother, who could seem to see every knight's weakness as if it were written in a book out in front of her.

Using the excuse of going to congratulate Ari, I managed to extract myself from the royal box. Father came with me, as he was off to fight in his first match. I watched, gratefully, as the royals we were with eagerly followed him to the Middle Arena, thrilled to see Father fight again. I quickly congratulated Ari before moving towards the Small Arena where I assumed Thomas and my children had been watching Al fight. It was more than upsetting to be hindered in that process by the unsettling presence of Lord Nicholas.

"You're too nice," he cheerfully told me, settling into my pace as he walked beside me.

I sighed as I looked back to where Oberon, Challa, Hugo, and my other knights walked behind me and briefly contemplated if I could order them to prevent Lord Nicholas from ever coming near me. This plan was, sadly, put to rest in my mind as I remembered that as Nevremerre's current noble representative, it would be next to impossible to ignore him. "Most people find kindness to be a virtue," I pointed out.

"Not if you're a pushover," Lord Nicholas casually insulted.

There was an angry snort made by one of the knights behind me, that I couldn't help but agree with, "I don't believe that is how many would describe me."

"Then why do you keep acting like one?"

A Queen does not punch High Council members in the face. A Queen does not punch High Council members in the face, I repeated to myself. Still, it took several deep breaths before I found it in me to respond civilly. "My behavior is in line with what is expected for a person in my position," I said with more condescension than was probably required.

"Well, that was better!" Nicholas smiled at me, and I watched in abject horror as a group of girls walking past us stumbled at the sight. "You need to speak to more people like they are beneath you, like you do with me."

"I don't talk to you like you are beneath me, I talk to you like you are annoying, which you are," I snapped at him. There was a snort of laughter, reminding me that Nicholas had chosen to have this conversation in full view of not just my knights but any passerby who felt the need to listen.

"It doesn't matter, the point is you are still acting like a Princess," Nicholas declared.

"Technically, in Nevremerre, I am a Princess," I argued.

"That's the problem!" Nicholas declared, "You are not a Princess, even here, you are a Queen of two different countries. Your Nevremerre title does not supersede that."

"So I should start talking to people as if they are beneath me?" I asked sarcastically.

"Yes!" Nicholas eagerly agreed.

I stopped then, right in the middle of the tournament grounds as I gaped at Nicholas who took a few seconds to realize that I was no longer walking alongside him. "You can't be serious," I told him, incredulously, when he doubled back to stand in front of me. "Have you learned nothing in the past seven years?"

"Oh relax," Nicholas said, impudently, "I don't mean about the people and your subjects. I am talking about the other royals. You are their equal in rank and power and yet you are unfailingly polite and kind-"

"Again, that's generally considered a good thing."

"Yes, but not with them! Be more firm! Be more rude! Set actual boundaries that they have to accept. Remind them you are their equal, if not more powerful. You are a Queen; you do not have to listen or respond to them if you do not wish."

"Exactly, I am a Queen, being rude could lead to an international incident, or a war! I cannot act without being endlessly cautious about that fact."

"As should they!" Nicholas argued back at me, "They must work just as hard to show you that they are willing to work with you as well. They need to ensure that you won't go to war with them as well. A war which, currently, you are in a far better position to win."

"Gods why does everything have to be so focused on war? Every action I take is so smothered in the question: will this end in a war?"

"You are a Queen. It is always an option. We are governed by people. People have started, fought in, and ended wars throughout all of our history. You are a ruler; you will never be able to escape the threat of war because you will always hold the power to start the next great war. It is an arsenal in your tool box and your last resort in times of hardship. War is in your hands more than any other person in this continent, save the other rulers of the known world."

I hated his words, and then tried not to hate them. Nana had once told me that to hate was to be stuck. When you hold hatred in you, you cannot move forward, and I always wanted to move forward. So, I hated Nicholas' words and then, bitterly, I had to accept them. He was right, infuriatingly so. War, the power to start it, was something I held in my hand. It was my responsibility to hold it. It was my responsibility to prevent it. If there ever was, truly and honestly, a need, it was my responsibility to start a war. It was a horrible thing to think about, and I suddenly found myself understanding the litany of curses my great grandfather had written out when he went to war with Calvine.

"Okay," I accepted, focusing once again on Nicholas, "then what do you suppose the limit is to how "rude" I am allowed to be to the other royals?"

Nicholas smirked at me, and I once again wrestled with the desire to punch him, "Like I said, Your Majesty, you're too nice, I doubt you'd ever actually cross any lines."

He gave me too much credit, I decided. For I was certain that punching him, as I very much desired to do, would cross the lines he spoke of and yet, I still very much desired it. It really was a shame he wasn't a knight, even with the work he'd done all those years ago, I would have liked to cross his path in training, or to crush him in a tournament like this. So, there certainly were some lines that, in my thoughts at least, I most definitely crossed. "Well, leave my sight then," I snapped at him, "I have no desire to speak with you any more."

"What a thing to say to someone who will decide if you are to become Queen of Nevremerre," Nicholas smirked.

"A truly terrible decision on the part of the nobles, if you ask me," I responded, although I found I did not mean it as much as I wished to. Lord Nicholas was not without skills as a negotiator and an advocate for the desires of the nobles in Nevremerre. "Still, Noble representative or not, I am going to meet with my family, so this conversation and your companionship on my journey has come to an end. Do be on your way," I told him, barely refraining from saying please before my request that he leave.

"Much better," Nicholas smiled, as if his approval was somehow my aim in taking his advice. "I shall bid you good day, Your

Majesty, and I wish you luck in this tournament," Nicholas then gave me a low bow before walking the opposite direction.

"He's an arrogant one," Challa commented then.

"You have no idea," I agreed, before continuing on my own journey towards the Small Arena.

I missed the end of Al's victory, but I found my children all dressed in Nevremerre purple and gold. With them, I was able to put aside any nerves that had gripped me about the fights I was to have this afternoon. We laughed and excitedly watched the morning matches. We saw Father win his first match by just a hair and watched the intense battle between Mateo and Carlos, in their second round of fighting. All the while I was whispering the fighter's weaknesses to Alder and Genevieve as Mother had done for my brothers and me as a child. I practiced being slightly rude to the other royals as I asked for the space to watch the fights with my children. Although, I suspected Nicholas would still believe that I did not use enough of my authority in doing so. Then, as we cheered Carlos exuberantly hugging Mateo, despite Mateo's incredible victory, it was time for me to get ready for my first match.

I walked alone to the knights' tents, or rather I walked with my knights until we reached the competitors' tents and all those not competing were barred from entry. My knights wished me luck and began to head to the arena to watch from the stands. I warmed up, stretched, and tried unsuccessfully to abate the nerves that always held me before a tournament. Over the years, many people have told me their methods of handling nerves, from phrases, exercising techniques or talking them out with someone else. I had heard a different solution from everyone I knew and I still hadn't found one for me. I simply had to live with the feeling that swirled in my stomach, making my lunch rebel inside me and causing me to put extra chalk onto sweaty palms. I could do no more than breathe through the uncomfortable sensations and know that as soon as the fight actually began, provided I could focus on the fight as opposed to my feelings, all my nerves would simply fade away.

It was just as I predicted, once the announcer said to begin, I fought Sir Rixton with a clear head. It was a quick match, I knew I needed to conserve energy, and Sir Rixton had never fought me before. He did not have the ability to adapt to my fighting style in such a short period of time. Just as Mama had suggested, in a one-on-one fight, I was stronger, faster, and smarter than in a group battle. With only one opponent, years of listening to Mother honed my mind to see any weaknesses in the fighter in front of me. With a body trained since childhood by the best knights in Nevremerre to take any blows and give me the speed and reflexes to beat my opponents, victory came easily to me.

With only an hour break, I went on to beat my second and third opponents as well. I then found myself in the final four, facing an opponent I'd wanted to beat since I was only eleven years old, my eldest brother, Al. Our match was to be held in the Middle Arena, but the sheer size of the crowd would suggest we were a much bigger venue. I was sure we'd somehow managed to go over the arena capacity despite the fact Nevremerre had hired people specifically to prevent such an occurrence. Still humans were fallible, and the carefully planned size control could only do so much. I could only hope that they could manage the rush that was sure to come once a victor had been named and all of these people would try to get into the Grand Arena to see the final.

It was perhaps a sign of how far I'd come as a Queen that my thoughts all veered towards safety and logistics when I should have been more concerned with fighting Al. Al was not some random knight, he trained with me all throughout my youth. All the advantages I had from growing up with our parents were something Al had as well. It also didn't hurt that he was four years older and he had an hour of rest prior to our match while I had been stuck fighting Dame Layana in order to get to this match. The universe really did feel like it was fighting against me, and still my main concern was the crowd before me. I even thought about going out before I had been called to fight to handle the situation. At least, I wasn't nervous for the fight, I supposed.

I was still debating going out to speak to the crowd when I heard a hush fall over the crowd, followed quickly by the resounding voice of my father, "Hello all." The second he spoke I knew it was all going to be okay. Father would take care of all my worries with the crowd; there was no one I would trust more and the core principles of Nevremerre's government meant that this trust in Father extended to all the people he ruled. The trust he inspired as King, is what kept Nevremerre comfortable and happy and it is what would be immediately transferred to whomever was named heir.

Father continued in his speech, acknowledging the people's excitement, but laying out strict rules for how the crowd was to exit the arena. The crowd was memorized by Father's words, nodding, cheering, and laughing in all the right places. When Father spoke to me yesterday about his battle being a show of his strength to the leaders of the visiting nations, I had known his demonstration would have the desired effect. Now, watching the tens of thousands of people in the arena hang desperately onto every word my father spoke, I wondered if this was not the greater show of power. Even if he lost to Galileo in his second match of the day, the people of Nevremerre still revered him. Their respect for Father as a leader seemed, to me, a far more powerful display of the strength of Nevremerre as a country.

The roar of the crowd revived me from my thoughts as the announcer called out my name to welcome me fully into the Middle Arena. The excitement from the crowd was palpable. It filled every sense that I had from the thunderous cheers, to the fading winter sunlight, to the glow of a hundred thousand lanterns. The heat of so many people in one space managed to keep the frigid cold away, even in the open space that Al and I would fight in. The scent of popcorn and arena snacks filled the air and I could taste the dry dust still floating unsettled after my previous match. It was so abundantly vibrant, my heart pounded in my chest as if it were desperately trying to echo the sheer amount of noise that exploded from the monstrous crowd.

"And, opposing her we have Prince Alveron of Nevremerre." I hadn't thought there was a way to increase the noise of the crowd and yet, as Al stepped into the arena, the cheers became almost deafening. I suppose I couldn't blame them for the excitement; the last time any of my siblings had fought against each other, Azar had still been alive. He'd actually only gotten to fight against Al in a tournament once before. It was his first year in the Open Tournament, and, after losing to Al, he vowed he'd get revenge. According to letters I had received from both brothers at the time, they each declared their battle was an intense match in which they were both fighting at peak form. However, I also had a note from Ari detailing how they'd both made a series of simple mistakes in their eagerness to battle each other.

Still, despite the fact that before Azar's death they'd both managed to win the Open Tournament at least once, they were never matched against each other again, so Azar never did get his revenge. That would make it somewhere around six years ago that my siblings had last faced each other in a tournament. It was no wonder the crowd was so excited. Then there was the addition of this week being the week the next Crown Prince or Princess would be chosen. I wondered if there were any in the crowd today who thought that this fight was some sort of indication of who would next take the throne. I even wondered if Al thought this way too. If I were younger, or perhaps if I'd lived a different life than the one I had for the past seven years, would I think the same thing?

And then, I didn't have time to think, as a whistle was blown and Al's aggression, strength, and agility gave me no room for further thought. Reflex was all that kept me going throughout the beginning of the match. Al was smart, and he knew the tricks I was prone to playing to deal with the fact that he was about a foot taller than I, and that my head was comparable to the size of his biceps. It was all I could do to spin, duck, and dodge his heavy blows as I hoped he'd give me an opportunity to strike. However, patience was a trait that had been forged in me through screams and cries of children with no concept that their parents had any wants or desires of their own. Waiting for Al to falter, even though he possessed strength and stamina of a truly exceptional knight was nothing to me.

When he did falter, when he accidentally did give me enough time to think of a strategy to use against him, I was surprised to find my brother becoming just like any other opponent to me. I had thought I would view our battle like Al and Azar had viewed theirs. I expected my thoughts to venture towards the epic melee that they'd both written me pages about, even if the outside observer (Ari) saw nothing more than a typical exchange. Yet, when I fought Al, he became nothing more than a normal opponent. The same pattern of finding a flaw, exposing the flaw, and seizing victory was the only thought process going on in my head. In the thick of our battle, the fact he was my brother did not even cross my mind. I, of course, felt the flare of pride and love when Al made a particularly clever move, but I never had the time to consciously register those feelings as I instead focused on getting in my next blow.

It was only after I won that I understood what was so special about fighting my brother. Al was in the dirt, sprawled and sweaty with my sword at his throat, and a radiant sibling rivalry rang through me as he snarled at me. I suddenly felt the vindication of years of being the small younger sister who could never catch up. Memories of tree branches too tall, dolls stolen, dresses ripped, and the indignant refusal to join my stuffed toys and me for a daily tea party filtered through my brain as I laughed down at Al. And, when he laughed, too, pushing away my sword to give me the tightest of hugs, I all but cried in his arms.

"Azar would be so proud of you," Al whispered to me.

"Nonsense," I whispered back, "He'd be terribly jealous that I accomplished his greatest dream and then you two would band together to get back at me. Just like you always did."

Al laughed then, putting me back on the ground and giving me the traditional handshake for my victory, "Too right we would and we'd be right too, Ava, you're getting far too strong as it is."

We laughed and headed out of the arena, the howling cheers and clasping from the arena threatened to echo across the whole of Nera. "Right," Al told me as we got to the fighters, tents, "drink plenty of water, and rest as much as you can now before the final. You must win the whole tournament now, Ava, or you'll make me look bad you see." Al handed me a cup of water.

"Perhaps I'll lose just to spite you," I joked, sipping at the water he'd gotten me and giving him a little smirk.

He wasn't Azar though, and refused to even nibble at the bait I had set. "Now we both know that won't happen," Al said, with a disapproving frown that was betrayed by the smile in his eyes. "Go on, off to the Grand Arena with you, and good luck."

Al successfully shooed me off and I was able to catch the last bit of Galileo's match with Dame Blanche. He came out victorious, and I had to smile at the irony of Nevremerre's best knights in this tournament were not actually living in Nevremerre. Still, at least my next opponent would be a familiar one. It would be just another battle to add to our ever-going series on the training grounds of Dolma and throughout our travels around Agremerre. There was also an added benefit that Galileo, like myself, was about to fight his third match in a row, so I could at least feel like we were on equal footing.

"Nicely done," I told Galileo as he exited the arena. "It seems that we will be facing each other for the final."

"I would expect nothing less, Your Majesty," Galileo smiled at me before his face quickly fell, "Where are your guards?"

"Most likely still trying to make it through the crowds at the Middle Arena."

"Then you should have waited for them," Galileo insisted, his eyes flashing dangerously as he inspected me once more, as if searching for an injury I might have sustained while out of the purview of my knights.

"I'm fine," I huffed, rather arrogantly as I let Galileo inspect me. "I can defend myself."

"No one is invincible," Galileo said seriously, his blue eyes begging me to understand that my life was not one conducive to independence or solitude.

I sighed as I watched him. I knew that he no more desired to give me another lecture on my safety and the importance of the knights that followed me any more than I wished to hear one. I also knew the point he was making: my life was not guaranteed to be safe, even here, not with all the many countries and rulers who feared the power I could potentially wield. I knew my knights served a purpose, I knew my safety was not a given, even if I felt safe; there were measures that had to be taken. I didn't really resent it; it was my choice after all and I still felt the pros of my position outweighed the loss of the independence I'd once carried. Still, every now and then, the presence of the knights could feel like a cage, even when they were my friends I so dearly loved.

"I know," I told Galileo, once again choosing to accept the truth of the matter. "I know, I should have waited, I just forgot."

"You forgot?" Galileo repeated, sounding less than impressed with my rationale, even if I rather thought he should be appreciating my easy acceptance of my error.

"Yes, I forgot," I repeated with confidence.

"You've had knights with you practically every day for the past seven years."

"But, not in Nevremerre," I protested, "When I was just Nevremerre's Princess, I never had knights. I moved around freely. I simply forgot things had changed."

Saying it aloud, I admit it sounded like a rather weak defense. There wasn't much to do about it though since it was the truth. "My Queen," Galileo sighed, shaking his head at me in dismay.

"I do appreciate you putting up with me for all these years," I said, earnestly remembering the many, many times Galileo had been forced to endure the whims, stubbornness, and rash impulses I felt I had been prone to, probably for my whole life.

"Queen Avalynn, you are my chosen Queen. I do not put up with you. I serve you, I work for you and I care for you, because I wish to do so more than any other occupation. It is a pleasure and you do not put up with pleasure, you actively and continuously seek it out."

"Yes Sir," I saluted, properly chastised, and damn near on the verge of crying at his sweet words to me.

Galileo gave me an exasperated smile before continuing, "Now, who should win this tournament?"

"What?" I looked back at him, a little thrown by his words.

"Obviously, we know our fighting record is pretty even, but this tournament is on a highly political stage. So, I will follow your lead, which of us should win?"

"Oh, I hadn't even thought about it!" I didn't mind admitting this failure, not to Galileo, not to any of my knights for my original party really. I trusted them with all my perceived failures, a goal we'd spent the past three years working towards.

"Am I overthinking this then?" Galileo asked, seemingly fully prepared to back down in this line of thinking, if I told him yes.

"No, no you're not," I told him, leaning my head against the stone wall of the Grand Arena, "On a public stage everything is a statement,"I repeated a lesson Father had told us several years ago, before Al had even reached the age of majority and we were all just kids. "Even if not everyone receives the message, someone will, and someone will always interpret every action as a message."

It had been silly of me to forget this lesson, really. I had nothing to blame except my own stress and nerves regarding the Crown Prince/Princess selection. There really was a message either way. If I won, it would be a show of strength that could scare my enemies either into a more passive role, or into a more active one. If I lost, it would show weakness in both the countries I was a Queen of, but it could also placate those who felt I was too powerful. There were about a million other reasons for or against my securing a victory, and perhaps there was a right answer that would have solved all my problems. I, however, was in no mood to try and think of it.

"There will be fallout either way," I sighed to Galileo, "Let's just fight at our best, and we shall deal with whatever the aftermath is once the match is over."

"As you wish, my Queen," Galileo smiled at me.

"Gods above there is a lot you have to think about when you are Queen," I complained to him.

Galileo laughed, "That's why you'd never see me in the position, my Queen. It's much better to just have one thing to focus on, even if that one thing is the rather unpredictable challenge of trying to keep you safe."

In the end, our match was rather anticlimactic, at least it was for the two of us. The day's fights had left us both mentally and physically exhausted. Our moves were sloppy and we both made silly mistakes in our sword work. It was hardly our usual battle of mental tactics and physical prowess. However, this did not appear to be noticeable to the crowd, whose cheers and applause were positively ear splitting as I eked out a victory from the older knight.

Perhaps it was because I knew we weren't fighting at our best that the victory felt hollow. In fact, all I really felt after disarming Galileo was relief. I was so relieved that I had time to bathe and be pampered before attending the tournament ball this evening. I wasn't alone in this though, as Galileo hugged me in celebration of my victory, we both sagged heavily against the weight of each other.

"Do you think it would be regal if I had someone carry me back to the royal palace?" I said, more seriously than I initially anticipated.

Galileo still laughed though, as he pulled back from the hug, "Perhaps, but you'll have to ask someone else, as it stands, I think I'll need someone to carry me back as well."

I laughed too, letting my feelings of relief, and finally, the joy of victory filled me as I turned towards Galileo once more, "Make sure you save me a dance tonight!"

"With pleasure," Galileo bowed.

In the end, Hugo carried me back and Challa held Galileo, much to the delight of Oberon and Leonard. Mateo, always far too polite to laugh at the slightly pink tinge that had taken up residence on Galileo's cheeks, did his best to switch the conversation to the various fights of the day. He tried valiantly to keep the teasing at bay, but was ultimately thwarted by Sir Lemmly, who took one look at Galileo before calling him a "Princess," stealing him from Challa's arms, and trying to carry Galileo back to the knights' rooms himself. He was highly unsuccessful in this endeavor, as Galileo decided he'd had enough teasing and shoved himself out of Lemmly's arms resulting in both men falling to the floor and the rest of my knights collapsed in laughter. Both men brushed it off with good humor, laughing along with the rest of us and Hugo soon deposited me safely back into my rooms where I was bathed and dressed for the late night of celebrations that was to come.

Chapter 25

The Queen's Choice

Thomas and I walked down to the ball together, after ensuring the kids were all tucked away in bed. Despite their many protests that they could stay awake for the event, both Genevieve and Marcus fell asleep quickly, Eliza having fallen asleep well before, too young to even know there was an event going on around her. Alder reluctantly accepted that he would have to wait another few years before he was allowed to attend, although I had a sneaking suspicion that his understanding would not stop him from trying to watch the festivities in secret.

The ball was magnificent. The grand ballroom was packed with nobles and foreign royalty. There were so many people that the dancing and festivities took over the whole first floor of the Royal Palace, and even then the active bodies of the many visitors and guests made the whole palace warm, despite the wintery evening chill that coated the outside of the palace. As Thomas and I walked down the stairs into the waiting crowd, a sea of colors and glittering jewels brightened up the gray stones that usually decorated the palace. When the footman, Henry, called out our arrival, cheers rang out from every person in sight. We were instantly swarmed by people congratulating me on my victory.

The talk focused primarily on my fighting style and the battle success of my family and knights. The fine dresses and polite conversations felt like something out of a fairytale. Now, to those who grew up outside of the royal life, my life, in all its facts, was a fantasy story, the kind parents would tell their children to ensure they had sweet dreams. But, for me, for my family, this was our lives. We were always grateful for the wealth and care our roles provided for us, but we rarely felt the magic and wonder that fairy tales had described ruling to be. We knew too much you see; we saw the work that our titles demanded; we knew the pressure and the continuous awareness of our actions that being in the public eye demanded. Our life was blessed with luxury, but it wasn't a fairy tale.

Still, tonight, being celebrated for an accomplishment that I felt I'd truly earned, in a colorful room vibrating with all the luxuries, wealth and circumstance provided, I felt like the Queens spoken about in fairy tales. I felt like I glowed. In this moment, I was the sun, dancing with bright abundance, shining with all I had, indifferent to the perils and concerns of the future. There were no passive aggressive or outright aggressive comments that could hurt me, for what does the sun care for the reviews of others. I danced with my husband, my knights, my friends, my family and anyone else who wished to partner with me. The night flew by with laughter and music in a dazzling haze of brilliant joy, and then, in what felt like an instant, all that color was gone.

The ball ended and the next morning, we woke up to silence. It was a heavy, stilted silence, maintained even by the cold castle walls. The freezing stone seemed to refuse even to carry the echo of footsteps. I wondered if this breathless silence was true of every previous selection week, or if ours was special somehow. Nevremerre tradition dictates that the week after the 21st birthday of the youngest heir be spent choosing the next Crown Prince or Princess. During this time the royals and High Council are not to be seen. There will be no events, no friends that can visit, all non-essential stuff and knights are even sent home.

Meals during this time consisted mostly of spending time with my children and brothers. Thank the Gods for Thomas and Cecil, who managed to keep the conversation flowing and the children entertained as my brothers and I fell into a nervous silence. Father, Mother, and Mama were consistently absent. They were cooped up behind the large wooden doors that held the main chamber of the High Council. Doors I knew from my youth were totally soundproof, but, still, I somehow found myself walking by them more frequently than could be explained by mere chance.

I felt like a kid again, in all of the worst ways really. I was nervously awaiting the judgment of my parents, stuck in my childhood home with little but my siblings to entertain me. The addition of my husband and children were new, of course, but even with them, I found it difficult to feel like the grown-up woman, not to mention the Queen that I was. I felt so very young, and a little unprepared for what was to come, even if I had decided that the outcome didn't really matter.

That, really was the oddest part, I was not nervous about whether I would or would not be picked– well, there might have been a little bit of that, but mostly it was the environ-ment that threw me off balance. It was the silent halls, the tense meals, the cumulation of really decades of competition that would all come to a close in merely a few days. I had the brief insane thought that I did not know myself without this competition, before I reassured myself that this was simply not true. However, this was most definitely the end of an era. It, one way or another, would set the stage for a new chapter in my life. If I thought about it, I could argue that as Queen of Dolma and Agremerre, that new stage of my life had already begun or that, as a mother, that new stage of my life was currently in place. But, somehow, beyond all of that, this selection still felt more real.

And, when I did think about it, despite my work, being the Queen of Dolma and Agremerre still felt surreal. Whether it was a byproduct of how quickly I seemed to acquire these titles, or the fact that I never grew up expecting to receive them, four years in, I still didn't feel like a Queen. Somehow, it seemed that this decision, no matter what it was, would free me from the surreal nature my titles currently held. Like being Nevremerre's Crown Princess would make me a Queen or being released from my role as heir would allow me to fully accept the titles Agremerre and Dolma had graced me with, even if, at least in Agremerre's case, I felt like nothing more than a mere placeholder until Genevieve came of age.

So, I was beyond nervous to hear a decision whose outcome I was happy with either way and I learned then that managing my worry and stress was a constant task. I was running through a daily mantra of "It will be okay. It will all be okay." And, it only sort of worked, but I kept at it, for I knew of nothing else I could do. Somehow, I survived that week and after what felt like both an eternity and an instant, Al, Ari, and I were sitting in a drawing room, an hour before the public announcement was to be made, waiting to learn the results for ourselves.

"Good afternoon," Father said as he walked in, sounding oddly stilted and formal as he spoke. "Thank you all for your patience and hard work during this process."

He's nervous, I suddenly thought, watching Father fiddle with his hands as his eyes nervously bounced around the room, settling anywhere but on the three of us. It was oddly amusing to watch. I don't think I had ever seen Father look so lost. He always managed to have at least some level of composure about him, but here he seemed to me to look more similar to the way Alder behaved when he'd done something wrong. I couldn't help but smile at the beast of a man my father typically looked like, as he curled in on himself in an unconscious attempt to appear smaller.

"It's okay, Father," Al smiled, realizing, as I had, Father's apprehension. He laid a hand on Father's shoulder and reassured him, "Just tell us who it will be."

Father sighed, and smiled at Al. He took a deep breath before announcing, "Ari will be the next King."

Relief flooded throughout my body in an astounding quantity. I waited for disappointment to seep in, but it never came, instead I was greeted with a profound and utter relief. Across from me, I saw Al's body sag as a brilliant smile held his face. Our eyes met, and I knew we both were feeling the same thing. With ease and sincerity, I beamed at Ari, "Congratulations, Crown Prince Ari of Nevremerre, may you serve this country with grace, compassion, and wisdom."

Al echoed my words adding a little bow and saying, "As the Duke of the South, I promise to honor and serve you in the name of Nevremerre."

Ari, unlike Al and I, looked very overwhelmed. His whole body was rigid and his teal eyes blinked at us, as though he wasn't sure what was going on. Al laughed at him before pulling him in for an awkward hug where Ari did nothing but stand stiff as a board while Al's muscular body encapsulated him.

"Let him breath Al," I laughed at them, as Al sheepishly backed away. "Now, Ari, this is the part where you're supposed to thank Al for his support."

"Thank you for your support," Ari repeated, still looking absolutely gobsmacked at the turn of events.

"As Queen of Agremerre, I look forward to working with you in the future."

"Oh, yes," Ari said, his eyes suddenly going wide with what looked like panic as he began flapping his hands around.

"What about Dolma?" Al joked at me as we continued to let Ari process.

"While Dolma and Nevremerre have treaties together, we have yet to establish the close relationship that Nevremerre and Agremerre have."

"Playing it cool then, dear Ava?" Al joked.

"Anything for the countries I rule," I said, more seriously than I intended. "How are you then, Father?" I asked, finally turning back to the nervous man in front of me.

Father stood on shaking legs, but they looked to be growing stronger as the color returned to his cheeks. "Better, my gift, you are all taking this better than expected."

"Should we burst out into tears then?" Al asked, "I confess I don't feel in the least bit sad, but I'm sure I could muster up something if that would make it easier for you."

Father laughed then, finally regaining his composure fully. "No, no love, I don't believe that will be necessary. I must say, that was easily the hardest moment of my career."

"Oh, don't say that," I laughed as Al added, "So far..." in a somewhat menacing tone.

"No, no, I mean it. I've had years, decades really, to prepare for that moment and yet I still didn't know what to say. Alveron, Avalynn, I hope you know how proud I am of you, even if you will not inherit the throne of Nevremerre."

"Don't fear, Father. It's a relief not to have it," Al smiled, patting Father's shoulder once more.

"For me, too, I'm afraid. I would have loved to rule Nevremerre, but three countries is rather a lot," I added.

"Good then," Father smiled, "Now, would you give me a moment with Ari? And, remember, nothing is to be said to anyone until the official announcement is made."

"Yes, Father," Al and I agreed before leaving the room. On my way out, I gave Ari a large, but awkward hug and whispered, "You'll be an amazing King."

Outside we spoke with Mother and Mama, and we reiterated our relief and excitement for Ari. Then we moved as a family to the Great Hall where all the nobles of Nevremerre had gathered to hear the long-awaited news. Father made a beautiful speech about Nevremerre's bright future under Crown Prince Ari and the nobles below pledged their loyalty to Ari, who had recovered enough to look every bit the shining Crown Prince he was. Father then brought out a glittering golden crown which replaced Ari's silver one marking him as the next ruler of Nevremerre and only then did I feel a rush of disappointment at missing out on these moments I once so desperately wanted.

It occurred to me then, in between the applause of the nobles, that I had lost any remaining connection to my home. Of course, I would always be welcome in Nevremerre and there was the Unajo festival I would attend each year, but I no longer held a position in Nevremerre. I would always be a Princess, technically, but my position as Queen of Agremerre and Dolma would always outrank that. I would have to spend my time in Agremerre and Dolma because those places were where my responsibilities lay. That may have been true for years now, but there was always the hope that I would come back and rule, even if it felt a little unrealistic. Now, this would be a final goodbye. Nevremerre would always be where I came from, but it was now time to make Agremerre and Dolma my home. Nevremerre raised me, but I must now grow old in Agremerre and Dolma.

We stayed only three more days in Nevremerre before we returned to Dolma. I celebrated Ari and prepared myself to say goodbye to Nevremerre. Many people, mostly foreign nobles and royalty, gave me their very relieved condolences. Each time this happened, and it happened quite a lot, I reminded the person that condolences were rather a strange thing to give me, considering I was still the Queen of two countries. This worked wonders at curbing any condescension some of these individuals seemed to believe necessary in their tone, and maintained Dolma and Agremerre's new combined status and power. Even if I wasn't to rule Nevremerre, I was not lacking in power, wealth, or status, and it felt just a little good to remind people of that fact.

Then we went home.Thomas and I ruled Dolma and I worked with the High Court to strengthen and rule Agremerre. The children grew and thrived. Ollifelle and Chanti got married and I came to call Dolma and Agremerre my homes. As I predicted, Ari becoming Crown Prince marked a shift for me. I began to truly settle into and accept my role as Queen in both countries. I found a rhythm and a joy that had eluded me in the years before and I finally felt I understood Nana's words: the joy that came from life's banality was unparalleled. I was content, thriving, and prepared for what I believed my life would look like going forward, which is what made it all the more surprising when exactly one year and eight days after his succession as Crown Prince, Ari turned up at my office in Dolma.

"I think I gave Sir Mateo quite a shock," were Ari's first words as he entered my office, as if he hadn't shown up, without guards, completely unannounced, having not even sent a letter to us beforehand saying he would be coming.

"Crown Prince Ari of Nevremerre," I said, not entirely warmly as I stared at him in a sort of shock, "what are you doing here?"

"I quit," Ari beamed at me, as if I was supposed to realize what he was talking about.

"You quit," I repeated, "I had not realized you had a drinking problem."

"What?" Ari paused, looking at me as if I'd somehow acquired a second head in the past two seconds. "I don't drink; it tastes funny."

"You can't have taken up smoking," I admonished.

"What? No. Why are we talking about this?"

"Well what else is there that you could have quit?"

"Being Crown Prince of course!" Ari told me as if this were the most obvious answer and not genuinely impossible.

"What?!" I all but screamed, finally standing up from my desk to come towards Ari, "You can't have quit! It's not allowed."

"It definitely is, I checked."

"Of course you did," I muttered, before sinking into the sofa in my office. Ari followed my lead, excitedly sitting on the couch opposite me.

"There have been a grand total of three Crown Prince and Princesses who have quit. One quit due to illness, one was chosen before the age of majority due to the kingdom being at war, so she resigned when peace returned. She was then later reselected as Crown Princess when her youngest sibling reached the age of majority. She then agreed to the job and became Queen Tilliana. And, finally, one Prince quit after a year on the job, after which he concluded that he'd rather pursue a career in acting. I have followed Prince Regus' model, minus becoming an actor, of course. I plan to take over Duke Austin's business, or perhaps strike out on my own, but I'll certainly start with Austin. By the way, we missed a step."

"What step could we possibly have missed?" I cried out, still reeling from what Ari had just said.

"We're supposed to say hello and tell each other how much we missed each other."

This sobered me up a little as I took a true look at my younger brother. He looked happy; his shoulders had finally fully widened making him look more like Father and he also looked more relaxed than I could ever remember him being as he earnestly looked around the room. "Hello Ari, I have missed you very much," I told him sincerely.

"Hello, Ava, I have missed you too," he smiled back.

"So, tell me again why you've quit being Crown Prince?"

"Well, I tried it for a year, a whole year, and it was not fun. There's a lot of talking to people and meetings and sometimes you have to stop projects right in the middle of working on them to go do another different project," Ari ranted at me.

"Yes, but surely you knew you would have to do that for a while now," I pointed out.

"I thought that I'd have more support in not having to do stuff like that. When I worked with Father after Azar died, I mostly got to do paperwork, and that was a lot of fun."

"If you need more help, you can certainly get it. You are the Crown Prince after all!"

"Well, I suppose, but the real issue is that I simply realized that I had more fun and joy working with Duke Austin than I ever did being Crown Prince, and there's no way I can stay Crown Prince when I know there is a job out there that I like more. So after I worked as Crown Prince for one year, I quit, just like Prince Regus."

"Okay, okay," I said, slowly wrapping my head around his words. "So, what happens now?"

"I'm taking a month off to see you and my nieces and nephews and then Austin says I can start working with him right away."

"Right, that's wonderful and we all love having you here -"

"Now that I'm not Crown Prince, I can come more often," Ari excitedly interrupted, "I can spend whole months of the year with you!"

I had to smile at that even if we were straying from my main question. "That's wonderful," I repeated as sincerely as possible while desperately needing an answer to my next question, "but I meant who will be the Crown Prince now?"

"Oh, you of course," Ari informed me.

"What?!" I demanded, back to being shocked.

"Yes, I tried asking Al, but he shot me down before I could even ask."

"So, I'm the last choice?" I asked, just a little offended, "And, what do you mean you asked? Surely this is a decision that has to be made by the council and Father?"

"Oh yes, but we needed to test interest to see who was still a candidate. I also needed to tell Al that I quit. It's rude to let the public find out things before you tell your family," Ari nodded and I couldn't help but uncomfortably think about my arranged marriage to Thomas and departure for Dolma. However, Ari's tone in no way implied an insult to me. "Al was thrilled of course. As you know he's been saying for ages that I wouldn't like being King. So, he got all superior and told me that he told me so. However, I reminded him that he said that about you, too, but you like ruling and he stopped being all superior after that."

I had rarely seen Ari so chatty, so I took a moment to just process the young man in front of me, "So you're here to gauge my interest, then visit us?" I finally asked him.

"No, I'm here to give you the job," Ari informed me bluntly.

"What, but I haven't said I'm interested yet! And, I'm not. I have quite enough work as it is," I said aghast at his gaul.

"You are interested," Ari informed me, "We all know you are."

"Oh, I hadn't realized the Nevremerre council is full of mind readers," I said sarcastically.

"I don't think any of us have the power to read minds," Ari said, seriously.

"Never mind, the point is my answer is no."

"If you refuse, the next choice is Lord Nicholas."

"I'll do it."

I am sure there are several rational explanations as to why impulse and a rabid desire not to see a very specific individual get something are not the best reasons to make a decision, however, in this case, I have no regrets about the choice I made. Ari then handed me several documents declaring that I had become Crown Princess of Nevremerre six days earlier and detailed the High Council's current ideas for how I may rule three countries at once when that time occurred. I reviewed them with Thomas that night and we made plans. We then confirmed those plans with our allies in Dolma and Agremerre's High Court. The word of my new title got around slowly and without the pomp and circumstance that had followed Ari's, but this was perhaps for the best as the neighboring countries had seemingly lost their fear around the power I would hold. Or, rather, it became too late for them to do much about it.

I held my title of Crown Princess of Nevremerre for five years until Father retired, hoping to spend more time with Mama and Mother as Mama's health began to worsen. It was a bright summer day when I was crowned Queen of Nevremerre alongside Thomas, as the new King of Nevremerre. It was the only coronation I remember enjoying. It was the only one I was familiar enough with that there was very little new information to memorize. It also was not preceded by the death of any loved ones, although Mama died less than a year later. I also was now and forever more sure and strengthened by the mutual love Thomas and I shared and having him by my side made everything easier. It also didn't hurt that all my children were old enough not to need constant monitoring, and so, with all of that, it was easy and joyful to be crowned Queen of Nevremerre.

I need not bore you all with the details of how I ruled each kingdom and it should be obvious by now how I got my title as the Triple Queen. After all, you were all there to watch me rule. You all experienced your own Crown Prince/Princess selection when Alder was chosen to rule Nevremerre and met his wife, Madeline, shortly thereafter. You know intimately how Genevieve refused to accept the role of Queen until I retired, running off to travel the continent for eight years and then came back with two husbands, Romesh and Patrick, and my first sweet little grandchild. You were all there when Marcus declared he would rather paint than rule and when he married Ki, who used to grace my sitting room with the other Dolmanian children. And, you were there when Eliza became the first Crown Princess of Dolma without a man by her side. You lived through the deaths of my father and Mama, and know that even in her 90s, we are still graced with the formidable presence of Mother.

But now, my dearest children, it is time for me to retire. Sixty is a good age to explore the continent. I think I must continue what Nana always told me– I would fly. I will take your father with me, of course, I would be lost without him. I will be around to visit; I will return as often as I am able; and I will be sure to be there for the birth of any more grandchildren. I will be back if Eliza decides to marry someone. But, until then, I am off to explore this world of ours.

Until those times in which I see you, darlings, I leave you these three books containing the parts of my life you didn't get to see, or perhaps that you were too young to remember, in the hopes that my experiences will help guide you through anything you may face. Alder will rule Nevremerre with wisdom, poise and an amazing ability to adapt to even the greatest change. Genevieve will rule Agremerre with a passion and furious determination that only the bravest of souls can manage. Eliza will rule Dolma with compassion as well as the demand for justice that Dolma still requires. I believe each of you will be the leader each of these three countries needs. Marcus will live a different life than ours, but I have no doubt that it will bring him joy.

So, my loves, this is where I leave you. Enjoy this time of your lives, but be sure to take breaks and to nurture yourselves as well. You shall always carry all my love. May the Gods bless you, for all time.

Love,
Your Mother
Queen Avalynn of Nevremerre, Agremerre, and Dolma

Acknowledgements

A big thank you to everyone who helped me create this book. The cover was designed by the amazing and talented Jen Leong. Check out more of her incredible art at www.jern-inc.com. The maps and family tree were the work of my wonderful mother, Julie Nelson. Thank you also to my editors, Julie Nelson and Diane Peterson Mathis. Finally, I am immensely grateful to all of you who have read and enjoyed this book. You have helped me bring my dream to life--literally--this story came to me in a dream!

Halle Clark grew up in Phoenix, Arizona. She moved to Scotland to attend the University of St. Andrews and graduated in 2020 with a degree in Honours Biology. She currently lives in Adelaide, Australia where she finished writing this book. Her hobbies include reading, walking along the beach, pole dancing, and flying through the air as much as possible.

While Avalynn's journey is now complete, Halle Clark's writing career is not. Keep your eyes peeled for her next book: The Dragon at Hedgefield Farm! For more updates follow @halle_cn on instagram.